ACCLAIM FOR LUANNE RICE AND CLOUD NINE

"A tightly paced story that is hard to put down . . . Rice's message remains a powerful one: the strength of precious family ties can ultimately set things right." —*Publishers Weekly*

"One of those rare reading experiences that we always hope for when cracking the cover of a book . . . A joy." —*Library Journal*

"Elegant . . . Rice hooks the reader on the first page."
—*Hartford Courant*

"Luanne Rice touches the deepest, most tender corners of the heart." —Tami Hoag, author of *Ashes to Ashes*

"Rice is a gifted storyteller with a keen eye for character and detail." —*Brunswick (ME) Times Record*

"A celebration of family and the healing power of love. Poignant and powerful . . . One of those rare books which refresh and renew the landscape of women's fiction for a new generation of readers." —Jayne Ann Krentz, author of *Sharp Edges*

AND MORE CRITICAL ACCLAIM FOR LUANNE RICE

"A rare combination of realism and romance."
—*New York Times Book Review*

"Luanne Rice proves heself a nimble virtuoso."—*Washington Post*

"Few writers evoke summer's translucent days so effortlessly, or better capture the bittersweet ties of family love."
—*Publishers Weekly*

ALSO BY LUANNE RICE

CLOUD NINE

A NOVEL ·

LUANNE RICE

Bantam Books

CLOUD NINE
A Bantam Book

PUBLISHING HISTORY
Bantam hardcover edition published January 1999
Bantam mass market edition / January 2000
Bantam trade paperback edition / September 2008

Published by
Bantam Dell
A Division of Random House, Inc.
New York, New York

Book design by Tanya Pérez-Rock

Library of Congress Catalog Card Number: 98-47796

Bantam Books and the rooster colophon are registered
trademarks of Random House, Inc.

ISBN 978-0-553-38584-7

Printed in the United States of America
Published simultaneously in Canada

www.bantamdell.com

BVG 10 9 8 7 6 5 4 3 2 1

To TIS:
Heather, Hannah, Nora, Carol,
Leslie, and Mia

CLOUD NINE

CHAPTER

1

ANOTHER AUTUMN HAD come to Fort Cromwell, New York, and Sarah Talbot was there to see it. She sat on the front porch of her small white house, drinking apple cinnamon tea, wondering what to do next. The college kids next door were washing their car. Spray from the hose misted her face. Wrapped in a red plaid blanket, she tilted her face to the sun, and imagined the drops were saltwater and she was home on Elk Island.

A blue sedan drove slowly down the street. It looked municipal, as if it might belong to an undercover police officer or street inspector. FORT CROMWELL VNA was stenciled on the side, and when it parked in Sarah's driveway, a small, trim woman in a white coat climbed out.

Sarah smiled to see her.

"What are you doing here?" Sarah asked.

"That's a fine greeting," the visiting nurse said.

"I thought you were done with me," Sarah said. Holding her blanket with one hand, she used the other to unconsciously ruffle her closely shorn white hair.

"Done with you? My daughter would kill me. Besides, do you think that's how I treat my friends?"

"I'm your patient, Meg," Sarah said, smiling.

"*Were,* Sarah. Were. We're here to take you for a ride."

"A ride? Where—" Sarah began. Glancing at the car, she noticed Mimi in the backseat.

"Happy birthday, Sarah," Meg said, bending down to hug her.

Sarah reached up. She put her arms around the visiting nurse and smelled her citrus-scented shampoo. Meg's pockets jangled with keys, pens, and a stethoscope. A colorful plastic teddy bear was pinned to her lapel, just above her name tag. Sarah could feel by the new padding between her bones and Meg's skin that she was putting on weight. The hug felt good, and she bit her lip.

"How did you know?" Sarah asked when they pulled apart. Today was her thirty-seventh birthday. She was having a quiet day: no party, no cards or calls from home. In the car's back window Mimi was waving with one hand, trying to paste up a bright pink sign with the other. In silver glitter she had written MANY HAPPY RETURNS OF THE DAY!

"I read your chart," Meg said, grinning. "Come on."

———

WILL BURKE STOOD in the hangar, his head under the hood of the Piper Aztec. Fall was his biggest season. He needed all three of the planes he owned serviced and ready to fly. The lake region was a tourist destination, with all the cider mills and foliage trails. He operated fifteen-minute aerial tours, especially popular during the Fort Cromwell Fair. The end of October brought parents' weekends at two area colleges, with scheduled flights back and forth to New York, shuttling parents to see the big games and visit their kids.

At the sound of tires crunching over the gravel outside, he wiped his socket wrench on a blue rag and placed it on his tall red toolbox. He checked his watch: four o'clock. A friend of his daughter's had booked a quick birthday tour, up and down, a fifteen-minute scenic loop of the lake and mountain. An easy thirty dollars, and he'd be back to the tune-up in no time.

Tucking his work shirt into his jeans, Will walked outside to greet his customers. He didn't really feel like taking a break, but the afternoon was sunny, and the fresh air felt good, so he found himself smiling at the car anyway. He waved as they pulled up.

Meg and Mimi Ferguson got out. Meg was the town visiting nurse, and she yelled hello with cheerful efficiency, making Will smile a little wider. He hung back, wondering which one had the birthday. His daughter sometimes baby-sat for Mimi, and judging from what he remembered, Mimi must be about ten.

But then someone new got out of the car, a woman Will had never seen. She was small and thin, the size of an underfed teenager. Her skin was pale and translucent, like high cloud cover on a fall day, and her head was covered with blond peach fuzz. It was the way she looked at the sky that caught Will's attention: with total rapture, as if she hadn't ever seen it so blue before, or as if she couldn't believe she was about to go up in it.

"Ready to fly?" he asked.

"Which plane, Mr. Burke?" Mimi asked, excited.

"That one," he said, pointing at the two-seater Piper Cub.

"We can't all fit?" Mimi asked, disappointed.

"Now, Mimi—" Meg began.

"Sorry, Mimi," Will said. "The big plane's getting an oil change. If I'd known..."

"You know what, Mimi?" the woman said eagerly. "Why don't you go up for me?"

"It's your birthday flight," Mimi said. "It was my idea, and we want *you* to go."

"Happy birthday," Will said to the woman.

"Thank you." Again, that expression of amazement, as if she had never been so happy. She stared at him directly, and he had that shock he felt when coming upon a person he knew from somewhere, hardly at all, but who has undergone a drastic change of appearance. A weight gain or loss, a different hairstyle, a drop in health. He had seen this woman around town looking quite different. Then, for some strange reason, he pointed at the sky.

"Ready?" he asked.

"I am," she said.

"Let's go," he said. Then, speaking to Mimi in a voice he tried to keep from sounding overly hopeful, he said, "Hey, Susan's in the office. She'd be glad to see you."

———————

SECRET'S DAD HAD brought her to the airport. Her allergies were out of control, and the school nurse had tried to call her mother, but of course she wasn't home. So Secret had told her to call Burke Aviation and ask for Will: Her father would definitely pick her up. And he had. She'd felt better almost immediately upon reaching the airport, but there was no point in going back to school: the day was almost over. She slouched at his desk, painting her nails. Craning her neck, she could just see the action outside, through the big window. Mimi and her mom and their friend were standing by the landing strip, talking to him.

Of all the kids Secret baby-sat for, Mimi was the best. She was a nice little kid. She listened to her parents, never tried to get Secret to pierce her ears in weird places, and wanted to be a veterinarian when she grew up. She had *Dreams* and *Goals,* she knew there was more to life than Emma Turnley, the only school in this one-horse town, just as Secret herself did.

"Hi, Susan," Mimi said, bursting through the door.

"'Susan'?" Secret said, barely looking up. "There's no one named Susan here."

"That's right, I forgot," Mimi said, grinning. "Secret. You changed your name. What're you doing?"

"October is the month for witchy doings, and since you know I'm a witch, I'm painting my nails accordingly," Secret said patiently, as if she were explaining something terribly obvious to a dim but cherished friend. She wiggled her fingers at Mimi, casting a spell.

"Wow," Mimi said, admiring the artwork. Secret had used India ink and a crow-quill pen to paint delicate spiderwebs on her iridescent pale blue nails. Being right-handed, her left hand was more intricately done, with microscopic spiders clinging to the silken strands.

"You brought that lady here for her plane ride, I see," Secret said, looking out the window again. The airport was tiny, and there wasn't much activity. "Was she surprised?"

"Very surprised," Mimi said. "I'm glad you suggested it."

"Mmm," Secret said, taking the compliment as her due. She was known for her great surprise and party ideas. Watching the woman walk toward the plane, she noticed a few things: She was too thin, her hair looked terrible, and she had the nicest face Secret had seen in a long time. "Is that lady really sick?" she asked.

"She *was*," Mimi said. "But she's getting better. My mom takes care of lots of people, and for a while she said Sarah was going to die. But now she says she's probably not. I'm really glad, but I don't get it."

"You're too young to get it," Secret said benevolently, although Mimi was older than Secret had been when her brother died. Secret's throat began tickling. Her chest got that heavy feeling, and she reached into her father's top drawer for the inhaler they always kept there. She took a hit.

"Are you okay?" Mimi asked, always looking so worried when Secret had an attack. This was nothing. Secret had asthma and allergies, and she had first met Mimi because Meg Ferguson had been *her* nurse. After a really bad attack, when she had stopped breathing and started turning blue, Secret had needed inhalation therapy for a few days, and her mother had called the visiting nurse.

"I'm fine."

"Good thing you have your inhaler."

"I didn't have it at school today, so I had to come home early." As soon as she said it, Secret felt bad for lying—to Mimi *and* to the school nurse. She *had* had her inhaler; it was buried deep in her book bag, beneath her art supplies and *Franny and Zooey*. But she had been bored at school, feeling lonely, and when the opportunity had presented itself with a choking fit, she had asked them to call her father.

Lonely: Secret felt it all the time, down to her toes. She missed her brother. Living with her mother, she missed her father. Right under the same roof, Secret missed her mother. Half the time she missed people when they were sitting right next to her. Walking through the mall with girls from her school, she missed her friends and they were right there.

Like now: Sitting here with Mimi, gazing out at the airstrip, she watched the sick lady with the terrible hair get into the plane, with this beautiful radiant look in her eyes, and Secret missed *her*. Missed her so badly her chest began to hurt, even though Secret had never met her before and didn't even know her name.

————

THEY FLEW NORTH. The pilot took her over the lake and western ridge, where the leaves blazed in the orange light. The craggy rocks glowed red, and the lake itself was deep blue-black. Sarah pressed her forehead against the cold window, looking out. She watched red-tailed hawks circling below the plane, their shadows dark and mysterious on the lake's smooth surface.

"Ever been up in a small plane before?" the pilot asked.

"Yes," Sarah said.

"Don't know why, I thought it was your first time," he said. "The way Mimi and her mom were so excited about arranging it for you."

"I think maybe I mentioned to Meg that I love flying," Sarah said. "Although I don't do it as much now as I used to. Lots of weekends, I'd be on a plane just slightly bigger than this, flying home to Maine from Boston."

"I'm from New England too," he nodded. "That lake's pretty, but it's not—"

"The Atlantic," she said, grinning.

He laughed too, the response of a man who had saltwater in his veins, who for some reason, like Sarah, had found himself living in upstate New York after a lifetime by the sea.

"I'm Will Burke," he said, taking his hand off the controls to shake her hand.

"Sarah Talbot."

"Hi, Sarah."

"Who was that I saw in the window back at the airport?" Sarah asked. "That young girl looking out?"

"My daughter, Susan," Will said.

"A teenager?"

"Fifteen," he said. "Going on thirty."

"I know the syndrome," Sarah said, glancing east, as if she could see across four states to a tiny island off the coast of Maine.

They kept heading north, even though they had reached the midway point, been in the air for seven and a half minutes, and should have turned for home. Down below was an endless pine forest. It covered the hills in all directions, an unfathomable expanse of green, and the dying sun threw glints of gold in the tall treetops. Sarah felt her eyes fill with tears.

Will glanced over.

"I didn't think I'd be here," Sarah said. "For another birthday."

"But you are," Will said.

He pulled back on the controls, and the plane began to climb. They left the earth behind, flying straight into the sky. Sarah felt the exhilaration of adventure, something new, of being alive. Her heart was in her throat, gravity pulling her shoulder blades against the leather seat. Will glanced quickly over.

The plane dove down. Holding tight, Sarah felt the plane do

one loop-de-loop, then another. Will's hand was so close, she wanted to grab for it. It was a sudden, mad impulse, and it passed. The plane steadied off. Sarah's fifteen minutes were up, but they kept flying north for a while longer before they turned for home.

CHAPTER

2

"DID SHE LIKE her ride?"

Sitting at the kitchen table, reading the paper, Will didn't quite hear the question. He had been up since five, servicing the planes and flying a mapmaker around the state. Updating his topographical maps, measuring elevations and plotting railroad lines, he had spent the morning directing Will to fly low and come around again for a better look; he'd be back again before dawn tomorrow.

"Sorry, Susan," he said, yawning. "Did you ask me something?"

" 'Susan'?" she asked, frowning as she sprinkled croutons into their salad.

"I mean . . . honey," he said, trying to remember the name she had decided to go by. "September?" he asked.

"Dad, I haven't been September for weeks. I can't believe you don't even know your own daughter's name. Try 'Secret.' "

"That's right," Will said, folding his paper so he wouldn't be tempted to read it anymore. He didn't understand this name-changing business, and he didn't like it, but his daughter had been traumatized by losing Fred, then the divorce, so he tended to give in on points that didn't seem that important. "Okay, Secret. What was the question?"

"Did she like her ride? That lady."

"Sarah?" Will asked, remembering her shining eyes. "I think so."

"You seemed to be gone a long time."

"Really? Didn't seem that long to me."

"Well, it was. I was timing you. Thirty-five minutes. It was only supposed to be fifteen."

"My watch must've stopped," Will said, trying not to smile. His daughter was so transparent. Anytime she sensed even a glimmer of interest on his part in a woman, she turned ultra-vigilant. She was probably afraid he'd do what her mother had done with Julian: go off skiing for a weekend and come back married.

"Your watch never stops, Dad. You are Mr. Time Man. Zero one hundred hours and counting. You've even got me trained." She glanced at the wall clock, which read six-thirty. "Like now, it's eighteen-thirty. From our years in the Navy, right?"

"Right, honey."

"So I don't believe your *watch* stopped."

"Well, we flew over the lake, and the leaves were so bright and pretty, we just kept going. I guess I just lost track of the time."

"You never lose track of the time, Dad. I know that. I just think—" She paused, trouble in her eyes. She had made a big salad for their dinner, and she carried it to the table. It was in the big wooden bowl his brother had given him and Alice for a wedding present, that Alice had let him keep when she'd moved in with Julian. Secret had filled it with lettuce, tomatoes, cucumbers, croutons, and white grapes, and she presented it with shy expectation in her wide blue eyes.

"Wow," he said. "That looks great."

"Thank you. Most people wouldn't think of including grapes, but I think they add a lot. Do you?"

"Yes, definitely," he said, taking a large helping, knowing he would stop by McDonald's for a double cheeseburger when he drove her home.

"Well, just don't get too attached to her."

"Who?" he asked, knowing.

"That lady. Sarah."

"Honey, I just took her up for a birthday ride. That's all."

"She's sick, Dad. It was like one of those trips to summer camp for dying kids. She's all alone in Fort Cromwell, and the Fergusons wanted to make sure her last birthday was happy."

"It wasn't her last birthday," Will said, surprised by how much the idea of that upset him.

"If it was mine, I'd want to know. I'd want to plan my last birthday and have a great old time. We'd go back to Rhode Island, for one thing. I'd take everyone on the Edaville Railroad. There'd be more cake than you could handle, and I'd give out presents. We'd just keep going round the track till I said everything I wanted to say. And I'd have my favorite music playing. I'd want to hear all the songs I like, my own top one hundred countdown."

"That won't happen for a long time," Will said, knowing he was in dangerous territory.

"What won't?"

"You dying."

"It did for Fred."

"Fred . . ." Will said, taking the chance to say his name.

"His last birthday passed, and he didn't know. When his last day came, he didn't even know *that*. How can it happen, Dad? That you wake up happy and fine one morning, and by fourteen hundred hours you're drowned?"

Will looked across the untouched salad plates. Secret was staring straight at him, no blame in her expression. Just the wide-open gaze of a child who still trusted her father, after everything he had failed to do, to give her a straight answer.

"I don't know, sweetheart," he said, because honesty was the best he could offer her now.

"Mom's over it," she said bitterly.

"She'll never get over it. You don't 'get over' losing one of your kids, honey."

"She never talks about him. Whenever I mention him, she tells me to shush, it upsets *Julian*. And he's just a rich bastard who spends all his time *car* racing and going to lectures. Is that where they are tonight?"

"Don't say 'bastard,' Susan. A play, I think she said." His ex-wife's life was a mad smorgasbord of cultural events at the local colleges.

"Jerk, then. Idiot. Numskull. Dickhead. Drip. Flaming creep. Full-dress weenie. Turdman. Shitbreath."

"Susan. Secret," Will said wearily. "Stop, okay?"

"Sorry, Dad," she said, drizzling plain vinegar onto her salad. She had taken only lettuce leaves, a pile of medium-sized shreds. Assuming she had left all the good stuff for him, Will took an extra helping to make her happy.

"The grapes were a good call," he said, taking a bite.

"Thank you," she said. "She looked nice."

"Who, honey?"

"That lady, Sarah."

"She was," Will said.

"I hope she's okay," she said. "Because death sucks."

SARAH HAD BEGUN to open the shop for a few hours every day, usually from ten until two. She loved how the morning sun streamed through the tall windows, throwing light and shadows on the pale yellow walls. Today she felt a little tired. She imagined curling up for a nap in the middle of the things she sold: quilts and pillows, some filled with white down from the geese on her father's saltwater farm in Maine.

The bell above the door tinkled. She glanced up from an inventory list she was perusing, and smiled at the two college students who walked in. They stared at Sarah for a second. She felt she still looked weird, with her tufty white hair, and she grinned to put them at ease.

"Hi," she said. "Let me know if I can help."

"We will. Thanks," the taller girl replied, smiling as her friend lay flat on the sample bed, prettily made up with a fluffy quilt in an ecru damask cover. Feather throw pillows covered with narrow umber stripes or golden swirls and hand-printed oak leaves were strewn around the headboard.

"I want this exact bed," the second girl sighed, sprawled amid the pillows.

"You do?" Sarah asked.

"The linen service at school doesn't exactly provide sumptuous bedding," the tall girl explained. "We're fantasizing."

"Be my guest," Sarah said. "Everyone deserves sweet dreams."

"I don't have a credit card," the other girl said. "But if I call my parents and they give you their account number, can I charge every single thing in your store and take it back to campus?"

"That can be arranged," Sarah said. "I'll deliver it myself in a silver sleigh."

The girl giggled and sighed again, the sounds muffled by all the padding around her.

Sarah remembered her own college days. Too-thin sheets and scratchy old blankets had been her inspiration for starting her own business, Cloud Nine. She had dropped out of Wellesley after her freshman year. Opening her first store in Boston, she had stocked it primarily with down products made by her father, back on the farm.

The farm had been on the verge of failing. Her mother had died when she was fourteen. Sarah and her father never talked about it, but she knew she had saved him. She had gotten her own financing, come up with all the ideas, expanded into mail order, taken on lines from France and Italy to supplement the stuff from Elk Island. The original store remained in Boston, but after eight years and the last in a series of ridiculous love affairs, Sarah had expanded to this college-rich valley in upstate New York. She had been here for ten years now, and her father had all the work he could handle.

The telephone rang, and Sarah answered it.

"Hello, Cloud Nine," Sarah said.

"Happy birthday," the deep voice said.

"Thank you," she said. Her heart contracted. She couldn't talk. She had the feeling if she breathed or sneezed, the line would go dead.

"I'm a day late. Sorry."

"That's okay, I didn't even notice," she lied.

"What'd you do? Go out for dinner or something?"

"I took a plane ride," she said. "To see the leaves. They looked beautiful, all red and orange and yellow, like a big bowl of Trix. I couldn't stop smiling, it made me think of you, and I knew it would make you laugh. I mean, flying over this beautiful fall landscape and thinking of Trix. Remember when that was your favorite cereal?"

"Huh. Not really."

"How are you?" she asked. She could picture him, standing in the big basement kitchen, with a fire burning in the old stone hearth. Closing her eyes, she was back on Elk Island, could see the dark bay, the prim white house, the fields full of white geese. She could hear the waves, smell the thick pines.

"Fine."

"Really? Do you still like living there? Are you honestly enjoying the work? Because—"

"What about you?" he asked, sounding sullen and accusatory. "How are you?"

"I'm great," she said.

"Yeah?"

"Yes." She turned her back, so the college girls wouldn't hear. "I finished chemo last month, and my X rays look good. There's no sign of any tumor. I had an MRI, and the doctor says I'm all clear. Good to go."

"You're cured?"

"Yes," Sarah said, biting her lip. She was the most optimistic person she knew—ferociously hopeful—and had often been accused by the very party on the other end of being annoyingly cheerful. She couldn't stop herself. She knew about statistics, five-year survival rates, worst-case scenarios. Here she was, saying she was cured, when she didn't even know if there was any such thing.

"Good," he said. A long silence passed, and then he cleared his throat. "That's good," he said.

"Is your grandfather there?" she asked.

"He's out in the barn. I just came in to get some lunch." He cleared his throat again. "Just thought I'd call to say happy birthday."

"I'm glad you did, Mike. I miss you."

"Huh."

"A lot. I wish you were here. I wish you'd decide to . . ."

"When're you coming to Maine? I mean, Grandpa was wondering. He told me to ask. And to say happy birthday. I almost forgot."

"Was it his idea for you to call?" Sarah asked suspiciously, feeling upset. She had been thinking it was Mike's idea.

"No. It was mine."

"Hmm," she said, smiling.

"So, when're you going to come?"

"I don't know," she said. The idea of going to the island filled her with more anxiety than she knew was good for her. Her doctor had told her to avoid stress, that a centered spirit was her best defense. Just thinking about seeing Mike in the barn with her bitter old father, knowing that Mike had put himself under his tutelage, sent Sarah's spirit careening.

"Thanksgiving would be good," Mike said.

"We'll see."

"Are you too sick to come?"

"No. I'm fine. I told you, I—"

"Then why not?"

"I said I'll see, Mike."

An uneasy silence developed between them. Sarah's mind

raced with questions, accusations, declarations of love. How
could her son have left her to go *there*? From the day of her
mother's death, Sarah couldn't wait to leave the island. She had
let her father down, and even in his bitter silence he refused to
let her forget. But Mike had gone to live with him while
searching for connections to Zeke Loring, the father who had
died before he was even born.

"Excuse me," called the girl who had been lying on the bed.
"I think I do want to buy some things. Can we call my mother
to get her Amex number? I know she'll say yes."

"Oh. Someone's there," Mike said abruptly, hearing the
background voices. "I guess I'd better go. Grandpa's waiting for
lunch."

"Honey, I'm glad you called. You can't imagine how happy
you made me," Sarah said. "It's ten times better than any present
I've ever gotten, even my favorite dollhouse when I was four,
and I'm not kidding you, I loved that dollhouse, I played with it
constantly, just ask my father. . . ."

"Bye, Mom," Mike said.

"Bye, honey," Sarah said.

When she turned back to the girls, she was smiling. Her face
was calm, her mouth steady. She nodded yes, the girl could call
her mother. Handing her the telephone, she told her to dial direct, not bother charging the call. She was going through the
motions of selling a quilt, cultivating the business of the girls at
Marcellus College, the students who were her bread and butter.

But her heart was far away with her son, Mike Talbot, her
seventeen-year-old dropout, the person Sarah loved more than
her own life, the boy who was single-handedly planning to
carry on the family traditions of quilt making and farm saving
under the wing of her father, the wrathful George Talbot, of Elk
Island, Maine.

It was at moments such as this that Sarah, writing a sales
ticket for a three-hundred-dollar quilt, wished that she had just
let the old farm die.

IN THE AIR with the mapmaker for the second day, Will criss-crossed Algonquin County eleven times. They plotted the Setauket River, the Robertson wilderness, Lake Cromwell, Eagle Peak, and the foothills of the Arrowhead Mountains. Will flew him over small towns and Wilsonia, the county seat. They counted windmills and silos, surveyed the patchwork of farms, fields dotted orange with pumpkins. He had climbed to six thousand feet, but on their way back to the airport, he flew one low circle over Fort Cromwell.

It looked like a toy town, like the miniature buildings that had come with Fred's model railroad. Will almost never thought of Fred's train, but with the mapmaker paying such close attention to track beds and crossing signals, he couldn't get it out of his mind. Fred's set-up had looked just like Fort Cromwell: pristine town green, redbrick buildings, railroad tracks winding through the low hills. Will had been stationed in Newport then, and Navy housing didn't leave much room for toys. Fred's railroad was super deluxe, from F.A.O. Schwarz in New York, the kind of railroad Will had wanted when he was a boy. It had taken up the entire dining alcove.

Alice had been a sport. Her mother had given them a nice cherry table, and he remembered how they had just pushed it off to one side. Susan's playhouse and Fred's railroad had been the main deals back then, and that was just fine. With Will out at sea so much, he didn't suppose Alice had much use for a fine dining table anyway.

But she used that table now. Will saw Julian's estate nestled in the trees on the top of Windemere Hill. Stone mansion, clay tennis court, circular drive, security gates worthy of a movie star or a corporate mogul. That's where they live, Will thought. While the mapmaker updated his notes, Will banked left. His port wing pointed straight down at the stone house, like a finger of God. Blessing his daughter, Will thought, but also cursing

Julian. For being in the right place at the right time, for stealing Will's family when they were all weakened—broken really— after losing Fred.

Catching sight of his daughter parking her bike against the fieldstone garage was too much for him. Feeling like he'd swallowed a fishhook, he gunned the engine and wheeled through the sky. The mapmaker gave him a terrified look.

"Sorry," Will said.

"Is the plane okay?"

"Fine, sir. Just a little turbulence."

"Ah," the mapmaker said, a deep line across his brow.

Flying home, Will wondered why his heart was pumping so hard. He could feel it pounding in his chest, as if he had just swum a hundred yards in a Force 10 sea. That had been his first job in the Navy: rescue swimmer aboard the *L. P. James*. He could slice through twenty-foot waves, weighed down with a two-hundred-and-fifty-pound man, and barely notice his breathing change.

Maybe it's all this freshwater, he thought, surveying the lakes, the river. Made him feel nervous, like something was missing. No ocean, no coastline in sight. Just like Sarah Talbot had said yesterday: It's not the Atlantic.

Then something strange happened. Thinking of Sarah Talbot, the whole thing went away. The speeding heart, the saltwater anxiety. Memories of life as a rescue swimmer, all the good and terrible reasons for leaving the ocean he loved so much. Will started to breathe easier. He pictured Sarah, kind and wise as a beautiful owl with her wide-open eyes and feathery hair, her way of staring at the sky with unblinking gratitude, and Will Burke felt calm. Like he could breathe again without cracking his chest wide open.

CHAPTER

3

SECRET RODE HER bike through town. The air was freezing cold and her fingers felt stiff in her new blue gloves. Sticking out her tongue, she caught the first snowflakes of the year. Her nose and cheeks stung. Halloween had barely passed, and clear ice had already started to form on the lake. Nowhere on earth was colder than Fort Cromwell. Newport had been tropical by comparison.

All the shops looked cozy. It got dark around five these days, practically before she got out of school, so everywhere glowed with that orange warmth she associated with England. She didn't know why; she had never been to England, but she had an extremely good imagination. When she was very small, her mother had read her books by Rumer Godden. Secret had loved the sound of scones and tea, and she wished she had some that very minute.

She had baby-sat for the Neumanns after school. On her way home now, she was in no particular hurry; her mother and Julian were having cocktails at Dean Sherry's house. Pedaling slower, she looked into the shops. A few still had jack-o'-lanterns in the window. Others had jumped the gun, entwined white lights with evergreen roping, getting ready for Christmas. The down shop looked especially inviting, with no holiday decorations whatsoever. The sign was enough: a magical cloud and a golden "9." Brass lamps glowed, the quilts appeared thick and enveloping. Wanting to warm up, Secret parked her bike and walked in.

"Hi," the lady called from the back.

"Hi," Secret said. Trying to look real, like a genuine shopper who might actually be in the market for pillows, Secret frowned and began looking at price tags.

"Just let me know if you need any help."

"I will," Secret said, flattening her voice and earnestly rifling through a bin of small silk-velvet pillows. She had accompanied her mother and Julian to the Antiques Corner, so she knew how people who spent money looked. Spiced cider was brewing somewhere in back. What she wanted was to sink into this soft pile of velvet-covered down. She found herself relaxing, forgetting to concentrate, leisurely browsing through the beautiful things.

"Would you like some hot cider?" the voice asked.

"Well, I shouldn't," Secret said, feeling guilty for defrauding the lady. She had absolutely no intention of buying a single thing.

"Are you sure? It's pretty cold out there."

"You can say that again," Secret said.

"Are you sure? It's pretty cold out there."

Secret chuckled. She glanced up, and for the first time she actually saw the shop owner. It was Sarah Talbot, the sick lady, Mimi Ferguson's friend.

"Oh, hi," Secret said.

"Hi," Sarah said. "I know you. You were in the airport office the day I took my birthday flight."

"Yes. My father's the pilot."

"An excellent pilot," Sarah said. "I've had some terrible ones, believe me."

"You have?"

"Absolutely. Small-plane pilots are the worst. I've had guys who taxi down the runway like bucking broncos. I know one pilot who flies under bridges, just for fun. When I was younger, I lived on an island, and some of them would fly when the fog was thicker than these quilts. Those pilots were the cowboys of the air."

"Half of them probably can't get jobs at major airlines," Secret said confidentially. She leaned against the bed in the middle of the store.

"I wouldn't be surprised," Sarah said. "Sure you wouldn't like a little cider?"

"Maybe a little," Secret said. She waited while Sarah filled two brown mugs. "The airlines would hire my dad though. He had offers from TWA, Delta. He could fly anywhere, but he likes being his own boss."

"He certainly seems capable to me," Sarah said, handing her a mug. Secret accepted it, smelling the spicy steam.

"The Navy trained him," Secret said. "But he was a pilot even before that. He learned to fly when he was just a little older than me. He was so valuable to the Navy, he could do everything. Fly, swim in times of disaster. Lead his men. He always kept his head in times of maneuvers."

"Maneuvers?"

"Yes, such as the Persian Gulf. He was there."

"You sound like a proud daughter."

"I am."

"Upstate New York is pretty far inland for a Navy family," Sarah said.

"Yes," Secret said, sipping her cider. She felt her asthma just waiting for the next questions: Why are you here? Do you have any brothers or sisters? But the questions never came. Instead, Sarah stuck out her hand.

"We haven't officially met. I'm Sarah Talbot."

"I'm Secret Burke."

"What a beautiful name!" Sarah said.

Secret glanced over to see if she was being fake. Certain older people tended to patronize her when they heard her name, but she could see that Sarah was being sincere. Sarah's eyes were full of admiration. She had a wonderful smile, with a slightly crooked front tooth.

"Thank you," Secret said. "I'm actually getting ready to change it."

"Really? To what?"

"I was thinking of Snow."

Sarah nodded, blowing on her cider. "Perfect for winter," she said.

"Is Sarah your real name?"

"Yes, it is," Sarah said. "I've lugged it around my whole life. For a while in seventh grade I tried out Sadie, but it wasn't me."

"No," Secret agreed. "You are definitely a Sarah."

For the first time since coming in, Secret focused on Sarah's hair. It had grown out about half an inch, and the color was somewhere between yellow and gray. She knew people having cancer treatments lost their hair. Beauty tips were one of Secret's best talents, and she eyed Sarah appraisingly.

"What?" Sarah said. The way she blushed, touching her hair with a stricken look in her eyes, made Secret feel so bad, she almost spilled her cider. Sarah was self-conscious! Secret had seen that same expression in the eyes of her friend Margie Drake when two of the cool girls, whispering and pointing, had made fun of her new perm.

"Well . . ." Secret said, trying to decide. She could lie, say nothing, pretend she had just been about to burp. Or she could tell the truth, offer to help. "I was just noticing your hair," she said bravely.

"My poor hair," Sarah said, still pink. "Yep, I lost it. It used to be dark brown, and now look. It came in such a funny color. Somewhere between old socks and dirty dishwater."

"You could bleach it," Secret suggested. "The way it's growing in, it's so cute and punky. You could get it pure white and look so great!"

"Like Annie Lennox," Sarah said, smiling.

"Who?" Secret asked.

Just then the bells above the door sounded. A cluster of tiny silver bells, just like you might find in England. A group of college girls walked in, hugging themselves to get warm. Sarah called hello to them, and they called back. She offered them cider.

Secret nestled into her spot on the edge of the bed. The bed took up most of the store. But it was a bed no one would ever sleep in. Like a toy bed in the bedroom of a beautiful dollhouse. Like her playhouse in the middle of their apartment in Newport. All they needed was Fred's toy train chugging around the room, sounding its happy whistle.

Sarah served the college girls cider, but when she was done she came back to sit beside Secret. Their mugs were cool enough to really drink now. Side by side they sipped their drinks, while outside the air grew colder. The girls' voices were cheerful and excited. Their parents had sent them money, and they were all buying new quilts for the winter. They were the paying customers, but Sarah was sitting with Secret. As if she were her friend. As if she were hers alone.

———

LATER THAT NIGHT, Sarah stood in front of her bathroom mirror. The lights were bright, and she thought she looked like a startled cat. Her ugly yellow-gray hair stuck straight up, like the soft bristles of a baby brush. Ever since closing the shop, she had found herself thinking about what Secret had said: She could bleach her hair.

Thinking about it felt radical. Sarah had never dyed her hair before, never even considered it. Growing up, she hadn't fooled around with her appearance much. She had never been much for makeup, especially lipstick. It always felt so heavy on her mouth, and she was always licking her lips to see if it was still on. It made her feel too obvious, as if she was drawing too much attention to herself. Beauty products were for other, more glamorous girls.

But now, ruffling her hair, she wanted to do *something*. She hated the way she looked. Ever since the chemo, she could hardly recognize herself. She looked either very old or very young, anything but her real age. Her hair had come in colorless, and she had lots of new lines around her eyes and mouth that put her close to forty, but she had an alarmed, perpetually surprised look at all times that made her look like an overgrown infant.

No one ever mentioned it, how weird she looked. Not even her friends—not even her wonderful nurse, Meg Ferguson. At the hospital, someone had come around with wigs to try on, but Sarah had said no to those. Wearing a wig would feel like having pantyhose on her head, sweaty and claustrophobic. The scalp equivalent to lipstick. Sarah had gone the distance for her brain tumor, trying every revolutionary treatment known to doctors anywhere, but when it came to her appearance she wouldn't try the simplest things.

Sighing, she walked into her bedroom. Annie Lennox played on the CD player; Sarah had put her on for moral support. Annie and Sarah. And Secret. She wondered if Secret Burke knew what a big favor she had done her, breaking the ice about something that had been driving her crazy with stupid worry.

Thanksgiving. What if she went? Aside from all the old sorrow with her father, their history of letdown and resentment, Sarah had an even bigger fear about the possibility of going home to Elk Island in less than three weeks. She was afraid to have Mike see her this way. She didn't want him to feel scared, or disgusted, by his own mother. She would have to hire extra help or close her shop for the long weekend.

She remembered naming her first shop. She was nineteen years old, a college student in Boston. Nineteen! Hardly older than Mike! Where had she gotten the confidence, the ambition? The shop was tiny, one single room with a brick wall and parquet floors. Sarah had walked through the door and filled the place with all her dreams. She would stock the shelves with Aunt Bess's quilts, become a successful businesswoman. Envisioning additional stores, catalogue sales, a chance to save the farm, a way to make her father happy on earth and her mother proud in heaven, Sarah had named her store Cloud Nine.

Cloud Nine. Leaning against her bureau, Sarah remembered designing her logo: a golden "9" on a white cloud superimposed on a blue oval, tiny white down feathers drifting down like snowflakes. She had commissioned David Walker, a woodcarver on Elk Island, to make the sign. Naming the store had given her so much pleasure, such a sense of dreams coming true, of knowing exactly who she was. She hadn't felt anything like it before and never would again until Mike was born.

Michael Ezekiel Loring Talbot.

Thinking her son's name filled Sarah with so much emotion she had to grip the bureau top. She had always loved the name Michael. It was strong, and it had belonged to an archangel, and it sounded poetic. She had given her son the name of a leader and an athlete, someone who had fun and took risks.

Sarah had wanted to name Michael for his father, but she had been free to give him "Loring" only as a middle name. Michael, like Sarah, was a Talbot. Perhaps that was why he was clinging so tenaciously to the island and his grandfather, to the old farm and the refuge it provided.

Her eyes brimmed with tears, and she blinked them away. No use crying about things she couldn't change. Mike had made his decision. She couldn't even say he had run away from home, because he hadn't even hidden his plans. And his destination wasn't New York or Los Angeles or even Albany: It was the family farm. Still, he was only seventeen, now living on Elk Island with the original recluse. In search of the truth about his own dead father. Mike would kill her if he knew she still thought of him as her baby, but she did.

Sitting on her window seat, Sarah took a sip of herbal tea.

She ate only healthful things now. She walked a little every day, as much as she felt able to. Some days she felt strong enough to run on the college track, like she had before getting sick, but she wasn't ready to push it. Her doctor had told her to take it slow, and Sarah listened to what he said. She wanted to live. She had brought a boy into this world, and she wanted to live to see him safely moving on a shining path.

———

ALICE VON FROELICH walked into her daughter's bedroom and tried to determine by her breathing whether she was actually asleep or just faking it. Several blankets and a quilt were piled high, pulled right over her head. The radio was playing, but Susan had been falling asleep to music for as long as Alice could remember.

Standing stock-still, hoping to catch her moving, Alice hardly breathed herself. She glanced around the room. The lamps were turned off, but the hall light illuminated certain things. Undeniably elegant, like the rest of Julian's house, Susan's room showed very few signs of being occupied by a teenage girl. Noticing this, as she did every time she entered, Alice crinkled her brow and exhaled worriedly.

Susan loved the idea of England, so Julian had let her choose two Gainsboroughs from his collection: a little girl in a blue dress, and two spaniels on a satin pillow. Her furniture and accoutrements were English too: the Queen Anne bed and dresser, the antique rocker covered in Susan's favorite shade of rose, the monogrammed sterling silver brush and mirror on the vanity. Julian had given them to her last Christmas, along with several sterling picture frames for her great collection of photos.

Stooping down, Alice took a closer look at the photos. Susan certainly did love her father: Will was in every one. There they were, in the cockpit of his Piper Cub, when Susan was four years old. Sitting on his lap under an umbrella at the Black

Pearl, the family's favorite restaurant in Newport. Standing on the dock just before he'd shipped out for the Middle East. Alice remembered taking all three pictures. And then her eyes fell upon the fourth.

"Freddie," she whispered.

There he was, his last Christmas, standing in front of a tree with Will. Her lanky, sleepy boy, braces on his smile, so beautiful and tall. In this shot, Fred was nearly the same height as Will. How had Alice never noticed that before? Was it just the perspective? She couldn't see their feet; had Fred been standing on a box, a stack of books?

"Mom?" Susan asked, shielding her eyes against the hall light.

"Honey, you're awake," Alice said, sitting on the edge of her bed.

"You weren't home."

"Didn't you get my message?" Alice asked, feeling that panicky guilt. "I called the machine."

"I got it."

"We had cocktails with Dean Sherry, and then a bunch of Julian's friends decided we should all cook dinner together. So we went to Martine's house and made Indonesian food and listened to Armando play some new pieces on his keyboard."

"God, how boring," Susan said, scowling.

"Did you eat?"

"Yes."

Alice worried. She stared at Susan, wondering what was going on in her head. She sounded so tense and sullen, almost as if she were *trying* to make her feel guilty. As if it weren't already a fait accompli.

"What did you have?"

"Dad took me to Chedder's. I had a salad."

"You called your father? Susan, you know there's a whole pantry full of food downstairs. Pansy bought every single thing you put on your list. The refrigerator is loaded with lettuce, all those strange kinds you love. Susan . . ."

" 'Susan'?" she asked, frowning. "If you expect me to answer you, you'd better call me by the right name."

Alice refused to play into Susan's trap. She had been acting out ever since Alice and Julian had gotten married, and one thing she knew worked best was the name game. Alice felt her blood pressure mounting through the roof. She had a sneaking suspicion that Will was enabling this. He was so easygoing, he'd let Susan get away with anything. He had gone to pieces when Fred died, and he wasn't even halfway put back together again.

"Honey?" Alice heard herself asking with an admirably even tone. She never spoke about Fred to Susan, not wanting to upset her. He had been her big brother, her hero. But she had to ask. The question just came out: Alice couldn't have held it back if she'd wanted to. "Was Freddie as tall as your dad? Almost as tall?"

Silence. Downstairs, she heard Julian and Armando laughing. Drinks were being poured. The clack of pool cues. The chime of the break.

"Susan, answer me."

"There's no Susan here," her daughter said dangerously from beneath her pile of quilts.

CHAPTER

4

THE FORT CROMWELL Fair was always held the Saturday midway between Halloween and Thanksgiving, to celebrate the harvest and the season of gratitude. Everyone went. The Old Fairgrounds were miles from town, in the middle of nowhere. Driving past at any other time of year, you might see a tractor chuffing down the road. You'd be lucky to see another car. But around fair time, traffic was backed up for miles. The now-bare fields surrounding the grounds swarmed with the expensive import cars of urban daytrippers in search of local color.

Sarah had come with Meg and Mimi. They wandered around, gazing at prize pigs and champion steers. Clydesdales clopped by on their way to the horse pull. Since the fair was held so late, someone had gotten the idea to put Santa in the hayride, and a wagon full of little kids singing "Jingle Bells" rattled past.

Mimi had gotten a camera for her birthday. She was taking pictures of everything, but she wanted to *do* everything too: eat cotton candy, take the hayride, run through the haunted house, ride the Ferris wheel. It was the conflict between being a total kid and starting to grow up a little. Sarah remembered Mike at that age and wished he were there.

"Want to ride the Ferris wheel?" Meg asked. "I think I'll take Mimi."

"You two go ahead," Sarah said. "I'm going to find some hot chocolate."

They agreed to meet by the paint-on-tattoo booth in an hour. Heading toward the refreshment area, Sarah felt exhilarated. Fairs always did this to her: the crowds, the animals, bells ringing everywhere. She said hello to a few people she knew, mainly college kids who came into her store.

She wore a black bowler hat, black jeans, and Zeke's old leather bomber jacket. For some reason, she had felt like wearing it. Since it had belonged to Mike's father, she hardly ever wore it when Mike was around. Seeing it brought forth too many questions. Sarah had so few of Zeke's things, and they all seemed to stir Mike into asking things Sarah couldn't answer. Once Mike had asked her why his father had given her his jacket, and Sarah couldn't even bring herself to tell him the truth: that Zeke hadn't given it to her at all. That she had borrowed it on her own and never given it back, that she had wanted so much more.

"One hot chocolate," she said to the elderly man behind the counter.

"Marshmallows in that?" he asked.

"No thanks," Sarah said, imagining the evil health risks of even one. She felt healthier all the time. She wasn't going to throw it all away on a marshmallow, even though she *really wanted it*.

The cardboard cup was scalding hot. Glancing around for napkins, she saw a separate counter with squeeze bottles of ketchup and mustard and napkins and straws. A man was blocking her way. He was tall and big-shouldered, and he was wearing a leather jacket almost exactly like hers.

"Excuse me," she said, leaning around him to get a napkin.

"Hi, Sarah," he said, sounding surprised and happy.

"Hi!" Sarah said. It was the pilot, Will Burke. She had worked herself practically under his arm to reach the napkins, and he was holding his hot dog aloft to keep the relish from spilling on her. They untwisted themselves and stood back, smiling.

"Good to see you," he said.

"You too. How have you been?"

"I've been fine," he said, tilting his head as if he were thinking that one over. "How about you?"

"Great," Sarah said. "Really great. What brings you to the fair? Are you here with Secret?"

"Secret?" he frowned. "Oh, Susan. You've met her?"

"She stopped by my store."

He laughed, shaking his head. " 'Secret.' It gets me every time. We gave her a perfectly nice name: Susan. Not that we didn't think of something more exotic. Delphine comes to mind for some reason, but we didn't want her to be embarrassed. You know?"

Sarah nodded. Will was laughing, but his eyes were barely smiling. He looked like a man with something weighing heavily on his mind, but she didn't know him well enough to ask. Maybe he and his wife weren't getting along. Never having been married herself, Sarah was no expert.

"She's a nice girl," Sarah said. "No matter what she calls herself. That's the important part."

"So you wouldn't worry about it?"

"Personally, no. I wouldn't."

"Hmm." He frowned again. He seemed to have lost all interest in his hot dog, which was piled high with relish, chili, and onions. "Because her mother thinks it's a danger sign. Some kind of call for help. I don't know."

"I wouldn't want to second-guess your wife," Sarah began.

"Ex-wife," Will said.

"But it doesn't seem all that dangerous to me. She's fifteen, just trying out new things. It could be worse—" Sarah said.

"Drugs," Will said solemnly.

"Exactly. She's just figuring out who she is. You know?"

Will nodded. He obviously felt better, because he started eating his hot dog again. His face and hands were weathered, the constant tan of a man who loved to be outside. He had curly graying brown hair with all-gray streaks at the temples. For a man who had been in the Navy, it looked a little long. His eyes were startling, as dark blue as a Maine bay.

"Is she here?" Sarah asked, looking around.

"Secret?" he asked, grinning. "No, she's home. I'm here for work. I take people up for rides—like the one I gave you—to see Fort Cromwell from the air."

"That was a great ride. I've thought of it often."

"You have?"

"Yes. It was the first time I knew—" She took a sip of hot chocolate to buy a little time, get past the emotion.

"Knew what?"

"That I'm okay again," she said. Smiling, she felt radiant, as if she were shining with health and happiness from the inside out. She shivered, but it was from the thrill of existing, of standing outside on a crisp fall day, not from the cold.

"I'm glad about that," Will said. He touched her arm.

An idea came upon her. It must have been brewing, because for the last few nights she had lain awake, wondering whether she should go home to Elk Island for Thanksgiving, how she would get there if she did. Because when she asked the question, it seemed as if she had it all planned.

"Do you ever take long-distance charters? To Maine, for example?"

"Yes," he said. "Lots of times. Where in Maine?"

"Elk Island."

He closed his eyes as if he were trying to picture it on a chart. Sarah helped him out.

"It's far up there," she said. "Past Penobscot Bay, almost to Mount Desert. Just a tiny little island way out at sea."

"Does it have an airport?"

"Not much of one. Just a grass strip."

"My planes like grass strips," he said, grinning. "When do you want to go?"

"That's the thing," she said. "Thanksgiving. I know you probably have plans, so . . . If you're even working that weekend."

"I am," he said.

"Well . . . do you want to think about it? You can work up a price and let me know?"

"Sounds good," he said. "We'll have to watch the weather. My big plane has the most instruments, and at this time of year you never know what to expect in the way of storms. But it's more expensive."

She nodded, swallowed hard. Making transportation arrangements brought her one step closer to actually going. Seeing Mike! Her throat vibrated with a laugh, and she started to let it out until she realized that by returning to Elk Island, she would be facing her father for the first time in many years. He had never gotten over her growing up, leaving the island for college, coming back just long enough to get pregnant and cause a scandal. Trapped by his grief for Sarah's mother, her father just grew more bitter as the years went by. Sarah had tried taking Mike there for summers long ago, but after a while her father's darkness had stopped her.

"I'll call you," she said, shaking Will's hand.

"Right," he said, glancing at his watch. It looked huge and heavy, about ten pounds' worth of chrome, a very high-tech chronometer. But it looked exactly right on his strong wrist. "Guess I'd better get back to work."

"Fly safe," she said.

"Thanks," Will said, starting to walk away. Sarah stood still, both hands holding her cup of hot chocolate. He started to disappear into the crowd. Then, turning, he called her name. "Hey, Sarah!"

Walking toward each other, they came together in a throng of teenagers. Bumped and jostled, Sarah brought her elbows into her body, making herself small. She and Will were standing in front of a booth festooned with burgundy paisley scarves, curved swords, and magic lamps. Mysterious sitar music wafted out. The sign read: GYPSY SECRETS OF THE ORIENT, FORTUNES READ BY THE LIGHT OF THE ETERNAL FLAME. A turbaned man flew out the door in pursuit of a young man.

"Stop him!" the turbaned Gypsy yelled. "He blew out the eternal flame!"

"The eternal flame!" the fortune-teller wailed, agonized. "Ahhh!"

"Wow," Will said. "That sounds serious."

Sarah smiled at him, shrugging her shoulders. "My son blew it out last year. Keeping up a tradition, I guess."

"Teenagers," he said. They stood there like two tourists being stampeded at Pamplona. Sarah stared into his eyes, which were bluer than the sky. He seemed to have forgotten why he'd called her back. Facing each other, their toes were touching.

"What was it?" she asked.

"Secret lives with her mother and stepfather," he said. "I mean, Secret is my family, but she doesn't live with me, and she's having Thanksgiving with Alice. So it's no problem to fly you to Maine."

"Oh," Sarah said. She was trying to think of what to say next, when another pack of boys charged by. Looking through their faces to see if she recognized any of Mike's old friends, she noticed they were wearing team jackets from a nearby town. One of them grabbed her bowler hat.

Sarah felt him drag the hat off her head. The brim scraped her scar, and she felt a flash of pain. The kids dropped it with embarrassment. "Sorry!" one of them yelled. Tears sprang to her eyes. Her mouth had dropped open, and for one terrible instant she looked at Will and registered her own shame in his eyes.

Ducking her head so he wouldn't see her cry, she felt his arms come around her. He held her against his chest. She felt his breath on her scalp, his hands covering the back of her head. She had moved freely without a hat all these weeks, but somehow the kids' cruelty and the idea of facing Mike had made her feel incredibly uncomfortable, self-conscious about her awful hair.

"It's pretty," he whispered. "It's so pretty."

"It's ugly," she wept. "My son's going to hate it."

"No, he won't," Will said.

"He ran away when I got sick," she said. "He's never seen me this way, it'll never grow out by Thanksgiving."

"Well, he'll see you then," Will whispered, his mouth against her ear. "I'm taking you there myself."

"If I even go."

"You'll go," he said. "You won't back out."

"How do you know?" she asked, leaning her head back to see his eyes.

"Because you're the bravest woman I've ever met," he said.

———

SECRET SAT IN the backseat of Julian's Range Rover. She was seething. Her mother and Julian had promised they could go to the fair, and they had started to, but now they were driving about a hundred miles an hour in the opposite direction. They had made the mistake of stopping at an antiques shop, and the dealer had given them a hot lead on a Victorian umbrella stand.

"I can't believe this," Secret said out loud.

"Believe what?" Julian asked.

"That you're making me miss the fair for a stupid umbrella stand."

He chuckled, glancing across the front seat at Secret's mother. Torn between wanting to support her husband and wanting to give in to Secret, Alice was gazing at him with a tight-lipped smile. As in, what-an-amusing-child-I-have-don't-be-mad-at-me. Alice was beautiful, a porcelain doll. She had golden hair and a perfect face, and three or four times a day she looked as if she might break.

"It's so unfair," Secret said.

"We'll get there —just be patient," Julian said, glancing at her in the rearview mirror. He lit a cigarette for himself and one for Alice. Another thing Secret hated about him: He had influenced her mother to start smoking again after having quit five years ago.

"It's not just an umbrella stand," her mother explained, blowing a quick puff of smoke into her lap, as if Secret couldn't see. "We're sorry about the fair, honey. But it's a great piece, a big old carved thing with hooks and a huge mirror and a bench. It's being auctioned off this afternoon, and it would look great in the south foyer."

"That's the thing about a big house," Julian said. "It needs lots of nice things to fill it up. Now that I have you and your mother with me, I want it to be even more beautiful."

"I'm not materialistic," Secret said. "I don't need *things*."

"Honey . . ." her mother warned.

"Let her be," Julian said, giving Alice a look that translated his words into "let her stew."

Secret settled lower into her seat, pulling her Red Sox cap down, leaving just enough space to look out the window. She watched the land fly by, farm after farm. Cows, cows, cows. She wanted to see boats so badly, her throat began to hurt. She wanted to smell salt air, feel the sea breeze on her face. Glancing at the back of Julian's head, she wished she had the powers necessary to make him disappear as dramatically as he had arrived.

For a year, he had only been her mother's boss. Then she divorced Secret's dad to marry him.

He owned a company called Von Froelich Precision that built race cars for rich guys. Prizefighters and rock stars would fly in from all over to order custom-designed cars made to go fast and look cool. Secret's mother had been the secretary, and she was always coming home with stories about the famous people she talked to, the movie stars who walked in wearing old jeans and scuffed-up shoes, seeming nervous about spending so much money, just like anyone else.

Suddenly, weeks after she had started working, she had started talking about Julian Von Froelich nonstop. How he was so *interesting*. He raced at Lime Rock and Laguna Seca and had once driven at Le Mans, he was world-renowned in the world of motorsports, but he was so *humble*. He hated when people asked him about Paul Newman, who happened to be a good friend. Every year he sponsored Grand Prix Day at the local high school, and he'd let all the kids sit in a race car and pretend they were driving.

Most of all, she talked about what a great boss he was, how he made Alice such a valued member of his staff: his *team*. She was just as integral a part of Von Froelich Precision as Julian's head mechanic, his pit crew chief. While Secret's dad buried himself in the newspaper and TV shows, Alice was building a new and fabulously glamorous life in the fast lane. Secret and her dad were numb zombies, too busy missing Fred to notice that her mother was leaving their family behind. Secret's parents got divorced a year earlier. Her mother married Julian a month after that.

"You know, the Queen of England drives a car like this," Julian said. When Secret looked up, she saw his eyes watching her in the rearview mirror.

"Lucky her," Secret said.

"A Range Rover. I thought you'd be interested, considering you're such an Anglophile."

"What I'm interested in is when we'll get to the fair," Secret said. She wanted to see her father. He was giving sight-seeing rides until three, and she wanted to get there before then. She checked her watch. "It's nearly fourteen hundred hours. It's going to be too late to go. If I'd known we were going to go looking for an umbrella stand, I'd have gone with my friends. . . ."

"People who think small usually end up with small lives," Julian said.

"I agree," Secret said.

"You're too good for the fair, Susan. A bunch of cheap garbage for sale and a lot of badly maintained rides. Mechanically, they're dangerous. Wanting to go to the fair is beneath you. I want to show you beautiful things. . . ."

"I was thinking of something else," she said. "About thinking small."

"Honey," her mother began, wanting to cut her off.

"You were? What?" Julian asked, meeting her gaze in the rearview mirror. He had eager, puppy-dog green eyes that made her feel terrible—he wanted her to like him, and she never would. He had long dark blond hair that he tied back in a tucked-under ponytail. Secret knew he thought he looked sexy, as if he were trying to be one of the rock-movie types he hung out with, but she thought he looked pretentious. She wondered how he'd feel if he knew he had a small bald spot on the back of his head, about the size of a silver dollar.

"What?" Julian pressed, tossing his head, not taking his eyes off her. "What's thinking small?"

"People who buy things all the time," Secret said quietly.

Julian drove in silence.

"I feel sorry for them," Secret said.

"Susan, you love shopping. Don't—"

"No, let her talk," Julian said, sounding hurt. "I want to hear."

"Nothing," Secret said, scrunching down. "Just that every time you have a free minute, you seem to be driving somewhere to buy something expensive. How many priceless antiques does one person need?" She thought of the carriage house, filled to the brim with mahogany tables, rosewood chests, teak benches. "You could open your own shop."

"Yes, but I don't need to," he said.

"I know," Secret said. For some reason she thought of Sarah Talbot; she sold beautiful things, but she did it to make people happy. She wanted the college kids in town to feel safe and warm, wrapped in thick down quilts and soft wool blankets. They might be far away from their parents, but they could feel all cozy and tucked-in with things from her store. She wondered if Sarah had gone to the fair.

"Honey, with all the beautiful things Julian gives you, you're not sounding very grateful," Alice said.

"Dad gives me everything I need."

Julian made a sound through his nose.

"What?" Secret asked, feeling something hard in her chest. Her breathing became faster, and her airway constricted.

"You're right, you're absolutely right," Julian said.

"Then why did you make that noise?" Secret asked. She felt the wheezing start.

"Oh, no reason. That's correct, what you said about your father. He puts clothes on your back, and he sends us money for your food. But . . ."

"What?" Secret nearly screamed.

"I guess it's a matter of where you like your clothes to come from. If Cromwell Casuals is okay for you, then fine."

"It is!"

"You're a little young, Susan. But one day the names Armani and Prada might mean something to you. Dolce & Gabbana, you know? I *want* to treat you like a princess. I don't *have* a daughter of my own. I haven't noticed you putting those Gainsboroughs out in the hall. Being a pilot is very cool, but the salary doesn't buy great paintings. You know?"

"Julian, I think that's enough," Alice said.

"I just want her to understand," Julian said, reaching across the seat to stroke his wife's head. "The way the world works."

"Don't talk about her father," Alice said, lowering her voice. "Don't say anything bad to her about Will."

Her mother was trying to defend her father, but it was too late. Secret was having an asthma attack. She fought to breathe. The air rasped through her mouth, into her lungs. Alone in the backseat, she gulped a sob. Her chest ached, and her throat stung, but that wasn't the worst part. Secret's heart was being squeezed. It was being crushed, as if two big hands had grabbed it and wanted to break it.

Reaching into her pocket, she found her inhaler. Pumping it once, she placed it in her mouth and took a breath. The aerosol hissed. Her lungs filled like a balloon; she could almost hear them inflate. Her mother looked back, and with her eyes asked Secret if she was okay. Secret nodded, her eyes glittering with tears. They stared at each other, each wanting something they could never have.

When her mother turned back to Julian, to try to cajole him out of the bad mood he had just fallen into, Secret was miles away. Her eyes closed, she was sailing. Out in Narragansett Bay, the white spire of Trinity Church sharp against the blue September sky, the sloop was flying across the water. Her father had the tiller, and Fred was trimming the jib, and Secret and the woman were just sitting back, their mouths open with joy, drinking the wind. The woman was so happy, her eyes shining with love. Secret knew she was supposed to be her mother, but in the fantasy she wasn't. In the fantasy her mother was off spending money with Julian.

With her eyes closed, as she sat in the backseat of Julian's Range Rover, speeding away from the fair, Secret clenched her fists to keep the fantasy going. The day was fine, the bay was calm, her father and Fred were laughing. The woman sitting beside her had brought a thermos of hot cider. They were sailing to an island, a secret island none of them had ever been to before, and they were going to have a picnic. The woman was smiling into the sun, and she turned to Secret and touched her hand, and now Secret could see her face, could see her kind and accepting face, could see she was Sarah Talbot.

CHAPTER

5

SARAH SAT IN a paper smock waiting for Dr. Goodacre to see her. Each monthly visit required long intervals of patience. He was a neurosurgeon, and most of his cases were, or had been, life-or-death. If you had a brain injury, you wanted Dr. Goodacre. He saw the head-on crash victims, the motorcyclists who spun out without their helmets, the children who dived into shallow water and broke their necks, the riders who flew off horses and severed their spines, the people who woke up with brain tumors.

His nurse, Vicky, walked in. She looked tense, driven. Opening a cabinet, she rummaged through with a fierce expression on her face. Sighing, she gave up, slammed the door, tried a drawer. She was small and slender, with auburn hair and a great figure, and Sarah thought she was probably very attractive away from work. But the pressures of working for Dr. Goodacre made her seem impatient and rather mean.

"Hi, Vicky," Sarah said.

"Oh, hi," Vicky said, abstracted.

"Has he got you running around?"

"He needs a prep kit, and he needs it last Christmas, you know?"

Sarah laughed. She had watched Dr. Goodacre in action for the last nine months, and she knew exactly what Vicky meant.

The quality that made him the doctor you wanted to save your life probably made him a nightmare as a boss.

Sarah sat at the edge of the exam table, watching Vicky flee from the room. She had wanted to ask about how long she had to wait, whether they could turn up the heat a little, but she held back. Her journey through illness had taught her to overlook certain details. She had trained herself to focus on the most important matters, let the small things fall into place.

Finally Dr. Goodacre walked through the door. He was tall and extremely thin, dressed in a dark suit covered by a white lab coat. A pale yellow tie was visible at the neck. He had short dark hair, and in spite of his round wire-rimmed glasses and lack of beard, he resembled Abraham Lincoln. Without smiling, he reached into a compartment behind the door and pulled out Sarah's chart.

"Hi, Doctor," she said.

"Hello, Sarah."

"Everyone seems so busy today."

"Mmm."

Frowning, he began to read. Sarah was unafraid of his severe expression. She understood it was just his manner, the way he protected himself from feeling too much about his worst cases. Dr. Goodacre had saved her life, and she adored him with all her heart.

"Any pain?"

"Only when I touch the scar."

"Numbness? Tingling?"

"No."

"No more seizures?" he asked, reading.

"Not since July." Sarah closed her eyes, saying a prayer. She hated seizures. She had had three, including the one that alerted her that something was wrong. Nine months before, she had been perfectly healthy, running seven miles a day, training to run in her first marathon. One day she woke up on the floor of her shower. The hot water had run out. She couldn't remember getting in, and she didn't know how long she had been lying there. It took all her strength to crawl to the phone and dial 911.

At first they thought she had had a stroke. She couldn't move, could barely talk. Her limbs felt heavy, and she had double vision. Cardiologists swarmed around her, hooking her up to heart monitors, ordering EKGs, CT scans, and EEGs. The EEG revealed seizure activity, and the heart doctors had handed Sarah over to the neurosurgery department for further tests. Within a day, they had found the brain tumor.

"Okay," he said, laying down her chart. He leaned close to look into her eyes. She smelled his spicy fragrance and smiled.

"If I had a boyfriend, I'd want to buy him that cologne," she said.

"Sit up straight and close your eyes," he said without smiling back. "Hold your arms straight out in front."

She did as she was told, knew he was watching to see whether she could keep her arms and hands steady.

"Now hold them straight out to the sides."

Like wings, she thought, like a plane flying to Maine.

"Touch your nose with your left index finger. Now your right. Eyes closed! Very good."

Sarah felt like a small child being tested by the school nurse. With her eyes closed, smelling Dr. Goodacre's familiar scent, she felt safe. She had first come to him for a second opinion. The first doctor, at a small hospital across town, had told her she had osteogenic sarcoma, the most deadly tumor possible. He had suggested that treatment would only prolong the inevitable, that even with surgery she would have only ten weeks to live. He had suggested she go to Paris, eat her favorite foods, say good-bye to the people she loved. Telling her this, he had held her hand. He was elderly and respected, and he had spoken in sonorous tones of regret.

He had sent her home. In shock, thinking of Paris and Mike

and death ten weeks away, Sarah had curled into a ball. Was this what her mother had gone through? Crying, Sarah had prayed to her. Weak and sick, she had needed the visiting nurse to check on her. Meg Ferguson had come to call. Six days into her death sentence, Mike had left for Maine. Ten days into it, pouring her terrors out to Meg, Sarah had listened to Meg's compassionate, logical reason: Get a second opinion.

A second opinion: the light in the dark, the hope after total despair. Suddenly Sarah saw with total clarity that she wasn't ready to accept the prognosis. Her mother had been too isolated on the island to fight her disease, but Sarah wasn't. Sarah was a mother, her son had run away to Maine, she didn't want to go to Paris, she couldn't be dying of a brain tumor. She couldn't—could *not*—die just then. Sarah could *not*. She could almost hear her mother begging her to fight. And so Meg had gotten Dr. Goodacre's name and number. And Sarah had called him.

"I'm thinking about taking a trip," she said to Dr. Goodacre now.

"You are?" he asked, examining the back of her head.

"To Maine. To see my son."

"Ah," he said, probing her scar. Her tumor had been located in the meninges, the lining between the skull and the brain. It had clung to the sinus nerve, making it a challenge to remove surgically without paralyzing or killing Sarah. But Dr. Goodacre had done an amazing job: he had gotten ninety-nine percent of it out. To get inside, he had cut a large flap in her scalp. U-shaped, it looked like a big red smile on the back of her head.

"Remember I told you about him?" she asked. "Mike? He left for Maine right about the time I met you?"

"At college?" the doctor asked, squinting at the incision.

"No, to live with my father." Sarah closed her eyes. She tried not to feel hurt. Just because Dr. Goodacre meant so much to her, why should he remember the mundane details of her life? With all his patients, that would be impossible. But just knowing she had thought the word "mundane" in connection with Mike made her feel worse, and she drew inward.

"Are you asking me if you should go?" he asked.

"Yes, I am."

"I see no reason why not," he said. He leaned against a low cabinet, and for the first time since entering the exam room, he really looked at her: into her eyes, as if she were a whole person, not just a collection of parts to study and assess. "Have you asked Dr. Boswell?"

"No," Sarah said. "Should I?" Dr. Boswell was her oncologist. While she was very important to Sarah's care, had administered two courses of chemotherapy and overseen the radiation treatment, Dr. Goodacre was the One. He was the one who had identified her tumor as large-cell lymphoma, eminently less deadly than osteogenic sarcoma, offering her the possibility of long-term recovery. He was the one in whom Sarah had placed her faith, to whom she entrusted her hopes and fears.

"I'll have Vicky give her a call," Dr. Goodacre said, making a note on Sarah's chart. "If she has no objection, neither do I."

"Really?" Sarah asked.

"You know the road we face, Sarah. You've done everything we've asked of you, and you've responded well."

"I just don't want a recurrence," she said, shivering. Did that sound dumb? Did anyone want a recurrence?

"I know. We can't predict . . . your tumor was very difficultly situated, and it is rather aggressive for a large-cell lym—" He cut himself off. The look on his face said it all. Dr. Goodacre gave Sarah credit for her intelligence and powers of intuition, and he didn't have to spell it all out. She might survive and she might not. Sarah knew the anguish of cancer: She had watched her own mother die in bed on Elk Island. She had watched her father wither and almost disappear with grief.

"I'd like to see my son," she said quietly, without emotion. "I'd like to go home."

He nodded. "Be alert," he said. "If you have any symptoms of numbness or tingling, you should call me immediately. But I see no reason for you not to go."

"Thank you," Sarah said, glowing as if she had just won a race.

"I'll see you back here in a month," Dr. Goodacre said as sternly as ever. Preparing to leave, on to the next case, his hand was on the doorknob.

"Dr. Goodacre," Sarah asked, needing to summon up a little courage. She had never asked him anything personal. "How's your father?" The last time she was there, she had heard Vicky saying his father had had a heart attack.

"Better," Dr. Goodacre said, pausing. He gave Sarah a curious look, as if he wondered how she knew to ask. "But he lives in Florida, and I can't be with him. It falls to my older brother to look after him."

"Does your brother do a good job?" Sarah asked.

"He's an angel!" Dr. Goodacre said with passion. He broke into a grin, staring straight into Sarah's eyes. Full of intensity, he looked at the ceiling, then back at Sarah. She understood how it felt to love someone far away, to worry yourself sick about him, to trust his care to another human being. In a way, Dr. Goodacre's brother was looking out for him—Dr. Goodacre—too.

"I'm glad," she said. "That you have such a wonderful brother."

"I wish everyone had someone like him," he said.

Sarah had never seen the doctor this way, and she nodded. He lingered for a moment, then walked away. The door closed softly behind him.

Alone in the room, Sarah closed her eyes. She felt her heart beating fast. Her exercises calmed her, so she held her arms out straight in front. Then out to the side again, like before. Sarah had never had a brother like the doctor's, had never had an angel in her life. But then she thought of Will Burke holding her at the fair, flying her home.

Taking her to see Mike.

———

WILL DROVE UP the long driveway. The road up Windemere Hill zigzagged through a forest of pin oaks and white pines. Snow had fallen the previous night, and the branches drooped low. At the top, the drive opened onto a wide, snow-covered lawn lined with white-capped boxwood hedges. It was late Friday afternoon, and he was there to pick up his daughter.

Julian's imposing stone mansion lorded over the wintry scene. Two old Ferraris were parked in the turnaround, and a Porsche 356 was visible in the carriage house. Will parked his car, trying not to feel resentful that one guy should have all this, and Alice and Susan too.

Expecting Susan, he was surprised to see Alice walk out the front door. The sight of her made him catch his breath. She was still the most beautiful woman he had ever seen, with her creamy skin and wide, almond-shaped blue eyes, silky golden hair, a shapely, feminine figure. She walked through the snow in short black boots.

She was wearing sleek gray workout clothes, revealing her body. In the fifteen years since their daughter's birth, she had never stopped trying to obliterate the slight roundness left in her tummy. Unable to help himself, Will checked to see if it was still there: It was.

"She asked me to tell you she'll be a few minutes late," Alice said hurriedly, her arms folded in front of her, her breath making white clouds.

"No problem," Will said. He got out of the car, leaned against the door. He wore jeans and an old green sweater. The air was freezing cold, and he had to fight the urge to offer Alice the leather jacket he had thrown in the backseat.

"Her asthma's been terrible lately."

"Really?"

"It's completely psychosomatic. We all know that. She works herself into attacks just to interrupt whatever's going on. I'm not blaming her, she's been through a lot, but she needs to be the center of attention."

"I did when I was fifteen," Will said, smiling.

"Like *that* ever stopped."

Was she kidding? Will couldn't tell. Her expression was stern, and she was staring at his boots. They were a pair of old Dunhams, the brown leather well worn and scuffed, recently resoled. He wondered if she remembered buying them for him their first winter in Fort Cromwell, five long years before.

"I wanted to ask you about Thanksgiving," Will began.

Her head snapped up. "Thanksgiving? She stays with me. We have plans—"

"Whoa," Will said, raising one hand. God, the smallest conversation became so tense, every point felt like a negotiation. He couldn't help thinking of other years, when a conversation about Thanksgiving with Alice revolved around Fred being John Alden in the school play, Susan playing a Pilgrim girl, whose parents' house they should go to, whether they should have mince or pumpkin pies or both for dinner.

"You know she stays with me on holidays, Will. It was part of the agreement."

"Yes, I know. Relax, Alice. I was just asking."

"My God. Everything is such a damn battle," she said, folding her arms even tighter.

"It's no battle. I just wanted to let you know I'll be out of town."

"Fine."

"Good."

"Where out of town?" she asked, glancing up, some new emotion in her cornflower-blue eyes: worry? Will had heard about wives who ran out on their marriages, started whole new lives, then developed intense curiosity about their ex-husbands' behavior. Was this what he was seeing in Alice? He somehow doubted it.

"I have a charter to Maine. I thought you should know, in

case her asthma gets really bad or she needs me for something else. You know?"

Alice nodded, her stern face back.

"She'll be okay," Will said. "Secret's going to be fine."

"Secret? Jesus, Will!" Alice exploded. "We named her Susan. You wanted to give her a name with *strength*, after someone she could look *up* to. . . ."

"Susan Mallory," he said, thinking of his grandmother.

"My God. Don't be indulging this 'Secret' crap. It's really unsettling, if you want to know how I feel about it. Julian thinks she needs more professional help."

"That's a good sign that she doesn't," Will said, feeling aggressively immature. "If Julian says she does. Didn't you tell him we went through that when we first got to Fort Cromwell?"

"Of course I did. He knows Dr. Darrow." Splaying her fingers with frustration, Alice revealed some of her jewels: the largest diamond ring Will had ever seen, and a wedding ring–style band of diamonds and emeralds. Will exhaled slowly.

"Hi!" their daughter called, bursting through the front door with her knapsack, duffel bag, and a small package.

She stood there like a star who had just burst onstage: radiant smile, theatrical pose, boundless energy, arms open wide to greet her adoring public. Her parents were too upset to applaud or even smile, but Will tried. He gave a half-smile, holding out his left arm to embrace her as she ran through the snow.

"Hi, Secret," he said.

"Jesus," Alice muttered.

"Hi, Dad. Can we drive through town? I have something I have to drop off for a friend."

"You bet," he said.

"I'll need a number for wherever you're going on Thanksgiving," Alice said brusquely. "Just in case."

"You're going somewhere for Thanksgiving?" Secret said, jerking her head back from Will's chest, looking up at him with worried eyes.

"Just for work," he said.

"You're going to *work* on *Thanksgiving*?"

"I'm flying the Fergusons' friend Sarah Talbot to Maine."

"That's who you're taking?" she asked with apparent amazement, staring at her small package.

"Do you have your inhaler?" Alice asked, pulling her away from Will for a hug. Seeing his ex-wife hold their daughter brought too much back for Will, and he had to look away. Glancing toward the carriage house, he saw Julian walking out with a man wearing a blue mechanic's uniform. Time to go.

"You ready, Secret?" Will asked, hoisting her bags.

"Please," Alice said. "I hate that name. You two can play make-believe when you're alone, but when you're around me, I can't have it."

"You don't have to call me Secret," she said. "I'm changing it. As of midnight last night, I'm Snow."

"Susan..." Alice said dangerously.

"Well, hello," Julian said, walking over. He had the tall, lean look of a man who worked out or ran a lot, with a stupid ponytail that looked idiotic with the lines on his face. He had to be fifty years old, Will thought. He wore an expensive suede jacket with his race car logo embroidered on the chest.

"Hi, Julian," Will said, shaking his hand.

"You know why I'm Snow?" his daughter asked, her voice high and tense. "Because of Freddie. He adored winter, it was his favorite season."

"Susan, honey, stop..." Alice said.

"Sledding, skiing. Remember when we all went to Mt. Tom? How much he loved it, he refused to stop all day, even for lunch, he skied and skied until the lifts stopped running and it was dark and we couldn't find him?"

"I can't bear it," Alice said, her face bright red.

"He taught me how to make angels in Newport. We lay in the snow at Trinity Church, looking out over the harbor, and we lay on our backs and spread our arms and legs and waved at the sky over and over until our prints were in the snow. Remember?"

"I remember," Will said, gazing into her glittering eyes.

"Stop, honey," Alice said, grabbing her wrist, tears rolling down her cheeks. "Changing your name won't bring him back."

"He just loved it so much," she went on as if she hadn't heard. "Falling out of the sky, lying on the docks. He didn't care. Snow. He died in September, so I was September, and he always kept my secrets, so I was Secret, and he loved, loved, loved snow, so I'm Snow."

"Oh, God," Alice said, burying her face in her hands and starting to sob.

"Can't you say something to your daughter?" Julian asked harshly, wrapping his arms around Alice as he glared at Will.

Will didn't speak. He took his daughter's hands, held them in his. Looking deeply into her eyes, he tried to reach her. She was wild, crazy with grief for Fred. Will felt it too, and so did Alice. Will had been so wrecked, he had resigned from the Navy before they could kick him out. The overpowering loss came over him again now. His heart pounding, he tried to pull his daughter close, but she wouldn't let him. She faced Julian with hatred in her gaze.

"Don't you talk to my dad that way," she said.

"Listen," Julian said. "I've had about as much as I'm going to take with you disrespecting your mother. If your father won't say it, I will. You're hurting your mother, Susan. If you need to go back to Dr. Darrow, we'll see that you do. But cut the name bullshit right now."

Will didn't even feel it coming. The punch started somewhere in his gut, and by the time it got to his fist, Julian was laid out on his driveway, blood from his nose turning the snow pink. Alice was screaming, the mechanic was rocking back and forth on his heels, and Susan was crying. Will's knuckles hurt, as if he might have broken them. His head pounded, an emotional hangover starting already.

"I'm sorry," he said calmly, standing over his ex-wife's husband. "But I can't have you speaking to my daughter that way."

"Fucking maniac," Julian said, struggling to sit up. "No wonder the Navy kicked you out. Fucking menace to society."

Will considered holding out his hand to help the man up, but he didn't want to add insult to injury. He gazed at Julian for an instant, making sure he could move okay, that he hadn't broken anything. He glanced at Alice, ashamed of himself for making her cry harder. Then he turned to his daughter, tried to reassure her with a smile.

"Sarah thinks it's a beautiful name," his daughter said, her eyes wide, full of panic, looking as if the world had betrayed her, as if she had just walked away from a cloister or asylum and been horrified by the real world, what she found outside. But she had said the name Sarah, and Will felt something give. The anger drained out of him. He wished he were with her now, flying wherever she wanted to go.

"Sarah? Who's Sarah?" Alice asked, but no one answered her.

"Come on, Snow," Will said, his hands shaking. "Time to leave."

Without another word, the pair climbed into Will's old blue Jeep, and they drove away.

———

THE COLOGNE PHILHARMONIC was playing in the Marcellus College Concert Series that night, and Julian was a subscriber. But his nose was broken, and his mood was foul, so he was lying on the sofa with an ice pack and a bottle of Courvoisier while Alice tried to read. They were in the library, listening to Sibelius. A fire crackled in the fieldstone fireplace.

When she heard Julian start to snore, Alice lowered her

book. She placed it on the low tiger-maple table and gazed at her sleeping husband. He loved her so much and tried so hard. Kissing him, she tiptoed out of the room. She wandered through the enormous house, listening to the wind outside. This was her home. She kept telling herself that, walking past portraits of people she had never met. Moving here, she had believed she was going to be so happy. She had found love, and it was going to save her.

At certain terrible moments in life, she had learned to make choices. At thirty-five years, set in ways she had been establishing for years, surrounded by people she thought she knew. Building a family with a man, raising his children, using his name. Going along, not happy, not unhappy, when the bottom just fell out.

Her only son died. They were all together when it happened. The scene was a nightmare, with no one doing what she would expect them to do and no one waking up in time. Everyone reacted in unexpected ways.

Nothing would bring him back, and Alice was left with the wreckage. A daughter who couldn't stop crying, a husband who lost his mind.

Lost in his own hell, her husband turned neglectful. Had she ever loved him to begin with? She wasn't sure. Being ignored when she had needed him so much made her start to hate him. He took his retirement, uprooted the family, and moved them far away from anything comforting or familiar. She had begged him to snap out of it, and he didn't even hear her. She got a job just to get out of the house. She loved her new job, she loved her new boss.

And her new boss loved her. He treated her like a queen, a lover, a woman. They had an affair, but suddenly he was her whole world, so "affair" didn't begin to describe what they felt for each other. *This* was right, *this* was what she was born for, *this* was what God intended. So much so, she was willing to break her husband's heart. Break up her daughter's family. Her son was buried, but she imagined him giving her his blessing. He would want his mother to be happy.

Did I do the right thing? She would ask herself that question for the rest of her life. She loved her new husband, cherished him with all her heart, lay beside him at night and thanked her lucky stars. She quit her job to volunteer at the hospital because she was now so rich. But there was so much pain. She saw it every time she looked into her daughter's face; she saw the broken man she left behind and blamed herself for all his sleepless nights. She knew he had them, because she knew him better than anyone else alive.

Walking through the big, empty house, Alice couldn't stop thinking of Will's rage, the fury in his eyes as he decked Julian. He'd been storing it up for a long time, just waiting for the right excuse. She blamed herself. Just as she blamed herself for Susan's crazy name-changing, just as Will blamed himself for what happened to Fred.

Her feet felt warm in her fleece-lined slippers as she strolled the dark halls like a tormented sleepwalker. With Susan at Will's, now might be the time to look through her drawers and see what she needed for clothes. With Christmas coming, she knew Julian wanted to buy her some special things.

But when she got to Susan's room, she stopped still.

There, standing in the hallway, leaning neatly against the walnut wainscoting, were the two Gainsboroughs that Julian had given her. Alice stared at them, the beautiful paintings in their large gold frames. The little girl, the two small dogs. She remembered what Julian had said in the car on their way to the auction, about Will not being able to afford paintings like these, and she closed her eyes.

This was too much for her. She felt the weight of her daughter's unhappiness bearing down on her shoulders, and she sank to the floor. Cold drafts of air blew through the rooms. Hugging herself, she lowered her head. Constantly preoccupied with Susan, she was too upset to be the woman Julian had fallen in love with. She was going to lose it all: her new marriage, her security, her daughter's respect.

Sitting there, alone in the upstairs hallway of Julian's stone chateau, she whispered one word: "Help."

6

SARAH HAD JUST opened her shop on Saturday morning when she heard the bells above her door tinkle. That fresh white-yellow early light was in her eyes, so she leaned down to see around the sunlight. Will Burke and his daughter stood there, holding two white bakery bags.

"We came last night, but you had already closed," the young girl said.

"You caught me," Sarah said. "I wanted to go to the movies in Wilsonia, so I closed a little early. What do you have there?"

"We brought you breakfast," Will said. He looked tan and sexy, bundled up in a hunter-green ski jacket. His ears were red from the cold, and the corners of his gray-blue eyes crinkled in the sunlight.

"You must have read my mind," she said, grinning. "I'm starved!"

"Are you really?" the girl asked.

"Yes, Snow," Sarah said. "My stomach is growling."

Snow's intake of breath was loud and dramatic. The teenager stood there, one mittened hand over her mouth; she looked pale, with dark circles under her eyes. "How did you know I'd changed my name?"

"You told me you wanted to be 'Snow' for winter, didn't

you? Just look outside," Sarah said, pointing at the snow-covered street, the new powder lying on all the rooftops and evergreens, on the statue of General Jameson Cromwell standing on the town green.

Snow and her father looked at each other. Some violent feeling was clouding the girl's eyes. She had been practically wringing her hands, but she began to calm down. She took a deep breath. Removing the plaid muffler from around her neck, she trailed it across the damask-covered bed.

"Let's sit back here," Sarah said, clearing a place on her desk for the doughnuts, coffee, and juice. Doughnuts weren't on her list of healthful foods, they were too sugary and fried for her, but there was no way in the world she wasn't going to have one just then.

With Snow and Will watching her, she selected a French cruller and tasted it, letting herself enjoy every bite. That was her motto: Once you decide to do something, you might as well love it. Such ease of mind didn't always come freely, but it was always worth the effort.

"You're going to Maine, I hear," Snow said, placing a small white bag on the desk. Sarah moved to open it, but Snow gestured for her to wait till later. Curious, Sarah slid it aside.

"Maine? Yes, I am," she said.

"The five-day forecast looks cold but clear," Will said. "No storms in sight."

"Why all the way to Maine?" Snow asked.

"To see my son."

"You have a son?" Snow asked, nearly dropping the doughnut she had just chosen.

"Yes. Mike. He's not much older than you."

"He doesn't live with you? How come? Does he live in Maine with his father?"

"Snow..." Will began.

"That's okay. I love talking about him. He's a man of strong beliefs and opinions, a total individual, and about a year ago he dropped out of high school to go home to Elk Island and save my father's farm."

"You grew up on a farm?" Snow asked.

"Yes," Sarah said. She gestured at a pile of quilts stacked in the corner. "See those? They were made on our farm. About nineteen years ago I started a store like this in Boston because the farm was about to go under. My mother had been sick when I was young, and when I was fourteen she died. My father was just so distracted . . . especially after she was gone. He found someone from Thomaston who wanted to buy all the geese, and he had a man from Camden who wanted to buy the land. None of that sat very well with me, so I dropped out of college to start my business and support the farm."

"Like mother, like son," Will said.

"Exactly. I have no one to blame but myself. Was that what you were going to say?"

"No, I was going to say your father is a lucky man," Will said, handing her a cardboard cup of coffee.

Sarah thanked him, taking a sip.

"Did you save the farm?" Snow asked, sitting on the edge of her seat.

"I can't actually say we *saved* it," Sarah said, picturing the ramshackle buildings, the tired old geese, the falling-down fences, her Aunt Bess with her ancient treadle sewing machine. "But so far he's been able to keep it."

"It's still running?" Will asked.

"Yes. They put out ten quilts a year, and I pay them. They sell geese. Together we just about cover the taxes."

"Your father must love you so much! He must be so ecstatic to have Mike living with him now," Snow said. The thought made her so happy, she popped two doughnut holes into her mouth, one in each cheek, and left them there as she closed her eyes, basking in the notion of a grateful old father.

"I'm not really sure how he feels," Sarah said.

"Ask him!" Snow said, stating what was so obvious to her.

It did sound simple. But Sarah and her father had years and layers of bitterness between them: disagreements over her mother's treatment, the aftermath of her death, the fact that Sarah had left the island. Sarah tried to smile.

"Why don't you?" Snow asked, looking troubled.

"You know how I said Mike's a man of strong opinions? Well, he got that from his grandfather. And most of his opinions collide with mine."

"Difficult," Will said, looking as if he understood.

"It is."

"That's no reason not to try," Snow said. "He's a person too. If I'd given up on you, Dad, I'd hate to think of where we'd be. Talk about difficult."

"Hey," Will said. Was he kidding or hurt? Sarah couldn't tell by his eyes.

"Worse than difficult," Snow said, glancing at Sarah.

"Fathers don't have it easy," Sarah said. Although for some reason her thoughts slid to Zeke, who had had it about as easy as it got: From the minute Sarah had told him about her pregnancy, he had never wanted to see her again. Her father had gone crazy. His fury at Zeke had distracted him, at least a little, from the long-standing grief he felt for Sarah's mother.

"They don't *make* it easy," Snow said.

"What did I do?" Will asked, taking another cruller. "To get me in such trouble?"

"I happen to be referring to the fact that you quit the Navy and dragged me and Mom way the hell into these ridiculous boondocks," Snow said, glaring at him. Then, afraid she was offending Sarah, she touched the back of her hand. "I'm sorry. They're nice for some people, but we need the ocean."

"I understand completely. My son used to say the same thing to me, and he was right. I moved us away from Boston to these—what did you call them—ridiculous boondocks? Mike used to call it the middle of nowhere."

"If I had a family farm to run away to, I just might go there," Snow said.

"Don't run away," Will said.

"He's right, Snow. Listen to your father. It's not worth it," Sarah said, feeling suddenly cold. She had worn a flowing silk jacket, rich with embroidery and brocade, and she pulled it tightly around herself. She looked at Will, saw that abstract fear in his face, and knew what he was feeling: the idea that his child could just disappear from him.

"I don't see why not," Snow said. "Mike took off and you're following him out there for Thanksgiving, so your family can be together. The way it's supposed to be."

"That's a nice thought, but the reality's going to be a little different," Sarah said. "My father doesn't believe in much anymore except high and low tide and the phases of the moon. He hasn't really celebrated a holiday for years—not since my mother died."

"Then why did they ask you?"

"Her son asked her," Will said, although she hadn't told him.

"He did," Sarah said. "He knows I love Thanksgiving more than any other holiday, and he knows I'll close the shop and give myself a few days off."

"More than any other holiday? More than *Christmas*?" Snow asked.

"Yes."

"Always? It's always been your favorite?"

"No, not when I was your age."

"Then when?"

"Why do you love it so much?" Will asked.

"It started the year my son was born," Sarah said, looking into Will's eyes. Seeing him with his daughter made her like him even more than before; she recognized his passion as a parent, and she knew he would understand.

Will nodded, riveted.

"I just never knew how—" Sarah paused, getting herself under control. "Incredible it would be. How it would change me from the inside out."

"Having children."

"Having Mike made me a different person. I fell madly in love with him, and when you're in love, everything looks so beautiful. You stare at a sunset, and you can't bear to think it won't last forever. You think your heart will break. You know?"

As if she knew this was between the adults, Snow was silent. She sat very still, perched on the chair, her knees drawn up to her chin, watching Sarah and her father. But Will nodded.

"I was so happy," Sarah said, her eyes shining. "The world made sense. I'd watch red finches at the bird feeder and imagine God made them for me and Mike. I felt so grateful. All I wanted to do was give thanks, and when Thanksgiving rolled around that year, it became my favorite holiday."

"And you told Mike?" Will asked.

"Every year. All the time."

"You can't tell them enough," Will said. "You have to tell them you love them all the time."

"That's why I'm going to Maine," Sarah said, bowing her head.

"It's been too long," Will said.

She nodded. Composing herself, she looked up.

"I'm afraid the farm is wrong for him. It's very isolated, there aren't any other kids around. His father was from the island, but he's dead. And my father..." She glanced at Snow. "Well, my father is difficult. Losing my mother made him unhappy. He never got over it. Never. The years did nothing to soften his pain."

"Death does that," Snow said.

Sarah nodded. "I'm afraid his misery will rub off on Mike. My Aunt Bess used to be the smilingest person you knew when she lived in Providence. But when her husband died, she moved back to the island, and you should see her now. Living alone with my father all this time has turned her into an old prune."

"It sounds interesting," Snow said.

Sarah stared at her. What kind of wonderful girl would think such a bleak scenario sounded "interesting"?

"I felt guilty for leaving," Sarah said. "But I had to."

"Did you take care of your mother?" Will asked.

"How did you know?"

"You just seem like someone who would," Snow volunteered.

"I did," Sarah said quietly, remembering her mother's loving presence, her steady gaze. "But I had to escape."

"And now you're going back," Will said, "for Mike."

"Exactly," Sarah said. Unconsciously, her hand strayed up to her head, where the cancer had been. "I want to set him straight before it's too late."

"Before he turns into a young prune," Snow said.

"Before he forgets why you love Thanksgiving so much," Will said.

"Fuel up the big plane, Dad," Snow said. "Because I'm coming with you."

"No!" Sarah said quickly. "The island's a mess. There's not enough heat in the house, the geese smell terrible." She felt worried, not wanting this to become a big excursion, a way for the Burkes to pass Snow's school break, to get through whatever trouble they were obviously having.

Sarah had a mission. She saw her son as lost, a piece of driftwood far at sea, and she needed to bring him back. Wanting to say more, to stop this before it went too far, her thoughts raced. She didn't want Snow, another person in need of attention, to distract her from Mike. But Will saved the day.

"You can't come, honey," he said. "It's my job, not a vacation. And your mother wouldn't like it. She needs you with her for Thanksgiving. You know that."

"She has Julian," Snow said.

"Yes, but she needs you," Will said.

"Dad, I—"

"No, Snow. You're staying with your mother. That's all there is to it."

Sitting back, Sarah knew that Will needed Snow every bit as much. He was big and strong, and he had a deep, calm voice that hid a lot. But he couldn't hide his love for his child. Sarah knew. She couldn't hide hers for Mike either.

———

THAT NIGHT AT home, Sarah opened the package Snow had left on her desk. It was a small cardboard box of bleach. She stood in the bathroom, staring at herself in the mirror. The thought of dyeing her hair felt weird, but Thanksgiving was less than a week away.

She lit the candle Meg had given her before her last surgery. It glowed from within. Staring at the candle, she thought of the red barn and white goose down of Elk Island, candles and quilts, the mysterious connection between the archaic and the modern.

She pictured Mike in the cold barn. She heard the geese honking, saw their feathers drifting like snow in the wind. As a baby he had loved the geese. He had cried one time, afraid his grandfather was hurting them to get their feathers. Holding him tight, Sarah had smelled his sweet neck, whispered in his ear that the geese didn't mind, that taking their down was no worse than combing a little boy's hair.

Her words had been a lie, and by now, working in the barn, Mike would have found that out. Ducking her head under the faucet, feeling the hot water on her head, she wondered what he thought about that.

Reaching blindly for the box of bleach, Sarah thought of Snow. She was another woman's daughter, and Sarah hoped she was as kind to her own mother as she had been to her, encouraging her to take this scary step. Sarah would never have bleached her hair on her own. Wondering what she would look like, she found herself imagining what Will might think of her.

Whether he would think she looked foolish, a middle-aged woman trying to look too young.

Or whether Will would think she looked pretty. Like he had said at the fair.

———

THE EVIL CASTLE was cold and forbidding, with everyone letting Snow know exactly how they felt about her. All the big, ugly, baronial furniture squatted along the walls like toady gnomes, closely watching her every move. Her mother and Julian sat on the love seat by the fire, sharing a bottle of wine. The old portraits leered at her, Julian's moon-faced ancestors. They didn't love her, but they were going to make sure she didn't escape.

"I want to go," Snow said again.

"Absolutely not," her mother said.

"Poor Dad. You're going to let him fly all the way to Maine with some stranger and no one who loves him on Thanksgiving?"

"He's a grown man, Susan," her mother said. "Accepting that charter was his choice. If he had wanted to stay in Fort Cromwell, he could have picked you up after dinner on Thursday and spent the whole weekend with you. I'm sure you'll see him when he gets back."

"Dinner's the important part," Snow said. "Last Thanksgiving he ate frozen turkey dinners. Six of them!"

"We want you to be here with us," Julian said, swirling his wine and appreciating the color in the firelight.

"Yeah, right," Snow said.

"We do," he said. "I've already told Pansy to make that sweet potato dish you like, with the marshmallows and pecans. . . ."

"Hazelnuts," Snow said. "I like it with hazelnuts."

"Ah. Well, we'll have to tell Pansy."

Snow wanted to walk right across the room and wipe that dumb grin off his face. He thought he was being such a great stepfather, telling his cook to make sweet potatoes for Thanksgiving while her father was being forced to fly practically to the tundra to rescue someone else's kid.

"They need me to go with them," Snow said.

"That's not what your father said," Alice said.

"That's only because he's trying to make things easy for you and not fight for me on the holidays. They need me, to help talk Mike into coming home."

"Who's Mike?" Julian asked.

"Sarah Talbot's son. He went home to Maine to save the family farm, he's practically a saint looking after his old grandfather and Aunt Bess, but he's throwing his life away. She wants to get him back before it's too late, and I know I can help. One kid to another, you know?"

"Mike Talbot," Julian said, smirking.

Snow was stirring the fire with a long poker. Its brass handle was shaped like a lynx's head. It had an evil little smile on its cat face, just the way Julian looked now. Snow felt like running upstairs before he spoke, not giving him the satisfaction of listening, but her curiosity got the better of her.

"Oh, do you know him?" Alice asked, leaning against his chest with his arm around her.

"Yeah, I do. He's a druggie."

"He *is*?"

"Yeah. He worked for me after school last year. He was my clean-up kid."

"That doesn't mean he took drugs," Snow said. She had been to Julian's shop. He owned a big garage with race cars up on lifts and mechanics drilling things underneath and some of the faster boys from high school hanging around, sprinkling Speedy-Dry on the spilled oil and sweeping it up with a wide broom.

"Mike Talbot did. My foreman caught him smoking pot

and fired him on the spot. Zero tolerance for drugs in my operation."

"I think that's wonderful," Alice said, gazing at him as if he had just discovered the cure for cancer.

"Thanks," he said, giving her that Elvis grin he thought was so sexy. The thing was, and Snow hated to admit it, his eyes shone with love every time he looked at her mother. "I felt terrible doing it, though. Firing Mike. He was a nice kid. A little on the edge, but basically good. His mother runs that great down shop in town."

"Cloud Nine? The quilt place?" Alice asked.

"Yes. I dated her once before you came along," Julian said, nuzzling her neck. "She used to be very beautiful before she got sick."

"I don't want to hear about beautiful women you once dated," Alice said, pretending to be huffy. She leaned away from Julian, and he pulled her back.

"She was never in your league. She had this New England thing going, high cheekbones and an aquiline nose and this rich dark hair all swept up on her head. Kind of a Boston de' Medici, real aristocratic. I bought some pillows and took her out for a drink, that's all. Gave her kid a job."

"Good," Alice said.

"I heard she got very sick. Frankly, I'm glad to hear she's still well enough to work," Julian said.

"Well, she is," Snow said.

"Sarah Talbot," Alice mused. "That name sounds familiar. I think maybe I've seen her at the hospital."

Snow watched her trying to picture Sarah. Since marrying Julian, her mother had quit her job to do good deeds at the hospital. She wore a pink smock and spent two days each week with other Fort Cromwell society women delivering flowers and offering to help sick people write letters or walk to the solarium. Snow admired her mother for doing it, and she wondered if she had ever helped Sarah. But just then her mother seemed to be drawing a blank.

"I wish her nothing but the best," Julian said.

"I'm going to Maine with her and Dad," Snow said.

"Susan," Alice said, leaning forward. "You are not invited. You are not allowed. You are not going."

"I'm going," Snow said softly.

"I hear you're sick of Gainsborough," Julian said, pouring more wine into his and Alice's glasses. "You're rotating the exhibit in your bedroom."

"Sorry," she said.

"Whatever you want, Susan," he said. "You pick out any paintings you want. What's mine is yours. You want sweet potatoes for Thanksgiving, you get sweet potatoes. This year you pick the pies. And what was that cranberry stuff you made last year? Delicious. I want the same exact thing this year, and you have to make it. It wouldn't be the same if Pansy did."

"I want to be with Dad," Snow whispered, gazing at her mother, who wouldn't meet her eyes.

CHAPTER

7

THE DAY BEFORE Thanksgiving, Sarah woke up with a slight fever. She felt hot, but when she pushed back the quilt, she felt cold. Her muscles ached. Her mouth felt dry, and when she swallowed, her throat hurt.

"Please, not today," she said. She could not come down with the flu right now, but that was what her symptoms felt like. Today Will Burke was flying her to Elk Island. Before dark tonight, she would see Mike. Slowly, she got out of bed. Pushing back her curtains, she could see the sun rising over the house across the street. The sky was clear and brilliant, already bright blue.

By the time she took a shower and drank some orange juice, she felt all better. Her skin was cool. The flu had merely lighted upon her instead of settling in for a real bout. It had reminded Sarah of being very sick, of all she had to be grateful for. She flexed her shoulders, stretched her spine. She thought of near-misses on the highway, an incredible white rose she had seen lingering in her garden last week. Instead of the flu, were the fatigue and aches cancer-related? She refused to think that way. Sarah had grown to believe in the small miracles of life, and she knew she had just received another.

Meg Ferguson picked her up at nine to drive her to the airport. Sarah was ready, dressed in traveling clothes: jeans, an Irish fisherman's sweater, a long navy wool jacket. She had two large bags packed, one filled with things Mike had left behind. At first she considered pulling on an old red felt hat, but when she saw Meg turn into the driveway, she took a deep breath and left the hat on the chair.

With her head in the trunk, rearranging things to make room for Sarah's bags, Meg didn't see Sarah right away. But when she looked up, her mouth fell open. Sarah was so nervous, her heart was pounding.

"Oh, my God," Meg said.

"Is it ridiculous?" Sarah asked, covering her head with her hands. Meg held Sarah by the elbows, easing her arms down. Sarah could hardly look at her.

"It's gorgeous. Let me see."

Meg, who wasn't exactly the done-hair type, stood back and gazed appraisingly at her friend. Meg had straight brown hair and bangs pushed off to one side. She wore her usual uniform of a skirt and sweater covered by a white lab coat. Her stethoscope dangled from the left pocket. She had a plastic turkey pinned to her lapel. But she was looking at Sarah as if she were a world-famous stylist and Sarah was a rare specimen of beauty.

"I can't believe the difference," Meg said.

"Is it too much? Do I look like myself?"

"I never knew you before," Meg said, and Sarah knew she meant before the illness. "And you do look different. I mean, it's like Paris. You've got that model's bone structure anyway, and now with that white-gold hair . . . Wow. Very chic, Sarah."

" 'Chic'?" Sarah asked, smiling.

"Will Burke had better keep his eyes on the sky," Meg said. "With you looking like that."

Sarah shook her head, embarrassed. "Will Burke? What would it matter to him? He won't even notice."

"He'll notice."

"Meg, he's just a nice pilot flying me to Maine."

"Bull," Meg said, grinning. "Mimi took a picture of you two at the fair. The look in his eyes . . ."

"He was just being nice," Sarah said. "Some kids had swiped my hat." But she found herself wishing she could see that picture, wondering about the look in Will's eyes.

"Well, you don't need any hat today. You look beautiful. Ready to go?"

"All set," Sarah said, climbing into the car.

"Dr. Goodacre gave you the green light?" Meg asked, backing out of the driveway.

"Yes," Sarah said, wondering if she should mention the fever. She touched her own forehead; it felt cool.

"His nurse is a piece of work," Meg said. "Vicky. I used to call her for questions about your dressing changes, whether he wanted me to keep using Silvadine or not, and first of all she'd never call me back, and second of all, when she finally did, she was so mean!"

"He runs a tight ship," Sarah said, smiling with recognition at the description of Vicky. "I keep hoping she's happier outside of work."

"Anyway, you feel fine, and that's what counts."

"Hmm," Sarah said. Her fever was gone, the flu had passed her by; she decided to say nothing to Meg. They were halfway to the airport, the day was shining, and she was on her way to see Mike.

"What?" Meg asked, glancing over.

"If it came back," Sarah said, so choked up she almost couldn't talk. "I couldn't stand it."

"Oh, Sarah," Meg said.

They had talked this over before: Sarah knew that when tumors like hers recurred and metastasized, the survival rates plummeted. The new treatment would be just as aggressive as the last, and the outcome would be uncertain. They would just be maintaining her life, keeping the cancer in check while she slipped away. The thought of living her life in cycles of pain and illness, steadily growing weaker, filled her with dread.

"I won't, you know," Sarah said.

"Won't what?"

"Have any more radiation or chemo." Sarah shivered. "This is my chance, and I'm going to grab it."

"Grab it, Sarah," Meg said, her voice catching. Reaching across the seat, she hugged her friend. "That's exactly what you should do."

"I have to," Sarah said. Her heart was pounding, but in the warmth of her friend's arms she suddenly relaxed. Her head cleared, she felt calm. She was healthy, free, on her way to a place that used to be home. Sarah Talbot felt bright as the day.

————

WILL HAD THE big plane all fueled up and ready to go. He had called the National Weather Service, learned that they could expect clear flying and a ten-knot tailwind the whole way. They had a high ceiling, clouds building in the west and weather blowing in for tomorrow. But for today, the line of high pressure would keep them safe.

He had thrown his duffel bag into the baggage compartment, and tossed an extra jacket into the backseat. The Piper Aztec was an older plane, all-weather, and it had significant range. It had six passenger seats and enough instruments to fly around the world in fog, so he felt prepared.

Even excited. It was Thanksgiving, and he had made no plans. With his daughter tied up with her mother and Julian, it wasn't going to be any fun hanging around Fort Cromwell. He remembered last year. He had decided to boycott the holiday, spent the afternoon watching football and drinking beer, but midway through the first game he got a craving for turkey.

Driving down to the A&P, he'd stocked up on frozen turkey dinners, but eating them had made him feel more depressed than he'd felt in years.

Seeing Meg Ferguson's blue car coming down the airport road, Will locked the office door behind him. He had his chart case. He checked his pockets, making sure he had his keys and wallet. Since Fred's death, he had become somewhat forgetful. Before she'd left, Alice used to tease him about having early Alzheimer's disease. Sometimes he had wondered how she did it, store all the facts and details of everyday life in with all that sorrow.

His daughter had begged him to let her fly to Maine with him, but he had held firm. It wasn't fair to Sarah, and it wasn't fair to Alice. Ultimately, it wouldn't be fair to his daughter. Selfishly, Will would have loved to have her along. But he had to do what was right. The thought of another holiday without either of his children struck him straight in the heart; he felt an actual pain, and he touched his chest.

This is my Thanksgiving, he thought, watching the car come. Flying a stranger to an island to see her family. He recognized the self-pity, hated himself for it. But then Sarah Talbot stepped out of the car and everything changed. The woman glowed. She looked around, gazing from the sky to the plane to Will. Waving, she opened both her arms and looked straight at him, as if to ask whether he had made this day for her.

Will looked up. For the first time that day, he saw the weather as something other than a system to fly through: a clear blue sky, shimmering sunshine. The sun sparkled on mica in the tarmac and some traces of snow left in the field. The sunlight was going to look like diamonds spread upon the ocean. In a few hours Will would see the Atlantic, the sea he loved so much.

It was nearly Thanksgiving, and he didn't have his daughter with him, but she was alive and well. Will walked toward Sarah and knew he was going to be fine. He had a feeling about her, and he had since the first time he'd seen her. Sarah Talbot was taking him home.

———

THE TWIN ENGINES hummed loudly. The sky surrounded them in endless blue. Sunlight turned the wings silver, and even though she wore dark glasses, Sarah couldn't stop squinting. The land below was vast and forested, filled with snowcapped pines standing on rocky hillsides. The mountains rose ahead.

Neither she nor Will spoke. They flew along in silence, watching the land unfold. A radio crackled, and voices spoke to them from down below. Occasionally Will would answer, using their call letters. Sarah had the sense of being passed from tower to tower, as if the air traffic controllers were a benevolent order, overseeing their progress from New York to Maine. At one point Will reached over to take her hand. He held it for a few minutes, until he had to use the radio again to call into Boston Center.

"Look," Will said, leaning toward Sarah to point out a bald eagle circling below. Its wings were long and broad, and it crossed its territory with very few beats. Seeing it filled Sarah with strong emotion.

"It's a big one," Sarah said, watching it fly over its nest. "We have eagles on the island." She was a patriot, and seeing eagles always made her proud. Her father had flown in World War II, and she had grown up singing anthems. That reminded her of something Snow had said, and she turned to Will. "You were in the Navy, weren't you?"

"Yes, I was."

"But it's not where you learned to fly?"

"No, I've always loved flying. I grew up in Waterford, Connecticut, near a small airport, and I learned how to fly before I could drive. My first job was taking charters out to Block Island."

"So this is nothing new to you. Flying people out to islands."

"No, it's old hat," he joked, laughing.

"Snow said you flew in the Navy."

"Some of the time. Yes, I did."

"She's so proud of you," Sarah said.

Will was silent for a while. "I don't know why," he said.

Sarah could hear the self-hatred in his voice. Whatever had happened had hurt everyone very badly. She could see it in Snow, in the way she dawdled on her way home from school and hung around the shop, and in the way she changed her name. She could read it in Will, the deep lines of sorrow in his face, the way he was spending his holiday flying her to Maine instead of with people who loved him.

"It doesn't matter why," Sarah said.

"Everything matters," Will said.

"Except 'why,'" Sarah said. "Why they're proud of you, why they love you, why they need you so much. All that matters is *that* they do."

"Is that how it is with you and Mike?" Will asked, turning to see her face.

"I do the best I can and try to let go of the results."

"If you can do that, you're very lucky," he said.

"I don't do it perfectly, that's for sure," Sarah said. "I remember the day he told me he was leaving. The words that come to mind are 'killing rage.'"

Will's gaze intensified, and he stared harder at the sky, as if it were a busy highway with dangerously merging rush hour traffic.

"Look!" Sarah said.

There, in the distance, far beyond the last hill and the tall buildings of the last city, was a line of silver.

"Wow, Sarah," he said. He had been concentrating so hard on his thoughts, he seemed shocked by the sudden appearance of the sea.

"Do you know how long it's been since I saw it?" Sarah asked, resting her fingertips on the dash.

"No, how long?"

"Three years. At least," Sarah said. "Three and a half, in Marblehead. How about you?"

Will stared at the Atlantic Ocean. It had appeared as a silver thread on the horizon, and it was spreading into a silver-blue sheet. The sun was behind the plane. It had risen high and was making the distant water glisten with bright light.

"I know exactly when I last saw it," he said.

"When?"

"When we moved up from Newport, five years ago. Right after I left the Navy. I haven't seen the ocean since."

"Well, you're seeing it now," she said gently, watching his face. Mentioning Newport, the lines in his face had hardened with pain. He felt her staring at him, so he looked over.

Sarah remembered one time at the hospital, lying on a table, terrified and claustrophobic about going in for an MRI. A young nurse she had never met had stroked her hand and held her gaze. That gentle human contact had calmed her so much, and she never forgot. Reaching for Will's hand, she pulled her sunglasses down to make sure he could really see her eyes. She smiled.

"I haven't wanted to go back," he said.

"I know," Sarah said. She felt the fear pouring out of him, although she didn't know what it was for. The reasons didn't matter.

"I see it, and I think of him in there."

"Who, Will?"

"My son Fred," Will said.

"What happened to him?" Sarah asked, afraid to hear.

"He drowned," Will said. "In the Atlantic."

"I'm sorry," Sarah said.

Will nodded. There was no anger or hardness left in his face.

The lines had relaxed, and his eyes were blank. He looked straight at Sarah and nodded.

They were getting closer. Although the plane was sealed tight, Sarah could almost imagine she could smell the salt air. She could see waves breaking over rocks, the foam pure white and solid looking. Ships left V-shaped wakes behind them. Small towns dotted the coves, and white spires seemed to stand on every hill.

Will called in to a new tower, and the familiar flat tones of a New England voice greeted them. Announcing plans to land and refuel, he received clearance. They circled the airport at Portsmouth, New Hampshire. Although Maine was just across the Piscataqua River, they still had a long flight to Elk Island. Sarah closed her eyes and felt Will bring the plane in for a landing, almost enjoying the loss of control.

She was lost in her thoughts, in the thrill of seeing the ocean again and moving closer to Mike. What did it cost to survive? Breathing deeply, she said a prayer for Will and a boy she had never met, overwhelmed with the uncomfortable gratitude that every parent feels when she hears that it was someone else's beloved child who has died, and not hers.

———

SNOW COULDN'T HOLD back another minute. She had curled herself into a ball and taken an extra-large hit of her inhaler, just in case of an inopportune midair asthma attack. She'd had some tense moments an hour or so back, when her nose had started itching. All she needed was one big sneeze, and her father would be turning the plane around, flying her back to Fort Cromwell, with an attitude the size of New York.

The plane had touched down, another one of her father's perfect landings. Snug in her hiding place behind the backseat, covered with the old green blanket her father kept stowed there for emergencies and picnics, she flexed her muscles. Poking her head up, she looked around.

There was Sarah walking into the hangar and her father talking to the fuel-pump guy. Snow really had to use the ladies' room. She figured that was where Sarah was heading, and if she timed it perfectly, which she knew she could, she could run behind her father's back and sneak into the other stall before Sarah was finished, without anyone seeing her.

Using other planes to hide behind, she ran into the hangar. She saw by the sign that they had landed in Portsmouth, so she knew they were near the sea. Running as fast as she could, she sniffed the air for salt, but all she got was the smell of fuel. Once inside the hangar, she found the ladies' room. Sarah was in one of the stalls, her feet visible beneath the door.

Snow went into a stall at the far end. The room was freezing cold. Drafts blew in from everywhere. She felt slightly guilty, peeing with such subterfuge. She liked Sarah, and she didn't enjoy hiding from her. Trying to eavesdrop on her father and Sarah, all she had been able to hear were wordless voices droning at a pitch just below that of the engines. It had been so frustrating.

Now, hearing Sarah flush the toilet, she knew she had very little time to sneak back aboard the plane. Peeking through the crack in the stall door, she caught sight of something that made her gasp out loud. Sarah stood there, her hair bleached and very short, looking gorgeous. For the first time, Snow saw that she was quite a young-looking woman, beautiful, with more style than anyone Snow had ever seen.

"Hi, Snow," Sarah said.

"How did you know it was me?" Snow asked, still peering through the crack.

"I recognized your voice."

"Just from that little gasp?"

"Yes." Stepping close to the beige metal door, Sarah brought herself eye to eye with Snow.

"Are you mad?"

"That's beside the point."

"Are you going to tell my father?"

"I think I should, don't you?"

"Don't, Sarah. Please."

"How long were you planning to hide?"

"Just till it was too late to turn back."

Sarah closed her eyes and bowed her head. Something came over her, and Snow had the feeling she was fighting herself to keep from crying or yelling, some very big emotion. Snow had seen her mother in the same state, mainly during bad fights with her father. Seeing Sarah like that scared her. But when Sarah spoke, her voice was gentle.

"We're not turning back," she said.

"Did you know I was aboard the whole time? Were you fooled? Or did you suspect I was there?"

"It occurred to me as a possibility, but I didn't really suspect," Sarah said, not sounding very friendly.

"I'm sorry." Slowly, Snow opened the door. Somehow she had expected Sarah to like what she had done, maybe even to help her hide the rest of the way. Sarah's angry mood confused her. But now that she was truly facing Sarah, she could get a good look. Her skin was glowing, her cheeks pink. Her hair had come out white and silky, so fine you just wanted to touch it.

"I gasped because I can't believe how great you look," Snow said quietly, because she didn't want Sarah to think she was trying to get on her good side.

"Oh," Sarah said, looking doubtful, glancing in the mirror.

"You really do. It's like a makeover in *Vogue*."

"Thank you," Sarah said, surprising Snow by sweeping her into a tight hug. Snow closed her eyes and hugged back. Sarah felt solid and strong, like a good mother. When it was time to quit, Snow didn't want to let go. She was so glad Sarah didn't hate her. She hung on, feeling tears in her throat.

"I would never have had the courage if it weren't for you," Sarah said.

"Didn't your mother dye her hair when it went gray?"

"No," Sarah said. "And when you see the island, you'll understand why."

Snow smiled. Sarah had said she would see the island.

"We'll stay out of the way," Snow said helpfully.

Sarah seemed to mull that over. She didn't seem angry anymore, but she wasn't smiling either.

"Let's go see your dad," Sarah said, her arm around Snow's shoulders.

They started walking toward the plane. Stepping into the bright sunshine, Snow reached into her pocket for the pair of sunglasses she always kept there. Being the daughter of an aviator had its advantages. Putting them on made her feel hidden, and she had the wild thought that maybe her father wouldn't recognize her. There he was, standing by the Piper Aztec with his back turned.

"One thing," Snow said to Sarah, tugging her sleeve.

"What?"

"How did you suspect that I was aboard? Did you see the toe of my shoe or something? Did I leave something showing?"

Sarah shook her head, for the first time really starting to smile. "No," she said, linking arms with Snow. "It's just something I would have done."

———

"WE HAVE A stowaway," Sarah said quietly.

Will turned around, coming face-to-face with his daughter. Trying to control his expression, to make it seem stern, he failed to block his initial reaction: delight.

"Susan!"

"Dad, don't make me go back."

"What the hell's going on here?"

"I want to be with you, that's all. I was *worried* about you."

"I made a promise to your mother, Susan. She wants you with her on holidays, and that's that."

"It's just Thanksgiving, Dad. You know she only cares about Christmas."

"Christmas might be her favorite, but she cares about them all. Jesus, Susan!"

"Please let me come with you. We must be more than halfway there—you can't do this to Sarah."

Sarah felt anxiety bordering on fury. She had gotten so good about accepting things. Being sick, she had learned to live by the schedules of other people, by the unknown timetable of her illness. She was a polite woman, and she cared about others. But here they were on their way to see *Mike,* wasting time arguing about whether to turn back to Fort Cromwell. She felt the physical sensations of anger, the light-headedness that precedes a blowup. Trying to stay calm, she reminded herself to breathe. There was injustice here that had nothing to do with her: Will knew the right thing was to deliver Snow back to her mother, but he wanted to keep her too.

"Please," she said quietly. "We need to leave. We need to be on our way."

"What?" Will asked.

"This is my charter. Do I have any say in this?"

"You should," Snow said boldly. "You're paying."

Sarah looked from one Burke to the other. Snow had her father's eyes. Both faces were full of guarded hope.

"If you fly this young lady all the way back to Fort Cromwell, we'll waste half the day. I hired you because you were the best pilot around." Sarah pointed at Snow. "She told me so herself."

"I did," Snow said, shrugging.

"Now I have a mission to accomplish, and an island to get to, and I want to see my son."

"I see," Will said.

"I'd like you to fly me to Maine. Now."

Sarah stepped back. Folding her arms to keep herself warm, she watched the Burkes and tried to keep from crying. Here she was, preventing another woman's child from returning to her on Thanksgiving, and all she could think of was seeing Mike. She nearly shook with the graveness of it, they were *this* close, just over the border from Maine, just a couple of hours from the island.

"Mom will understand," Snow said, stepping closer to her father, tugging his sleeve. "She will."

"You'd better call her, then. Tell her what's going on, then let me talk to her."

"Sorry about almost screwing up your charter."

"Just don't let it happen again," Will said, his voice stern but that same flash of serious delight behind his eyes.

———

THEY MADE THE call. Snow dialed, but after a few seconds Will took the phone away from her. He knew this wasn't going to go smoothly, and he wanted to protect her from the worst of it.

"Hello?"

Shit, it's him, Will thought. "Julian? Is Alice there?"

"Yes." He hesitated, picking up instantly on the fact that something was wrong. "What is it? Something with Susan?"

"Yeah, she's with me on the way to Maine, but I'd like to tell Alice myself."

"Okay," Julian said. The response was quick and respectful, and Will could tell by the way he covered the mouthpiece that he was doing his best to break it to Alice gently.

"Will?" Alice asked, her voice high and nervous. "What's going on?"

"Alice, Snow is with me."

"Where are you?"

"New Hampshire. I'm flying that charter I told you about, and she decided to come along." Aware of both Sarah and his daughter watching him, he spoke carefully. "Now we're halfway there, and we can't turn back. She's coming all the way."

"Did you plan this?" Alice asked. "I swear, Will. If you—"

"No, no," Will said quickly, and to his surprise he could hear Julian in the background trying to calm her down, saying something about how they loved Susan's impetuosity, that's all this was. "Julian's right," Will said, amazed by his unlikely ally. "She decided all on her own."

"I'm furious," Alice said.

"I don't blame you," Will said.

"She's in for it when she gets home."

"Uh-huh," Will said, watching the light fill his daughter's eyes, the smile illuminating her face.

"I'm so mad, I don't think I should even talk to her right now. Just put the phone to her ear for *one second*."

Doing what he was told, Will held the receiver close to Snow's ear.

"Be a good girl," he heard Alice say loudly.

"I will," Snow said. "I'll see you very soon."

When Will tried to continue the conversation, he found that Alice had already hung up. He reached out to give Snow a hug, but she had already turned away. She was running across the wide tarmac, the black surface glittering in sunlight, her feet flying. She was fifteen, but she ran like a young girl: with the knowledge of being passionately wanted by both her parents, with all the thrilling hope and abandon of being on a fantastic adventure with her father.

Will and Sarah watched her go, not really daring to look at each other. He got the feeling if Sarah looked into his eyes, something was going to happen. She was going to start laughing or crying, he wasn't sure which. But it was going to be full force, and he knew it wasn't going to be easy to stop. So she just continued to stare straight ahead. The expression on her face was neutral, that of a woman who was paying good money to charter a plane, trying to remain patient until they got under way again.

8

MIKE TALBOT KEPT looking at the sky. He was sweeping out the picking shack, shutting it down for the first time since coming to the island. Grandpa was a driven man. He'd work twenty-four hours a day, Sundays included, if Aunt Bess didn't ring the dinner bell at six sharp and keep ringing it until the men walked through the kitchen door and took their boots off. He probably planned to work Thanksgiving—say it was just another day—but Mike had other ideas.

"What the hell's going on here?" Grandpa asked, following two geese down the snowy path. His face was windburned and wrinkled. Gelsey, the lame collie, limped along by his side. Grandpa looked around. He filled his days with more work than he could keep up with just so he didn't have to think. Mike had watched him do it.

"Closing up," Mike said.

"Who told you to do that?"

"Thought of it myself."

The old man's eyes narrowed. He took out his pipe but didn't light it. Mike felt his face redden; he had done the wrong thing, and he could feel his grandfather's disapproval.

"Never considered you as being dimwitted before, but what kind of goose farmer shuts down the day before Thanksgiving?" Grandpa asked finally.

"They're not turkeys, Grandpa. Besides, Mom's coming today—"

"Fowl is fowl, Mike," Grandpa growled, cutting him off on the subject of his mother. "Some folks likes their birds nice and gamy, not all dried out like those big, stupid turkeys. All white meat. Makes me sick."

"Yeah, but—"

"Did I ever tell you about the time those Butterball fuckers came up and tried convincing me to quit geese and take on turkeys instead? Rose had to hold me back, I had my shotgun cocked and ready...." Frowning, Grandpa sat down on the chopping stump and stared at his boots. He was winded from old age and old memories, and he had to catch his breath.

"You okay, Grandpa?"

"'Course I'm okay," he said darkly, rising to his feet again. He picked up the ax, looking around for any goose.

Snow had fallen every day that week, so the white birds blended in. Mike saw them pecking for grain down by the bay. After all this time, he couldn't help wishing the dumb birds would just waddle down to the water and swim away. Waves broke on the rocky shore. Mike counted eight seals, curved like bananas, sunning themselves on the cold rocks.

Mike remembered those nice growing-up-on-a-farm stories his mother had told him. He'd be lying in bed, wide-awake from a nightmare or something, and she'd sit beside him, stroking his hair, and tell him about combing the geese for their feathers. The farm had sounded so wonderful, the geese combing so peaceful. He had imagined it felt as good to the geese as her soft hand touching his hair. Boy, was that a lie.

"I'll get them, Grandpa," he said. Still wearing his bloody hip boots, he slipped and nearly lost his footing on the icy trail to the bay. The geese honked loudly. Mike came around behind, shooing them up the path.

"Go," he hissed so Grandpa couldn't hear. "Take off, you stupid birds. Fly away!"

Of course they didn't fly away; they never did. They padded along so trustingly to the picking shack. Their little black eyes looked up at Mike. He had seen these guys hatch last spring, watched them fatten up all summer, told them time and time again to swim or fly away. He had done his best.

"We'd better get busy," Grandpa said brusquely. "Some fellow from the Wayport Inn's bringing his boat over this afternoon to pick them up."

Grandpa staggered a little from his arthritis. He almost lost his balance, but Mike steadied him. Grandpa felt embarrassed about needing help. He never said thank you, or looked Mike in the eye. Pictures revealed that George Talbot had once stood nearly six feet tall, but old age had hunched him over and shrunken his bones. He was small and withered, with hair as white as his geese and skin as tan as tree bark.

Still, George moved fast. He grabbed a goose, lay its neck on the stump, and with one horrible whack, he cut its head off. The second goose was always worse, because Mike believed it knew what was coming. But his grandfather was so quick, it was over before you could blink.

"Now, aren't you sorry you cleaned the place up?" Grandpa asked. He hadn't put his teeth in, and his lips were invisible, but Mike was happy to see him smile. Grandpa loved being right.

"It's okay," Mike said.

They carried the dead geese into the picking shack. The main room was small and square, windowless except for one cut-out hole in the wall. It was the domain of an old trapper: dead muskrats covered the walls. Skinned, their fur sold to someone on the mainland, they were nailed spread-eagle to dry on the wall; to Mike, the little critters looked like flying squirrels soaring over some field.

Mike started the generator, and the feather machine began chugging. His grandfather pulled on his hip boots, and they both put on gloves. Grandpa worked so fast, Mike could hardly keep up. Rotating the goose over the machine, it worked like magic fingers, wiggling the feather tips out of the skin. Loosened by the machine, the feathers came out easily by hand.

Mike ran his gloved fingers through the feathers, throwing them through the small hole into the tiny anteroom. The good down was thickest on the goose's chest, and Mike paid special attention to getting it all. His fingers combed the dead geese, trying to keep the feathers clean. He heard his grandfather swearing. Mike's mother was coming, and it put his grandfather in a weird mood.

"This guy has a lot of down on him, Gramps," Mike called.

"Yep."

"More quilts for Mom."

"Yep."

"She's on her way here now," Mike said. "Should be here anytime."

"Surprised she's bothering to come at all," he said, squinting at his hands.

"She's coming."

"What time's she getting here anyway?"

"Sometime before dark. That's all she said."

"She's always been that way," Grandpa said. "Never could pin her down. She'll make you a promise, but if something comes along, gets in her way, forget it. She's on to the next thing."

"Huh. I don't know..." Mike said, not wanting to be impolite but disagreeing with his grandfather. "If Mom says she'll be here, she will. That's what counts," Mike said, feeling defensive. Usually he was quicker to attack his mother than anyone.

"Lots of things count in this world, Mike," Grandpa said, reaching into the geese to pull their guts out.

"Yeah," Mike said.

"She couldn't get off the island fast enough after her mother died."

Mike didn't even want to look. Practically every time his grandfather mentioned his wife, he got hoarse. Aunt Bess would play one of Grandma Rose's favorite songs on the piano, and he would have to leave the room. Mike knew he went out to Rose's grave sometimes; he had seen him at the old graveyard more than once.

"You okay, Grandpa?" Mike asked.

The old man nodded. He frowned as he blew his nose, as if that could disguise the fact he was all choked up. Mike hadn't known what to expect, asking his mother to come out. He had been fighting with her since eighth grade. She and Grandpa hadn't gotten along even longer than that, since before Mike was born. For years Mike had assumed that *he* was the reason for the rift: His parents hadn't been married, Mike was their bastard child. Having him must have made his mother the scandal of the island, maybe that was why she and Grandpa kept their distance. But as time went on, he was learning that the trouble had started earlier, around the time of his grandmother's cancer.

"Well, well," Grandpa said, surveying the dried muskrats hanging on the wall.

"What?" Mike asked.

"Grab me those two right there," Grandpa said, pointing.

Mike reached up, yanked two leathery carcasses down from their pegs. He practically gagged, doing it.

"We'll feed her good while she's here," Grandpa said. "Muskrat stew'll put some meat on her bones and get her back some health in no time."

"She is healthy," Mike said.

Grandpa gave him a funny look. He was frowning with his mouth scrunched up, his eyebrows angling down between his nose. He hosed down the dressed geese, placed them in a wooden crate, left it by the door to be picked up later. Then he walked around to the anteroom to grab a plastic garbage bag crammed with feathers to carry up the hill to Aunt Bess.

"She is healthy," Mike said again, because his grandfather's silence was making him feel nervous.

"That what she told you?"

"Well, yeah."

"That's what her mother kept saying too," Grandpa said, his frown taking up his whole face.

"But—" Mike began, looking into the clear blue sky for any sign of an approaching plane.

"What, are you just like them?" Grandpa exploded, planting his feet shoulder-width apart. "Believing what you want to believe? People sicken and die and that's that. Hasn't your time out here taught you anything realistic?"

"I'm realistic," Mike said.

His grandfather laughed.

"I am."

"You got a long way to go."

"No, I—"

"You want fairy tales, that's what you want," Grandpa said angrily. He was on his way up to the house, and he wouldn't be stopped. He yanked his pipe out of his pocket and practically broke the stem off, trying to get it lit.

Mike stayed where he was, feeling the cold seep through his boots into his toes. Tall pines ringed the property, and the sun had disappeared behind them. They were black silhouettes, their long shadows spreading far out into the bay. He watched his grandfather limp up the path, his anger making him swing the dry muskrats as if they were paddles. The house was old and crooked. Smoke wisped out of the leaning chimney.

"Hey," Mike yelled, but his grandfather gave no sign of having heard. If anything, he moved faster. His old shoulders hunched in on themselves, his spine curling over. He gave his head a violent shake.

"Killing geese makes me sick!" Mike said. But only when he was absolutely sure his grandfather couldn't hear, and even though it wasn't what he wanted to say in the first place. His heart was pounding. His icy breath came out in furious white clouds. Mike Talbot stood right where he was, straining his ears for the sound of an airplane engine approaching from the west. He gazed up, scanning the sky for his mother.

———————

THE HOUSE WAS quiet. Bess was lying down. She took up the whole sofa, covered from toe to chin with one of her old afghans. She breathed in and out through her mouth, making a ratchety little snore. The grandfather clock ticked loudly. Barn cats lay coiled around the room, watching her with yellow eyes. Bess kept the curtains pulled most of the day to keep the light from fading everything in sight, so the room was sepia-toned and rather somber, with most of the furnishings and wallpaper done in browns or shades of beige. The pipe smoke blended in fine.

George stood over his sister, watching her sleep. She looked mighty old. She had blued her hair for the occasion of Sarah's homecoming, and it didn't help a whit. Her face was a wrinkle-fest, and she had her teeth out. The fire had died down, and George stared at her accusingly. Hadn't he told her he wanted the house nice and warm for when Sarah got there? Mike had gotten him all worked up, and nothing looked right or good. The house smelled bad, and the decor reminded him of funeral parlors that had seen better days. George sighed and decided to try waking Bess up the nice way.

"Good morning, lazybones," he said.

Bess stirred a little. Feeling hopeful, George took a spin around the room. Barn cats were sleeping everywhere. He shuffled over to Rose's old piano, and this close up he could smell the lemon polish. No one could say his sister wasn't a good cleaner. All the picture frames were polished, neatly arranged like troops on the piano. She had laundered the curtains, washed the plaid flannel dog and cat beds, waxed the floor. But the place still smelled like two old coots and a teenager.

He poked around the corner into Bess's sewing room. He deposited the big bag of feathers in a wicker bin. The space was so poky, he could barely move without knocking everything over. Once his rheumatism started acting up, his joints all creaky and sore, he was like a bull in a china shop. He stepped on a sleeping cat, and it howled. George swore loudly. He steadied himself, grabbing on to one of the bolts of white cotton, dirtying it with the muskrat he had in his right hand.

"Shoot!" he said, noticing he had left a stain. Well, nothing to be done about it now, he thought, heading back to see how Bess was making out. He caught sight of three finished quilts, new since their last shipment to Sarah, neatly folded and stacked on a chair in the corner. Just seeing them made him frown. Why the hell didn't she just close that stupid shop of hers and relax a little? Working too hard could kill a person.

When he got back out to the living room, he noticed that Bess had gone right back to snoring. George's blood pressure shot up. He peered at his watch, but he couldn't see it in this light. So he checked the grandfather's clock: quarter past three! Sarah would be here anytime now.

He clacked the muskrats together over Bess's head. They made a sound just like cleaning erasers when he was a boy: loud and sharp. All the cats scattered.

"Wake up!" he yelled.

"George, what is it?" Bess asked, coming awake all at once.

"Will you look at the time, Bess? Do you want your niece to walk in after all this time and find you sleeping the day away?"

"I was just resting my eyes," Bess said, her frown causing about a million more wrinkles.

"Well, muskrat stew's not going to get made with you acting like the Queen of Sheba. And what the hell happened to the fire? It's as cold as a tomb," he said.

"In more ways than one," Bess said, sniffing. Composing herself, she slid her feet into her black leather buckle shoes. She primped her hair, then pulled her sleeves down. George watched his sister; she had always been a lady. She was elegant and cultured from all her married years in Providence. But getting to her feet took some effort. George grabbed her under the arms and tried to hoist her up.

"Oh, George, you're hurting me!" she said.

Easing off, he dropped her entirely and went tumbling after her onto the sofa.

"Goddammit, Bess," he yelled. They were all tangled up in her afghan and each other, and she was starting to giggle, making him so mad. They'd turned around, facing forward as if they were watching TV, their rumps all the way back on the cushions, trying to push themselves up. It was like a race, all the rocking and effort they were giving to the enterprise, and George felt like he might burst a blood vessel.

"Hey, Grandpa," Mike said, walking into the room. At the sight of the spectacle, he stopped short.

"What do you want?" George asked defiantly, expecting the boy to start laughing.

"Nothing," Mike said. His face was serious, his big eyes showing little. He reached out one hand and George pulled himself up. Then Mike leaned down, let Bessie grip his forearms, gently helped her to her feet.

"Thank you, dear," Bess said. Then she grabbed onto her walker and, with dignity, made her way out to the kitchen.

"Good boy, Mike," George said.

"No problem, Grandpa."

"That Bess. She's like lifting a sack of flour. Gives you no help at all, all flip-flopping like dead weight. Pull you right down if you're not careful."

"She's okay," Mike said. "Grandpa, that guy from the Wayport Inn just came in his boat. You want me to bill him for those two geese?"

"Hell no! Take his money. Don't let him sweet-talk you into giving him credit. That's a boy. Can't say your old grandfather isn't teaching you the way of the world, can you?"

"Nope, I can't," Mike said, easing out the door.

"Any sign of your mother yet?"

"Not yet," Mike said. Then he was gone.

Still holding the muskrats, George Talbot felt it all crash in. His daughter was on her way there. He walked over to Rose's piano and sat down. George had never learned to play a note. The women in his life had always made the music. Sitting on the old bench made him feel closer to his wife.

"Sarah's coming," he said out loud. She had had cancer, just like Rose. The thought of it was so terrible, so fearsome, it made his heart hurt just to think it. Lowering his head to the piano, he banged a few keys. How did people survive, getting so attached to each other?

Now there was Mike. What would George do without him? George didn't like to rely on anyone, but he was a practical man, and he liked to face facts. The boy was only seventeen, but he had descended upon their house like an angel from afar. George had never expected him to come. He knew he had no right to expect the boy to stay. Just like his mother, just like his grandmother. They came and they went.

———

THE SEA LAY below, an unending sheet of dark satin. Not quite blue—nearly black—it reflected the mysterious northern light. Snow-covered islands dotted the bays. The sun was setting, orange fire behind the plane. They flew into the darkening night, watching the early stars come out. Sarah held tight to her seat.

Will banked right, turning south-southeast. The plane leveled off, and Sarah scanned the islands.

"There," she said, pointing. Just the sight of home made her heart flip.

"That one?" Will asked. "The one farthest out?"

"The island all by itself."

Will nodded. He adjusted his heading, spoke into the microphone, checking with Boston Center. There was no one to call on Elk Island, no hangars or tower, just an old grass landing strip. Mike had promised he would contact Mr. Blackburn, the island caretaker, to plow it that morning.

From the air Sarah could see how remote her island really was. On the map it appeared at the far end of a curved cluster of islands dotted off the tip of the Tamaquid Peninsula, the dot at the end of a question mark. But from up there she could see that those miles of empty sea left Elk Island all alone, hardly part of the archipelago at all. She shivered, gazing down. She had loved it more than any place on earth, but she had been unable to get away from it fast enough.

"You grew up there?" Snow asked, leaning against the window.

"I did," Sarah said.

"That's where Mike is now?"

"That white house right there," Sarah said, pointing. She could see the farm; it took up half the southeastern corner of the island, two hundred acres of pine woods and salt meadows. The old house sat beside a red barn, and rickety white fences marked the pens and paddock. Smoke curled from the chimney.

"All the houses are white," Snow said, counting. "All fourteen of them. Are there only fourteen families on the island?"

"A few more," Sarah said, pressing her forehead against the window as Will banked right. She felt so excited. She must have sighed or gasped, because she felt Will's hand on her shoulder.

"Are you okay?" he asked.

"I'm so happy," Sarah said, her eyes brimming. She couldn't stop smiling. If Will opened the door to the plane, she felt she could step out and fly. "I'm about to see Mike."

Will squeezed her hand, then turned the plane around for its final approach. The tiny harbor veered off to the right. The lighthouse blinked green and white, short and long. The land whirled, and the stars straightened out. Pine trees stood thick as brush bristles. They flew over the treetops, pointing straight at a narrow landing strip. The landing gear growled into place.

"This is real trust," Will said. "Blind faith."

"What do you mean?" Sarah asked.

"Landing at a place I've never been before, trusting that someone did a decent job of clearing the strip."

"Mike said he'd call—"

"I'm sure he did," Will said, his jaw set, his gaze fixed on the runway. It was a narrow swath of greenish-brown in a field of white, and Sarah knew if the strip wasn't plowed right, their wheels could stick in the snow and spin the plane out. She wasn't scared; if Mike said he'd call Mr. Blackburn, he'd do it.

"Is Mike meeting you here?" Will asked, throttling back.

"I don't think so. He didn't know exactly what time we'd be landing," Sarah said. "Why?"

Will adjusted the wing flaps. He held the wheel, brought the nose down, kept the wings steady. The pine trees whispered beneath them, and Sarah could almost hear their top branches ticking against the wheels.

"Because that guy standing there," Will said, concentrating as he stared straight ahead. "Looks an awful lot like you."

"Mike!" Sarah yelled, her palms against the cold glass, her mouth open with sheer delight as the plane touched down on the frozen ground and bumped past the tall and handsome young man standing off to the side, his hands stuck deep in his pockets, his beautiful head bare in spite of how often his mother had told him to wear a hat.

9

MIKE HUNG BACK, watching his mother's plane land. Since Mr. Blackburn was laid up with gout, Mike had plowed the grass strip himself. He had done it twice that day, once after last night's dusting and again after the midday sun had melted the ice right down to the dry grass. His heart was pounding. He had never plowed a landing strip before, and he worried that he might have messed up. The shaky little plane jounced along something fierce, hitting every rut left by his plow. Until it came to a complete stop, Mike couldn't let himself really breathe.

Starting up the big Jeep, he drove through the snow to the end of the strip. He parked beside the plane, then climbed out. His mother was stuck. She had her door open, waving at him like crazy, but she couldn't get her seat belt off.

"Hi, Mike!" she called.

"Hi, Mom," he called back.

The pilot gave him a sort of wave, coming around the plane to unhook his mother's seat belt. The guy was really tall with big shoulders and a dark five o'clock shadow, just like some movie pilot. Mike watched how tenderly he acted and figured he was probably in love with her. Another man. Big surprise. But the belt unclicked, and she jumped out of the plane.

"Mike," his mother said, barreling through the snow at him.

He folded his arms. He didn't mean to; the action took him

by surprise. Looking forward to seeing her all week, he didn't understand why he suddenly felt like walking away. His mother must have read it in his face, because she stopped just short of giving him a hug.

"Hi, Mom," he said again.

"Mike, you grew three inches," she said.

"Yeah," he said.

Her blue eyes were darting back and forth. She was looking at his eyes, his hair, his skin, taking everything in. He wondered whether she could tell he had to shave every other day now. He tried not to show that he was doing the same thing to her: checking her out to see if she was really as healthy as she said.

"Your hair looks great," she said. "Grandpa's making you keep it short?"

"I want to." He shrugged.

He let his arms fall to his sides. It was okay with him if she hugged him now. She didn't. He kind of smiled, but she was looking very serious. She had her head tilted, not saying anything at all. Her mouth was open in a small "O."

"What?" he asked.

"I'm looking at you," she said. "That's all."

The wind had picked up, and it was whipping snow across the field. Darkness moved in fast this far north; an hour later would have been too late. Mike had driven over the minute he heard the plane overhead. If it hadn't come when it did, he would have lit flares for landing lights, would have stayed there parked with his headlights on. But such measures hadn't been necessary.

The pilot was tying the plane down. He had four stakes and a big mallet. The beam from the lighthouse flashed across the sky. Each mallet strike sounded harsh and metallic. Mike nodded at the pilot.

"He's staying?"

"Yes," Sarah said. "It didn't make sense to have him drop me off, then come all the way back to pick me up."

Planning to leave, of course. She had planned her escape route even before she'd arrived. His mother had abandoned the island a long time ago, just like Grandpa had said. She had brought a guy to keep her company for a few days, then fly her away. Mike didn't say anything though. He just walked over to help the pilot. The guy worked fast, not unlike Mike's grandfather. Mike watched him whack the stakes into the frozen ground, thread lines through the wings and wheels, tie them down with a sailor's precision.

"Need a hand?" Mike asked.

"Thanks," the pilot said, handing him a line, a stake, and the mallet. "Want to run this aft?"

"Sure," Mike said.

"I'm Will Burke," the pilot said.

"Mike Talbot," Mike said.

They shook hands. The guy didn't smile too long. His handshake was firm, but not suspiciously earnest. Mike felt his stomach relax a little. Will didn't seem like one of the idiot suitors wanting to win Mike over so he could sleep with his mother. Mike wondered how his grandfather would take it, the pilot staying.

Mike estimated the proper distance from the plane for the most effective hold. He kicked away a patch of snow, positioned the metal rod, and drove it deep into the icy earth. Then he yanked the nylon line, eased it through the steel eye, tied a solid sheepshank. When he looked up, his mother was standing there. She had those proud eyes that made her look sleepy, like she was about to cry at the national anthem or something.

"What?" Mike asked, still crouching.

"I'm so—" She swallowed. "Glad to see you."

"Yeah," he said. "Me too."

"Then hug me," she said.

Mike dropped the mallet, brushed the snow off his gloves, and did what she asked. They stayed there, not moving, with the wind rocking them from side to side. His mother felt small, built like a bird, ten pounds lighter than the last time he'd seen her. His eyes were squeezed shut. She was crying. He felt her body shaking. Tears felt hot in his own eyes. With some of the news he had gotten through the last year, he wasn't sure he'd ever see her again.

"Mike," she managed to say.

"Hey, Mom," he said. "Don't, huh?"

"I know." She bowed her head, took a half-step back. She fumbled in her pocket for a Kleenex. She never had one. When he was a little kid with a runny nose at the playground, she had been the only mother with no tissues in her pocketbook. Mike had grown accustomed to taking care of himself, so he reached inside his jacket, then handed her a handkerchief.

"Thanks," she said, blowing her nose like a goose. She handed the white square back to him. It was stiff with starch. "No one does laundry like Aunt Bessie."

"Nope," he said. Returning the handkerchief to his inside pocket, he was just about to suggest driving his mother and the pilot home, when he lost his breath. Totally, football-in-the-solar-plexus, couldn't breathe.

"Who's she?" he asked, looking over his mother's shoulder.

This beautiful young girl was climbing out of the plane. She had huge eyes, a glistening mouth, glowing skin. She wore a big navy jacket, tight jeans, brand-new sneakers. Her fingernails were painted brown and orange. Stretching, she looked as if she had just woken up. She glanced around her surroundings, but when she caught sight of Mike, she smiled and started walking over.

"That," his mother said, smiling too, "is Snow."

"Snow?" Mike asked.

"You must be Mike," Snow said with a voice like someone who should be singing on a CD.

"Yeah," Mike said. "Hi."

"We're friends of your mother's," she said. "My dad and I."

"Oh," Mike said, blushing at her beauty and direct way of speaking.

"Good friends," his mother said, placing her arm around Snow's narrow shoulders. Snow was just a couple of inches shorter than his mother, and having just hugged *her,* Mike had a pretty good idea of how it might feel to hold Snow. His face got even redder.

"Huh," Mike said.

"Your mother couldn't wait to get here," the pilot said.

"I couldn't!" his mother exclaimed, hugging Snow tighter. Mike saw how happy her eyes looked. They were glistening, and she was staring straight at him. As if it were he she wanted to be hugging instead of this new girl, as if she wished the space between them would magically close. Mike took a half-step toward her, but that couldn't close the space.

"You look different," Mike said.

"I do?" his mother asked, looking hurt. He didn't know how to tell her she looked beautiful, so he just stared.

"Sarah, can I ask him if he likes . . ." Standing on tiptoe, Snow whispered something in his mother's ear. It felt weird, to hear a kid his age calling his mother "Sarah." Mike forced himself to look disinterested in what particular like of his she might be wondering about.

"Go ahead," his mother said.

"Do you like her hair?" Snow asked.

"Huh?" Mike asked, frowning. Glancing at his mother's hair, he could see that it was something new. Really short and really blond. It looked good, maybe it was part of what was making her look so beautiful. He nodded. "Yeah, it's okay," he said, smiling.

"My idea," Snow said, beaming.

"Huh," the pilot said, smiling like Mike. "It does look good. It's different, isn't it?"

"Yes," Sarah said, smiling.

"Dad, you are so blind. All the way to Maine, and you're just noticing *now*?" Snow asked with affection. "Guess you are too, Mike. Blind!"

"Sorry," Mike said, feeling stung. He stared at Snow, determined to become more observant right away. He noticed her wide eyes, her long, chestnut-brown hair, the way it curled so softly over her shoulders. He noticed her throat, how white and delicate it looked. Swallowing, he had to look away to keep from being so observant that he'd explode on the spot.

"It's cold," Mike said. "I'll drive everyone home."

"That's fantastic! I'm freezing," Snow said, beaming as if he were her hero.

"I'll get the bags," the pilot said, heading toward the plane.

Without saying anything, Mike went to help, leaving his mother and the lovely stranger to climb into the Jeep and get warm.

———

THEY ALL PULLED up in front of the old farmhouse. Sarah and Will walked ahead of the kids. The memories of her entire childhood swept over her. She had lived in this house until she went to college. She hadn't even gone off the island until she was eleven. Her mother had died upstairs, in the front bedroom.

"I can't believe I'm here," she whispered. Her hands were shaking.

"You sound scared," he whispered back.

"I am!"

"It's your home," he said.

"That's why!" she said, and it sounded so funny, she laughed. Will put his arm around her. They stood still on the stone walk, letting her get her breath. Now that she was calmer, she really looked the old place over. It was an ancient saltbox, one of the oldest houses in Maine. The historical plaque had fallen off the wall, leaving nail holes visible. The white paint was peeling. One of the front steps had cracked in the middle.

"I haven't gotten around to replacing that yet," Mike said.

"You?" Sarah asked, surprised. Maintaining the house had always been her father's job. She hadn't seen her father in several years, and all of a sudden she realized that she was afraid of what she was going to find.

"What are you, a handyman?" Snow asked.

"Yeah," Mike said, sounding proud.

"You ready?" Will asked, his hand on Sarah's arm.

"Yes," she said, giving three knocks on the big brass door knocker, then turning the knob and walking in.

George Talbot stood right inside the front hall. He must have seen the headlights, been waiting for them to enter. He might have opened the door, yelled hello, greeted them as they came up the walk, but that wasn't his way. Sarah stared at her father. He's gotten old, she thought. My father is an old man.

"Well," he said, looking at her. "Well, Sarah."

Sarah felt the blood rush to her face.

"Hi, Dad," she said.

"What did you do, bring the troops?" he asked, glaring at Will and Snow.

"I'm Will Burke, sir," Will said, shaking his hand. "And this is my daughter, Snow."

Sarah smiled at the fact that he had said "Snow" instead of "Susan."

"How do you do. You're the new boyfriend?"

"The pilot, Grandpa," Mike said, stepping in.

"Your daughter hired me to fly her up here," Will said.

"Pretty expensive, a private pilot all the way from New York to Elk Island."

"I guess that shows how much she wanted to get here," Will said.

"Oh," George Talbot said. Sarah watched the confusion cloud

his eyes. He had such little contact with other people, he had never really known how to interact. He was terribly shy, but it always came out as hostile. Sarah felt embarrassed and protective toward him, and she walked across the hallway to take his hands.

They felt dry and gnarled, as if they were old tree roots. She squeezed them gently, looking into his eyes. The gray hair he had had for as long as she could remember had gone all white.

"Hi, Dad," she said again.

"Hi, Sarah," he said. His pale blue eyes were sunk deep in the sockets, washed by an entire lifetime of living by the sea. Jutting forward, his sharp chin gave him a perpetual pose of contention, as if he were daring you to a challenge. Just about eye to eye with Sarah now, he had lost at least two inches in height. His posture was fierce, but his body had gotten so old.

"My friends are going to fly me home on Sunday, so I thought it would be better for them to stay. I'll make up some beds for them—"

"You come all this way, and you're only staying four days?" he asked.

"Yes. I had to close the shop completely to come, and I don't feel right being gone for longer. . . ."

Her father regarded her, then shifted his gaze to Mike. He took a step toward his grandson, as if allying himself with him. Sarah couldn't take her eyes off them. In the dim hall light she looked at her handsome, strong son, and saw the affection he had for his grandfather. George gave him an elbow jab, and Mike pretended to double over, jabbing back.

"Knock it off now, Mike," her father said sternly. "You behave yourself in front of our company. You like muskrat stew, young lady?"

"Who, me?" Snow asked.

"Yes, you."

"Um, I'm a vegetarian."

"You eat only vegetables?" he asked.

"Yes. I don't believe in eating animals."

Mike looked uncomfortable, and George appeared perplexed.

"Aren't you worried about her having a balanced diet?" he asked Will.

Will laughed. He shook his head. "She has a mind of her own, Mr. Talbot. She's my daughter, but she has her own ways."

"I know what that's like, Mr. Burke," he said, glaring at Sarah. "Exactly. You got any boys?"

"No," Will said.

Sarah couldn't see any sign in his face, or in Snow's, of the boy they had once had. Fred. Leaning closer to Will, she accidentally touched her shoulder to his. Almost automatically they stepped apart, their eyes meeting for just a second.

"Boys are easier," her father said. Strange, Sarah thought, considering he didn't have any sons. But then she saw him looking at Mike. "Well, we'd better get down to dinner. Bessie's deaf as a doorpost, or she'd have been up to welcome you. We don't want to leave her out."

"Okay, Dad."

Her father paused, giving her a long look. His eyes seemed to soften, and all at once they filled with tears. He was brutally sentimental, and Sarah knew that seeing her reminded him of the past. "Seems strange your mother isn't here, doesn't it, Sarah? I never get used to it, no matter how much time passes."

"Me neither, Dad." Stepping forward to hug him, Sarah was too late. He had turned away. Shuffling toward the stairs, he started down.

"She'll fix you any vegetables you want," Mike said to Snow.

"I don't want to put anyone to any trouble," Snow said, following Mike.

Sarah and Will were alone. Their bags were piled by the door, their children had followed her father down to the basement kitchen. Light, not much brighter than a candle, flickered from pewter sconces. Sarah's heart was racing from the joys and terrors of coming home.

"Are you okay?" Will asked.

Sarah nodded. She wanted to smile, to say yes, but if she spoke or moved at that very moment, she would begin to sob. She heard Mike's voice downstairs, introducing Snow to Aunt Bess, and he sounded so steady and mature and incredible, she could hardly believe it was the same boy she had fought with so terribly a year before.

"You can stop missing him, Sarah," Will said. "He's right here."

"I know. Thank you."

"For flying you here? That's—"

"For being with me," Sarah said.

Overcome with emotion, Sarah grabbed his hand. It happened so fast, before she had the chance to think about it, her heart racing. Instead of looking into her eyes, he was staring down at their hands, at the way they were joined, their fingers laced together. He brought her hand up to his lips, kissed the back of it, and let go. Raising his eyes to meet hers, he smiled.

"The same to you," he said. "Thanks."

"You're welcome," she said.

Together they walked down the narrow stairs to dinner.

————

THE BASEMENT KITCHEN ran the entire length of the house. Five large windows overlooked Elk Bay; a window seat stretched beneath them, covered with one long cushion and many small down pillows, each covered with bright fabric and cut-out stars. The house was built on a granite ledge, and it was deeper by one whole story here in back. A fire crackled in the big stone hearth. Trophies covered the whitewashed walls: heads of boar, elk, deer, and moose. Hooves had been hollowed out, and now were used as containers to hold Bess's cooking utensils. Antlers had been employed as coatracks.

The table was hewn from one enormous fallen oak, the grain

visible and mysterious under many coats of shiny varnish. A large cast-iron kettle held the stew. Aunt Bess stood by the stove, supervising Mike, doling it into rough brown crockery bowls. Aunt Bess was plump, as filled out as her brother was gaunt, and made her way around the kitchen on her walker. Sarah watched her, wondering how she got up and down stairs, thinking her the perfect example of how hard life could be on the farm. Wearing her special-occasion navy blue dress with white polka dots, she took her seat between Sarah and Snow with a big smile on her face. Her scent was an amalgam of perspiration, mothballs, and Arpège.

"It's so nice to have some girls around," she said. "Gets kind of lonely with just the men to talk to."

"It's good to see you, Aunt Bess," Sarah said.

"The same to you, Sarah." Looking from Snow to Will, she said, "Sarah's like the daughter I never had."

"Sarah had a mother," George said, frowning at Bess.

Sarah couldn't bring herself to look at him, wondering why he would want to hurt his sister that way. Aunt Bess steeled herself, setting her mouth. But at Sarah's glance, she raised her eyebrows and shrugged her shoulders. The mood at the table was as tense as Sarah had remembered, and she found herself looking at her son, wondering how he stood it.

"This stew is delicious," Will said.

"A Maine specialty," George said.

"Glad you like it," Aunt Bess said, the praise making her happy again.

"Don't know what you're missing, young lady," George said to Snow. "Muskrat stew puts hair on your chest."

"My dinner is just fine," Snow said, eating the plate of carrots, turnips, and kale Mike had chopped and Bess had steamed for her.

"This is real New England eating," George said.

Snow paused, tilted her head. "We never ate muskrat stew, and we're from New England," she said.

"Oh, really? I thought Sarah said Fort Cromwell," Aunt Bess said.

"Snow was born in Newport, Rhode Island," Will said. "When I was in the Navy."

"Newport? Oh, my goodness, my husband and I lived in Providence, and we just loved Newport. Our favorite restaurant was the Pier—do you know it?"

"Lobster bisque," Snow said. "I loved the Pier's lobster bisque before I became a vegetarian. And Fred loved their seafood stuffing. Remember how he'd always have baked stuffed lobster, Dad?"

"I do," Will said.

"We'd drive down to Newport nearly every Saturday, just to ride around and see the mansions and go to the Pier. Oh, I—"

"Navy man, eh?" George asked, cutting Bess right off, peering at Will with new interest.

"Yes, sir."

"See any action?"

"Some."

"Like what?"

"Like the Persian Gulf!" Snow said proudly.

"Yeah?" Mike asked.

"Yes," Will said, looking across the table at George. "Sarah told me you served in World War Two."

"That's right. Army Air Corps, Eighth Air Force in Europe. Yep."

"Grandpa flew in the lead plane," Mike said.

"On D day, he was one of the first planes over Normandy," Sarah said, feeling as proud as Snow. She always had for the fact that her father had been a hero in the war. He was passionate about the cause he had fought for. She watched him turn to glare at her.

"Surprised you remember," he said.

"Oh, I remember," she said softly. She had heard all the stories. He had told her most of them himself, but a few had come

from her mother before she died. About how he had bombed
Cologne and left the cathedral standing; about how the crew he
had trained with in Colorado had been shot down over the
North Sea, all killed except her father. Sarah kept his medals—
the Air Medal, the Distinguished Flying Cross—in a small pink
satin jewel case back in Fort Cromwell.

"Persian Gulf, eh?" George asked Will as if the others were
not there.

"Yes, sir."

"What was your rank?" he asked, a glint in his eye.

"Commander."

Sarah watched her father's face fall. He hated being out-
ranked. She wondered whether he would offer the information
that upon discharge from the air corps he had attained the rank
of first lieutenant, but he didn't. Pushing his chair back, he went
to the refrigerator and took out a big pitcher. He poured himself a tall glass of milk, and one for Mike.

"Anyone else?" he asked.

"I'll take one, sir," Will said.

George gave him a sidelong glance. He had heard the "sir,"
the tone of respect, and was deciding whether to forgive Will
for being a commander as he filled another glass with milk.
Sarah watched him replace the pitcher, his eyes hard with anger.
Why was life so harsh for her father? She had never been able to
understand. The island days that had been bliss for Sarah had
seemed to weigh her father down.

"George was only a few years older than Mike is now when
he went off to war," Bess said to Snow. "He was so brave, and
we were all so afraid for him. My father was the meanest lobsterman you ever saw, he'd slice the buoys off a competitor's
pots without thinking twice, but, oh, he cried like a baby when
we drove Georgie to the train."

"Bess, that's enough," George said.

But this time he couldn't ruin her mood of nostalgic affection. A gentle smile on her wrinkled face, she gazed at him with

love, her brother who had gone to war. The siblings were elderly now, George and Bess, but watching them stare at each other, Sarah could see the unending connection.

"She doesn't mean anything by it," Snow said.

"What?" George asked.

"She's just teasing you. It's what sisters do. They don't do it to hurt you," she said.

George gave a long, exasperated exhalation that sounded dangerously like an angry whistle. He glared at her, holding back whatever poisonous comment he wanted to make. He didn't like being spoken up to; whenever it happened, he usually retaliated sharply. But Snow was new to him, a guest in his home, a young girl. Saved by those factors, he let her off with a cantankerous scowl instead. With awe and admiration Sarah watched Snow in action.

"You're very lucky to still have each other. At your ages," she said.

"Lucky?" George snorted. "Hah! She's a millstone around my neck."

Even Bess couldn't take it. "Lucky he still goes to work every day, that's about it," she said. "I pray to God I die before he retires."

Will caught Sarah's eye, trying not to smile. Mike was openly grinning.

"You don't want to say that," Snow said confidentially to Bess. "You'll miss him when he's gone."

Bess raised her gaze to meet her brother's. He stood there, frowning at the outspoken child. His teeth were slipping, and he gave them a shove back into place with his thumb. A log collapsed in the fireplace, sending a galaxy of orange sparks up the chimney.

"Hear what she says?" George said, looking at Bess.

"I hear," Bess said.

"You'd better start being nicer to me."

"Take your own advice. Your own daughter walks in after six

years, and you're acting as mean as a black bear in a thicket. We have houseguests, and we're bickering like blue jays."

"We're nothing like blue jays," George said, his tone softening by way of almost-apology. "Are we, Mike?"

"Not at all," Mike said. He and his grandfather exchanged manly nods, and Sarah sensed something protective toward Bess in the gesture. Her son had become part of this Elk Island household, and he wanted to make sure everyone knew it. Sarah could almost feel him averting his gaze from her.

CHAPTER

10

THANKSGIVING MORNING WAS crystal clear and very cold. The sun came up like thunder here, and Sarah made sure she woke up in time to see it. Again she felt the ripple of fever. It ran through her body as she got dressed. Her father was cheap with oil, so he kept the house cold at night. Standing in her freezing room, her skin felt hot. She stood naked by her bed, glistening with a fine sweat, trying to remember her dreams. They had been busy and passionate, causing her to toss around the bed all night, twisting in the sheets. Will's was the face she recalled, as if he had been the one responsible for her fever.

But by the time she had pulled on thermal underwear, jeans, turtleneck, and a heavy sweater, she felt normal again. Her temperature was down. No one else stirred. She paused outside Mike's bedroom door, listening for his deep, steady breathing. The sound contented her, as it always had. Knowing he would be there when she got back, she left the house and walked down the snowy path to the bay.

The stars were still out. They hung in the deep blue sky, low globes of light that someone had forgotten to extinguish. Sarah stood by the water, her hands stuck in her pockets. The geese were beginning to cackle in the barn, and the seals were starting to bark on the rocks. Again, returning to a place she loved so much after thinking she would never see it again, moved her immeasurably. Grateful for dawn, Maine, her family farm, her beautiful son, she opened her arms.

But she wasn't alone. In the darkness she hadn't noticed the man sitting on the rock. Hearing her footsteps, he rose and walked across the tidal flats. She saw him coming, silhouetted against the cold auroral fire. Looking up into his kind face, into eyes that hadn't seen much sleep last night, she smiled.

"Good morning," Will said.

"You're up early," she said.

"I figured if I was the first one up, being this far east, I'd be the first person in the United States to see the sun rise."

"Do you mind company?" she asked.

"No," he said, standing beside her as they faced the sea. "Not at all."

His leather jacket crinkled as he unfolded his arms. They listened to the wildlife growing noisier as the horizon blazed brighter. Waves broke over rocks fifty yards away. The tide was low, and Elk Island tides were notoriously extreme. The exposed sea bottom was rippled, the silver mud scored with rivulets of water running out to sea. Lobsters and crabs scuttled beneath the rockweed. Boulders changed shape and slid into the bay, and Sarah touched Will's hand and pointed.

"Seals," she said.

"Those rocks?" he asked. The animals did look rocklike, sleek and gray and thrown together in haphazard fashion, the water rising around them.

"A whole colony," she said, watching the creatures arch their backs, pointing their noses toward the sky, fifty or sixty adults and at least a dozen young.

"I'll be damned," he said.

"You didn't have seals in Newport?"

"Maybe one or two, spending the winter in Narragansett Bay. That's about it. Someone would spot one, and the word would get out, and the kids would beg us to take them to Castle

Hill or Beavertail to see if we could look for them. Wait till Susan sees these guys."

"Kids love seals," Sarah agreed. "When Mike was little, I couldn't get him off the rocks. He wanted to chase seals all day long."

"He's a nice kid," Will said. "He did a good job yesterday, getting the airstrip ready for us. And he's glad to see you."

"Hmm," Sarah said, trying to be strong. But her insecurities got the better of her. "Why do you say that?"

"I can just tell. The way he mentioned fixing that step last night. He wants you to see he's indispensable. It's a man-of-the-house kind of attitude. He wants you to be proud of him."

"I was thinking...something different."

"Like what?"

"That he wants me to see he doesn't need me at all. He's adopted my father and Bess as his new family, he's theirs now."

The sun had broken out of the sea. It was a red ball shining through the outer islands dotted throughout the bay, turning the tall pines black and spiky and sharp against the golden light. The air was still frigid, and thinking of Mike in his new life in her old family made Sarah's arms feel numb.

"Why is he here?" Will asked quietly.

"He ran away."

"From home?"

Sarah paused, thinking of their last, and worst, fight. "From me," she said.

"Isn't that normal at his age? Guys go through a stage where they can't stand their mothers. Or at least they can't show it."

"He had his things packed," Sarah said, closing her eyes as she remembered. "Ready to hitchhike to Maine, to catch the ferry out here from Bethlehem. We fought, and then I caught up with him on the highway. I asked him to think of his future, stay with me just until he finished high school, and he just looked at me and said he couldn't. He wouldn't even listen." She took a breath. "He looked like he hated me."

"Why would he?"

"Lots of reasons," Sarah said.

Will didn't speak right away. He seemed to be watching the seals. As the sun rose, they were more visible. They looked bonded to the rocks, hardly separate at all, like infants pressed up against their mothers. Sarah had to lower her eyes.

"He doesn't hate you," Will said.

Sarah looked up at him. His face was dark with whiskers, sexy, and kind; he hadn't shaved yet. He looked disturbed, as if he wanted more than anything for the words he was saying to be true.

"How can you tell?" she asked, praying he would tell her something she could stand to hear.

"Because no one could hate you," he said.

Sarah's heart fell. She had started to shiver, and she couldn't quite get it under control. She had wanted something specific, some observation Will Burke had made after watching her and Mike, some revelation she could let herself believe. She didn't say anything, but she didn't have to. Will knew he had to give her more.

"Because a boy who hates his mother doesn't ask her to come all the way to Elk Island to spend Thanksgiving with him," Will said.

"He didn't want to be with me last year. I know it's not why he left, but I found out I had cancer and he couldn't get away fast enough."

"He was scared," Will said.

Sarah nodded. That was part of the reason; she knew, deep in her heart, that any son would be afraid of losing his mother, no matter how self-sufficient he was, no matter how many years he had been letting himself into the house after school while she worked hard to pay their rent, to sustain this old farm.

"He wouldn't want to lose you, Sarah. No one would."

"Oh, God, that sunrise is so beautiful," Sarah said, watching

the sky turn from dark gray to blue, watching the last star fading
into the light of the new day.

"Happy Thanksgiving, Sarah."

"Happy Thanksgiving, Will."

Ready for coffee and breakfast, wanting to see their children,
they walked slowly up the frozen path to the still-dark house.

———

WHILE ALL THE adults were busy fixing Thanksgiving dinner,
Snow decided she needed a tour of Elk Island. She bundled into
her parka and checked all the rooms in the crooked little house.
Her favorite was Aunt Bess's sewing room. It was full of tiny
white feathers. They stuck to every surface, including the ancient black sewing machine. A stack of finished quilts stood in
the corner, and it made Snow happy to think of them on the
shelves in Sarah's shop, ready to make the people of Fort
Cromwell feel safe and warm.

Finally she found Mike down by the bay. He was coming out
the door of a tiny little shack, and he looked guilty the minute
he saw her. He held a bushel basket full of feathers.

"What's in there, secret treasure?" she asked, walking straight
over to the shack.

"Uh, no," he said.

"Then how come you look so afraid I'll open the door?"

"Believe me, you don't want to," he said.

Snow stood very still. She tilted her head, looking him over.
She hadn't spent twenty minutes freezing cold in front of a
bathroom mirror for nothing that morning. Zero eight hundred, out of bed, and beautifying. Applying eye shadow, dark
liner, mascara, and lip gloss here in the wilderness of deepest,
darkest Maine, she had been thinking the whole time how cute
Mike Talbot was. And now they were face-to-face. Tall, dark,
and wow.

"Why not?" she asked. "What is it?"

"The picking shack."

"The what? Why can't I go in?"

"It's kind of gross."

"Gross? How?"

"It's where we take the feathers off the geese."

"Really?" she asked, her eyes lighting up as she looked at the basket. "Are there a bunch of naked little geese running around in there?"

"No, they're dead."

"Dead?" she asked, unbelieving.

"Yeah."

"You have to *kill* them? To get their *feathers*?"

"Well, yeah."

"Oh, my God," Snow said. This threw new light on Sarah's shop. Snow hated killing animals. She refused to eat meat, not even chicken or fish. She despised rich women who wore fur coats, imagining the suffering endured by the tiny creatures. So what if they were rodents? She cringed, thinking of the sable coat Julian had given her mother. And geese were no different. She couldn't believe this of Sarah.

"Are you okay?" Mike asked.

"No, I'm not," Snow said. "Not really okay at all. Does your mother know about this?"

"About what?"

"Killing the geese?"

"Well, yeah. Of course. She grew up with it."

"I just can't believe it. I just can't." Snow felt sick. Compared to all the other adults she knew, even compared to her own mother, Sarah was the best person in the world. But here she was, selling products that required the slaughter of beautiful birds! A pair of geese waddled by, nuzzling against Mike's boots, which Snow suddenly noticed were streaked with reddish-brown.

"Is that blood? On your boots?" she asked.

"Yeah," he said, looking down for an instant.

"Go on," Snow said, scaring the geese. She waved her arms, chasing the birds down the path. They ran ahead of her, looking over their backs as if she were a madwoman with an ax. All the way to the edge of the cove, which was filling fast as the tide poured in. The geese veered off just as they reached the water's edge. Snow stood there, watching them run back to Mike.

"They can't fly," he explained. "Their wings are clipped."

"More cruelty," she said. "I can't believe they die for their feathers. For quilts!"

"We kill them for food," Mike said. "My grandfather and aunt would starve if we didn't have the geese to sell."

"No one should starve," Snow said nobly, her lower lip quivering as she stared at the geese. "But quilts!"

"I know how you feel," Mike said. "When I was little, my mother told me the geese liked having their feathers taken. I pictured this really serene procedure, combing the geese . . . but it's not that way."

"When did you find out?"

"Not till I moved up here," Mike said.

"Oh," Snow said, shuddering. She tilted her head again, suddenly feeling sorry for Mike. What a horrible thing to learn. And now he was trapped on this island, taking care of his mean old grandfather and killing geese. Staring at Snow, seeing her terrible distress, he looked very worried.

"Grandpa handed me an ax one day and told me what to do," he explained. "If we didn't need the money so badly, I'd never kill another goose."

"Stop the death," Snow said. "You have to stand on your principles."

Mike shrugged. He looked as if he were about to laugh, but he turned serious instead. "That's what I'm doing," he said. "Keeping the farm alive."

Suddenly he reminded Snow so much of his mother. His eyes were really beautiful, deep and full of some amazing yearning. He wanted something so badly: Snow felt she could almost peer inside his soul. She had seen that same intensity in Sarah's face. It was the thing that had initially drawn them together. Just remembering that feeling made Snow forgive Sarah for the geese. What she wanted more than anything in the world was to reunite, really reunite Sarah and her son.

"You don't have to kill the geese anymore," Snow said softly.

"What?"

Snow took a step toward him. The sun was in her eyes, and as she squinted she felt herself start to smile. They were so close, she could feel the warmth of his body. A shiver ran down her spine, and she felt herself wanting to save the day, to make everything better between Mike and Sarah.

"You can come home with us," she said. "When we leave on Sunday. There's room on the plane."

Mike was breathing funny. His mouth was open slightly, and he licked his lips. She could see by the way he blinked and looked away that he was very nervous, and she wondered what he was thinking. They were wearing gloves, but she touched the bare spot on his wrist, between the cuff of his sleeve and the top of his glove. The connection shocked them both.

"I can't go back with you," he said, his voice nearly a croak.

"Why not?" she asked.

"Because I have things I have to do here."

"Oh . . ." Snow said, tipping her head back.

Mike just stood there, paralyzed by Snow's touch. He dropped the basket, and it clattered against a rock. Drifts of white down rose around them like a private snowstorm. The feathers swirled in eddies, flying on the air currents, sticking to whatever they landed on.

"Sorry," Mike whispered, still just staring at her.

"For what?" she whispered back.

He could barely talk, he was breathing so hard. "For getting feathers in your hair."

"You're forgiven," she said.

And then they didn't talk anymore, until Snow's neck ached

from bending back for so long as she stared up at Mike, wondering why she felt this way, until they heard Aunt Bess ringing the bell, telling them that Thanksgiving dinner was served.

————

THE MAIN COURSE was goose. It was roasted golden brown, its skin crackling. Sarah had made her mother's apple stuffing, and Will had mashed the potatoes. They had turnips and parsnips from the root cellar, and Bess had prepared prunes soaked in brandy and stuffed with goose liver, a recipe she had saved from her entertaining days as the wife of a jewelry manufacturer.

"Isn't this a little swanky?" George asked, frowning at the spread. He seemed particularly upset by the candles, tall white tapers Bess had unearthed from one of her boxes from Providence.

"It's a holiday celebration, George," Bess said.

"I don't like candles. I like to see what I'm eating."

"The Pilgrims ate by candlelight," Snow said.

"The Pilgrims didn't have electricity, but we do," George reasoned. "Now, that's something to be thankful for."

"I think it's romantic," Snow said, and Sarah noticed Mike starting to blush.

"Come carve the goose, George," Bess called.

"I brought it to the table. Let's give Will the honors."

"Thanks," Will said as George handed him the Sheffield cutlery set.

Everyone had changed into their best clothes. Snow wore a short plaid jumper, Will wore soft gray corduroys and a navy blue sweater. Aunt Bess kept on the same blue dress with pearls, Mike had put on clean khakis and a blue oxford shirt, and Sarah wore a long hunter-green velvet dress.

Her father wore gray flannels and a white shirt. The shirt was yellowed with age, stiff with starch. Sarah knew he hadn't worn it in years, and she felt touched by his effort. She wondered whether her mother had been the one to iron it. Sarah watched him limp around the kitchen, knocking the fireplace tools over as he added another log to the dwindling fire.

"Goddammit," he said, burning his hand as he pulled the poker out of the flames.

"Come here," Sarah said, pulling him over to the sink, turning on the faucet. Water, icy from the well, came gushing out, and she pushed her father's hand into the stream.

"Can't see a thing with those damn candles," he said.

"Dad, it's only three o'clock. It's broad daylight. If it makes Aunt Bess happy to have candles, let her."

"It's hoity-toity," he grumbled. "Just to let the company know she used to live in grand style, down there in Providence with old what's-his-name."

"Uncle Arthur."

"The executive. Get a load of those stuffed prunes. Can't you just imagine serving them up to the country club set? They'd have the runs to last them till Christmas. Makes me so damn mad. Blow those candles out, will you, Sarah?"

"Mom loved candlelight," Sarah said.

She had been holding her father's rough hand under the faucet, amazed at the strength and tension in his wrist and forearm, but suddenly it went slack. At the mention of Sarah's mother, all the fight went out of him. His whole body relaxed. For the first time since arriving on the island, Sarah could look at her father and not think about how angry he was.

"Yes, she did," he said.

"Especially around the holidays," Sarah said. "We always had candles for Thanksgiving and Christmas, remember? Beautiful tall ones, just like these."

"They had to be white," her father said. "Boats and candles, she always said, had to be white. I miss her every day."

"I know you do, Dad."

His anger was back, or something close to it. George Talbot peered into his daughter's eyes as if he wanted to catch her in a lie. As a teenager she had sometimes come home after dances on the mainland, and he had stared at her in this same intense way, with protective suspicion, as if he would see in her eyes the reflection of boys she had kissed, beers she had drunk.

"How's that sickness of yours?" he asked.

"It's fine."

"What d'you mean, it's fine? It can't be fine. It's over or it's not. But it can't be fine."

"Dad, medicine has come a long way since Mom died," Sarah said. She had turned off the cold water, but she continued holding his hand. Wanting to reassure him she was all better, she didn't understand why her heart was pounding like mad. And then she noticed Mike. He was leaning against a counter across the room. Will was carving the goose, and Snow was tempting Mike to pull the wishbone, but he was looking over her head at his mother, listening intently.

"I'm fine," Sarah said again.

Her father waved his hand. "What a bunch of double-talk. If you can't answer a straight question, I won't bother asking. Blow them candles out, Bess. I mean it, now."

———————

BUT THE CANDLES stayed lit. The families sat at the big table, in the seats they had claimed last night. Already, it felt like a tradition. Will had been honored to be asked to carve the goose, and watching Bess and Sarah fill the plates, it pleased him to be told how well he had sliced the meat. He had thought that Snow would miss her mother, but he shouldn't have worried. She was lost in adolescent rapture for Mike Talbot, unable to take her eyes off him.

Will felt the same way about Sarah. She wore a long, beautiful velvet dress that hugged her body perfectly and made him want to take her in his arms and give thanks of a very quiet and private nature. Watching her reach for a silver dish on a high shelf, he caught sight of her collarbone, delicate and pale, and imagined kissing it. She kept glancing at him. Moving around the kitchen, she gazed over with those deep blue eyes.

She took the seat across from him. Will had not felt anything close to all right for several Thanksgivings now, but he felt that way today. All right. Sitting near Sarah made him happy. She calmed him and excited him at the same time, a way he couldn't remember feeling for a long time. He felt as though he knew her well, had known her forever, better than anyone else in the world, and she knew him too. It was impossible, but it was the truest thing he knew.

George had gone out to the barn for a jug of hard cider, and everyone was waiting for him to return. Bess seemed impatient with her brother's bad mood, and the kids were oblivious, but Sarah took it in stride. Will wondered whether she knew her father's rotten manners were the result of missing her mother. He wondered whether George knew it himself. He figured they must: they had had enough time to figure it out.

Will had learned more recently. The grief he felt for Fred had barely dulled to an ache. After five years it had just begun to feel manageable. He recognized the emptiness in the old man's eyes. He had seen the same blank look in his own eyes in the bathroom mirror. Listening to George question Sarah about her own health had shaken Will, but just for a minute. She was fine, she had said so herself. Her bright eyes were testament, her glowing skin, her amazing energy.

Finally George slammed through the door, set the jug down on the table.

"Storm's here," he said. "We got high clouds moving in fast, flurries just starting to come down."

"Winter's too early this year," Bess said.

"We're having a storm?" Sarah asked. "Oh, I hope so. I'd love you guys to see a real Maine gale."

"Should hit around midnight," Will said. He had checked with the weather service, and the storm fit right in with their travel plans: an early snowstorm would end by noon tomorrow, give way to an Alberta clipper, dry Arctic air that wouldn't interfere with their flight home. Although, looking around the warm basement kitchen, seeing the excitement in Sarah's eyes, he wouldn't mind being snowed in for a few extra days.

"It's only November, and we've already had two big snowstorms," Bess said, sounding worried.

"What do you expect?" George asked. "You're in Maine, not Florida."

"Don't worry," Mike said. "We have the plow, and there's enough firewood cut to take us into spring."

"Our beautiful goose is getting cold," Bess said, still upset.

"Let's eat," George said, agreeing with her for once.

"I'd like to say grace," Sarah said.

George slouched, a sullen look on his face, but everyone else folded their hands and bowed their heads. The candles flickered. Will closed his eyes. He heard Sarah clear her throat and take a deep breath.

"Bless us, O Lord," she said. "Thank you for the food we are about to eat, thank you for our health. Thank you for bringing us together on this island, thank you for one another. Thank you for everyone we love, especially for those who can't be with us right now."

"Fred," Snow whispered.

"Fred," Will repeated.

"Mom," Sarah said.

"Yep," George said. "My Rose."

"Arthur," Bess said.

"Can I say something?" Mike said, immediately getting everyone's attention.

"Of course, honey," Sarah said, blinking at him with such hope and love in her eyes that Will wanted to reach over and hold her forever.

"Just this," Mike said, clasping his hands and bowing his head even lower than before. "I'm thankful you're well. And you're here." He paused, then stared at her very hard. "Okay?"

"Okay," Will said, because suddenly Sarah could not speak. "Amen."

Mike glared at him, and Will figured it was because he'd answered for his mother. His eyes reflected anger, but he nodded.

"Amen," they all said.

Will had caught Sarah's eye, and she didn't look away. The table was laden with food, the fire was warming the cozy room, six people of three generations were gathered closely together. Sarah was home with her son, and for one amazing moment, looking at her, Will could almost imagine that they were all part of the same family. They were connected by some mysterious and nameless love. Even Fred was with them.

―――――

LATER, WHEN THE house was quiet and everyone had gone to bed, Sarah came down to sit by the fire. She felt too churned up to sleep. The house was full of old memories of her mother and father, of the family the three of them had been. And seeing Mike again was incredible. Staring at the glowing embers, she sat on the window seat feeling quiet and content from just being under the same roof as him.

"I thought I'd be the first one up and the last one to bed, but here you are," Will said, surprising her as he entered the room.

"Can't sleep?" she asked.

"I haven't tried yet," he said. Coming closer, she saw he was wearing his parka and boots, both dusted with snow. "The storm's starting. I was just outside."

"Get warm," Sarah said, sliding down the window seat.

Will slid off his boots and placed them by the door. He hung his jacket on the coatrack. He held back, standing in the shadows. Sarah watched him reach into his parka pocket, transfer something into his jeans. He was big but very graceful, and she realized that she enjoyed watching him.

"I keep interrupting your solitude," he said.

"That's good," Sarah said. "I have enough of it in Fort Cromwell."

Will nodded. "It gets quiet without them around."

"It does," Sarah said, knowing he was referring to the kids.

The snow had begun to fall outside. It blew against the windows, driven off the sea by the wind. Across the room the dying fire crackled. Sarah looked over at Will and smiled.

"This is nice," he said.

"I know. I'm glad you came in."

"No, I mean all of it. Thanksgiving with your family. Thank you for inviting us."

"You're welcome," Sarah said. "I've been feeling guilty about bringing you all the way out here. Is there somewhere else you usually go?"

Will paused. "Used to go, maybe."

"Like where?"

"Well, we used to have Thanksgiving with my parents. We lived in Newport and they lived in Connecticut, so it was easy. Every year we'd drive down."

"Your mother cooked?"

Will nodded. "Yes. She was a good cook too. She had this thing about Thanksgiving—everyone had to have everything they wanted. So if one person liked one kind of cranberry sauce and someone else liked another, we had both."

"Bountiful," Sarah said. "The old Pilgrim spirit."

Will nodded. He got quiet. Maybe he felt he had said enough about it, but he seemed to enjoy talking. He kept going. "My father grew up in Mamaroneck—in Westchester County—and his family smoked their turkeys. So instead of choosing between smoked and roasted, we had both. When I married Alice, my mother sat her down and found out everything she'd had at her family Thanksgivings in Northampton. Like sweet potatoes, creamed corn, chocolate cream pie. Things that were sort of different for us. We didn't do away with our things, we just added hers."

"Sounds like a wonderful time," Sarah said, curious about Alice.

"It was. I miss them. My parents died within six months of each other, about five years ago."

"That's recent," Sarah said, looking over.

"It is. I feel it today," Will said. "My mother went first, a sudden heart attack one spring morning. My father just didn't want to live without her. It was so obvious—he just got tired. Stopped going out, doing the things he always did. Never even put his boat in the water that summer. He just died in his sleep one night in September."

"I've heard of couples like that," Sarah said. "Who love each other so much, they can't live without each other."

"That was them," he said.

"My father didn't die after my mother did," Sarah said. "But he changed. He wasn't always so . . . hard," she said finally, trying to think of the right word. "He was so mad at God for taking her, he's never forgiven anyone. Especially me."

"When did she die?"

"When I was fourteen," Sarah said.

"Why especially you?"

"I remind him of her," Sarah said, although she knew that wasn't the real answer.

Will nodded. They listened to the storm for a few minutes. With the fire dying, the room was getting cold. Sarah didn't want to stop talking, so she walked over to the fireplace and stirred the embers. Mike had brought in a stack of wood earlier. Sarah chose a small log and threw it on. There was a bed of hot coals, so the outer bark started to catch and blaze immediately.

"Did Alice take over Thanksgiving after your mother died?" Sarah asked.

Will shook his head. "Alice isn't much of a traditionalist," he said. "She likes everyone to be together, but she'd be just as happy with roast beef as turkey. And by the time my mother died five years ago, so had Fred. Thanksgiving kind of faded away."

"I can imagine," Sarah said.

"Thanksgiving seemed . . . beside the point," Will said. "Without Fred."

Sarah nodded. She thought of Mike, of what she would do if something ever happened to him. The idea of any feast or celebration, any holiday at all, would be impossible.

"We didn't last long afterward," Will said. "Alice and I."

"I'm sorry," Sarah said.

"I believed in marriage," he said. "I did. I thought it was supposed to carry people through."

"I know," Sarah said. Because although she had no firsthand experience, she had always believed that too.

"It didn't though," Will said. "Ours just fell apart."

"Do you know why?" Sarah asked.

"I couldn't save Fred."

Sarah waited, listening. She heard Will breathing harder. The snow slanted against the windows. Could it be that simple? Could the end of an entire marriage really be condensed into those four terrible words?

"She was there too," Will said. "She got to watch me not save her son."

"What happened?" Sarah asked.

"We were sailing, all four of us. The boom came across, and Fred didn't see. It hit him so hard, it . . . It would have knocked anyone over, and he just fell in."

"Oh, Will," Sarah said, taking his hand.

"He was such a great kid."

"What was he like?"

"He loved sports. Baseball, hockey. He was a great sailor, loved the water. Living in Newport, he got his feet wet every day. You know? He'd skip school to go fishing, and I couldn't even get mad."

"I used to skip school to go fishing," Sarah said, smiling at the description of a boy she would have liked very much.

"Whenever I was away, which was often, he'd look after his mother and sister. I'd get these letters from Fred, telling me about Susan learning to swim or winning a spelling bee. He'd hear his mother say she didn't have enough money to buy new tires, and he'd write me telling me he was afraid she'd skid into something."

"Did you take care of the tires?"

"Yes."

"Fred saw to it. What a good son," Sarah said.

"He was."

Sarah looked at the fire. She supposed he was thinking about his marriage. What was Alice like? she wondered. She found herself feeling jealous of a woman she had never met, the ex-wife of a man she hardly knew. If Snow looked anything like her mother, Alice must be beautiful. Those wide eyes, that lustrous hair. Sarah thought of herself, her skinny bones and scruffy white hair, her owl eyes, and she blushed.

"I don't know much about marriage," Sarah said. "But to me, couples like our parents are right. The ones who stick together through everything, and when one of them dies, it's the end of the world."

"Yes," Will said.

"You asked me this morning why I think Mike hates me. That's part of the reason. I didn't marry his father. I had Mike when I was very young."

"That bothers him?"

Sarah nodded. "When he was in second grade, I went to school for parent-teacher night. His teacher asked me when my husband was coming back from sea. Mike had told her his father was an explorer, sailing around the world on a lobster boat."

"They make teachers gullible these days," Will said, smiling.

"That's what I thought."

"It's nothing to hate you for."

"He was ashamed."

"About what? Lots of kids have parents who live apart."

"I know, but we were never together at all. Married anyway." She cringed, drew her knees up to her chest, hugged herself tightly. She remembered how hurt she had been, how she had cried her eyes out. Her father had stood across this very kitchen, waving a poker and threatening to kill Zeke; all these years later, the shame was still damaging Mike. Wondering what Will thought of her, she looked over the tops of her knees.

"I'm sorry," Will said.

Sarah shrugged, tried to smile. "Poor little kid," she said.

"Hmm."

"He didn't like it when I was away from him. I worked a lot, and . . . I was young. I had boyfriends. His friends had nice, stable homes, and he wanted that too. He was always tagging along with his friends' fathers to the hardware store. They couldn't get rid of him."

"Needed male companionship."

Sarah nodded. "Looking for fathers everywhere he went. He didn't really like the guys I went out with. Or he'd start to, and they wouldn't stay around. We just couldn't win."

Will was staring at her. Sarah knew she didn't have any hair falling across her eyes, her hair was too short for that, but he reached over and gently brushed his hand against her cheek as if he were pushing back a stray lock. She did the same to him. They nodded, listening to the storm grow stronger outside.

At the sound of footsteps on the stairs, they both looked up. Mike walked into the kitchen. Seeing the fire still burning, he stopped and frowned.

"Hi," Sarah said, her heart rising at the sight of him.

Mike jumped. He peered into the shadows.

"God, you scared me," he said.

"Hi, Mike," Will said. "I'm just keeping your mother company."

"Huh," Mike said, sounding not quite sullen.

"What brings you downstairs, honey?" Sarah asked. He had always been such a sound sleeper. He would fall asleep on the couch almost every night. She would have to wake him, ask if he'd done his homework, tell him to go to bed. Sleeping through the night, he wouldn't even wake up when the phone rang or someone came to the door, when Sarah got home late. Yet here he was.

"Just checking the fire," he said. "I heard the wind start, and there's something banging down by the dock. I want to tie down the tarp better."

"I'll help you," Will said, rising.

"It's no big deal," Mike said flatly. "I can do it myself."

"I know you can," Will said, pulling on his boots. "But I'd like some air, if you don't mind company."

"Whatever you want," Mike said. He sounded indifferent, but he was staring at Will. Sarah's heart twisted. Her talk with Will had left her feeling raw, thinking of how she had let her son down.

"In the Navy," Will said, "we always sent two out on deck, especially at night. In storms like this—always."

"There's nothing dangerous out there. What do you think? One of Grandpa's muskrats might come to life?" Mike asked rudely. "Fly out of the picking shack and attack us?"

"Those poor little critters," Sarah said. This was so familiar to her: the men she knew trying to be nice to Mike, him acting tough and rude, Sarah right in the middle. She felt it again, that in-between anxiety, and she and Will weren't even romantic. She just kept talking. "All dried out and strung up. He still hunts them?"

"When he can," Mike said, sounding protective. "He's getting pretty lame. I'm afraid he'll trip when he's out in the woods. We wouldn't know where to find him."

"That's why you take someone along," Will said, slapping Mike's back.

"You said you wanted air," Mike said. "I'm not 'taking' you."

"Are you always such a jerk to your mother's friends?" Will asked.

Mike just stared. He seemed shocked by Will's words; for years he had mouthed off at men, and usually they had disappeared rather than talk back.

"I wasn't mouthing off," he said, glancing at his mother to see what she had to say about Will's retort. Sarah forced herself to remain impassive. She just sat there, pretending to be stone deaf.

"Don't worry about it. I was in the Navy a long time. I've heard people be rude before. But you seem like a good guy. You might grow out of it."

Mike didn't speak. Grabbing his gloves and a flashlight, he led Will out the back door.

Sarah sat still, watching the men go out into the night. She heard the wind, felt her own breath in her chest. No one ever talked to Mike like that. She had felt his tension all the way across the room, imagined him wanting to throw a punch. But he hadn't; he'd quieted down and led Will out to batten down the hatches.

She thought of allegiances and loyalties, shifting around, realigning, old connections shattering. Her son had come to her island to find his father, and here he was taking care of George. And now Will was out in the darkness with him, Sarah's hostile son, when his own Fred was drowned, taken by the sea.

The fire had died down again. Sarah took a deep breath. A gust of air from the door being opened and closed knifed through the room. Rising, she walked over to the fireplace and added one more log. She wanted the room to be nice and warm when the men returned.

CHAPTER

11

MIKE LAY ON the floor on his back. Everyone was gathered around, waiting for the storm to pass. His mother and Will were doing a jigsaw puzzle. Eyes almost closed, Mike pretended to be asleep and watched them. He was trying to get over being called a jerk last night.

He'd been shocked at first, then outraged. He had expected his mother to yell at Will, at least apologize to Mike for him, but she had just sat there. That was new. His mother's attitude toward Will had Mike thinking. Will had a stealth thing going, he wasn't always coming on with a smile.

Mike respected guys who didn't grin too much. His mother was always going out with men who went around shaking hands and nodding their heads. Pretending to agree with every stupid thing he said, taking all the abuse Mike felt like handing out. Most of them had been super-respectable types, the pharmacist and the accountant, the lawyer and the paving specialist. Nine-to-five guys Mike figured his mother had chosen so he could look up to them.

She had always had someone around. Mike remembered asking her how bridges were built, and the next thing he knew she was bringing home a civil engineer. He had inquired about constellations one time, and within a month his mother was dating an astronomy professor at Harvard. He guessed she didn't want to be alone, and she wanted him to have a father figure, so she tried killing two birds with one stone.

It had always pissed Mike off. By now it was habit to act hostile to the men she brought home. How could he respect bureaucrats when his father had been a maverick lobsterman? As a kid, he had told his friends his father was like Jacques Cousteau, exploring the world on an oceanographic lobster boat.

Peering across the room, he tried to tell whether Will and his mother were more than just friends. They weren't giving anything away. He got the feeling Snow was doing the same thing, scoping out the romance angle between their parents. Wondering also what she thought about him, Mike tried to see her now. She was sitting right there, just across the room. But to actually check her out, he would have had to move his head. They'd all know he was awake, and he would lose his advantage.

Will was the kind of guy someone could respect. A Navy pilot wasn't too bad. Coming to Maine, Mike had learned his father wasn't exactly the lobsterman hero he had once dreamed of. But he didn't have to let anyone else know that.

———

SNOW QUILTED ELK Island from the north cliffs to the bay, and it kept falling. All the barn cats had come into the house, seeking the warmth of the fireplace, and they lay curled in all their secret places: on top of the bookcases, inside the piano, in the sweater drawers, in the springs of the old sofa, in the baskets of down. Gelsey, the ancient collie, lay at Aunt Bess's feet, right on the braided rug she was working on.

All these animals and so many feathers, and Snow hadn't had one asthma attack! Her airways were free and clear. She felt the peace and love of Elk Island taking over her body, and she imagined never leaving. She could live here forever. Lying on the sofa, reading by the fire, she watched the snow coming down and considered the logistics.

Her dad would stay with her. He and Sarah got along very well, so he'd have a friend his own age. Plus, he and George had their military days in common. Aunt Bess liked everyone. Sarah would be like a mother to Snow, a kind of maternal best friend and eventual mother-in-law. Snow was going to marry Mike.

He lay across the room, stretched out with a pillow over his eyes. Snow watched him carefully, the way he flexed every muscle in his wonderful arms. They looked so strong. She imagined them wrapping her in a sweet embrace, lifting her against his chest, carrying her over the threshold. The whole family would be so happy.

Sarah and her dad were working on a jigsaw puzzle. They sat at a card table by the window, their heads bent together over the emerging picture of a mountain scene. One of the cats kept rubbing against Sarah's cheek, wanting to be petted, messing up the puzzle pieces. Her father whispered something, making Sarah laugh.

Had she ever seen her parents having so much fun? Snow racked her brain, trying to remember. Silence, anger, unspoken accusations and then *spoken* accusations: Those were the elements she recalled from her parents' marriage. Way back, when Fred was still with them, they had loved each other and had a ball. But the details of that time were hazy, receding like the land from a sailboat at sea.

Snow sighed, thinking of her mother.

Sarah glanced over, alert and smiling quizzically. "Are you okay?" she asked.

"Mmm," Snow said, smiling back.

"Bored?" Sarah asked.

"Not at *all*," Snow replied. Did Sarah know how wonderful this was, being snowbound on an island with people who cared about her? Snuggled under a scratchy plaid blanket, surrounded by mangy cats, Snow wondered if Sarah knew that she was the center of everything, the person who had brought everyone together. She was Mike's mom, George's daughter, Bess's niece,

Snow and her father's friend. It seemed like such a generous existence, regardless of the goose killing.

Thinking of her mother, all wrapped up in Julian and their selfish life, made Snow feel sad. She shrunk inward, and for the first time since coming to the island she started wheezing.

"Have you called your mother?" Sarah asked quietly, as if she could read Snow's mind. How had she done that? How was such clairvoyance humanly possible?

Her mind boggled, Snow shook her head. She attempted to channel, to see what her mother was doing right now. Maybe it was snowing in Fort Cromwell, and she was up in her bedroom giving herself a manicure. Or possibly she was snowmobiling with Julian. Or, perhaps, and this was the image that came through the clearest, she was crying on her bed, missing Snow and Fred.

"Why don't you call?" Sarah asked.

"It's a good idea, honey," her father said.

"The phone's in the hall," Sarah said.

"I'll show you," Mike said, easing himself onto his elbows, off the floor. He stood over Snow, looking down at her with that soft mouth of his half open, and Snow's wheezing stopped dead. She smiled up at him, her brown hair falling across her eyes, hoping she looked alluring and mysterious.

"You will?" she asked, her voice low and miraculously wheeze free.

"Sure."

"Thank you," said the future Mrs. Michael Talbot, and she followed him out of the room, down the hall, into the great unknown.

———

WHEN THE MAIN snow stopped, the sky stayed white and flurries continued to fall. Housebound for too long, everyone but George and Bess put on warm clothes and went out for a walk.

Snow lay heavy on the dark pines, the witch-bone oaks. The barn roof sagged under the snow's weight. Juncos and sparrows roosted in low bushes beside the house, and smoke wisped from the chimney. The sea was dark and silky.

The mudroom contained snowshoes and cross-country skis, but not enough pairs of either to go around. The men strapped on snowshoes, while Sarah and Snow took the skis. They all pushed off, aiming for the trail that would lead them to Great South Head. Overjoyed to be outside and moving, Sarah felt her heart pounding. Skiing in heavy powder gave her a work-out comparable to many miles at the track, but she knew she was up to it. She gave Dr. Goodacre a passing thought, telling herself she would stop if she got tired.

Mike led the way. He and Will made snowshoeing look ef-fortless, which it was not. Will walked beside her, never letting her get too far ahead. Sarah felt something happening between them. She glanced over, smiling at him over the muffler that was wrapped around her chin.

"I'll race you," she said.

"How much time do I have to give you?" Will asked.

"None. I'll beat you fair and square."

He laughed. They kept up a fast pace, just behind their chil-dren, forging along through unmarked snow. They crossed a wide field, mounted a headland with the pine forest on their left and a rickety rail fence on their right, and the trail became nar-row. The land rose gradually. Everyone unzipped their parkas, sweating and breathing hard. They proceeded in single file.

As the trail grew steeper, they tried different tactics. Sarah and Snow sidestepped, their skis perpendicular to the trail. Will and Mike ran ahead, toes out, herringboning uphill. The old fence needed mending, and at certain spots it had broken down. The cliff dropped one hundred feet to the sea. Sarah shielded Snow, shouldering her closer to the trees. She was almost afraid to look at her fearless son. He was bombing along, racing Will. Suddenly he stopped.

"Hey, Mom," Mike said. Waiting for her to catch up, he pointed at the sky. "There he is."

"Who?" Snow asked.

Circling overhead was a bald eagle. He lived in the northern cliffs, at the far end of the island, but he had come down to fish the bay. Sarah stood beside Mike, catching her breath. Their heads back, they stared upward, watching the eagle soar in great circles, his wings spread straight and wide.

"Oh, Mike! Do you remember...when?" Sarah asked when she had paused long enough to talk. Her body ached from exertion, and her chest hurt with each deep breath. She leaned over, her hands gripping her thighs.

Mike knew what she meant, and he interrupted so she wouldn't have to keep talking. "When we first saw him? Yeah."

Mike had been eleven. They had come out to the island for summer vacation, and they'd spent a whole amazing week lobstering and eagle watching.

"It can't be the same guy," she said.

"Eagles live a long time," Mike said. "He's still around."

"But is that *him*?" It surprised Sarah how much she wanted it to be.

"It is," Mike said. "He's always been missing a few pinions. See?"

The last, long, fingerlike feathers at the ends of his wings. Mike was right; Sarah could see a wide space where several pinions should have been. She nodded, gulping for air. She held her right fist just under her breasts, trying to stop the painful stabs of every breath.

"I am out of...shape," she said.

"You're doing great, Mom," he said.

"I am?" she asked, loving his praise.

"Yeah," he said. He had been staring up at the eagle, but now he looked directly into her eyes. His face was red from the cold, but it was so handsome and grown-up, it took her breath away even more. She could hardly see the baby he used to be. His cheeks were lean, his jaw strong, his eyes steady as a man's, no longer questioning like a boy's.

"You are," he said. "A mile in the snow? That's better than great."

"I feel so much better," Sarah said, thinking of how sick she had been.

"Did you and Dad ever ski? Or snowshoe?"

Sarah shook her head. "No. He was always lobstering."

"Everyone here remembers him," Mike said.

"It's a small island," Sarah said carefully, wondering what people were telling Mike they remembered him for.

"Why do you always put him down?" Mike asked hotly.

"Mike, I'm sorry," she said quickly.

Suddenly Snow squealed. Pointing her ski pole seaward, she began to jump up and down. She went down in a heap, but she kept pointing. Gazing out, Sarah saw the wide, dark bay. It was deep blue-gray, like unpolished steel, unmarred by waves or whitecaps. It was the calm after the storm, and there was barely a whisper of wind on the water's surface. The only movement was a series of large, concentric rings rumbling outward from an earthquake-like epicenter.

Sarah and Mike glanced at each other, old Maine hands, knowing exactly what they were seeing. The whale breached a second time, coming clear out of the sea. Its sleek, gigantic body launched skyward, water streaming off, and landed with a violent splash.

"Oh, my God!" Snow yelled.

Mike bumbled over to help her up. Grabbing for his hands, she accidentally pulled him down with her. Amazed, Mike didn't even move.

"What is it?" Snow asked.

"A whale," Mike replied.

"It's a humpback," Will said, scanning the sea for the same whale or its mate, a big smile on his face. "We'd see them all the time, crossing the North Atlantic."

"How can you tell?" Snow asked. "Dad, how do you know it's a humpback?"

"The white flukes," Mike said. "Those long white fins."

"That's right," Will said.

"Angel wings," Snow said. "That's what those white things looked like to me."

"Angel wings," Sarah said, trying to breathe right again. Angel wings. She stood back, surprising herself by realizing that she loved all three of these people staring at the sea for a whale who had disappeared.

"My father set his pots in there," Mike said to everyone, pointing at the bay.

"Lobster pots?" Will asked.

Mike nodded, saying nothing. He stared at the section where his father's buoys once had been. Mike had never seen them, so someone must have told him.

"Elk Island lobstermen only go out in winter," Mike said.

"They must be tough," Will said.

Mike turned, his eyes narrowed as if he suspected the Navy man of being sarcastic. But Will's face was open, his expression kind. Watching him be kind to her son, Sarah felt her throat ache and wondered why.

"The toughest lobstermen in Maine," Mike said.

———

AT THE TOP of Great South Head, they turned inland. Will and Sarah hung back, letting the kids lead them wherever they wanted to go. The trees closed in. The snowfall was thinner here, but even so, four inches covered the ground. Following the twin tracks, fat snowshoe prints and unbroken ski marks, Will made himself move slower than he had to. Sarah seemed tired.

"Do you want to rest?" he asked.

She shook her head. Her cheeks were pink, her eyes bright.

She looked amazing in her black stretch pants, a bulky red sweater patterned with snowflakes, a black cashmere scarf around her throat, and a black headband around her short white hair. Her eyes were big and dark.

"I'm fine," she said.

"So am I," he said, smiling. By standing there, holding them up, he hoped to be giving her the chance to catch her breath.

She nodded. "You and my son have called a truce," she said. "Thanks for what you said about Elk Island lobstermen."

"I meant it."

"He was really off base last night."

"He's protecting you, that's all."

"I'm sorry."

"Don't be," Will said, not wanting her to worry. The bad manners of a seventeen-year-old meant nothing to him, and he trusted they would get better on their own. All he could think of was Sarah, the way she looked just then. He was glad the kids had gone on ahead. Something was building between him and Sarah, and he wanted to be alone with her.

They kept on. At first, they could hear the kids' voices. But after several minutes, as Will and Sarah slowed even more, the voices faded. The smell of pine was thick, intoxicating. They came to a fallen tree, and Will stopped. Without asking, he dusted off a patch of snow. They sat down.

Sarah undid her scarf. She closed her eyes and let out one long cloud of breath. Her eyelashes were blue-black on her pale skin. The forest was so still. He gazed at Sarah.

"Do you always arrange to have eagles and whales show up?" he asked.

"Only for you," she said.

Will took her ski poles. He lay them beside the log. She seemed to smile, as if she knew what he was going to do. Which was odd, because Will hadn't known himself.

He slid his arms around her. He kissed her. She felt so small, as delicate as a child, but her embrace was so strong, he felt her heart beating through her thick sweater. Her lips were cold, but her kiss was so hot. It turned Will's heart to fire, set it blazing with a passion he had never felt in his life. Her eyelashes fluttered against his cold cheek, and his eyes flew open.

They smiled at each other, leaning back a little, still holding tight.

"Eagles and whales are nothing," he said, "compared to you."

"That whale was an angel," she said. "Like your daughter said."

"You think so?"

"I know so."

He kissed her again, reaching up to hold her head. His fingers found a long, hard scar under her hair. His heart jolted, but she calmed him with the way she didn't flinch, the way she didn't duck. Sarah Talbot didn't hide from anything. She was kissing him with all her heart, letting him know it all. Will just kept caressing her, drawing her against his body.

"This is very interesting," she said after a minute.

"It is?"

She had her hands pressed against his cheeks, looking directly into his eyes. She spoke with humor, and there was amusement in her eyes, but there was great seriousness as well. Will waited for her to speak.

"They asked me who you were, what you were doing here with me—my father and my son—and I told them with total honesty and truthfulness that you were my pilot. And also my friend."

"Definitely your friend," Will said, tucking a fringe of silver-gold hair under her woolen headband.

"But, oh," Sarah said. "Will."

"More than friends?" he asked.

"Don't you think so?"

When something was this right, everything made sense. Holding Sarah, Will knew he could never go back to the old ways. The shock of having Fred ripped from his life had torn him in half. He had been walking around, ruined, all these years, waiting for some kind of explanation. A translation that would reveal to him the workings of God and the universe, the key to being human and feeling this kind of pain.

The key was Sarah. Will understood now. Sitting up, he let go of her just to see if he could. They faced each other, their noses six inches apart. Ten inches. A clump of snow fell from a tree limb, and they looked away entirely. A snowy owl pounded through the trees, hard on the trail of a field mouse. The mouse escaped. Will watched Sarah watching the owl fly away and knew they would remember this day for the rest of their lives.

A scream shattered the peace.

It was Snow, far off, crying for help.

On their feet, Will and Sarah ran and skied as fast as they could.

CHAPTER

12

THE KIDS WERE a quarter mile ahead. Will followed the tracks, hearing the echo of his daughter's scream. Sarah skied behind, nearly keeping up. They emerged from the woods into a white field spreading across the island. Snow stood alone at the edge of a sunken circle. Covered with snow, just like the rest of the landscape, Will could tell it was a pond.

"Mike went through the ice!" Snow cried.

"No," Sarah breathed.

Will doubled his strides. He was unstrapping his snowshoes even before he reached his daughter. She was hysterical, tears pouring down her red cheeks. Her eyes were panicked, darting from side to side. She stared at Sarah with horror.

"I told him not to go, I told him not to go!"

Sarah grabbed her hand. "When? How long?" she asked.

Will didn't hear the answer. Untying his boots, he kicked them off. He dropped his parka on the snow as he aimed at the hole in the ice. The Navy had taught him procedures for ice rescue. He knew about forming a human chain, tying a safety line to a sturdy tree. He understood the dangers of hypothermia, the risks of diving into a frozen pond.

His training had taught him to reason, but right now his only thought was for Mike Talbot. Throwing his heavy sweater aside, leaving only his jeans and T-shirt as protection against the frigid water, Commander William Burke, rescue swimmer for the United States Navy, dived into the hole in the ice.

———

FOR EXACTLY TEN seconds, Mike thought it was funny. Trying to show off, clear the ice so Snow could slide around on her skis, then he had gone crashing into the pond. He had expected it to be frozen solid. He had not expected it to be this deep, over his head, a lot over his head. He sank and sank.

The water was unbelievably cold. His heart seemed to stop, then started up again. He felt it chugging in his chest, a rusty old engine. Landing on the bottom, he tried to swim up. He moved his arms, attempting the breaststroke, going nowhere. His clothes and snowshoes were anchoring him down. He was dead weight. Sliding his feet around the slimy bottom, he tried to walk to the edge.

That was the part that struck him funny: snowshoeing at the bottom of Talbot Pond. Trying to impress Snow. But within ten seconds reality struck him: It was dark as a cave, ice cold, and his lungs were about to explode. Ten seconds, eleven, twelve.

Mike was going to die down there.

———

SILENCE FILLED THE air. The sound of Will's splash had echoed for a moment, but now it was gone. He had disappeared into the pond. Sarah ran back and forth along the edge of the ice like a dog with its eyes on a ball.

"How long, Snow?"

"A minute, Sarah. I think about a minute."

Sarah tried to ease out on the ice. It held firm under her feet. She inched out more. The ice creaked, and she stepped back.

"A branch," Snow yelled. "We can hold it out, and they can grab it!"

Trees had fallen in storms, and broken branches lay under the snow. Together, Sarah and Snow ran to the closest pile of fallen timber. Sarah grabbed the fat end of a long oak branch, and they used all their might to drag it free. Sarah's heart was pounding, and her breathing was labored. They lugged the branch to the pond.

"Now what?" Snow cried. "What do we do?"

Sarah didn't know. Her hands and feet moved, the desire to save her son and Will driving her into action. She stepped onto the ice. She took one step, another. The ice creaked, but it didn't give way.

"Slide it out," she said.

Snow gave the branch a shove.

"More! Hurry," Sarah commanded, wild inside.

"Okay," Snow said. She pushed the crooked branch hard, hitting Sarah's boot. As Sarah hopped over it, the ice cracked. The sound was loud, like fabric tearing, and Sarah went straight through. Standing in water to her knees, she heard a groan of agony: her own voice.

"I'm sorry, I'm sorry!" Snow wept.

Slogging onto land, Sarah wanted to rip out her hair, scratch her face, scream her guts out. Snow grabbed her. The child was shaking violently, and Sarah found herself stroking her back.

"Shhh," Sarah said, trembling.

They clung to each other, staring at the hole in the ice. Their breath was white frost, balloons drifting away. Snow filled her balloons with pictures: of Fred drowning, of Mike under the ice, of her father dying trying to save him. Sarah squeezed her tight, trembling hard. Snow's knees buckled.

"Do you pray, Snow? Pray now!" Sarah said.

"Sarah, help me," Snow wept.

"Pray," Sarah said.

"I'm too scared," Snow cried. "I don't know what to say."

"But you do," Sarah said, holding her. "You just think you don't."

Sarah shivered, staring at the black hole, as if her gaze alone could pull her son and Will from the ice, as if her mother were standing beside her, reaching into the cold darkness, saving the men who were meant to still live.

"Please pray," Sarah whispered. "Please."

"Oh, Freddie," Snow said.

How long could a man survive underwater in such freezing temperatures? How long could two? Sarah didn't know, but nothing could convince her that it would be very long. Holding the girl, trying to give comfort but actually supporting herself by the young girl's steadiness, Sarah closed her eyes.

Will was going to save her son.

She remembered Christmas shopping in Boston, one time when Mike was six and the crowds were mighty. Holding his hand, taking him to see Santa, she had been so careful to not let go. But the friction of shoppers, people grinding by, ripped his hand from hers. She could hear him yell, hear his voice fade away. His hand still felt real, but it was no longer in hers. Her child had been ripped from her grasp, and for one second she had thought she was dead.

"Mike," she said now, just as she had said then.

"Sarah, he can't hear you under the water," Snow sobbed.

"Mike!" Sarah called louder. "Mike!"

Bring him back to me, Sarah had prayed that bright Christmas on Newbury Street. Give me back Mike, and I promise I'll never ask for anything else.

But of course she had. Sarah had asked for many things since then. She had asked for romance, for exclusive status as the purveyor of certain linen lines, for good parking places, for a decent third quarter, for an extra hour's sleep, for life itself.

Closing her eyes, she thought of her brain tumor. When she was really sick, she could actually feel it, pressing against her sinus nerve, taking up space in her cranium. She had prayed to live, and God had seen fit to let it be so. She had been given so much in her life, why not this one other thing? Why not Mike?

Standing by the pond, Sarah knew she would take back her sickness if Will could just save Mike.

Sarah would trade her life for Mike's in one instant.

Sarah knew: Mike had been returned to her in Boston, and he would be brought back to her now. Blinking slowly, taking a deep breath, she stared at the surface of the pond. It had to be so. God couldn't take her beautiful child.

Snow sobbed beside her, melting into her arms.

"It's okay, Snow," Sarah whispered.

"No," Snow said. "It's been too long."

"Wait," Sarah said, feeling more alive than she ever had, full of hope and intense yearning for whatever the rest of her life would bring.

The black water rippled, and the surface parted. Gulping for air, the humans sounded more massive than whales. One head emerged, then the other. Will had Mike in a lifesaving tow-hold. He sidestroked his way to the edge of the pond, breaking the ice with pounding, powerful strokes of his clenched fist.

"Dad," Snow yelled. "Oh, Dad!"

Wet, dripping, their hair already turning to ice, Will and Mike lay on the snowy ground. Mike threw up pond water, choking for air. Will pulled him higher, onto safer ground, while Snow struggled to get the snowshoes off his limp feet.

"I saved him," Will said, looking into Sarah's eyes, his cheeks glistening with ice or maybe tears.

Sarah crouched to kiss first her son, then Will Burke. Their lips were blue. Their faces were white. She pressed her cheek to theirs, completely calm and without fear. They would both be fine.

"I saved him for you," Will said again, tears pouring from his eyes.

"I know you did," Sarah said, her eyes warm with joy and unending gratitude and something that felt like love. "I'll never forget it."

———

BACK AT THE house, Aunt Bess made hot chocolate and George dragged heavy wool horse blankets out of an oak chest in the mudroom. He brought them into the kitchen, where Mike lay, as close to the fire as they could get him. Snow sat by his feet.

"We've got to take him to a hospital," Sarah said.

"What hospital?" George snapped.

"On the mainland," she said.

"Hypothermia's nothing to fool with," Aunt Bess said, her voice trembling with panic.

"The ferry ride would freeze him even worse," George said.

Sarah sat beside Mike, rubbing his ice-cold hands. Will stood beside her. Even though he was half frozen himself, he wouldn't lie down, wouldn't leave her side. On the way home they had had to practically carry Mike. Will told her Mike had just about lost consciousness by the time he got to him. Churning up the pond like an outboard motor, flailing his arms as he tried to swim to the surface, he'd socked Will in the eye.

"I'll fly him," Will said, trying to keep his teeth from chattering.

"Bullshit, you'll fly him," George said, throwing him a blanket. "You're in no condition to do anything but dry off and warm up."

"Not these old scratchy blankets," Aunt Bess wailed. "Get them some nice soft quilts."

"Shush, Bess," George said, tucking blankets around Mike. "Quilts are too fluffy. We need big, weighty wool right now, got to hold the heat in and force it into the bones. There, boy. How's that?"

"Good, Grandpa," Mike tried to say. He made eye contact with his grandfather, and the look that passed between them nearly broke Sarah's heart. It was full of love and trust, the way you might have expected a boy to look at his father.

"Sweetheart," Sarah said, trying to catch his eye the same way. "Wow, honey. Thank God you're here. I was so . . ."

"Mom," Mike said, shaking his head. "Come on, okay?"

"Let the boy warm up," George said more gently than he usually spoke to Sarah. "Why don't you tend to Will? He's got a hell of an eye there."

"No, I . . ." Sarah began, but she couldn't finish her own sentence.

She felt Will's hands on her shoulders. His long fingers were cold even through her sweater. Pulling her slightly, he eased her to her feet. She wanted to face him with gratitude for saving her son, but she felt despair deep inside. At this amazing time, with Mike brought back from near death, he was turning more to her father than to her.

"He'll be fine," Will said.

"Thank you," Sarah said again. "I mean it. Thank you."

"You're welcome," Will said.

"Your lips are blue," she said.

He nodded, a great shiver running through his body.

Sarah reached down for a blanket on top of the heap. Standing on tiptoe, she wrapped it around Will's shoulders, over the one her father had just thrown on him. Will smiled, nodding very happily. Sarah reached for a third blanket, and put it on top of the others.

"Better?" she asked.

"Much," he said.

"Another?" she asked.

He shook his head. His hair had thawed out, but it was still sopping wet. Sarah went to the laundry room, returned with some towels. Reaching up, she began to dry his hair. She had to stand very close to him, and she was aware of their legs touching, their chests. Toweling his hair, she gazed directly into his eyes.

"Hi," he said quietly.

"Hi, Will," she said.

All the action was happening ten feet away. Her father, Snow, and Aunt Bess were huddled around Mike, checking his color, rubbing his hands and feet. Sarah glanced over, but Will reached up to take her hands. She dropped the towel.

"You have a black eye," she said.

"You should see the other guy," he said.

Sarah tried to laugh, but Will held her hands a little tighter. She took a step closer. Now she felt his breath, warm on her forehead. Her face was tilted up, looking straight into Will's eyes. The whole family was at their feet, but she felt as if she were alone with him. Will had gone into the icy water after her son, and now Sarah felt that she was the one who needed to be saved. She heard her father telling a joke, Mike laughing. Her eyes filled with tears.

Will didn't say anything. He just dropped her hands, slid his arms around her body, drew her into a close embrace. The wool blankets felt scratchy against her cheek. They were outside blankets—for picnics, boat rides, stargazing. How many times had she lain on them with Mike when he was a baby?

The memories were sweet and strong, and they made her cry. Will held her, letting her sob silently in his arms as she remembered the babyhood of the boy she had almost just lost. It made her cry harder to hear him talk to the others. His voice was steady, growing stronger. But it wasn't directed at her, and it made Sarah feel he didn't even care whether she was there or not.

———

WHEN MIKE WAS out of danger, they moved him upstairs. Will was sort of in charge, considering he had the most medical training, had been on ice rescues before. The kid would be fine. Aunt Bess finally got her way, retrieved the old wool blankets and put the men to bed, covering them to the nose with down quilts. That was okay with Will. He lay on his back, letting massive shivers pass through his body.

"Dad, you look like you're possessed," Snow said.

"I'm not," he said.

"But your body's shaking like crazy." She frowned, terribly worried.

"That's how it warms up," he said, feeling another tremor run down his back.

"Are you frostbitten?" she asked.

He shook his head, momentarily unable to speak.

"Is Mike?"

"No," he said. "We were under for less than three minutes. Once our temperatures get back to normal, we'll be fine. Why don't you go check on him?"

She hesitated.

Will felt guilty for wanting to get rid of his daughter, but Sarah was standing in the doorway right behind her. She smiled in a way Will had never seen before.

"Why don't you stop in on Mike?" Sarah said, stepping forward. "I know he'd like to see you."

Snow looked over her shoulders with complete affection in her eyes. "Hi, Sarah," she said. "Forgive me?"

"For what?"

"For luring Mike to the pond. For being the one who stayed safe while he fell in. For having that stupid idea about the branch. I don't know!"

Sarah shook her head. "Mike falling in had nothing to do with you," she said. "And the branch wasn't a stupid idea."

Snow looked unconvinced, and Will wondered how much she was thinking of Fred. "I'm glad he's okay," she said finally.

"Go see him," Sarah urged.

Kissing her father, Snow started out the door. She paused, kissed Sarah, then kept going.

"Wow," Sarah said. "That was nice."

Will waited for another fit of shivering to pass. "What?" he asked.

"That kiss."

He was half naked under the quilt, and he was thinking of kissing Sarah himself. It was all he could think about, as a matter of fact, and he had to struggle to keep from pulling her close, kissing her for the rest of the night.

"It was?" he asked instead.

"I have to threaten Mike to get him to kiss me. Or bribe him. Come to think of it, neither has worked for years. I'm sorry I lost it downstairs."

"You didn't lose it," he said.

"Crying like a lunatic," she said. "Considering how happy I was. Am. You know."

"I know," he said, reaching for her hand.

"I mean, you saved his life. How much happier could I be?"

Will smiled, stroking her palm.

"Have you ever done that before?" she asked. "Gone charging into frozen water?"

"Once, off Martha's Vineyard," he said.

"It was unbelievable," Sarah said, kissing each one of his fingers.

"It was?"

"You're my hero."

"I'm no hero," he said.

"You have no say in the matter."

"I'm an old Navy guy," Will said. "I had no choice, doing anything different." But he was thinking: This time it worked.

Pulling Mike to the surface of the pond, he had known he was alive the whole time. The kid had fought him tooth and nail, boxing in the desperate manner of all drowning men. Dragging Mike to shore, Will's heart had been full of Fred. Lying in the soft, warm bed, he closed his eyes and pictured his son.

Sarah breathed on his hands, her hot breath making his fingers ache. Will felt as if she were the one saving him. Just a few hours before he had sat on a snowy log, kissing her, and she'd kissed him back. His body shook with the pain of getting back to normal, his heart pumping heat to the coldest parts. Will Burke was certain his heart had always worked just fine, always been in top shape. It was just that, to the best of his knowledge, his heart had never worked like this.

"I feel like a brat," she said, her eyes filling with more tears.

"Why?"

"Grrr," she said, exasperated, wiping her eyes. "Crying again."

"It's okay," he said.

"He doesn't want me around," she said. "My father's been in there for the last hour, sitting in a chair, talking about the whale. Mike's listening as if he can't hear enough."

"Don't worry, Sarah."

"He doesn't even know I'm here. I took his temperature, and he didn't even look at me."

"Guys don't want their mothers taking their temperatures...."

"But he's listening to his grandfather as if it's a wonderful bedtime story he's never heard before."

"About a whale?"

"The whale we saw," Sarah said. "My father's full of nature stories, island lore. The old coot and the sea." She blew her nose.

"You sent Snow to drive him out?" Will asked.

"No." Sarah smiled. "I just know Mike would love to see her. He keeps glancing at the door to see if she's there."

"She'd probably love to hear about the whale."

"I think Dad's onto herring now. How herring school, when they mate, who eats them, what they eat, how whales eat plankton instead of herring..." Sarah sighed.

"Hey..." Will said.

"What?" she asked.

"Mike's embarrassed," he said.

"Embarrassed?" she asked. "How do you know?"

"Trust me on this," Will said. "Guys with timber don't go falling through the ice. Mike's got to be tight about that. He went in right in front of Snow, and he had to get rescued. By me. Mike's a tough guy, and he's embarrassed."

Sarah started to smile; Will had suddenly set her mind at ease.

"Timber?" she asked.

"Yeah," Will said. "The opposite of wimp. Macho guys have timber."

"You have timber," she said, smiling.

"You think so?" Will asked. His heart was pounding. The sheets felt smooth on his legs, and his mouth was dry.

"Oh, yeah," Sarah said, leaning over to kiss him on the lips. But he pulled her close and held her body against his, feeling her heat against his bare chest. Was it timber that made him feel like this? He was lying still, but there was nothing inside him that was calm.

———

LESS THAN FIVE minutes after entering Mike's room, Snow watched old George just push out of his chair and walk down the hall. He didn't even say good-bye.

"How come your grandfather just left like that?" Snow asked.

"Guess he had something to do," Mike said.

"He sure knows a lot about herring."

"I guess," Mike said offhandedly, although Snow could see how much he admired his grandfather. It was in his eyes, in the way he listened to George without interrupting, the way he dropped that sullenness he wore around Sarah.

"You're at my mercy," Snow said, sitting at the end of Mike's bed.

"Yeah?" he asked.

"I'm going to torture you."

"How?" he asked, sounding intrigued.

She didn't really have an answer for him. She was just so happy to be sitting there, watching the blood come back to his cheeks, feeling his feet move under the quilts. Several cats had wandered into his room, and they had arranged themselves beneath the quilt beside lumps that Snow knew to be Mike's feet, left knee, and abdomen.

"Were you scared?" she asked.

"No," he said.

"Did you think you were going to make it?"

"Yeah." He paused. "Well, maybe not in the last minute."

"We weren't too sure ourselves. Your mother and I."

"I made it, though. Your dad was pretty cool."

"I know," Snow said simply. Why deny the obvious?

"Pilot, ice diver . . . what else does he do?"

"He could have been a secret agent," Snow said, although she wasn't sure, strictly speaking, that this was true. "If he hadn't left the Navy."

"Why'd he leave? With so much James Bond stuff going for him?"

"Hmm." Snow looked at Mike, leaning against his pillows, and thought he sounded pretty excited and patriotic for the troubled kid Julian said he was.

"Why did he?" Mike asked.

"What?"

"Why did your dad leave the Navy?"

"Oh," Snow said. "Because of Fred."

"I kind of wondered who Fred was, on Thanksgiving," Mike said. "When you mentioned his name during grace."

"He was my brother, and he drowned," Snow said. "I was with him when it happened."

"I'm sorry," Mike said.

"We all were with him," Snow said.

"Was it cold, like today?"

"Oh, no. It wasn't winter," Snow said, picturing the day. The golden sky of Indian summer, a bright September day just out-side Newport harbor. Storms blew up so fast in the fall, when you least expected it.

"Couldn't he swim?"

"He was a great swimmer," Snow said. She pictured her brother teaching her to float, showing her how to do the scissor kick.

"How, then?"

"We were all sailing," Snow said. "My parents, Fred, and I. A storm blew up, and we were heading back to port, and my dad let Fred take the helm. He was almost your age. Big enough to handle it, you know?"

"Yeah."

"A big gust came along, and we jibed."

"Shit," Mike said, and that's when Snow knew he was a sailor. She didn't suppose you could live on an island and not be, but she hadn't known for sure. His eyes looked so sad, and he winced, as though he anticipated what was about to happen.

"The boom swung across, and everyone except Fred ducked. It hit him right in the head and knocked him over-board."

"Snow, that's terrible," Mike said. He sounded so nice, and he was moving his hand down the covers as if he wanted to touch Snow's hand, which was just lying there. All of a sudden, more than anything, she felt the urge to hold hands with Mike Talbot, but it didn't seem right, happening in the middle of telling about Fred. So she made a small fist and pulled her hand away.

"My father went in after him, just like he did after you. He swam and swam, and my mother and I stood up, trying to see where Fred had gone, but we couldn't. Two days went by be-fore he ... washed up."

"Drowned."

"My father just about died. I mean it," Snow said, her voice hollow and her eyes wide. She could still hear her father wailing behind the closed door of his study when they came to tell him they had found Fred.

"Shit," Mike said.

"My dad was a rescue swimmer," Snow said. "For the Navy. So you can imagine what it did to him."

"Yeah," Mike said, the reality dawning in his eyes.

"And you can probably imagine how incredible it was for him to pull you out today."

"Nothing could make up for your brother."

"No," Snow said.

"Fred Burke?" Mike said, asking his full name. He had left his hand where it was, palm up. Snow wiped the tears out of her eyes, looking at Mike's hand. She nodded, putting her hand in Mike's.

"Fred Burke," she said.

"I'll remember that."

"Your mother was scared, Mike. Really scared."

"Huh." He paused, then cleared his throat. "I want to thank your father."

"I think you should let him fly you home with us," Snow said. "When we go."

Mike didn't reply. He closed his eyes, as if he might be giving it some thought. Wanting to kiss him, Snow just stared. His lips weren't blue anymore, and his cheeks were actually pink. Snow squeezed his hand, which felt almost as warm as a normal person's, and he squeezed back.

———

SARAH SAT BESIDE Will until he fell asleep. Being so cold had made him tired, and he drifted off, propped up on pillows, late in the afternoon. She watched him without moving, just sitting on the edge of the bed. He looked so peaceful. His graying hair looked soft, just barely curling around his ears and neck. She wanted to touch him, to kiss him and thank him again and again, but she was afraid of waking him up.

How does someone thank a person who saves her son? What words does she say and how many times does she say them? She had no doubt that Mike would have drowned if Will hadn't gone in after him. It wasn't like that Christmastime in Boston, where he might have come home to her anyway. It was an honest, irrefutable case of one man saving another man's life.

Sarah looked around. Her mother had once slept in this room. After she got sick, when her coughing would keep her father awake at night, she had moved in here for a while. Sarah could remember sitting in this very spot, holding her mother's hand. The wallpaper was the same but very faded: pale blue with a pattern of old-fashioned roses. The tall mahogany chest held her mother's wedding portrait in a gilt frame.

There she was, Sarah's mother. Rising carefully, to avoid disturbing Will, Sarah walked over to the picture. The frame was cheap for such a beautiful photo, but her father had always made her mother buy things at a dime store like Woolworth's, on trips to the mainland. Sarah held the picture, looking into her mother's face.

Rose Talbot had such life in her eyes. Tall and graceful, her wedding gown flowing to the floor, dark hair under her lace veil, she held a small bouquet of island flowers. She looked almost alive, as if she was gazing with intense love at her grown daughter. So often, in the hospital during her own illness, Sarah had talked to her mother, begged her for strength, imagined her sitting there beside her. When the treatments worked and Sarah got better, Sarah had imagined how happy her mother would be.

Rose had never met her grandson. It was one of Sarah's great sorrows, that her mother had never known Mike.

"You would love him, Mom," Sarah whispered. "I thought I'd lost him today."

She closed her eyes, holding the picture to her chest. It

seemed impossible, but she felt her mother's love flowing within her. She could almost imagine her mother standing there, taking Sarah into her arms, telling her how much she loved her.

Turning to look over her shoulder, she stared at Will, still asleep. She wanted her mother to know what he had done. Then it occurred to her, all at once: She wanted to tell her mother that she was falling in love.

"Is this really happening?" she whispered to the picture, feeling the catch in her throat. She glanced at Will and felt it even stronger: She was thirty-seven years old, just finished with chemotherapy, falling in love with the strong man in the bed behind her. She felt light-headed with emotion, with gratitude. Wiping the dust off her mother's picture, she gently replaced it on the tall chest. She walked to the window, watching darkness settle on the bay.

The snow had stopped falling, but the night seemed full of grace. The constellations blazed with wings, and she thought she saw whale fire in the bay, streaks of bioluminescence left, she imagined, by the whale they had seen. Wiping her eyes, she looked from Will to the picture of her mother.

People looking after each other, taking care of the ones they loved. Sarah pulled the old curtains to keep the cold night air from blowing in. She wanted to keep Will from getting chilled. If he was awake, she might take his hands, look him deeply in the eye, and tell him the words that were in her heart. But he was fast asleep, breathing steadily.

"I love you," she said in a normal voice.

Will didn't move. He lay there, blue shadows on his lean and angular face. Beneath the white comforter, his body was large and still. Sitting quietly beside him, Sarah kept watch over Will while he slept.

CHAPTER

13

WHEN WILL WOKE up the next morning, Sarah was in the rocking chair across the room. Asleep, her chin touching her chest, she was dressed in the clothes she had been wearing the previous night, a small blanket pulled around her. Will stirred under the covers, watching her. More than anything, he wanted to call her, have her come to him. He felt crazy, passionate, full of feelings he hadn't experienced in a long time.

"Good morning," he said.

"What?" Sarah asked, waking with a start.

Propped up on his elbow, Will stared at her. What would she think if he climbed out of bed, walked over to her chair, leaned down, and kissed her as they had last night? The down quilts had done the trick, warmed him through to the bone.

"You slept in that chair?" he asked.

"Mmm," she said, rubbing her eyes. "Guess I did."

"Couldn't have been too comfortable," he said. "Does your neck hurt?"

She arched her back, shook her shoulders. Without waiting for an answer, Will got out of bed. Walking over, he kissed the top of her head. The room was colder than it had seemed when he was still under the quilt. He rubbed the back of her neck and her shoulders. She leaned into his hand.

"That feels good," she said.

"I dreamed last night . . ." he began, trying to remember.

Waiting for him to go on, Sarah didn't speak. But she was sitting in a rocking chair, and very softly she began to glide back and forth. Will's mind filled with images from the night: feelings of fear and love, soaring flights over water, boys playing at the bottom of a frozen pond, he and Sarah holding each other and refusing to let go.

"What did you dream?" she asked after a few seconds.

"Of you," he said simply.

Sarah reached up, caught his hand. He had been rubbing her neck, but he stopped. He felt her nod, and she glanced up.

"So did I," she said. "Dream of you."

There was so much more Will wanted to say, but he couldn't find the right words. He was battling with himself; he wanted to carry Sarah across the room, take her to bed. And he wanted to tell her to wait while he got dressed, go outside together, and watch the sunrise as they had on Thanksgiving morning.

Her chair creaked on the old floorboards. Will laced fingers with Sarah, kissed the back of her hand. Her blue eyes were bright, alert in spite of the fact she had just spent the night sitting up. He didn't trust himself to speak, because what he wanted to tell her seemed so unbelievable. Will was in love with Sarah.

———

EVERYONE HAD BREAKFAST at the kitchen table, then went off to do their own things. Will and George took the Jeep across the island to make sure the storm didn't do any damage to the plane. Mike went out to the barn, and after a while Sarah went after him. Hearing Aunt Bess in her sewing room, Snow knocked quietly on the door.

"Come in, dear," Aunt Bess said, sitting at her huge black

sewing machine. With half-glasses resting on the tip of her nose, she wore a cherry-red wool dress covered by a soft charcoal-gray shawl.

"Am I disturbing you?" Snow asked.

"No, not a bit. Is there something you need?"

"Just," Snow blurted out, "I think we should have a party!"

"A party?"

"Yes, it's our last night, and we have so much to celebrate, Mike being rescued, and . . ."

"I was thinking the same thing," Bess said, smiling up from her work. "I sent over to Hillyer Crawford's for some lobsters, and I have a cake all ready to mix up and stick in the oven. I adore parties, and we never get to have them around here."

"Oh. Well, I'm glad we're having one tonight," Snow said, nodding with recognition at a fellow party planner. She backed toward the door. "Guess I'd better leave you to your work."

"Please stay," Bess said with an edge that let Snow know she really meant it. "I'm just finishing up another quilt for Sarah to carry back with her. We might as well save the shipping charges, right? Oh, just push those magazines aside and sit on the window seat. Give that kitty a nudge."

"Right," Snow said, making room for herself. Carefully lifting the sleeping cat, she held him on her lap. She watched Aunt Bess smooth the field of white, her fingers magically spreading the down into place, stitching so fast, Snow could hardly follow the motion.

"Have you seen Sarah's shop?" Aunt Bess asked.

"Yes," Snow said. "Have you?"

"The one in Boston, many years ago. I've never visited her place in Fort Cromwell."

"Her shop is beautiful," Snow said. "Like a place you might find in England."

"I loved England," Bess said. "Arthur took me there once, and we went to London and Stonehenge . . . it was marvelous."

"You're lucky," Snow said. "Maybe you'll go again someday."

"I don't get off the island much," Bess said, pressing lightly on the treadle. Peering down, she saw that she had run out of thread. She stopped, dropped her glasses from her nose, and let them dangle on the chain around her neck while she reached for a small tray of bobbins.

"Let me get that for you," Snow said, passing them over.

"Thank you," Aunt Bess said, selecting a small metal spool of white thread. "It's been so nice having you and your father here with Sarah. Especially considering what happened yesterday . . . we would have lost Mike if it weren't for your father."

"I know," Snow said solemnly.

"I suppose Sarah plans to take him home with her."

"I don't know," Snow said, sensing that Aunt Bess was trying to get the story out of her.

"We certainly love having him here."

"Oh," Snow said, feeling guilty for how badly she wanted Mike to fly home with them. Mainly for Sarah, but also because she wanted him to return with them to Fort Cromwell so they could do fun things together.

"He makes us laugh, especially when he and his grandfather get going . . ."

"Really?" Snow asked. She hadn't heard Mike crack many jokes; in fact, she had heard him say very few words.

"He's an island boy, just like his father."

"His father?" Snow asked, her curiosity piqued ever since Mike had mentioned him the day before.

"Yes, although I probably shouldn't have mentioned him. We don't look very kindly on Zeke Loring here in this house," Bess said, concentrating on threading the needle. She licked the end of the thread, twisted it, then bent down toward the presser foot until her cheek rested on the section of quilt she was sewing.

"Can I get that for you?" Snow asked.

"That's so helpful, just like Mike," Bess said, sitting back.

Snow did a little thread magic. She poked the thread through the eye of the needle in one try: It had never failed, not once. Once she had done it with her eyes closed. Her mother couldn't believe it.

"Wonderful," Bess said, fitting the bobbin into its little silver case.

"You don't look kindly on Mike's father?" Snow asked in a calm voice, very gentle, not wanting to spook Aunt Bess.

"Not *because* he's Mike's father," Aunt Bess said. "We've adored Mike since the day he was born. But because he hurt Sarah so badly. Left her standing at the altar."

Snow gasped. "No!"

"Oh, yes," Aunt Bess said, her lips set tight. "On her wedding day, or what would have *been* her wedding day. She was with child, although none of us knew it at the time. I made her dress myself."

"She was wearing it, and he just..."

"Never showed up," Aunt Bess whispered, shaking her head.

"That's horrible!" Snow felt crushed, thinking of Sarah being left at the altar.

"I know. She was a beautiful girl. So bright and happy and *kind*. A truly unusual child, the way she cared so much for other people. She lost her mother so young, and she looked after her father all those years. Then, finally, she went off to college in Boston. I was so thrilled, a chance for her to really live life and get away from this lonely place, and what do you think happens?"

"What?"

"She came home for the summer and fell madly in love with the biggest troublemaker on the island."

"Zeke Loring."

"That's right."

"If he was so bad, why did Sarah love him?"

"He was handsome and terribly funny. Sarah would bring him by, and he'd make us all laugh for hours at his stories. Everything had a dangerous, hilarious edge. But honestly,

Snow? Sarah was beautiful herself, sweet just the way she is to-day, and she could have had any boy in Boston. I think she chose Zeke because he was from the island. This is Sarah's place."

"She was pregnant with his baby," Snow said sadly. "And you made her dress, and he just left her ... where was the wedding? In Boston?"

"Oh, no, dear. Right here. In the island chapel," Aunt Bess said.

Snow gasped again. That such a terrible thing could have happened right here, in Sarah's place. This idyllic island! More magnificent than Yorkshire, more enchanted than Stonehenge, she loved Elk Island even more than she could imagine loving England.

"I don't think we saw it on our walk," Snow said.

"The other direction, dear. Way across the eastern moors. A tiny little church facing the Atlantic, nothing but the sea be-tween the congregation and France."

"I wish I'd seen it," Snow said.

"It's a pretty spot," Bess said, plumping up the quilt. A cat scooted out from underneath.

"Does Zeke still live here, on the island?"

"No, he's dead. Drove into a tree that same summer he was supposed to marry Sarah, with one of those summer girls from up-island. Both of them killed instantly. Zeke never even got to see his son."

"Poor Sarah and Mike."

"He's buried in the churchyard. Just like his parents and Sarah's mother and all the other islanders. That's where George'll go when his time comes. I'll lie with Arthur in Rhode Island, though sometimes I wish I'd brought him up here instead."

"I can understand," Snow said. "I love it here."

"I love having you."

"But we have to leave tomorrow."

"Too soon, too soon."

"I wish we didn't have to go."

"So do I," Bess said. "And Sarah's father..." She gave an exaggerated shiver. "We'll have to take cover for a week after your plane takes off. He won't be fit to live with. You have no idea how he feels about Sarah. The apple of his eye, not that he'd ever show it. And if she takes Mike with her..."

Aunt Bess shivered again, staring out the frosty window at the fields of endless white, her wrinkled old hands smoothing out the snowy quilt that resembled the outside landscape. Snow thought of that white wedding dress, just a little older than Mike, and wondered where it was now, whether Sarah might ever wear it again.

"Well, it'll be a special dinner tonight," Aunt Bess was saying. "Even though it's sad to think we'll be seeing you off tomorrow."

"If we even go..." Snow said, wishing they could all just stay on the island forever.

————

SARAH SAT ON a tall crate, watching Mike take apart the old lobster boat engine. He had installed a woodstove in one of the old sheds, and he had the place very warm. Sarah arched backward, trying to get comfortable. She had woken up with an ache in her lower back. Will had been rubbing her neck, and nothing in the world would have made her tell him to stop, that the pain was much lower. It ached in a knot at the bottom of her spine, shooting down her legs.

The lapstrake boat took up most of the space. Dressed in navy blue work clothes, Mike was covered with grease from head to toe. Frowning as he worked, he reminded Sarah so much of his father that she blinked hard to shake the vision. Seeing Zeke when she looked at her son didn't make her happy.

"Are you sure you're warm enough?" Sarah asked again.

"Mom," he said warningly.

"Well, sorry. It's not every day my son falls through the ice. Excuse me for thinking you might still have a chill."

"What about Will? Aren't you worried about him?"

"He's—" Sarah stopped herself. She didn't trust herself to say one word about Will Burke. The conversation stalled, but Mike didn't seem to notice. He was a good mechanic, and he loved working with engines. He had been so upset, getting fired from Von Froelich Precision. According to Mike, he had gotten caught trying pot with another mechanic. He said he hadn't liked it, and he wouldn't necessarily smoke it again. Sarah believed him. She didn't approve of every single thing he did, but she trusted him to tell the truth about it.

"Do you miss working on race cars?" she asked.

"No," he said. "It never felt real."

"Really?" she asked, surprised.

"Toys for rich guys," Mike said.

Sarah hid her smile. She felt so proud that her boy would have such a down-to-earth attitude. All the high school boys had envied him, and he had worked late every Saturday on cars that most men would only dream of driving.

"You'd rather mess around with an old lobster boat?" she asked.

"Any day," he said.

"Just like your father," she said.

Mike nodded. He didn't say anything, but he glanced over. Pushing the hair out of his eyes, he left a black streak on his forehead. Knowing how Sarah didn't like talking about Zeke, he just waited.

"Is he the reason you came out here?" she asked.

Mike shrugged.

"I'd rather think that than what I've been thinking all along," she said, her heart pounding almost as hard as it had been yesterday when he was deep in the pond.

"What's that?" he asked.

"That you hate me."

He exhaled impatiently. Reaching for a wrench, he knocked over a whole tray of lug nuts. Crouching down, he began to locate the nuts with his right hand, place them into his cupped left. His hands were dirty, and to Sarah they looked so big. Her son was enormous, and staring at him as she wanted to deny what she had just said, she felt her eyes fill with tears.

"Mike?"

"I don't hate you, Mom."

"Then why'd you run away?"

"I didn't run away."

"You did! You quit school just like that, left your job, walked out of our house with your backpack, and started hitchhiking. I know, I was there. Don't you remember how I found you on the highway, you had your thumb out and—"

"I wasn't running away," he said, looking straight at her.

"Then what?"

"I was *coming* here."

Running to something, not away from it...Sarah understood the difference. Sitting on the crate, she drew her knees up, trying to make herself small and tight. In spite of the woodstove, she felt so cold.

"Because of your father?"

"He's dead," Mike said. "Why would it be because of him?"

"To find out where he was from?" Sarah asked.

"I don't know," Mike said.

"It would make sense to me, your wanting to know more about your father. I know I've never talked about him much."

"I've found out a lot," he said. "But you can tell me more."

Sarah nodded. It took effort to push Will from her mind, but Ezekiel Loring had been the sun, the moon, and the stars to her for a hundred days. She had counted one time, from their first date in the spring of her freshman year until the day he wrapped his pickup truck around an oak on Birdsong Road.

"Zeke could fix anything," she said. "You get that from him.

He was funny, and irreverent, and smart. He was a beautiful boy. I know I should say handsome, but that doesn't do justice . . . he was beautiful, Mike. Just like you."

"Huh."

"We'd known each other forever, but we met again one night in April. I was home for school break, walking along the bay. There was a half-moon, and I was staring at it. I remember hearing an engine, it was Zeke on his motorcycle. He just pulled over, and I got on. Just like that. He drove me all over the island, looking at the moon."

"Yeah?" Mike said.

"Did you find his little house? Over by the Hollow, fifty or so acres in from his parents' farm? I showed you once when you were young."

"I remember," Mike said, trying to sound sullen, but not truly succeeding.

"So you found it?"

"Yeah. It's just a little fishing shack, abandoned now. Weeds growing inside, and ivy climbing out the windows."

"Really?" Sarah asked, surprised by how that made her feel sad. "I loved it there. We fixed it up. I made white curtains on Aunt Bess's sewing machine, and we planted a garden. Zeke found a big, hollowed-out rock, and we used it for a birdbath."

"Oh," Mike said. He had always liked watching birds, more than any of his friends did, and maybe it was dawning on him that he had gotten that from his father. Sarah had always believed he had.

"We loved each other, Mike," Sarah said. "We fought like crazy, but we wanted to be together. One time we almost broke up. I ran out of the house and left my white sweater behind. When I went back to get it, Zeke wasn't there. But he had arranged my sweater beside his leather jacket, as if they were people sitting up straight on the love seat, with the arm of his jacket around my sweater."

"He wanted you to stay," Mike said.

Sarah smiled sadly, because that was only part of the story.

"Was that where we were going to live after I was born?"

"I wanted him to come back to Boston with me," Sarah said. "I was starting the shop, you know? He wasn't making much of a living out here, but he didn't care. He loved it. I guess it's why he stood me up. We hadn't done a very good job of talking things through." Sarah spoke mildly, as if to counteract the devastation of that last day, being left at the church.

She had wanted to take her island lobsterman and fix his life. She remembered all the plans and dreams: hers for him. He was handsome and smart; he could go to college, maybe to business school. As soon as he got successful in whatever field he wanted to try, they could buy a house on Beacon Hill, a cottage on the Cape, a dory for their kids, a recreational lobster license for him.

"He wanted to stay here," Mike said.

"Yes, he did."

"Instead of moving to Boston?"

"Instead of marrying me, I think."

"I don't get it."

"We were too young to get married, Mike," Sarah said gently. "But we had you coming."

"He knew about me?" Mike asked, looking scared. Was he afraid of hearing the answer? That Zeke had known he was going to be a father and abandoned them anyway? That he had died with another woman? Sarah could hardly bear to tell him, but she didn't want to lie.

"That I was pregnant, yes. But he didn't know about you, honey. He didn't know he was going to have Michael Talbot."

"Whatever."

"If he'd known you, it would have been different," Sarah said, lying now, unable to stand the hurt in Mike's voice. She doubted that any baby, no matter how amazing, could have induced Zeke to stay. He was on a wild ride, and a wife and child weren't invited along.

"Life would have been better if he'd been with us," Mike said. "We could have been happy, all of us living together."

"It didn't happen that way," Sarah said sharply. "Your father had other plans."

"You're the one who wanted to leave the island!"

"He wouldn't have stayed anyway, Mike. He wasn't ready to marry me."

"We could ask him, Mom," Mike said, turning back to the engine. "But he's dead."

"I know," Sarah said.

"I saw his grave."

Sarah sat still. Her son's shoulders were so stiff, his voice so hard. He was banging on the engine as if he wanted to demolish it. Pain shot through her own back, making her flinch. "I'm sorry, honey," she said softly. In all their visits to the island, she had never taken him to visit where Zeke was buried.

"In the churchyard, have you ever seen it?"

"I've seen it," Sarah said, keeping her voice steady.

"That's where you're going to be buried, isn't it?"

"Yes," Sarah said, knowing she had never seen Mike this upset before.

"Mom," Mike said, dropping his hands to the workbench.

"What, honey?"

"Why'd you get sick?"

Sarah stood and walked around the broken-down old boat and engine. Mike was crying now, trying to hide it. Maybe it was the aftermath of falling through the ice or the letdown after a family Thanksgiving or the things they had just said about Zeke or the first time he had ever told her he'd hated her being sick, but Mike's face was twisted in tears just like when he was a little boy.

"Mike," she whispered, putting her arm around him.

"Are you better?" he asked. "Because Grandpa says you're not."

"I am! Look at me, I'm here, aren't I?"

"That doesn't mean anything. You never looked bad, like you had cancer. You looked fine the whole time."

Sarah didn't reply. She had looked bad. He hadn't seen her after surgery, the experimental procedure that had torn up her back, deformed her head until it had started to heal. He hadn't been around during the radiation and chemotherapy. Mike had taken off right after the diagnosis, the one that had her flying to Paris and back, dead within ten weeks. She had known he was upset, but until that moment she hadn't realized exactly how much. He had been sixteen at the time, and if Sarah had died, he would have been an orphan.

"Look at me," she said, holding his face between her hands.

He blinked, trying to avoid her gaze. After ten seconds, he gave up and stared into her eyes. His cheeks were streaked with tears and grease, and his eyes wore the wounded expression she remembered from the worst sadnesses of his childhood. He blinked. "Yeah?" he asked.

"Platinum blonde," she said.

"Is that supposed to be a joke?" he exploded.

"No, Mike! I was just—" Just trying to make light of talking about my death, she thought, unable to finish.

"You don't know me at all," he said. "You never have. You think bringing some turkey around is gonna make up for not having a father, and you think joking about your hair is gonna make me forget you have cancer!"

She shook her head. "I don't—"

"Say what you want, but you do," he said. "You do."

"I want to talk to you. More than anything," Sarah said, breathless. "I want our relationship to be better. I want you to come home when I leave, finish school, and get your future in order. If you had any idea how much—"

"I'm staying, Mom," Mike said flatly.

Sarah couldn't speak. Was she doing the same thing with Mike she had done with his father? Wishing for a future that didn't rightly belong to him? Planning a course that suited her instead of him? Sarah couldn't believe that. Mike had his father's strong will and passion, but he was Sarah's responsibility. He was her son, and he was only seventeen.

"I'm only asking you to think about it," she said. She wanted to scream and rave, to take him by the shoulders and shake some sense into him. It took all her will to keep her tone measured and even, to prevent her voice from trembling, to sound pleasant.

"I'm staying," he said.

CHAPTER

14

GEORGE TALBOT WATCHED Will Burke brush the snow off his plane the way some other guy might clear his station wagon and knew he was looking at a man after his own heart. A man's man, did things the big way, the hard way. No making excuses or looking for shortcuts. Will did right by his plane. He swept it off stem to stern, shoveled out the snow around the wheels, undid the tie-downs, then pushed the plane back so George could plow the runway. Then Will started her up, made sure the engine wasn't dead, let the propellers wag around. When all the work was done, he put her back and secured her down proper.

"Got yourself a nice plane," George said.

"Thank you, sir."

"What's flying, your hobby?"

"It's my work."

"Thought maybe you just did it as a favor to Sarah."

"I own a little aviation company in Fort Cromwell. Corporate charters, mainly. There are lots of big companies relocating around Wilsonia, in the valley."

George nodded. He lit his pipe and puffed away. His rheumatism got cranked up in cold weather like this, and there was nothing like a good pipe to soothe the rough spots. "Lucky man, to get paid for what you enjoy. Time was, I spent quite a bit of time in the air."

"Over in Europe?"

"Yep. I flew forty-two missions. Cologne, Dresden, Normandy. Some of the big ones."

"Forty-two is a lot."

"Seventeen more than I was supposed to," George said, grateful that Will would know that. He didn't get to talk about the war much anymore. Rose had been the only one he'd ever told the whole story to. She would listen for hours, anytime he felt like talking. Shoveling out a plane with a young Navy man made George feel more like himself than he had in years.

"Why so many?"

"We had a lot of bombs to drop. They'd pump us up on coffee and reds, send us up and out. We'd no sooner get back than they'd send us up again."

"Did you ever get hit?"

George nodded. "Got shot down over Alsace. Hit the silk and landed in a tree. But that was nothing."

"You lost friends," Will said. It was a statement, not a question. He knew, just like all good soldiers knew. Even if it hadn't happened to you, you knew someone destroyed in the war. Your best friend, your bunk mate, your pilot, your medic: killed in action.

"My first crew," George said. "We trained together one entire year, flew ten missions once we got to England. Then for some crazy reason I got promoted to navigator-bombardier in the lead plane."

"Sarah said."

"Proud daughter," George said. But he didn't smile. He didn't feel proud of what had happened, not like it was any achievement of his own. It was wartime, and he'd gone where he was needed. Not willingly; his new crew had had to carry his cot and things and him into his new hut. "The very first mission they flew without me, they got hit, went down over Helgoland. Little island, no bigger than this, in the North Sea."

"I'm sorry," Will said.

"All dead."

"I'm sorry," Will said again.

"Yep," George said, drawing on his pipe. Still brought tears to his eyes: He couldn't believe those wonderful guys, his best friends, were gone. Losing them had scarred him early. Death was final, and it hurt, and there weren't two ways around it. You carried on, or you turned bitter, or in some cases you did both. "You flew in the Gulf?" he asked.

"Yes, I did."

George nodded. "Good man," he said. "Pilot?"

"Yes, sir."

"Sarah tells me you did a stint as rescue swimmer."

"Yes, I trained at NAS Jacksonville, served for a while aboard the USS *James*. But then I moved to a carrier. So I know how you feel, leaving your old crew. I did it myself."

George chewed his pipe. They were done at the airplane, climbing back into the Jeep for the ride home. He backed around, glanced across the seat at Will. The younger man had wartime torment in his eyes, or maybe it was family torment, the stuff that came later, that you couldn't help and brought on yourself because you'd turned so hard after all the crap you saw happen over there.

"What'd you do, son? Lose a man?"

"Yes, sir," Will replied. He waited a minute, gripping onto the seat with his gloved hands, and then he said, "Lost my son."

"Your son? Holy Christ," George said.

George sat in the driver's seat, watching Will stare straight ahead, haunted by the boy's face. George recognized the look in his eyes: He saw it in his own sometimes, when he passed a mirror early in the morning, before his dreams of Rose, of his old crew, had completely faded.

He sat tight, gripping the steering wheel. Wasn't often he found himself at such a loss for words. He wanted to ask where it had happened, what the circumstances had been. But what would his motive be? Making Will feel good, that's all. These days the world saw grief like a boil. They wanted you to lance it, let all the bad stuff out to keep it from infecting everything else. But George thought that was too easy. He knew that grief and sorrow were what kept people human, that it linked them forever to the ones they had lost.

George cleared his throat, spit out the window. The cold air flowed through the Jeep, giving them a shot to the spine: icy and bracing. George patted Will's shoulder.

"You did your old ship, the *James,* proud yesterday," he said. "Saving Mike."

"Thanks, sir."

"Did us proud too. Don't suppose Sarah will ever get over it."

"Hmmm."

George shook Will's hand. "Welcome aboard, Commander," he said. Then he shifted the big Jeep into gear and headed for home.

————

WHEN WILL AND her father walked through the back door, Sarah met them in the hall. She could still hear Aunt Bess on the phone with Hillyer Crawford, trying to convince him to deliver the lobsters himself. Feeling upset about Mike, she tried to sound upbeat.

"Aunt Bess and Snow planned a celebration for tonight," she said, "but Hillyer is too busy to drive the lobsters over. Can I take the Jeep to pick them up?"

"The brakes are spongy," her father said doubtfully. "Mike ordered new pads just the other day. Hasn't had the chance to put them on yet."

Sarah smiled. "I'll be careful," she said.

"I'll go with you," Will said.

"You drive, Will," her father ordered. "She'll show you the way."

"Okay," Sarah said. She and her father had so many battles,

this one hardly counted. She was way past being insulted that he didn't think she could drive an island car as well as any man. It had taken her many years to realize that this was her father's way of protecting her, clunkily trying to show love. Kissing him on the forehead, she accepted the offering.

"Pick out nice ones," her father said, scowling. "If he tells you they're two-pounders, make him weigh them right in front of you."

"Dad, he's not going to short you. You've known Hillyer your whole life. You went to Island School together."

"That's why I know what I'm talking about! He's got quite a little racket going over there. Just watch him, I'm warning you. He's got a nasty trick, leaving his shellfish shears in the scale pan. Them shears'll up the price by nearly a pound! Watch him, Commander."

"I will, sir," Will said.

Out in the Jeep, still warm from its trip to the airstrip, Sarah and Will embraced. They sat in the front seat, holding each other tight. Hours had gone by without seeing each other, but it felt like days. Will kissed her lips. Sarah slipped her arms under his parka and wished she could feel like this forever. No one from the house seemed to be watching, but she wouldn't have cared if they were.

Will backed out of the driveway. Several geese had gotten out of the barn. Waddling around, looking for feed, they were right in the way. Sarah rolled down her window to wave her arms. The pain in her back shot down her leg.

"Aah," she said, seeing stars.

"What's wrong?" Will asked.

Straightening out, she felt the pain go away.

"Nothing," she said.

"That was a loud yell for nothing," he said.

"I might have a pinched nerve," she said, praying that's what it was. "Or maybe it's Mike. I had a fight with him."

"That would cause your back to hurt?" Will asked.

"Tension," Sarah said. "I blame it for everything."

"What was the fight about?"

"Me," she said, and she smiled so he wouldn't see how hurt she was.

She directed Will to drive north, along the single-track road that bisected the island. They passed the pond where Mike had fallen through, the pine woods, the house where Zeke's parents had lived. Sarah knew every inch of Elk Island. She pointed out the Island School, where she had gone from kindergarten through twelfth grade; the best places to pick blueberries; the road leading down to Kestrel Point, where all the big summer houses were and Zeke's summer girl had lived.

They bounced down Harbor Road, rutted from the autumn storms, to the lobster wharf. Hardly any boats were in. Elk Island lobstermen fished from September until April every year, allowing the lobsters to fatten up all summer. The season was profitable but grueling. Lobstering in winter was hazardous. The fleet lost a man every four years or so, but their lobsters were considered the best in the United States, and they brought the highest prices.

Three trawlers lined the docks. Hundreds of lobster pots were stacked high. Bright buoys and old lines lay in a corner of the yard. Seagulls circled, hoping for a morsel of bait or an undetected lobster. The air was tangy with salt and herring. Parking in the shell-strewn lot, Will and Sarah walked into one of the old lobster shacks.

Hillyer Crawford was the same age as Sarah's father, but he looked older. His tan skin had more wrinkles, his arthritis had him even more stooped over. Island life was hard, but George Talbot had always claimed that goose farming was a tropical vacation compared to lobster fishing. From the looks of old Hillyer, he was right.

"How do, Sarah!" Hillyer said. He wore tall rubber boots, exactly like the ones her father wore to kill the geese. His jacket was stained, his khakis wrinkled. Sarah smiled, thinking of his wife, Sophia. She had been a friend of her mother's. Sophia Crawford had been proper and elegant, and she never would have let Hillyer out of the house looking so rumpled; she had starched and ironed his clothes, sent his woolens out to a dry cleaner on the mainland. But she had died last summer.

"Hi, Hillyer," she said, walking around the big wooden lobster tank to kiss him. He hugged her hard, not letting go for a long time. He smelled a little of whiskey. Her father was lucky to have Aunt Bess living with him, Sarah thought. These poor old island men had a lonely time of it.

"We lost Sophia, Sarah," he said into her neck.

"I know, Hillyer. I'm so sorry."

"Yep, she's gone. She was quite a lady, like your mother."

"She loved you," Sarah said. "That's what I remember. Sophia standing on your front porch, waiting for your boat to come home. I know you miss her."

"And *how*," Hillyer said, wiping his eyes. "You the pilot pulled young Mike out of the pond?" he asked, peering at Will.

"News travels fast," Sarah said. "Hillyer, this is Will Burke. Will, this is our old friend Hillyer Crawford."

The men shook hands, and Hillyer began to complain. He told about his old boat, his ulcer, his broken satellite dish, the end of his plans to move to Florida. "That was more Sophia's idea than mine," he said, reaching into the tank for the lobsters. "We took a few vacations down in Naples, and she loved it. We thought maybe we'd sell off the business, try moving down for a winter. Keep the house up here for summers, you know?"

"You could still do it," Sarah said.

"Nah," Hillyer said. "Wouldn't be any fun without Sophia."

"Maybe she'd want you to," Sarah said, watching how slowly he moved from the noisy tanks to the hanging scale. He weighed each lobster, wrote the price down on a paper bag, placed the lobsters in a wooden crate.

"Maybe she would," Hillyer said, "but I still ain't going without her. How many lobsters do you want?"

"Let's see," Sarah said, looking at Will. She did a mental count. "Six."

"Five," Will said. "Snow won't eat it."

"Mike'll have two."

"Bess said two-pounders, right? Want me to throw in some clams? They're nice and plump, had some for my dinner last night."

"Sure. Thanks, Hillyer."

"No problem," he said. He handed Will the crate, lobsters scrabbling around inside. He moved slowly, without purpose. Sarah had forgotten her father's admonition to watch that Hillyer gave good weight, but she suspected that he needn't have worried. Hillyer didn't seem to care enough to bother trying to get away with anything.

"Are you all right?" Sarah asked, taking his old, cold hands.

"Getting old, Sarah," he said.

"Take care of yourself, Hillyer."

He nodded halfheartedly. Will stepped forward to shake his hand. "Your wife sounded like a wonderful lady," he said. "You were very lucky."

"I was," Hillyer said, his eyes fierce.

————

BEHIND THE WHEEL, Will didn't want to go home right away. Without discussing it with Sarah, he turned east instead of south at the top of Harbor Road. He wanted to see the whole island before he left, so he would know his way around the next time they came. Driving through the town, they passed a general store, a post office, and two freestanding gas pumps.

"That's Hillyer and Sophia's house," Sarah said, pointing out a proud white colonial. It sat close to the road, the yard surrounded by a boxwood hedge. In spite of the fact it was one of four houses on the street, this was clearly "in town," and until recently, it had been something of a showplace. The house itself was stately; an American flag flew from a tall white mast in front. But dead geraniums and dried ivy filled the window boxes, untended since summer. One black shutter hung from a broken hinge. Bits of spilled garbage lay in the driveway.

"Oh, just look at that beautiful house," Sarah said. "I used to want to live there more than anything when I was little."

"Your farm is wonderful."

"I thought this was so elegant and sophisticated," Sarah said. "Downtown, with the flowers and big houses. I loved going to visit Sophia with my mother. But look ... without Sophia, it's falling apart. She must have done everything."

"It's not the house," Will said.

"What do you mean?"

"It's Hillyer. Without Sophia, he's falling apart."

"You're right."

"I don't know him," Will said, "but he seems like someone who won't live long without her. He's just deciding to give up."

"I wish he'd go to Florida," Sarah said, gazing out the window.

The "town" ended abruptly. Main Street gave way to a narrow road, hardly wide enough for two cars. Pine trees closed in for a few miles. Then the sea appeared again. They passed two small harbors, a light station, a tidal creek. The water flowed hard, under a graceful arched bridge, flooding out to sea.

"Artists used to paint that bridge," Sarah said. "They'd come all the way from New York and Boston. There's a famous painting of it at the Metropolitan Museum of Art. I saw it once, and all I could think of was crabbing in the creek."

"For blue crabs?" Will asked.

"Yes."

"I loved crabbing. I knew a place, under a train bridge in South Lyme. Are they big up here?"

"Huge," she said. "We'd use bacon and minnows for bait."

"I used chicken bones," Will said. "My record was twenty crabs in one day."

"Were they good-sized?" she asked, sounding skeptical. "Connecticut blue crabs?"

"What do you think, Talbot? Maine's got a lock on shell-fish?" he asked, laughing. "They were legal, pretty decent size. My mother would steam them for dinner, and she always acted like they were a big treat."

"So did my mother," Sarah said.

"Show me somewhere else," Will said. "I've seen your school, the lobster wharf, your crabbing creek. I want to know all the important places."

"Let's go visit my mother," Sarah said.

"Which way?" Will asked, and Sarah pointed farther east.

They passed the northern cliffs, the tall granite peaks that housed the nesting eagles. While Will drove, Sarah craned her neck for a glimpse of the bald eagles. A nest was visible, a thatch of sticks and brambles on a high ledge, but the birds were out hunting. Sarah told him to turn left, off the main road. Will pulled onto a narrow track, recently plowed but covered with last night's dusting of snow, so he shifted into four-wheel drive. The road meandered through a field, then into a forest of tall oaks, their branches interlocking overhead.

They emerged at the edge of the Atlantic Ocean. A stone chapel stood alone, surrounded by snowy fields. Beside it, en-closed by a wrought-iron fence, was a small graveyard. Will sensed a change come over Sarah. Parking the Jeep, he reached over to hold her hand. She gazed out to sea with a certain deter-mination, as if she had come there for a reason.

They walked through the snow. The chapel was dark stone, small and medieval, something you might expect to find in Oxford or Cambridge. Its sturdy steeple held a stone cross, at-tached to the slate roof with strong wires, against the Atlantic winds. Three granite steps led to an arched wooden door. Someone had hung a fir wreath, decorated with pine cones, sil-ver bayberries, dried blueberries, and a purple ribbon.

"My father was here," Sarah said, her eyes bright.

"George hung the wreath?"

"He puts one up every year, the day after Thanksgiving. He doesn't care about holidays, but my mother loved Christmas. He does it for her."

"Is she here?" Will asked, holding Sarah close as they walked toward the cemetery.

"Right there," she said, pointing to a grave with an angel on the headstone.

Will lifted the latch, letting the iron gate clank behind them. The wind whipped off the sea, blowing salt spray and loose snow into their faces. This was the coldest spot he'd found on the island. The wind put the chill back into his bones, and he remembered being in the pond. Standing among the graves, he bowed his head and thought of Fred.

Sarah knelt by her mother's grave. She looked so beautiful, lost in memories and prayer, her silver hair like the cap of snow on the angel's head. The monument was intricately carved, with a small angel flying over the sea. The name of Sarah's mother, Rose Talbot, was chiseled above the dates of her birth and death. Beside it, without any dates, was the name George Talbot. Beneath it was the name Sarah.

Seeing Sarah's name on a gravestone filled Will with dread. His feet were frozen to the ground, unable to move. All he could do was stare at the stone. He looked from the name to the woman. Sarah was right there, kneeling beside him, praying for her mother. All he had to do was reach out his hand, touch her shoulder. He had removed his glove, and his finger brushed her neck. Her skin felt warm. She moved at his touch, leaning into his hand.

"Sarah," he said, kneeling beside her.

"This is Will," she said, taking his hand. "I wish you could know him. And Mike . . . I wish you could know my son."

"Hi, Rose," Will said, locking fingers with Sarah.

"Mom, I miss you," Sarah whispered. "I miss you very much."

Will almost couldn't stand it. He had prayed to Fred many times since the day he drowned, but hearing Sarah talk to her dead mother, seeing her name there on the gravestone, was too much for him. He wrapped his arms around her, pulled her to her feet.

"What?" Sarah asked, sounding scared. The wind blew hard, turning her cheeks pink, bringing tears to both of their eyes.

"It's cold," Will said. "I want to get you warm."

"Should we go inside?"

"The Jeep?"

"The church," Sarah said.

"Isn't it locked?" Will asked, frowning. He had assumed that because of its isolated spot and the very few people who lived on the island, it would be locked up.

"I know where to find the key," Sarah said. Smiling, she walked around the leeward side. Behind a holly bush, about two feet off the ground, hidden behind a piece of loose mortar in the church stonework, she removed an old iron key. Four inches in length, with lacy curlicues, it didn't look real.

But the key worked. Sarah unlocked the heavy door with one turn in the lock. Inside, the old church was dark and musty. Six rows of carved oak benches filled the space. The stained-glass windows were dark blue and wine, depicting saints and boats. A plain wooden cross stood behind the altar, more New England than Oxford.

Sarah looked around. She walked over to a pew, ran her fingers along the oak, continued on. The expression in her eyes was angry and confused. If she had entered the church seeking peace, she hadn't found it yet.

"What's wrong?" Will asked.

"I don't know."

"Your mother's gravestone," he said. He wanted to touch her, but he didn't know how. He couldn't quite look in her eyes. "Why did it have your name on it?"

"My parents' and mine," she corrected him.

"Yours," Will said, "is the one I saw."

"It's a family monument," she said.

"I didn't like seeing it," he said.

Sarah nodded, almost smiling. "Is it weird? I can't tell. I'm used to it—been seeing it since my mother died. It's the way we do things on the island. We get born here, and we get buried here."

"Were you christened here?" Will asked, trying to think of happier things, forcing his heart to go back to normal. They faced the altar.

"I was," Sarah said, her voice cracking. "And Mike was. Twenty years apart, we were baptized right there," she said, pointing to the marble baptismal font. It was shaped like a clam shell, and Will imagined all the island babies crying as the water was poured on their heads. "I was nearly married here too."

"To the lobsterman?" Will asked, feeling strange to know Sarah had stood in this aisle with another man.

"He didn't show up," Sarah said. "He didn't want me."

"He was an idiot."

Sarah shrugged. She seemed so upset. Standing by the marble shell, she touched the holy water. It had frozen solid. She tapped it with her fingers. "He's buried outside," she said softly. "Mike's father. I know he's the reason Mike came out to the island."

"You do?" Will asked, inexpressibly glad that he was dead, whoever he was, the man who had gotten Sarah pregnant and stood her up at this altar.

"He's needed a father his whole life," Sarah said, thinking of the fight they had just had.

"He's a good kid," Will said. "He's going to be fine."

"He is, but he doesn't believe it yet. He wanted to find his father, that's what I think. He came all the way out here to learn the ways of a dead man. He did, Will. Island life, it's so crazy... there's no future. Look at my father, look at Hillyer! I want him with me, Will. I want him to come home with us."

"I know," Will said, holding her.

Sarah sobbed in his arms. She was trying to grab on to her son, and he didn't want to be grabbed. Will didn't know what was going to happen tomorrow, and he felt worried for Sarah. She had more at stake than what her son planned to do for the next six months; he could tell by the way her shoulders shook and her gasps knifed in.

"Let him be, Sarah," Will said. "That's all you can do."

"I tell myself that, but how?" she asked. "I'm his mother."

Will stroked her hair, thinking of Fred. How did you let your child go? Alive or dead, it was the most impossible thing in the world. But Will had learned the secret: You don't really have a choice. They don't belong to you, your children, they never did. They are entrusted to you for a short time. You do your best, you protect them wisely. If they change their names, you ask them what they want to be called. If they want to go sailing, you help them find the wind.

"You love him from wherever you are," Will said. "You know that already."

"I do?"

"Look at you and your mother," Will said.

"I love her from wherever I am," Sarah said, sniffling.

"You already know how to do it as a daughter." He smiled, wiping her tears. "Now you just have to do it as a mother."

Sarah nodded. Will had seen her cry before, and it amazed him how fluid her emotions were. Ten seconds ago she was a wreck, sobbing in his arms. But now she looked radiant, incandescent, glowing like a bride. He imagined her walking down this very aisle, standing at the altar, waiting for a man who wasn't going to show.

"Sarah," he said, taking her hands.

"Mmm?" she asked as if she didn't quite trust herself to speak yet.

The words caught in his throat. His eyes stung, gazing at her beautiful clear eyes. He had come so far in such a short time.

Sarah had brought him back to life, a place he had left the day Fred died. If Will could help her ease the suffering of her own son, maybe that's what he was there for.

They didn't say anything. Giving each other one long look, holding hands, they walked off the altar, toward the back of the church. Will thought of the man who had left Sarah waiting there long ago, who had died without marrying her and giving their baby a name. Will felt sorry for him, not because he was dead but because he had walked away from Sarah Talbot.

Walking her back down the aisle, Will stopped at the back door. He gazed into her eyes. Then, brushing his hand back over her hair the way a man might lift a veil, he stood in the middle of the aisle and kissed the woman who had never been a bride. Pushing open the door, they stepped outside into the cold wind.

15

SNOW CALLED HER mother in Fort Cromwell but she got the answering machine instead. She heard Julian's ask-me-if-I-do-voice-overs voice, with its loathsome announcement: "Alice and I are out dashing through the snow ... or watching the car win at Monza ... or possibly skiing down Saxon Hill ... or *very* possibly lounging by the fire and not answering the phone, so please do us the kindness of leaving your message."

"Hi, Mom, it's me," Snow said. "We're still on Elk Island, flying home tomorrow. Guess Dad'll drive me to the house. So don't worry about picking me up. I'll get a ride. I'll just get Dad to drive me. So you don't have to." Then, in a softer tone, "Love you. Bye."

Hanging up the hall phone, Snow had a terrible feeling that something was wrong. Why hadn't her mother answered the phone? Snow had the feeling she was terribly mad and hurt. What kind of daughter just up and left, without saying a word, for Thanksgiving? On Wednesday, Snow had justified her plan, telling herself she wouldn't be missed by her mother and Julian, that her father needed her more than they did.

But now, on Saturday, the clock was ticking and Snow knew she was going to have to face the music. She imagined her mother feeling sad and Julian feeling angry. He was probably whispering in her ear, like those evil advisers in Shakespeare-like plays, giving the confused queen bad information. For Christmas last year, Julian had paid for Snow to attend Saturdays with the Bard, a theater class for high school kids at Marcellus College, and if there was one thing she had learned, it was that her life had had enough tragedy, betrayal, and farce for Shakespeare himself.

Dialing her number one more time, she prayed for her mother to answer. What if something terrible had happened? What if thieves had broken in to steal Julian's art collection and antique cars and slit everyone's throat? What if they were serial killers? Gripping the phone, Snow bit her lip. She felt the fantasy filling her mind: the lonely house on a hill, the demented criminals, the fear in her mother's and Julian's eyes. What if they killed Julian outright and left her mother for dead, but even now her mother was stirring, hearing the phone ring, saved from oblivion by her very own daughter. . . .

"Hello?" her mother answered.

"Oh, my God!" Snow gasped.

"Susan, is that you?"

"Yes, hi, Mom. I've been calling you for days, I haven't talked to you since I first got here, remember?"

"I remember," her mother said dryly.

"How've you been? How was Thanksgiving?"

"We've been fine. Julian has a little cold."

"Oh," Snow said, making herself sound concerned. "I hope he feels better." Her mother didn't say anything, and Snow felt anxiety building in her chest. Why did she have to feel so nervous with her own mother? She was constantly feeling as if she were disappointing her, or making her mad, or somehow coming between her mother and Julian.

"How—" her mother began. She stopped, cleared her throat. "How was *your* Thanksgiving?"

"It was okay," Snow said, toning it down. She didn't want to tell her mother how wonderful it had been, what an incredible time she was having.

"I'm glad," her mother said, and Snow could practically see her lips disappearing into a tight, tight line.

"What's wrong?" Snow asked.

"It's just...it's just...that was our first holiday *apart,*" her mother said, bursting into tears. "Since you were a baby, since the day you were born, we've been together for every Thanksgiving, every Christmas."

"I'm sorry, Mom," Snow whispered, stunned by the sadness in her mother's voice.

"Even most Fourth of Julys. Except that one time when you and Freddie were little and your father took you out on the *James* to watch fireworks. I had the flu or something, so I didn't go."

"But we were home in time for dinner," Snow said, getting her mother's point.

"Sweetheart, I—" she began. Cutting herself off, she turned her attention to Julian, suddenly going on about something in the background.

"What's wrong?" Snow asked.

"Nothing," her mother said, and now it seemed to Snow that her mother's words were colored by Julian's presence, as if she were putting on a certain kind of show for him. "Except I'm very disappointed in the way you chose to do this. If you had asked permission properly, some arrangements could have been made. As it is, I'm very, very disappointed in you."

"I know," Snow said, catching sight of Mike at the other end of the hall.

"Very disappointed."

"Mom, I'm sorry," Snow said, distressed. Mike saw her. He just stood there, not moving.

"There will be consequences," her mother said ominously. "When you get home."

"Consequences?" Snow asked.

"We'll talk. When you get home. Now, hold the line. Julian wants to say Happy Thanksgiving."

"I have to go, Mom," Snow said quickly. "Someone has to use the phone. Love you, bye."

She placed the phone in the cradle as if it were burning her hand. Closing her eyes, she could hardly breathe. Her mother was so mad. Snow had hardly ever heard ther so angry, except during the worst days of the divorce. And there was no way she was talking to Julian.

"I wasn't waiting to use the phone," Mike said apologetically.

"Oh, I know," Snow said. "It was just a white lie so I wouldn't have to talk to my stepfather."

"You've got a stepfather?" Mike asked.

Snow nodded, feeling miserable. She felt so cornered and down. The clear knowledge of what awaited her back in Fort Cromwell came crashing in on her, life with her mother and Julian. Her mother seemed less her mother than Julian's wife these days. All her feelings revolved around Julian. Even her re-action on the phone: She had been fine, nice and sweetly emo-tional, until Julian had walked in.

"I hate him," Snow whispered. "I shouldn't hate anyone, I know, but I do...."

"Sometimes you can't help it."

"If I had an island to run away to," Snow said, "I would. Like you."

"You're here," Mike said. "Aren't you?"

Trying to smile, Snow let Mike lead her down the hallway. They walked up the back stairs. Dark and dusty, every stair tread held a sleeping cat. The cats uncoiled, sliding out of their way. As they neared the top, the air grew colder. This part of the house was not insulated; Snow could see daylight through the wallboards. They came to a closed door. Turning the knob, Mike let her inside.

They were in the attic. The open space was filled with old beds and chests, a broken mirror, trunks and boxes. Mike had roped off a section at the far end, and he led Snow through the maze of broken furniture to get there. Tattered blankets hung from lengths of fishing line, forming a makeshift tent. Pushing aside a plaid blanket, Mike let Snow enter first.

"It's so cozy!" she said.

"Yeah," he said, pleased.

A space heater threw plenty of heat. He had dragged an old mattress in there. It was covered with two down quilts. Three shelves were filled with books. A small window overlooked the front, the fields leading down to the bay. Snow explored every inch. She felt like she had just entered a grown-up playhouse.

"Is this where you sleep?" she asked.

"No, my room's downstairs."

"Then what's this for?"

"It's where I come to get away," he said.

"Your island on the island?" she asked.

He nodded. He didn't even think that sounded strange. He leaned his forehead against the windowpane, scanning the yard. His grandfather was standing outside the picking shed, warming his hands over a brazier. Goose blood covered the snow. Snow had to turn her head.

"Why'd you run away?" she asked.

"I keep telling everyone, I didn't run away," he said. "I wanted to come here. It's where my family's from, you know? Both my parents, my grandparents."

"Aunt Bess told me about your father. I'm sorry he died."

"I didn't know him," Mike said, as if that made it less terrible. Snow shivered, imagining either of her parents dying, and then she thought of something that hadn't occurred to her in a long time: Sarah had been very sick.

"You must have been so worried about your mother," she said.

"Yeah," he nodded.

"Luckily she's better."

Mike nodded again. Standing there in his secret island room, Snow thought of them as two kids who had been through a lot. He had never met his father, his mother had raised him alone,

Snow's parents had gotten a terrible divorce, her mother had married a jerk. And then there were the deaths, his father's and her brother's, his mother's illness.

Reeling from just thinking about it all, Snow flopped down on the mattress. She looked at him in amazement.

"How do normal kids do it? Don't they get bored?" she asked.

"What do you mean?"

"You and I could keep two shrinks working overtime for the next ten years!"

He laughed. "Did they ever send you to a shrink?"

"Of course. Right after Fred drowned, then again, during the divorce. Did Sarah send you?"

"She tried, a couple of years after we moved away from Boston. But I hardly ever went."

"You asked if they *sent* me," Snow corrected him. "I didn't say I *went*. Well, I did go some of the time, but I used to skip whenever possible. I had the faux flu a lot."

"The what?"

"I faked being sick." She gave him a sample of a phony coughing fit. "You know?"

"I just wouldn't show up. He made me nervous."

"Was yours a psychiatrist?"

"Yeah. Dr. Darrow, in one of those brick buildings out by Marcellus, and he'd just sit there for the whole hour with this really intense look on his—"

"Dr. Darrow?" Snow asked, her hand up to her mouth. "You went to Dr. Darrow?"

"Yeah."

"Tall guy? Stickpin under his tie? Never says a word?"

"All his diplomas right behind his desk, so you can't miss noticing he went to Princeton and Cornell the whole time you're supposedly spilling your guts?"

"Pictures of him and his wife on vacation in the Bahamas with their perfect twin sons?"

"Yeah," Mike said. "Everyone smiling, so you can't help noticing how happy the Darrows look compared to your family."

"We used to look that way . . ." Snow said.

"I can't believe you went to Dr. Darrow," Mike said. "Meeting you out here, I kind of forget we both come from Fort Cromwell."

"I come from Newport, Rhode Island," Snow corrected him.

"I come from Boston," Mike said. "But you know what I mean. That we both wound up in Fort Cromwell."

"I hate it there," Snow said, realizing it was her second time using the word "hate" that afternoon. She disliked negativity so much, people who went around complaining, disliking their own lives. It made her see how low she had been sinking. She had needed this trip to Elk Island.

Mike sat beside her on the bed. He was leaning against the wall; she had to half turn to see his face. He looked peaceful, glad to be with her. They both started to laugh.

"Dr. Darrow," he said, shaking his head.

"Are those twin boys scary, or what?" Snow asked, giggling. "With their perfect blond hair and matching swim trunks?"

"Their water wings," Mike said. "Those inflatable rubber things on their skinny arms, to keep them afloat. I could've used a pair yesterday."

"Can you imagine one of them falling through the ice?" Snow asked, breaking into a laughing fit. "Dr. Darrow would have him on the couch so fast, he wouldn't know what hit him. Did you get the couch?"

"He wanted me to, but I said no way."

"Why'd Sarah send you in the first place?" Snow asked.

"I had a problem with school."

"Your grades?" Snow asked.

"No," Mike said. "Going."

"At all," Snow said, cracking up. "I hear you."

They leaned back, laughing till their sides hurt. Picturing Mike in Dr. Darrow's office made her feel strangely close to him.

They were sitting right next to each other, their elbows touching, and Snow didn't even want him to kiss her. Lip contact was the furthest thing from her mind. Shoulders bumping, they were lost in the hilarity of being fellow patients of the silentest psychiatrist in Fort Cromwell.

"Does this look familiar?" Mike asked, balancing his chin on his left thumb, squinting with one eye. The imitation of Dr. Darrow was perfect.

"His wife in the picture," Snow said, leaping to her feet, striking a bathing-beauty pose. She could just see the doctor's wife with her red hair, her gold jewelry, her pseudo-demure stance.

"Mrs. Darrow," Mike said, shaking his head. "He has to see a lot of patients to take her to the Bahamas."

"And buy her that jewelry."

"Why'd your parents send you?" Mike asked. "Did you faux-flu your way through school?"

"No, I don't mind school," Snow said. "They just wanted to help me get over Fred."

"Old Fred," Mike said. "What makes them think you can get over him?"

"They're grown-ups," Snow said sensibly.

"It has to be something else," Mike said.

"Why, do you think I'm crazy?" Snow asked, making a face.

"Yeah," Mike said, tickling her. She felt the heat in her ribs and stomach, and she squirmed on the bed, just like horsing around with her brother.

"Zymptoms," Snow said, trying to sound Austrian. "Zey zent me on account of zymptoms."

"What symptoms?"

"Oh, nightmares. Changing my name every few months. Wearing my brother's socks."

"You wear his socks?"

Snow nodded. She pulled up her pants legs, revealing a pair of navy blue and maroon argyles. They had been Fred's favorites, but she was just as partial to his old gray ones, the navy blues, his dirty old white pairs. Some of them had holes, but she didn't care. She'd just darn them and wear them forever.

"Huh," Mike said with admiration.

"Coming to the island," she said, "is that like wearing your father's old socks?"

"And my mom's," he laughed. "One of each."

"Dr. Darrow was right about you," Snow said, happily staring at the attic eaves. A wasp had built its nest there last summer, its gray hive lurking up in the cobwebs, its papery layers giving it the look of a disembodied face. "You are mad."

"And you are insane," he said. "What'd you change your name from, Snow? Or should I zay 'Znow'?"

"Zusan," she replied. "I used to go by the name of Zusan, but that was BDF."

"What's BDF?"

"Before the Death of Fred," she said. "Of course."

"They shouldn't die," Mike said. "Any of them."

"You mean the people we love?" Snow asked.

"Yeah," Mike said.

"Well, no kidding," Snow said, giving the back of his hand a sisterly pat. "But if they didn't, what would Dr. Darrow do for a living? There wouldn't be enough sad people to pay for him to take Mrs. Darrow and the twins to the Bahamas."

"You've got a point," Mike said, lying on his back, staring at the wasp's nest with his hands laced across his chest, sounding as if he had no choice but to agree.

CHAPTER

16

GEORGE STOOD IN the basement kitchen, waiting for Sarah to get the crate of lobsters open. She was such a beauty, just like her mother. Small but strong, with long limbs and delicate hands. Sarah's face could stop a man's heart. Her blue eyes were so gentle, her mouth full of kind words. His daughter's face belonged on a Christmas stamp.

Her hair was another story. George had remembered it long and dark, full of glints and luster. But here it was, all patchy and sticking up every which way, like some of those backwoods Mainers who couldn't afford good barber shears. The color was too bright, a kind of silver-gold that reminded George of tinsel or the foil you might find wrapped around a chocolate candy. Understanding that Sarah's hair had something to do with her cancer treatment, George had said nothing.

Finally Sarah had the crate opened. George peered inside, counting the lobsters. Then he reached in and pulled out one at random. Peering at it, he first determined that the critter was male.

"Damn Hillyer," he muttered. "He knows she-lobsters have the sweetest meat. Figures he'd send males."

"I don't think he did it on purpose," Sarah said. "I didn't even see him check."

"Bet he did," George said. He hated being taken advantage

of. His heart was pounding, and he tapped his chest and sat down. Lobsters cost a fortune, and he had so many expenses. New brakes, a new roof, mouths to feed. He thought of Mike, who ate like a horse.

"You get yourself so upset," Sarah said. She had slid her hand down his wrist as if she were taking his pulse. George felt like slapping her fingers away, but he didn't have the oomph. As a matter of fact, he had a pain in his chest, and he was a little worried. With his daughter sitting right beside him, he got a good look at her eyes. They were so deep and blue, but they were surrounded by fine lines.

"Why don't you come home, where you belong?" he asked.

"I have a business to run, Dad."

"Business," he said quietly. "What's business compared to your family?"

She smiled, and in her face he could see the memory of other times when he had said the very same thing. Way back, after Rose died and Sarah had wanted to go to college. Then when she had decided to open her first store.

"I'm here, Dad," she said. "Aren't I?"

He scowled. He knew what she was driving at. They had been estranged. That was the terrible word to describe the months of silence, the years since she had come home. Bess had tried telling him to soften up, to take Sarah for who she was. But it wasn't that easy. After Rose's death, George had had to be mother and father to her, and he had made some mistakes. When she'd first told him about the baby coming, he'd thought she'd thrown her life away.

"You'd be better off staying," he said, stating his case. "You got Mike to think of. He seems happy here, you know."

"I've noticed," she said.

"I'd have killed Zeke Loring if he hadn't killed himself. But I thank him for Mike."

"I know."

He patted his pockets, looking for his pipe. He didn't have an inkling about talking to a daughter, never had. One hour at the plane with Will, and he was conversing with him like they'd known each other their whole lives. But Sarah; she demanded a whole different outlook and language to get along properly. George felt as if he were swimming blind in foreign waters.

"Stay," he said, keeping it basic.

"I can't," she said. "And I want Mike to come home with me."

George stared at her. He had expected as much. His heart banged around a bit, but not as bad as before. Mike was old enough to decide for himself, and George had confidence in what way the boy would go. Sarah was where his worst heart pounding came from: those little lines around her eyes, her strange metallic hair. His little baby had been mighty sick. The signs were right there.

"You look like your mother," he blurted out.

"I do?" she asked.

George nodded. He reached over, touched her cheek. Her skin was so creamy soft. She had been born in this very house, right upstairs. George had boiled the water himself at the stove behind him. He had held her in one hand; she was hardly as big as a small goose. Their eyes had met, and that was that.

He colored, caught dreaming about the past. How happy they had been, the three of them. George, Rose, and Sarah. This was their island.

"Do you have happy memories?" he made himself ask.

"Oh, Dad," she said, smiling. "The best."

"You do?"

She nodded. Putting her arms around him, she rested her head on his shoulder. She had done that so many times as a little girl. In the Jeep, driving around the island, in the boat, going out fishing. Sarah sitting beside him, her head leaning on his shoulder. He felt a big lump in his throat and couldn't swallow past it. He thought of Rose; the cancer had taken her quick, before they marshaled themselves enough to send her to a medical center off-island somewhere.

"The mainland's probably a better place for you," he heard himself say.

"Well . . ." she began.

There were fine hospitals in New York State. Top-notch doctors, all the right medicines, universities conducting modern research. If she got sick again, that was where he wanted her to be. Not out here, stranded on Elk Island like her mother. Dr. Miller had done his best, but it wasn't much. Now Miller was long dead, and no one new had come along to take his place.

"I'd better keep my shop open," she said. "To sell Aunt Bess's quilts."

"If you think I want the money," George said hotly, "I don't. All I want is you well. You understand, Sarah?"

She just stared, those big eyes filling.

"I want an answer."

She nodded, and then she let go. Bowing over, she started to weep. George exhaled. He was always making some woman cry at this kitchen table. Sarah, her mother . . . he put his arm around her, held her tight. She covered her eyes with one hand, sobbing quietly.

"There, dear," he said. "There, now."

"Dad—" she breathed.

"Shhh, Sarah. Let's not be mad anymore. Just stay well."

She nodded, her tears soaking through his wool shirt.

"If you ever need me," he began, trying to get the words out. "In any way. I know about cases where the daughter's sick and they need a kidney or some bone marrow. Anything. Anything I have, I want to give."

Luckily she didn't look up. She just held on tight, just like when she was a little girl sailing and George took her too far out in the bay. The sloop had heeled over, George trimming in the sheet and yanking on the tiller, with Sarah clinging to his chest like a scared little monkey. She felt like that now. A grown-up woman holding on to her father for dear life.

"Shhh, Sarah," he kept saying. "Shhh."

When she was good and ready, she stopped crying. She dried her eyes without raising her head. Her breathing was under control, and by the time she lifted her head, she had some color back in her cheeks. George checked her over. She was delicate, his Sarah, for a woman who acted so strong, who went through life all alone. She was her own captain. In some ways, he was proud of her for doing without a man all these years. But in another way, George wished she would find what he had had with Rose.

George pushed himself up from his seat. They hadn't solved the problem of Mike, but time would tell. It always did. If she thought she was taking Mike home with her, she was in for a letdown. The boy wasn't going anywhere, but George didn't want to be the one to break it to her.

———————

THE SUN BEGAN to set. It was Saturday, their last full day on Elk Island, and Sarah stood at the kitchen window, watching the violet shadows lengthen on the snowy field sloping to the bay. Her father had just walked out the door. She saw him limping through the yard with Gelsey, waving his arms to herd the geese into the barn.

Gelsey barked, hobbling just like her master. The geese waddled ahead, honking loudly. Sarah had watched the same scene a hundred times, but she couldn't ever remember it making her cry before. She touched the cold window, tears running down her cheeks. Her father had just offered her a kidney, his bone marrow. Her father, who couldn't stand the physical reality of someone else's headache, had been thinking that Sarah might need a transplant.

Her cancer wasn't the kind that could be helped by a blood transfusion, by new organs. It had originated in her lymph nodes, spread into her brain. Dr. Goodacre had done his best.

She had gone through all the treatment her doctors had deemed necessary, and now she was in the hands of fate. Of God.

Standing in the chapel with Will that morning, she had prayed for health. She wasn't supposed to ask Him for specific things, she knew. She was supposed to take action, do what her doctors told her to do, and trust that He would take care of her. But life was so sweet! Sarah's heart was so full of love for the people here on earth, her father and son and Snow and Will. Seeing her mother's grave had reminded her of heaven, that they would all be together someday, but for now she wanted to be here.

Right here. Sarah had so much to do. She had to run her shop, take advantage of the winter cold and Christmas spirit to sell a lot of quilts. Sarah wanted to help Snow, urge her to mend whatever rift with her mother had caused her to sneak aboard the plane and fly away for Thanksgiving. Sarah's father and Aunt Bess needed her help, the financial assistance she would continue to give them. She pictured Mike. Just the thought of him had her breathing harder. She had to set her boy on the right road.

And Will. Sarah needed him right now. Her heart was racing, and her hands felt cold. The icy air knifed through the old kitchen windows. Outside, her father shuffled into the red barn after the geese. Sarah watched, her forehead against the frosty pane, until he disappeared from sight. The first star hung in the twilight sky.

Slowly, Sarah turned away from the window and walked up the kitchen stairs. The house was quiet. Aunt Bess was taking her afternoon nap, and the kids were up in the attic. Sarah could hear music playing, the sounds of Mike and Snow laughing. Feeling clandestine, she knocked on Will's door.

"Come in," he called.

Sarah slipped inside, letting the door close softly behind her. The room was dark, the only light coming from windows overlooking the sea. Will lay on the bed, on top of the covers. Perhaps he had been reading, fallen asleep; a book lay open beside him, but the click of the door wakened him. Seeing Sarah, he hiked up on one elbow.

"Everything okay?" he asked.

Nodding, Sarah walked closer. She couldn't have explained why, but she had a lump in her throat that made her feel like crying. Without speaking, she stood by the side of the bed.

Will moved over. He held his arms out, and Sarah lay down beside him. He wrapped her in his arms, and she felt his warm body along the length of hers. She couldn't believe how solid he felt. It almost made her laugh.

"You know what's amazing?" he asked, stroking her back.

"What?" she whispered.

"I was hoping you'd come up."

"You were?"

"Yeah. Just before I dozed off, I thought, Maybe Sarah will wake me up. I really did."

"I feel funny, sneaking into your room."

"I know," he said, squeezing her. "We're acting more like kids than the kids."

Upstairs, their teenagers were having a raucous old time. Sarah heard Snow squealing and Mike laughing, running through the attic, their heavy boots pounding the old floorboards.

"How much time do we have before dinner?" Will asked, kissing her forehead, her cheeks.

"Hours," she said, running her hands down his chest. "At least two."

He pulled her sweater over her head, and she unbuttoned his chamois shirt. They fumbled with each other's belts, and Will unzipped Sarah's jeans while she pulled open his five-button front.

Down to their underwear, they slid under the quilt. The bed was warm from Will's nap, heated through by his body. Snuggling together, Sarah felt his fingers tracing her back, the length of her spine, sliding under the elastic of her panties. They kissed, their mouths seeking each other, every part of them touching.

Will's hands moved up toward Sarah's shoulders, and they found the scar. Sarah froze the minute he touched it. Her eyes flew open, and she saw him stop the kiss, open his eyes, wonder what he was feeling. Sarah felt ashamed. She was glad the lights were off.

"I had an operation," she said. "For my brain tumor."

"That's your scar."

"Yes, I hate it. Just pretend it's not there."

"If it's part of you, it's beautiful."

"If you saw it, you'd know that's not true."

"Then let me see and prove it to you."

She shook her head. No one but doctors and nurses had seen Sarah's scars. During radiation treatments, she had developed an infection in her scalp. It had spread to her skull, turned into osteomyelitis. Dr. Goodacre had had to debride the bone, remove a portion of her skull. He had had to make a large incision to get to the skull and to supply a blood source, and although Sarah had had plastic surgery, the scars still remained.

It was so ugly. Sarah knew she would never wear a bathing suit again. She loved air-conditioning in hot summer because it permitted her to dress completely, cover every portion of her back and shoulders.

"Show me," he said. "You can, Sarah."

"I want to, but I'm afraid," she said.

"You don't have to be."

"It's hideous," she said.

"I don't believe that," he whispered, holding her tight.

But even before he finished his words, Sarah reached past him. She pulled the cord, turning on the bedside lamp. Sitting straight and tall, she bowed her head so he could see the entire thing. Holding her with one arm, Will leaned back to look. She could feel him draw a breath, trying to keep from reacting. The first time Meg Ferguson had removed the bandages, she had burst into tears.

"Oh, Sarah," Will said.

He couldn't even pretend. It was so horrible, her mangled back, a shunt still in place, ugly and thick, to divert blood from her back to her head. Bowing his face to her back, he kissed her skin. She felt him shaking, weeping as he kissed her back, her shoulders, the side of her neck. His face was wet with tears, and she tasted them as she met his lips, their mouths open as they clung to each other in the old bed.

"It's awful, I know," she said.

"It saved your life, didn't it?" he asked.

"Yes," she whispered.

"Then it's beautiful. Just as I said." He caressed her body, letting her know that he loved her. She felt it in his hands. They touched her as if she were fragile and precious, as if it were his responsibility to see that she was never hurt again.

Sarah felt herself letting go bit by bit, believing him in inches. She had been so betrayed by Zeke, she had never really trusted anyone since. Sarah lay against Will's chest, feeling a great shudder pass through her body. All the tension and anxiety went out of her. She gave herself to him then. She really did, from deep in her heart, in a way she had never done before.

Sarah's scar was her secret. It marked her, like a map of her illness. Reminding her of life and death, she had always felt afraid of it. But suddenly it seemed like a gift, a different way to reveal herself to Will. She kissed him so tenderly. She felt more alive than she ever had, aware of every sensation, every whisper of breath on her skin.

Their bodies weren't young, but they were strong and full of passion. Sarah had narrow hips with a long waist and high, small breasts. Her legs were long and powerful, and as she felt Will caressing them, touching the insides of her thighs, Sarah had the incongruous thought of running a marathon, of Will being there when she crossed the finish line.

She kissed him all over, exploring his strong body. He had scars here and there, none as bad as her own, but they all told a story and she looked forward to hearing them. For now she lay beside him in bed, watching his eyes as he hovered over her.

They were in complete synch. Sarah had never felt a connection like this before. Will didn't have to ask her what she liked, he just knew. He took control so gently, letting her know she was safe, driving her to the crazy edge of passion. She was losing herself, letting go of control, leaving herself in the hands of someone else.

The sheets tangled around them, and the old bedsprings creaked. Sarah half wanted to laugh, but she was too far gone. Clutching Will, she stared into his eyes while he moved inside her, her legs wrapped around his back and her fingernails digging into his muscles.

You obsess over men like this, she thought. You fantasize that you will feel this way, so deep into another person that you don't know where the skin stops. The look in his eyes, so intense and full of love and it's all for *you*. Sarah moaned, trying to turn her head, to avert her gaze, it was all too much. But she couldn't. Will's eyes kept drawing her back.

"Hold on," he said. He smiled, getting her attention. Pulling her in, making love to her in her old house, trying to be quiet so everyone didn't hear. Everyone: Her mind conjured them up, all the people under this roof, listening to the bedsprings squeak, but Will stopped her. Lowering his head to hers, kissing her, their hot mouths open, he moved faster. Placing his lips against her ear, he whispered, "Stay with me, Sarah."

That was all she needed to hear. The house flew away. They were alone in the desert, a million miles from the sea, stars rushing overhead, the heat of the sands rising around them. Sarah and Will locked in an embrace so tight they would never let go, loving each other from the inside out, hard as ivory and soft as cream.

She was mad. She tore at his back, begged for his kiss, thrust in a frenzy and felt him thrust back. She had lugged her body around all these months, a battered old valise to contain her spirit, but now it was serving her well. Her body was quivering and vibrating. It felt every sensation known to woman, all at once, from an amazing place in her groin she had never known existed.

"Will," she said just to hear his name, to make sure he was still there. Her body was covered with sweat, her heart was beating so fast and her breaths came in gasps as her head moved from side to side.

"Sarah," he said, seemingly for the same reason. His hair fell into his eyes. He had a demented sex-look in his eyes, tempered with pure love, that made Sarah wonder if he knew where he was.

She felt it like a freight train. An orgasm rumbling deep inside, down in that dark place behind her belly button, making itself known. It began, went away. Sarah emptied her mind, but the more she thought of nothing the more she was aware of trying to think of nothing. She was conscious of trying not to think of children and parents and this house and that plane and the doctor and a tiny pain and—whoa.

"Sarah," Will said, and he had her in his sights again. They locked eyes, she felt his lips on hers, the thoughts went away. All thoughts, and she didn't have to try this time. Her body told her what to do. She and Will were together, really together, their bodies doing all the work. Sarah's mind drifted.

It got stronger, the rumbling, and it made her legs shake. She felt such pleasure spreading through her lower body, starting far inside and warming its way out, elusive at first, as if it might just suddenly stop, but then stronger. The feeling had her in its grip, and it wouldn't let go as long as she kept gazing into Will's eyes.

He was so hard, and he filled her so deeply, and her breasts rubbed against his broad chest with every thrust, the sensations in her nipples making her moan softly, adding to the heat down below. The feeling had been general, but now it became specific. It centered itself lower, right in the depths of her body, and it gave her such incredible pleasure, she didn't think she could stand it.

Now she and Will were in it together, holding on, loving each other with their hearts and souls and bodies; it was all the same thing, Sarah understood now, the great link of two spirits in love, finding each other after an eternity of searching. She wanted, wanted, wanted everything: love, health, life, this chance to make love. But it wasn't until she let go, stopped wanting, stopped even caring, that it happened. That, her legs locked around the body of this man she loved, she crashed into oblivion, the wicked wilderness of losing total control, of throwing caution to the winds, coming so hard and fast she hardly even noticed the words coming out of her mouth, out of Will's: "I love you, I love you."

17

ON ELK ISLAND there was only one way to cook lobsters: steamed in rockweed. The tide was out, so Mike and Snow offered to go down to the bay to gather seaweed and mussels. Everyone teased Mike, telling him to make sure he wore a life preserver, to kick off his snowshoes before deciding to take his next swim. Sarah was happy, and surprised, to see him taking the banter so well. Her son might act as if he had timber, but inside he was very sensitive.

"It's a new sport," he said. "I'm going to enter the next Olympics."

"Pond walking!" Snow said.

"Yeah, snowshoes are optional, but you have to fall through the ice and land on your feet. Making it out alive wins you a medal."

"Mike Talbot takes the gold for pond walking," Snow said, speaking into a saltshaker as if she were a TV sportscaster.

"Maybe," Mike said, looking nowhere in particular, "the gold should go to your dad."

Sarah said nothing, flabbergasted.

"That's a nice thing to say," George said. "But the tide's flooding in, and if you don't move fast, you'll never get that rockweed."

"Come with us, George," Snow said, pulling his hand. "Show us the best spot for mussels."

"Ah, Mike knows. He'll show you."

"Come on, George," Snow said. "Let's take a walk down."

Her father and the kids pulled on boots and parka and went down to the bay. Aunt Bess walked out of the room. Coming over to the stove, Will put his arms around Sarah. He kissed her throat, the side of her neck. Sarah's skin tingled, and she wanted to take Will by the hand and go upstairs with him.

He wore old jeans and an untucked chamois shirt. The fabric was soft under her hands, and his arms were strong and hard. Kissing his mouth, Sarah leaned back and closed her eyes. But something clattered, Aunt Bess cleared her throat, and they were interrupted.

"Let me help you," Will said, crossing the kitchen to take the battered old box from her.

"Thank you," she said. "I took these out to get a head start on Christmas, but I think I'll leave them to you two. Sarah knows where they go."

"Stay, Aunt Bess," Sarah said.

Bess shook her head. She smiled enigmatically, looking from Sarah to Will. Sarah knew she wanted to leave them alone. She had seen them kissing.

"Discreet," Will said, his arm around Sarah as Bess disappeared into her sewing room.

"I know," Sarah said.

"Let's open the box," Will said.

Every ornament meant something. There were glass balls from her mother's aunt in England, angels from her grandmother, tiny clam shells strung with red ribbon by Sarah when she was ten.

"I haven't seen this in so long," she said, holding a glass angel. Her mother's mother had given it to them the year Sarah was born, just before she died; her mother had reminded her every year.

"When's the last time you were here for Christmas?" Will asked.

Sarah closed her eyes, tried to remember. "A long time ago," she said. "Before Mike was born."

"I thought you'd have brought him out."

"I didn't want to come to the island for Christmas," she said.

"Why not?"

"It reminded me of everything we didn't have. An island family, a father for Mike. It was easier in Boston, with all the other single parents."

"It must have been sad," Will said. "Considering how much you love it here."

"I love Elk Island," Sarah said, leaning against him. She felt his breath against her head, drew closer. "But for a long time I wanted to stay away."

"I'm glad I brought you back," Will said.

"So am I."

They went outside to cut greens. The air was sharp, and their breath turned white. Will had a knife in his jeans pocket, and he used it to slice branches of white pine from a row of trees in the field. Sarah walked beside him, holding the boughs in her arms. Her eyes filled with tears; she couldn't help it. She couldn't believe this was happening to her: decorating a house for Christmas with a man who wanted to help, a man she loved.

"That enough?" he asked, looking down.

"Yes, plenty," she said. He took the branches from her, and they walked back inside.

They covered the mantel with evergreens, placing Christmas balls among the boughs. Sarah's mother had always tied red ribbons to everything at Christmas, around the pine branches and brass candlesticks and all the light fixtures, but Sarah's hands were trembling too much. She felt such intense emotion, such passion and happiness.

"What's this?" Will asked, holding up a paper decoration from the box.

"Oh," Sarah said. The sight of it pierced her through.

Mike's star. He had made it in first grade. They had been living in Boston and wanted to send something to her father for Christmas. Sarah had cut a star out of cardboard and Mike had colored it with crayons. They had driven up to Swampscott, to gather sand and tiny shells and bits of seaweed, and he had glued them on. Sarah had sprayed it with shellac. Together they had mailed it.

"My son made it when he was six," Sarah said.

"It's a good star," Will said.

"My father kept it," Sarah said.

"Why are you surprised?"

"He can be so angry sometimes," Sarah said. "I always think of him throwing things out."

"I wonder why," Will said. "Considering the way he lives. With everything from the past, from your life, all around him."

Sarah didn't reply. She looked around, knowing Will was right. Was it because she had sometimes felt thrown away herself? That she hadn't pleased her father by leaving this island to live in Boston, by getting pregnant, by being stood up at the altar? Gazing at Mike's star, she knew: He hadn't thrown her away. She had left on her own.

"I'm hard on him," Sarah said.

"No, you're hard on yourself, Sarah," Will said.

She looked up at him. More than anything, she wanted to hear this man who seemed to know her so well explain her to herself. Her heart was going fast, and the pain in her back seemed worse.

"You don't seem to trust how much people love you," Will said quietly, holding her against his chest.

"I don't?"

"Your father, your son. You can go easy," Will said, touching her hair.

"How?" she asked.

"They love you, Sarah," he said. "They just can't show it right."

"If I can't see it," she began slowly, "how will I ever be able to know that it's there?"

Will held her face in his hands. He looked her straight in the eye, his expression serious and unwavering. He held her gaze so long, she started to smile. Seconds were ticking by, a whole minute.

"What?" she laughed.

"I just want to make sure you can see it," Will said.

"See what?"

"That I'm here," he said.

———

MIKE WADED INTO the tidal pool, filling a bushel basket with rockweed. The saltwater felt cold through his thick rubber boots, but nothing like the frozen pond. Here they were, almost as far north as you could get on the Atlantic coast, and the sea still held its warmth. Mike had asked some of the old lobstermen why this was so, and they had told him the Gulf Stream swept in here.

Mike wasn't interested in lobstering, but sometimes he thought about being an oceanographer. He loved the sea so much, he missed it completely in Fort Cromwell. He wanted to study tides and currents, lobsters and whales, understand why the coastline was rocky in Maine and sandy in Florida. Use the same information lobstermen needed, but in a different way.

Mike had plenty of dreams. His grandfather subscribed to *National Geographic,* and Mike spent hours looking through back issues. He had learned that there was a profession called cultural anthropology, and it appealed to him a lot. You got to study the ways of different groups of people, figure out why they lived how they did. Mike thought it would be cool to observe the lobstermen in Elk Island and contrast them with the ones in Matinicus. It might be a way to know his father better.

Or maybe he'd just be a goose farmer. Take over the farm, raise geese, and work the land. Sell fowl and produce down quilts. Get someone else to kill the geese. Keep the family art alive.

"Hey," his grandfather said, clucking at Snow. "Over here."

She sloshed through the shallow pool, leaning over to see what he was pointing at.

"Mussels!" she gasped.

"Biggest colony on the island. Don't tell anyone," Grandpa warned.

Mike smiled. His grandfather was amazing. He ruled his land like a king. He knew where everything was, and he worked every bit of what he had. Last spring he had showed Mike the fiddlehead ferns. Growing on the shady side of a bog, curled so tightly into themselves, they were hidden from sight. Mike and his grandfather had picked some, fried them in butter, and had a feast.

Mushrooms. In October they had gone into the woods, looking for chanterelles, little golden things that Mike would have called toadstools if his grandfather hadn't pointed out the difference. "Good eating," Grandpa had said, handing him a chanterelle. Then he had handed him a toadstool, saying, "Puke your guts out and then you die." Returning home, Aunt Bess had mixed the chanterelles with heavy cream and served them on toast. So now Mike knew.

The mussels were blue-black, the color of the evening sky. Everyone picked a few, throwing them into a different basket from the seaweed. This could be his, Mike knew. This life of mussel picking at the edge of the Atlantic, two hundred acres of rolling hills and pine forests and a white house that had been in his family for over a century. Elk Island was in his blood.

"Everyone, look!" his grandfather bellowed.

They stopped what they were doing, dropped seaweed and mussels into the baskets, and gazed at the sky. It danced with cold fire. There, in the north, just over the house, was the aurora borealis.

"What is it?" Snow asked reverently.

"Never seen it before?" Grandpa asked.

Shaking her head, she didn't speak. Mike moved closer, just

so his arm could be touching hers while she saw something so incredible for the first time. The air shimmered gold and green, a forest of celestial Christmas trees. The trees shook and trembled, bending in some terrific wind. If he were an oceanographer, Mike could study the phenomenon. He would specialize in the waters of northern Maine, and any seaside activity, even atmospheric, high in the sky, would be fair game.

He wondered whether Marcellus College had programs in oceanography. He was pretty sure Cornell did.

"What is it?" Snow asked again.

"Tell her, Mike."

"The northern lights," Mike said, gazing over the house. "The aurora borealis."

"No way!" Snow said.

"Yep," Grandpa said, sounding satisfied, as if he had arranged to have them appear, as if he owned the land and everything on, over, and around it. If he were a cultural anthropologist, Mike could include Grandpa in his study. Old Maine farmers and their ways of life. Mike could write a book about him.

"The aurora borealis! Oh, my God!" Snow said. She pushed back the sleeve of her jacket, peered closely at her watch. It was too dark to see, but she kept trying.

"What are you looking at your wrist for?" Grandpa asked, sounding exasperated. "The show's up in the sky."

"I want to know the time . . ." Snow said.

Mike stepped in. His mother had given him a Timex Indiglo for his fifteenth birthday. All it took was the push of a button, and the time appeared, flooded in blue light. He stuck his wrist in front of Snow's face, pressed the button, and there it was: a luminous display, just for her alone. Good thing the evening was so dark, or she'd see him turning red.

"Eighteen hundred hours!" she said.

"Yeah."

"I saw the northern lights for the first time at eighteen hundred hours on November thirtieth," Snow said, holding on to

Mike's wrist even after she was finished looking at the time. This girl was incredible, Mike thought. His first sight of Snow had hit him like a ton of bricks, and here it came again.

"Eighteen hundred hours," Mike said, thinking it was so cool to know a girl who talked like a Navy man.

"Let's go get your mother," Grandpa said, already starting for the house. "To show her."

Mike hung back. Snow stayed with him, watching his grand-father go.

"Snow," he said.

"What?" she asked breathlessly.

"Nothing," Mike said, bending down to kiss her. It wasn't the first time he'd kissed a girl, but it was the first time he'd kissed Snow. She grabbed the sleeves of his jacket with tiny bare hands, her weight pulling him down as if her knees had given out, and forget the aurora borealis: Mike was seeing stars.

———

THE WHOLE FAMILY had stepped outside to see the northern lights, but thank goodness there was no way anyone could read Snow's mind. She was thinking, "My first kiss, first kiss, Mike Talbot, Mrs. Michael Talbot." She was standing between Sarah and her dad, just a few steps away from Mike, and she couldn't stop smiling. Her lips were tingling, as if she had rubbed Ben-Gay on them.

"Oh, my!" Aunt Bess kept saying, clasping her old hands. "Oh, my!"

"It's not like we don't see it plenty," George said.

"Every time is like the first time," Bess said, staring at the sky.

"You're not a young girl, Bess," George scowled. "First time, nothing. Don't we see it plenty, Mike? You don't get air shows like this down New York way, do you?"

"It's amazing," Mike said. Snow smiled at his diplomacy. He was so mature. Just by answering so noncommittally, he had avoided hurting Aunt Bess's feelings, George's feelings, *and* his mother's feelings.

Inching toward him, Snow slipped her hand behind his leg, found his hand hanging down, touched his fingers. His hand closed around hers, and all of a sudden she was holding hands with Mike Talbot. Right in the midst of their families! She felt the blood rush to her head.

"Dad," Sarah was saying. "Remember when you and I were coming home from fishing one night, just bringing the boat into the bay, and—"

"That's right, that's right," George said. "The aurora was red that night. We saw it from offshore, thought the house was afire."

"We did," Sarah said, talking straight to Will. She had her head tipped back, a love-smile in her eyes, looking up at him. And Will was gazing right back. He looked lost, bleary-eyed with love. Snow frowned a little. She wasn't quite sure how to take what she was seeing.

But Mike laced fingers with her, and Snow felt that hot rush again.

"We'll be seeing the aurora till April up here, won't we, Mike? Maybe even May?" George asked, staring straight at Mike's and Snow's hands. Staring hard, as if he had X-ray eyes and wanted to pulverize the connection.

"I don't know, Grandpa. We saw it in the middle of May last year," Mike said. By his answer, he wasn't making any promises about staying on the island. In fact, it sounded to Snow as if he was planning to leave.

"And we'll see it again!" George exclaimed. "Dammit, come spring, we'll be out here looking at the sky while all the people in New York State are gazing at the pollution. Right, Mike?"

"Aurora is a good name," Snow said, partly to get Mike off the hook. She hadn't decided what she was going to call herself next, and she liked "Aurora." But as pretty as it was, it didn't have any connection to Fred.

"Right, Mike?" George asked again, his voice tight.

Aunt Bess clapped her hands. "All right, everyone," she said. "We've got lobsters to cook. Let's get back inside."

"Lobsters and the northern lights," George said sullenly, looking from the hand-holding to Mike's eyes, as if he knew he was losing the contest to keep him. "Two things no place does better than Maine."

"I know, Grandpa," Mike said helplessly, unable to reassure him. But he slipped his hand out of Snow's to pat his grandfather on the shoulder.

Snow shrunk a little, trying not to feel hurt. He'd hold her hand again, she was pretty sure. But losing someone, even a little, even for a moment, felt awful to her. She didn't know why Mike's taking his hand away should make her feel so lonely. Standing among all these people she loved, Snow had an empty place deep inside. The hole made her heart ache, and it chilled her through and through. She blinked back mysterious tears. And it didn't help, not one bit, when she looked at her father and saw him holding hands with Sarah secretly, out of everyone else's sight, just as Snow had been doing with Mike one minute earlier.

————

NO ONE COULD remember exactly how many minutes it took to steam the lobsters, but it didn't matter. The Talbots had cooked them so often, they instinctively knew. The clams and mussels were done first, piled into one steaming bowl and set on the table with pots of melted butter. The lobsters came next, scarlet and festive, heaped on a big platter. There were baked potatoes for everyone, with an extra for Snow. Sarah made sure everyone had enough butter, and she couldn't stop smiling at Will.

"Maine lobsters, Maine potatoes. Ever been to Aroostook

County?" her father asked. "They grow the best potatoes in the country there."

"Not me," Snow said.

"Can't say I have," Will said.

"Lot of potato farms up Aroostook way," George said. He leaned over toward Mike. "I'll take you there come spring. We'll herd up the extra cats and drop them off. Good ratting up in Aroostook."

"Which are the extra cats?" Snow asked politely, looking around the kitchen. Cats of all sizes and colors had swarmed in from the fields and barn. Smelling the lobster, they circled warily. The boldest ones had approached the table, reaching wily paws toward the bowl of empty clam and mussel shells. Shyer cats lurked in the shadows, behind the andirons, on top of the cupboards. There might be thirty altogether.

Sarah smiled. "These cats are all descendants of Desdemona," she said. "The kitten my mother had when she was young." She broke off a shred of lobster meat and fed it to the scrawny black cat rubbing against her legs.

"I saw that," her father said ominously.

"Sorry," Sarah said.

"Feeding animals was always your specialty," he said. "Even when you knew better. How many times did your mother have to tell you they don't do that in good families?"

"I always forget," Sarah said, feeling extra benevolent toward her father since her talk with Will.

"Which *are* the extra cats?" Snow asked, sounding upset.

"They're all extra," George said. "If every one of them fell down the well, it'd suit me just fine."

Sarah heard the bad mood closing in fast. She ate a piece of lobster meat, chewing slowly. This was their last dinner together, and her father was feeling it. He took a bite of claw meat, grimacing.

"Blech," he said, spitting it into his napkin.

"What's wrong, George?" Bess asked.

"Garbage," he said. "Hillyer sent us all males. He knows damn well she-lobsters have the sweetest meat. Here, kitty." He put his plate on the floor, and two big brown coon cats began fighting over the carcass.

"George!" Bess said, dismayed.

"I thought you weren't supposed to feed the cats, Grandpa," Mike said jokingly.

"What's it to you?" he asked, pushing his chair back. "When you're just passing through? Don't quote house rules unless you're planning to stay in the house."

"Grandpa . . ." Mike began, turning red.

"Well?" George asked. He had toppled his chair over, but he didn't stoop to right it. Reaching over, Will quietly set the chair on its legs. Sarah felt the pressure of his knee against hers, but she couldn't look away from her father.

"Dad," she said softly. "Don't. Please?"

"Don't what? Please what?" he asked. His voice was furious, but his eyes were even worse. She caught him staring at her mother's mother's angel as if he wanted to break it.

"What's gotten into you?" she asked.

"What's gotten into *him*?" he asked, pointing at Mike. "That's more like it!"

"Nothing, Grandpa," Mike said steadily. "Come on, sit down and let's finish dinner."

"Why, on account of it's your last?"

Mike didn't reply. Sarah felt her heart pounding. He had made up his mind. She could see by the way he was gazing at his grandfather with such love and regret. Bess was right; she had raised a good boy. He cared about the people he loved, didn't want to hurt them or let them down. Now he looked at Sarah. His lips twitched, unable to smile.

"Grandpa," Mike said.

"Love gets folks into trouble around here," George said,

glaring from Mike to Snow. He looked at Sarah. "Doesn't it? Tell him."

"Dad, stop. Mike has to finish his education. You want that for him, don't you? You know how important it is?" Sarah asked. Her back had been feeling better, but suddenly the tension had returned. She felt the knot in her lower back, throbbing hard.

"You got a college degree, Will?" George asked.

"Yes, from Trinity College!" Snow blurted out, frowning at George as if he were her enemy.

"It's true, sir," Will said.

"That what you want, Mike?" George asked, his eyes steely. "You want more school?"

Mike shrugged. "Maybe," he said.

"You do, honey?" Sarah asked, her heart flooding with surprise and almost relief.

"Yeah," he said. "I've been thinking maybe I do."

The half-eaten lobsters lay on everyone's plates. No one but the cats was interested in food. George stared at the fire. Sarah couldn't take her eyes off her son.

"That's marvelous," Aunt Bess said. No one could have told from her tone how disappointed she might be feeling at the thought of Mike leaving the island. "Finishing high school is admirable, and a college education is priceless. Not only for the career opportunities, but for the enrichment. To go through life with a working knowledge of, oh, art and music . . . literature. Arthur always said he never would have advanced the way he did if he hadn't gone to Brown University. I only finished eighth grade, but traveling with Arthur was such an experience. As if I'd graduated from Pembroke!"

George looked over at her, then turned to Mike.

"How did this happen?" George asked. "I thought you were happy on the farm."

"I am," Mike said.

"I don't get it," George said.

"All I wanted was to come to Maine," Mike said. "See where my parents were from. I was sick of school and sick of—"

"What?" George asked.

"Life," Mike said, looking apologetically at Sarah. His gaze broke her heart, because how could she bear knowing her boy had been sick of life? When she, of all people, knew how precious and fleeting it was?

"Who wouldn't be without any ocean around?" George asked.

"Amen," Snow said, looking at him as if she wanted to mend their friendship. But George wouldn't even blink.

"When I came here, I got interested," Mike said, speaking straight to his grandfather. "That's all I know. We're just this little island in the middle of nowhere, and it's so incredible. There's so much to learn about. You know, the way the whales move through the passage between Elk Island and Little Gull? And why the mussels grow so thick here in the south, but you can't find any in Otter Cove or Kings Bight? You have to practically be a scientist to lobster right—"

"What else?" Sarah asked.

"The northern lights," Mike said. "Everyone thinks they happen when the air is cold, but that's not true. When Grandpa and I saw them last May, the air was warm. That day had been eighty degrees . . ."

"They occur at high latitudes," George said sullenly. "The aurora's got nothing to do with air temperature. The closer to the poles you get, the better you see them."

"That's the kind of stuff I mean," Mike said, ignoring everyone but his grandfather. "You tell me all these things, and I want to go off and learn more. I never had anyone talking to me like you."

Sarah blinked, unable to move. She had done her best, instilling in Mike all the curiosity, thirst for knowledge, desire to learn that she could. Loving him with all she had, she had tried to be both parents to him, but all along she had known she wasn't enough. Mike was all boy, and he had squirmed out of his mother's reach early. Hearing him talk like this brought tears flooding to her eyes.

"Like your *National Geographics*, Grandpa . . . they're so interesting."

"Glad to be of service," George said. "Go on up in the attic and read them all you want."

"I'm coming back," Mike said. "That's my plan. I want to go to college, and then I want to come back and run the farm."

"Round about the time we're dead?" George asked.

"George, you look pretty healthy to me," Will said.

"So did the American elm," George said. "And then the Dutch elm disease came along." His eyes shifted to Sarah, then away. She felt his stare, a reminder of how sick she had been, of how fast her mother had died. Tears were running down her cheeks. She was overwhelmed. Mike was coming home. That was all she wanted, but she couldn't stand to see how hurt her father was. She leaned toward him.

"Thank you, Dad," she said.

"For what?" he asked.

"For helping Mike the way you have. Just listen to him! He wants to keep on with school, and it's because of you. Thank you." She meant it with all she had, but her father wouldn't even look at her.

"Goddamn animals," he said as the cats, emboldened by their hunger, began climbing onto the table to sniff the plates. The lobsters had grown cold. The melted butter had hardened, and pools of brine had formed on the platter.

The pain in Sarah's back numbed her right leg slightly. Shaking her foot, she accidentally kicked Snow under the table. Looking up to apologize, she caught Snow gazing at Mike.

"I hate seeing these lobsters go to waste," Aunt Bess said, shaking her head. "We all left very sassy plates."

"That's the good thing about being a vegetarian," Snow said. "You don't feel so bad about leaving a potato."

"Don't cry for the lobsters," George said bitterly, sticking his pipe into his mouth, biting down hard. "Here in Maine we've got plenty."

18

THE DAY HAD come. It was time to leave the island. That was Sarah's first thought, waking up as the sun rose over the land. Her second thought was, *I have a fever.* Even before she opened her eyes she felt the chills under her skin, the aches in her joints and bones. Sleep had not eased the pain in her back. The pain had settled into her lower spine, radiating down into her legs and up into her ribs. Dinner had been upsetting, and that only made the ache worse. Gritting her teeth, she took a deep breath.

This fever was the real thing. She had fought this for over a week. It had lurked in her system while she took vitamins and drank juice, breathed fresh air and fell in love. A dark corner of her mind harbored fears of cancer, but this felt like the flu. The imminence of departure had lowered her resistance; Sarah had never liked saying good-bye. Sundays on Elk Island always seemed to be the day she left, and she dreaded the sadness of farewell, the prospect of leaving her father and Aunt Bess one more time.

At least Mike was coming with her. Rising from her warm bed, she found her slippers on the cold floor. Her stomach felt upset, and she shivered from the chills. She had a bottle of Tylenol in her toiletries kit. She'd take an extra, just to take the edge off her back pain. They would be taking off in just two hours.

GEORGE STOOD IN the kitchen, waiting for the coffee to perk. The fire had died down during the night, leaving the place as cold as a tomb. If it were Monday, he'd already be about his chores, killing geese for restaurants all over New England, going about his business. Forgetting all about the crap with Sarah and Mike.

Sarah and Mike. Just thinking their names took all his effort, the way it used to feel to think "Rose." George had to sit down. It wasn't six A.M. yet, and he was already tired. He had a whole day to face, with a lot of pointless crap. A cat meowed at his feet. George tried to ignore it, but it jumped onto his lap.

"What do you want?" he asked. It was one of the mangy ones, yellow fur with bald patches, eyes all blinky and stuck together with goop.

It meowed, purring like a motor. For such a sickly-looking cat, it sounded mighty healthy. George stuck it under his arm and walked to the sink. He turned on the water, letting it run till it turned warm. Then, taking a corner of one of Bess's clean washcloths, he wet it and cleaned out the cat's eyes.

Suddenly the cat's eyes were wide open. It looked straight at George, its scrawny face full of surprise. The purring stopped, and the cat sprang away. George didn't see where it went, it moved so fast. And it scratched his hand in the process.

The scratch wasn't bad, but it bled a little. George held his hand under the running water. Perking hard, the coffee started spitting all over the stove. George got to it just before it boiled over. He spied the yellow cat crouched on top of the refrigerator. The cat was watching him, but George turned away.

"Goddamn cat," he said. A year ago he was perfectly happy, running his farm and sharing meals with Bess, thinking Sarah and her son were lost to him. While not exactly estranged, no one ever found much reason to call or write. They certainly didn't visit. But then Mike came to stay and life got different. It got better, George would have said. He had the boy's company, the notion of reuniting with Sarah, the reality of his own flesh and blood. Frozen up since Rose's death, George had let down his guard. He had started caring.

He had to check the geese. Not even bothering to put on his jacket, he opened the kitchen door and headed outside. The thermometer registered twenty-five degrees. George moved stiffly over the frozen ground. Maybe he'd get new boots this year, with more tread. Just thinking about a long winter without Mike to help made him walk slower. Reaching the barn door, he grabbed the handle.

The latch was frozen.

"Goddammit," George said, yanking hard. He wedged his foot against the boards, trying for a better grip. His body felt so old and feeble, it made him swear harder. Frustrated, he threw all his weight behind one last tug and landed flat on his back.

"Shit," he said, looking up at the sky.

"You okay, Grandpa?" Mike asked, looking down at him.

"I'm fine," George said.

Mike reached down a hand. Taking hold, George pulled himself up. Mike stared off at the sun rising, pretending nothing had happened. George felt furious at himself, embarrassed and old. His bones hurt; even the cat scratch stung like the devil. While George brushed himself off, Mike opened the barn door. Inside, the geese began cackling loudly.

"What are you doing out here?" George asked.

"Feeding the geese, Grandpa," Mike said, walking into the barn without another word.

———

ONE BY ONE, they all helped themselves to breakfast. There was a big pot of oatmeal on a back burner, a pitcher of orange juice, and the battered old pot of coffee. Will ate by himself, at one end of the kitchen table. He had been up for hours; bor-

rowing the Jeep, he had driven over to the airstrip, cleared the
snow away from the plane, and readied the field. Eating slowly,
he gazed across the snow at the sea. It was dark blue, rolling
with big, unbroken waves. In about an hour they'd fly away,
leaving it behind. He had left the Atlantic before, but this time
it was different.

Alone at the table, Will thought of Fred. Staring at the sea, he
felt his son was right beside him. Will could hear his voice, see
his eyes. As if Fred were growing older, becoming the age he
would have been, Will could imagine how he would look now.
After all these years of trying to block the image, he now wel-
comed it.

Coming to Maine, he had fallen in love with Sarah Talbot.
He had spent Thanksgiving with her, gotten to know her family. He had spent time with Snow, the first four full days without
having to return her to her mother since the divorce. He had
done all those things, but in some ways this trip to Maine had
been as much about Fred as anyone else. Will had found a way
back to his son.

Pushing back his chair, he washed his bowl and coffee cup,
left them to dry beside the porcelain sink. Everyone was busy,
preparing in their own ways to leave or stay, to say good-bye.
He could hear footsteps upstairs, Snow's voice down the hall.
He hadn't seen Sarah yet that morning; he supposed she had
arrangements to make, things she needed to say to her father.
And her mother.

Will checked his watch: seven-thirty. They'd be leaving the
house in half an hour, taking off from the airstrip as soon as
possible to take advantage of the prevailing winds. Aunt Bess
had set a pile of finished quilts by the door. Will tucked his
green chamois shirt into faded jeans, then pulled on his leather
jacket. He lifted a few quilts under each arm, carried them out
to the Jeep. The plane would be fuller this trip, with Mike and
the quilts, but there would still be plenty of room. Nothing to
worry about.

SNOW SAT ON the edge of her bed, wondering when she would be back again. She had loved her time on Elk Island for so many reasons. Spending time in a family with just as many problems as hers had been great. Back home, her friends from school and all the kids she baby-sat for seemed to have such perfect lives, with parents who stayed together and brothers who never died. Snow's friends never changed their names; their parents never sent them to shrinks.

Thanksgiving with the Talbots had proved something to her. You could love someone imperfectly but still love them. Just look at Sarah, the way she felt about Mike. Snow could see it in her eyes, hear it in her voice. At the same time, you could look at George and read how much he loved Sarah. And they were a mess! They got so upset with each other, had so many resentments, it was almost comical. A bunch of people bumbling along, trying to just get along, hurting each other more the harder they tried not to.

Poor George. Snow knew how upset he'd be when Mike left. She believed that Mike wanted to come back, but it wouldn't be easy. Keeping on the course you set for yourself didn't always work out the way you planned. Like, Snow hoped Mike would hang out with her back in Fort Cromwell, maybe even be her boyfriend. She'd been so excited about the idea of flying home with him, she'd been unable to sleep. But she didn't want to get her hopes up; people seemed to veer away from each other all the time. They just did.

Someone knocked on her door. Hoping it was Mike, she checked herself in the mirror. But when she opened the door, it was her father standing there.

"Are you almost ready?" he asked.

"Yes, Dad," she said. She must have sounded uncertain, because he just stood there. Looking past her, he seemed to be gazing out the window.

"Will you miss Elk Island?" he asked.

"So much!" she said.

"I have a feeling we'll be back sometime."

Snow nodded. She knew her father's reply had to do with him and Sarah, and she wanted to ask him about it. At the same time, she didn't want to know. The conflict gave her a slight stomach-ache. She liked Sarah, she wanted her father to be happy, so why wasn't she overjoyed about the idea of them together?

"Mom's going to kill me when I get home," she said instead.

"I'll talk to her," he said.

"Aren't you mad? That I stowed away?"

"I should say yes," he said, hugging her. "But I can't. This has been a wonderful time, and I'm glad you were here."

"Me too," Snow said. "Dad, will George and Bess be okay without Mike?"

Her father wouldn't lie to her. He tried to smile, but he couldn't even really do that. "It'll be hard," he said. "You know how long it takes to get over missing someone."

"Freddie," Snow said. "And you when you moved out."

"Yep," her father said.

"It wasn't so bad seeing the ocean again, was it, Dad?" Snow asked. She had never told him how worried—scared—she had been when he had turned away from the sea, never wanted to sail again, moved the whole family inland to Fort Cromwell.

"It was great."

"I thought so too." Snow paused. She suddenly wished, as she had wished off and on since arriving on the island, that they didn't have to leave. Returning to Fort Cromwell would mean leaving her father again, going back to Julian's. She'd get to see him whenever she wanted, but it wasn't the same as always having him around, waking up and knowing he was just down the hall. The thought made her heart ache. It was the kind of thing she always thought she should talk to Dr. Darrow about but never quite could.

"What are you thinking?" her father asked.

"Oh, just that Julian's house is so drafty. It's never warm enough," she said, because it was too hard to put her real thoughts into words.

"Wear extra socks," her father said. "Are you running out?"

Snow grinned. Everyone but her father thought she was cracked for wearing Freddie's socks. That was one of the main reasons she had been sent to Dr. Darrow, and one of the best parts about Mike flying home with them: He understood too.

"Have no fear," Snow said. "Fred's socks will never run out."

"You're pretty good with a darning needle for a kid your age," her father said.

"Mom thinks wearing them is strange. She thinks I should go back to Dr. Darrow."

"I know," her father said. She could tell by the way he sounded that he disagreed with her mother, but Snow had known that all along.

"Mike went to him too, Dad. Do you think Mike's crazy?"

"No, Snow. And I don't think you are either."

"Dad," Snow said, swallowing hard. "What if we start forgetting him? Sometimes I wake up and I don't even think of him till I'm eating breakfast. Or waiting for the bus. I used to think of him all the time."

"We'll never forget Fred," her father said. "I promise, Snow."

Snow nodded.

"Come on," her father said, reaching toward her.

Snow Burke, even though she was a little too old to be holding her father's hand—especially in the house of a boy she hoped would become her boyfriend—laced fingers with her father and walked downstairs.

————

SARAH WALKED INTO the room where Will had been sleeping. He was downstairs, loading the car, so she was alone. She walked straight to the dresser, looked at her mother's picture. She felt chilly. The fever ran through her, making her shiver, but her hands were trembling with something else.

She picked up her mother's picture. Although she had photographs of her mother in Fort Cromwell, there was something about this wedding portrait that made Sarah feel so close to her. Perhaps it was the fact that her mother had died in this room, with this very same picture on the dresser beside her.

"Mom," she said out loud. Was she expecting her mother to answer? She knew it was crazy, but there was something in the air. It felt charged, different than it had ever felt before. No one was standing there, but Sarah felt that she was not alone.

Sitting on the edge of the bed, she looked around. This was where her mother had lain, the things Sarah was seeing were the things she had seen. The same faded wallpaper, the mahogany dresser, the paintings on the wall, the white curtains at the window. Lying here, she would have had to lift her head to see outside, to look at the sea.

She had been so weak. Sarah remembered coming in to sit with her, scared of what she might find each time. The smells of sickness were so strong that people who had never smelled them before knew exactly what they meant. Her mother had always been such a clean person, and Sarah remembered how happy it made her, the times Sarah would offer to wash her face.

How often had she actually done it? Once a day? Such a small thing, and she had done it so few times. She would fill the basin with warm water, use a white washcloth and a bar of her mother's favorite soap. The whole time, she had felt a pit in her stomach. Her mother would be smiling, so grateful for such a little thing, and Sarah would just want to get it over with. Looking back all those years, she understood that her mother's smile had less to do with getting her face washed than having her daughter sit beside her. The realization made her feel ashamed that she couldn't have done more.

"I'm sorry, Mom," she whispered.

Rising, she walked to the window. She leaned against the narrow sill, watching the early sun peeking through the pines, throwing orange light on the snow and rocks. The seals covered their rocks, curved upward. Thanksgiving was over. In just a few weeks Christmas would be here, her mother's favorite holiday, and Sarah remembered something else.

For her mother's last Christmas, too sick to get out of bed much, let alone leave this room, Sarah had spoken to her father about a tree. Bitter and full of fear, he had said it wouldn't be proper, that her mother couldn't get down to the parlor to see it anyway. There would be no tree that year. In some ways, Sarah had known he was right. Her mother was dying. They had no business celebrating.

But she wanted her mother to have a tree. She remembered the planning, the preparations. For one whole day she had worked in the shed, fixing everything she needed. She had made candleholders out of muffin tins, tinfoil, and electrical clips. She had gone outside, hollowed out spots in the snow, made a path across the yard to a small white spruce, a perfect Christmas tree growing on the edge of the woods.

That night, just as it was growing dark, Sarah had come into this room. Her mother had been lying there, almost too ill to move but so happy to see her. Sarah had helped her up, hurrying her along because time was short. She had brought her mother her robe, helped her into her slippers. Placing the chair beside the window, she had supported her mother for the achingly hard walk over. It was only ten steps, but it had seemed like a hundred.

Sarah remembered her mother's gasp. She had stood there, fingers pressed to her lips. Sarah had placed candles in the snow, on the branches of the tree. She had used up the entire emergency supply. The pathway blazed, from the back door to the Christmas tree, and the tree itself was lit with fifty flickering lights. Sarah had tied red bows to the boughs, but it had gotten too dark to see. She and her mother had stood by the window, just holding each other without speaking, until one by one each white candle went out.

"Our Christmas, Mom," she said, standing at the window, remembering. Her mother had taught her so much. Holidays were important, you couldn't let them pass by. No matter how sad, no matter how afraid you felt, you had to celebrate with the people you loved. Because you never knew when memories would be all you had left.

Turning away from the window, kissing her mother's picture for the last time, Sarah paused by the door. Her back hurt, and she knew she would never be able to lift her mother today as she had done then. She took a deep breath, saying good-bye. Then she went downstairs to find Will, to find her son and take him home.

————

AUNT BESS DECIDED to stay home, so everyone said good-bye to her in the front hall. She kept her dignity and good humor, hugging Mike only a minute longer than the others, telling him to be sure to write. When she hugged Sarah, she pulled back slightly, a worried look on her face.

"Is that a fever?" she asked, touching Sarah's forehead.

"Just a slight one," Sarah said. She kept her voice low, not wanting anyone else to know she was sick.

"Go to bed the minute you get home," Aunt Bess said, and Sarah felt relieved that she didn't act more concerned, didn't try to convince her to stay an extra day to recuperate. Now that the moment had come to leave, Sarah felt a sense of urgency. She wanted the good-byes to be over, to be up in the air on their way, to get Mike back home as soon as possible.

Her father was quiet this morning. He carried the luggage out to the Jeep, cramming it in back as if he were taking a load of trash to the dump. Gelsey needed a little help getting into the front seat, and George gave her a shove under the rump. Climbing behind the wheel, he sat there silently, like a reluctant chauffeur with a job he wished were already over. Sarah tried to let Will sit in front, but he refused. He kissed her on the cheek as he got into the backseat with Mike and Snow. She got in, and Gelsey climbed onto her lap.

They drove across the island. Sarah watched the landscape go by. Nothing changed on Elk Island. The island was too far away, too hard to get to, to attract builders and developers. Storms might topple trees, the sea might change the shore, but Sarah took comfort in knowing that when she returned again, the island would look about the same as it did now.

She had such mixed feelings. Leaving her father made her sad. But she was flying home with Mike, and that was the main thing. Was it greedy to hope for more, for her father to see it her way and feel happy? Driving the Jeep, he looked so hunched over and miserably turned inward. What would he and Aunt Bess talk about? Sarah could imagine him returning to the house, not saying another word until the spring thaw. Mike must have brought such light to his bitter life.

"Dad," she said in a low voice.

"Hmmmm," he growled.

"He'll be back."

No comment. He just gripped the steering wheel tighter, pressed on the gas pedal a little harder. Sarah tried not to think about how rusty the Jeep was, how dilapidated the farm. Mike had done his best to stem the tide of disrepair, but he'd been powerless against the brutal weather, the dwindling income. Sarah would slip some extra money into the next check she sent, hoping her father wouldn't be so proud that he'd send it back.

"We're here!" Snow exclaimed as they turned the corner and the plane came into sight.

George parked the Jeep, and Will and Mike unloaded it.

Sarah sat in the front seat, watching Snow run to the plane, her arms open wide as if she wanted to embrace it. Sarah's fever seemed to be getting a little worse. She had felt hot during the drive over, but when everyone got out of the Jeep, the cold air had knifed through her and left her shivering. Her back ached. Tylenol, chicken soup, and bed, she was thinking, watching everyone bustling around the plane. But overriding her discomfort, this onslaught of flu, was the knowledge that Mike was coming home. My son, Sarah thought.

———————

MIKE STOWED EVERYTHING carefully in the cargo area. He had heard about bags coming loose, flying through the air when small planes hit turbulence. With all these people he cared so much about, he wanted to make sure he did things right. That he loaded the bags as safely as possible.

In small planes you really got the sensation of flight. You were a bird, soaring into the clouds. Thinking of birds, Mike looked up and saw the eagle.

"Mom," he called.

She was still in the Jeep. Sitting in the front seat, petting Gelsey, watching everyone load the plane. Was something wrong? Mike felt worried, but then she smiled and waved and he felt okay again. He pointed at the sky.

"There he is," he yelled.

His mother looked up. She had that expression on her face, that what-have-I-done-to-deserve-something-so-wonderful look that only she got. Smiling at the sky, at the bald eagle circling overhead, she tilted her head back for a moment. Mike got a lump in his throat. She looked pale and a little tired, and he worried because he knew how sick she had been. She had come to see him, and that meant more to him than Mike could understand.

They had spent Thanksgiving together. Hadn't they spent

about a million before? Sitting at a table, eating some bird, waiting for pie? They had spent Thanksgivings alone, Thanksgivings with friends. They had had years of traditional cooking and years of experimentation, like the Thanksgiving his mother had decided to mix the turnips and mashed potatoes together, the time she had made apple crumble instead of apple pie. But no Thanksgiving had ever been as great as the one they'd just had.

"Mike, shouldn't he be going south?" his mother called. "Don't eagles migrate?"

"I think they do," Mike called back. "Maybe he's on his way now."

"My son the scientist!" she called.

Mike shook his head. He felt the smile drain from his face. She sounded so happy. He had seen her last night when he had talked about wanting to finish school, study oceanography, go on to college. All she wanted was to make things right, make sure Mike wasn't going to turn out a loser. Mike could understand that.

Parents loved their kids, wanted the best. He could see it with Will and Snow; he had experienced it all last winter, with his grandfather worrying about his mother. Every letter they *didn't* get from Fort Cromwell during the weeks when his mother had been too sick to write had affected his grandfather like a sliver under his skin. Mike had watched his body slouch, his scowl deepen. Scared of losing Sarah, his grandfather had clung tighter to Mike.

How did people do it? Mike wondered, wedging the last of the bags into the cargo door. How did they manage loving their kids, keep it from breaking them in half? Looking at Will, he tried to imagine what it had been like to see his son disappear under the waves. How did people let each other out of their sight?

"Hey, where's yours?" Will asked, counting the bags.

Mike didn't reply.

Will stood there, counting. He was the pilot, and he kept track of weight, of the number of bags that went into his plane. He and Mike were still wary of each other; Mike felt it. Frowning, Will turned to Mike.

"That's the same number we had coming out," Will said.

"I know," Mike said.

His mother had finally gotten out of the car. She was moving slowly, limping a little. Snow bounded over, put her arm around her, practically danced her over to the plane. The look on his mother's face was strange, kind of pained, but Mike figured that was because she hated leaving. She always had.

"You'd better get going," Grandpa said, the first thing he'd said all morning. He was speaking to everyone, but he directed his words to Mike.

It was a perfect day. The sky was bright blue, the sun brilliant. Mike knew it would be a beautiful flight back to Fort Cromwell. Looking at his grandfather, he kept his gaze steady. His grandfather couldn't do it alone. Mike knew; he had watched him all the last year, seen how hard the easiest chores were. He couldn't always catch the geese. His eyes were failing, and Mike was afraid he'd cut off his own hand someday. That morning, when Mike had found him lying on the ice, he had realized how bad it was.

"What's the story?" Will asked, lowering his voice. His eyes were blazing.

Mike half turned to keep the others from hearing.

"I'm not leaving," he said.

"What?"

"I can't. My grandfather needs—"

"Look," Will said sharply, "don't do this to your mother. She thinks you're coming home with us, and that's what you're going to do."

"I can't," Mike said. For him, that was all there was to it. He couldn't live with himself if he got on that plane, left his grand-father and Aunt Bess alone. They'd die this winter without him. Mike was sure of it. His mother would feel bad, but she'd be okay. She had good friends to help her. And it wouldn't be for-ever. Mike knew that. This might be the last winter they could keep the farm going.

Will looked like he wanted to kill him. His eyes were flash-ing, his jaw set tight. He gave his head a quick shake, as if he couldn't believe what was happening. Mike tried to breathe, knowing he was doing the right thing.

"Then tell her," Will said harshly. "Don't leave her hoping. Tell her right now."

Mike nodded. Turning around, the first person he saw was Snow. His mother was right there, but he couldn't look at her yet. Snow's eyes were so huge, her smile so pretty. She was looking up at him, and Mike remembered kissing her last night. He blushed, and Snow noticed. She smiled wider.

Will stepped between Mike and his mother as if he could somehow shield her from what was about to happen. He put his arm around her, slowly turning to face Mike. Mike saw his ex-pression, somber and watchful, and Mike felt glad his mother wasn't alone.

"I'm not going," Mike said.

His mother didn't reply. She cocked her head slightly, as if she hadn't heard him right. But Snow got it right away. Her smile disappeared all at once.

"You have to!" Snow said. "I'm going to get my dad to fly us over Boston, so we can see where you used to live!"

"Mike?" his mother asked.

"I'm sorry, Mom," he said. He stepped forward, wanting to make her feel better. He wanted to hug her, or hold her hands, or something, but all he could do was stand there.

"What about school?" she asked, her voice trembling.

"I know."

"You said you wanted to finish, didn't you? What about your future, honey?"

"I'll finish, Mom."

"When?" Sarah asked, growing agitated.

"Soon," Mike said.

"You're already older than a senior," Snow said, hands on her hips.

"It's your life you're throwing away," his mother said. "Don't you see that, Mike? Life is so short! You think you have all the time in the world, but a year will pass and you'll never go back. It will seem like too much trouble, honey. Or you'll feel too old."

"No, I won't," Mike said.

"But you will!" his mother said, her voice catching. She must have pulled a muscle or something, because she winced with pain. "Oh," she said.

"Sarah," Will said, holding her close. "He'll be fine."

"He won't," she said, pushing Will away. She walked straight to Mike and held his hands. She stared him in the eye, and he couldn't stand to see the tears rolling down her cheeks. "Come home," she said.

"Mom," he said, wanting to look away but forcing himself to hold her gaze.

"Come home," she said, her voice breaking. "Please."

"You should listen to your mother," his grandfather said half-heartedly. "Finish your schooling."

"Come with us," Snow begged. "We'll have fun."

"I can't," Mike said, speaking to all of them but focusing on his mother. "I never knew where I belonged before, but I do now. I'm staying on the island."

His mother was sobbing. She wasn't being strong at all. She had pulled her hands back, bowed her head, and started weeping into her palms. Will was holding her again, and even Grandpa looked concerned. Snow just stood there, staring at her feet. Mike reached into the cargo hold for a small pouch he'd stuck in with Snow's bag.

"Here," he said.

"What is it?" she asked sullenly.

"One of the extra cats," he said.

Seemingly against her will, but unable to stop herself, Snow reached into the sack and pulled out one of the black kittens. It was the smallest one Mike could find, with a white throat and bright blue eyes.

"Wow," Snow said. She kissed the cat's nose. "What's its name?"

"I don't know," Mike said. "You're good with names. It's a boy."

"Dr. Darrow," Snow said immediately, her smile flooding back.

"Yeah," Mike said, smiling at her. "Dr. Darrow." He looked at his mother, and his smile died. The light had gone out of her. She looked gray. Her face was pale, her eyes dull. She wasn't sobbing as hard, but her body seemed to be trembling.

"Sarah, are you okay?" Will was asking, supporting her with his arm.

"My back," she said, gulping past those last knifelike gasps, "hurts a little."

"You got a touch of the family rheumatism," Grandpa said. Now that Mike was staying, he could afford to be magnanimous. Will took one arm and Grandpa took the other, and they helped Sarah sit down in the front seat of the plane.

Mike walked over. The older men stepped away, and he was left face-to-face with his mother. She looked full of sorrow, as if she had lost the thing she loved most in the world. Mike couldn't quite understand how upset she was seeming. Mothers wanted their kids to get educated, but Mike had never been an A student. She couldn't be all that surprised.

"Mom," he said, crouching by the plane door. "I'm going to

finish school. I promise. Even if it's just a GED. I'll write the high school."

"What about being an oceanographer?" she asked, her voice weak.

"What oceanographer ever had it better than me?" Mike asked. "I get to live it, not just study it."

She nodded as if that made sense to her. But her eyes were bereft.

"Maybe I'll go someday. Just not right now."

"Oh, Mike," she said.

"I know you think I have to do it all at once, that if I don't go to school now, I never will. But there's time. There's plenty of time."

Mike must have said the wrong thing. His mother had started crying again. She wasn't sobbing like before, she hardly even shook. But the tears were welling in her eyes, and she was staring into his face as if she wanted to memorize every detail.

"I want you to be right," she said.

Mike nodded. This was it. Will had better get Snow into the plane, take off before his mother started crying hard again. Mike knew Will loved his mother, he could see it. At that moment he decided to trust him to take care of her. While Mike manned the island, looking after Grandpa and Aunt Bess, running the farm, Will could make sure his mother was okay. And Snow.

"You'd better go," Mike said to Will.

"Yeah," Will said, shaking Mike's hand.

Snow threw herself into his arms. Her body felt so small and beautiful, she smelled so sweet, he felt the ground shake beneath his feet. He pushed her away, not roughly but firmly, knowing he couldn't hold her an instant longer. Dr. Darrow meowed.

"One less cat. Good," his grandfather said. He said his good-byes, shaking hands with Will and Snow, leaning into the plane to hug his daughter. Mike watched the way Grandpa leaned down, holding Sarah's face between his gnarled old hands. She was looking straight at him, nodding at whatever he was saying. When Grandpa turned around, he looked straight at Mike. Mike might have expected an expression of friendliness, but instead, Grandpa looked as if he wanted to kill him for upsetting his mother. It was Mike's turn.

"Bye, Mom," he said, kissing her cheek.

She caught him with her arms. Hugging him so hard, he could hardly believe his mother had that kind of strength, she said something he couldn't quite hear.

"What?" he asked, leaning even closer.

"I have to tell you something," she said.

"Okay," he said.

"Grandpa says he'll send you home whenever you want. Just ask."

"Okay," Mike said, waiting.

"I have never," she said slowly, as if she were afraid of not saying exactly what she wanted to, "loved anyone as much as I love you."

"Mom—" Mike said.

"No one, Mike."

"My dad," Mike said. "And..." He trailed off, first glancing at Will.

"No one," Sarah said again. "From the minute I saw you, that was it. True love, and forever. You changed my world."

"Yeah," Mike said, his throat hurting because he had something to say but didn't know what it was.

"I know you love me, Mike," his mother said. "Don't ever think I don't."

"Uh..." Mike said. He wanted to say more, something about loving her too, thanking her for being such a good mother. The old problems just didn't seem so big anymore. But those thoughts were so huge, and Mike couldn't imagine himself saying them out loud. So he just nodded.

She pulled him close again, giving him another hard hug. Mike found himself thinking, what if this is the last time? What if we never see each other again? But those were crazy thoughts, and he looked up at the sky to drive them away.

"Bye," his mother said.

"Bye," Mike said. And then Will came around to close the plane door, to say good-bye to Mike, to fly the women Mike loved back to Fort Cromwell.

CHAPTER

19

EVERYONE WAS SO quiet. The grown-ups weren't talking at all. Snow sat in the back of the plane, playing with Dr. Darrow, wishing Mike were sitting beside her. She looked at things out the window and imagined how great it would be to be seeing them with Mike. The day was so sunny, the ocean was a golden mirror. She had planned to give Mike the best seat, but since he hadn't come, she was sitting on the left side, to get the maximum view of the sea. Once they passed New Hampshire, there would be no more saltwater at all.

So Snow stared at fishing boats and tankers, lobster villages and resort towns, hundreds of tiny pine-studded islands in the great Maine bays. She saw docks and jetties covered with snow, shadows underwater that might be shoals or reefs or even whales. Mike would know, and so would Fred, and thinking about her gone boys made her sigh.

Such a big ocean, Snow thought, watching it spread into eternity. That very same Atlantic flowed past Newport, into the bay where Fred had died. The sea had taken her brother, so how could she love it so much? She didn't understand. Mike had given her a wonderful idea about becoming an oceanographer. If she couldn't live beside the sea, she could go to some university and study it. She felt like announcing her plan, but she didn't want to upset Sarah.

Sarah was just sitting there, all clenched up with her arms wrapped around herself, lost in thought. Snow would have thought Sarah would be someone to make the best of things, to accept the fact that Mike had decided to stay on Elk Island, but she obviously wasn't. You just never knew how people would react to upsetting events. Just look at Snow's parents. Just when you expected them to stay calm, they exploded.

Dr. Darrow cheered Snow up. He was so adorable, no bigger than a coffee mug with legs. He had a nice full belly, a scrawny little tail, big blue eyes like Mike's and Sarah's. He didn't walk, he skipped. Snow watched him skip across the seat. He explored the door panels, the window, Snow's leg. Tired out, he plopped right down with his chin on her thigh.

Snow picked him up. She held him against her throat, his body resting on her collarbone. He could feel her pulse there, and it was nice and warm. The minute he felt her skin, he started to purr. Closing her eyes, Snow felt the kitten rumbling against her neck. He nestled closer, trying to get right into the curve under her chin. He tickled. Snow just sat there, not flinching.

When she opened her eyes again, they were just leaving the coastline behind. She had to turn, to watch the Atlantic recede into a thin golden line. Dr. Darrow adjusted his little body to her movement, but he didn't quite wake up. The grown-ups didn't say a word. Snow noticed her father reach across the seat, take Sarah's hand. Wishing she had Mike to do the same thing, Snow felt sad.

Flying deeper inland, she felt the wheezing start. Her chest tightened. Having trouble getting air, she fumbled in her pocket for her inhaler. She hadn't used it once the whole time they were on Elk Island. Her mother would say she needed it now because of Dr. Darrow. She would tell Snow the cat had to go, that cat fur made her wheeze. That asthma was nothing to fool with, cats only made it worse. But Snow knew this allergy attack had nothing to do with Dr. Darrow or any other cat.

She was allergic to leaving the sea behind. Being inland made her heart heavy, her spirits dark, and it was too much for her respiratory system to handle. Snow needed salt air. Breathing the other kind took too much effort. Taking a hit of her inhaler, she tried to think calming thoughts.

Christmas was coming. She'd make a tiny stocking for Dr. Darrow and fill it with catnip and bell toys. It was time to change her name again, and Christmas provided many possibilities. Star, Bethlehem, Blitzen, and Cratchit were just a few. While Cratchit didn't sound as pretty as the others, it was probably the most appropriate. Fred had loved *A Christmas Carol*. Their parents had read it to them all through the month of December every year. And the Christmas before he died, Fred had played Bob Cratchit in the school play.

Flying over the mountains instead of the sea, cuddling her kitten and trying to breathe, Snow tried thinking of herself as Cratchit. No. It didn't quite fit, didn't sound as peaceful as a new name should be. She had adopted a pattern of "S" names, and she saw no reason to interrupt that now. Snow's names brought her serenity as well as a connection to her brother, and returning to the lair of Julian and her mother, she needed all the serenity and connection she could get.

———

THEY STOPPED TO refuel in Lebanon. Everyone went into the hangar to use the bathrooms and get coffee and hot chocolate. Sarah felt like she was in a fog. Her head was thick from all the tears she had cried. Every time she thought of Mike, her eyes welled up. Her fever was getting worse, which seemed to make her even more emotional. And the pain in her back was intensifying.

Will brought her a cup of coffee. Sarah smiled as their fingers touched. She hated the way she was being. Since leaving Elk Island, she had been unable to talk. Why had Mike's decision to stay affected her this way? Flying out, she honestly hadn't expected to convince him to come home. But seeing him made her realize how much she missed him, how badly she wanted to see him go back to school. Seeing him on Elk Island had reminded her of how easy it would be for him to turn into an island man, watching the seasons pass, turning more bitter with every harvest moon. Her resistance to disappointment was painfully low, and she blamed it on the flu.

"I'm sorry," she said.

"For what?" Will asked.

She shook her head, trying to sip the coffee. "For being so upset."

"I don't blame you. He's not my son, and I feel the same way."

"What way?" Sarah asked.

"Like I'd like to stick him in the backseat and fly him home whether he likes it or not."

Sarah smiled. She couldn't drink her coffee. It smelled too strong, made her feel sick. Not wanting to hurt Will's feelings, she held the cup. But she felt pale, and she knew she had beads of sweat on her forehead. She had taken some more Tylenol an hour earlier, but she didn't feel any better. If anything, her back was getting worse.

"What is it?" Will asked. He took the cardboard cup out of her hand and placed it on a window ledge. The air was freezing cold, even inside the hangar. Sarah shivered uncontrollably.

"Nothing," she said. She made herself smile, take Will's hands. They felt so strong and solid. He put his arms around her, holding her tight. Somehow his embrace took the pressure off her spine. While Will hugged her, the pain was gone.

"Let's go," Will said into her hair. "The sooner we take off, the sooner I get you home. I'm coming over, by the way."

"You don't have to," Sarah said. "You've spent the last four days with me. Aren't you sick of me by now?"

"Not even slightly," Will said, still hugging her.

They stood still, neither one of them wanting to move. After a few minutes someone walked over to tell Will the plane was refueled and ready. If he hadn't, Sarah had the feeling they could have stayed there an hour or more, not thinking anything except that everything was going to be okay.

————

TAKING OFF JUST before noon, they encountered significant headwinds. Will had looked at the weather map, and this was nothing unexpected. A big system sweeping down from Canada was bringing the clear air, but also high winds. They hit some turbulence right away, and he suspected they were in for a rough ride.

"Hang on," he said. "It's going to be bumpy."

Sarah nodded, giving him a reassuring smile.

"Daddy . . ." Snow said warningly, as if she wanted him to stop it.

"Don't worry," he said over her shoulder. "It's going to be fine."

"The kitten's scared," she said.

"Just hold him," Sarah said. "That will make him feel safe."

Snow had never liked flying in rough air, just as when sailing she had never liked heeling too far over. She mistrusted the sense of motion, of feeling the earth slide away, seeing the horizon teeter. She would grip her seat, cling to her mother: Fred had been the opposite. He couldn't go fast enough. He had loved sailing to windward, putting the rail under water, looking straight down into the waves. Flying, he had enjoyed the turbulence that frightened his sister. He would have teased her for her fear today, made her so mad she would almost forget it.

"Aah," Sarah exclaimed.

"What is it?" Will asked.

"It's nothing," she said.

But when he looked over, her face was pure white. She was clutching her seat, but from pain, not fear of flying.

"Sarah," he said, alarmed.

"My back hurts," she said quietly. "That's all."

"Did you strain it? Lifting the bags or something?"

"I don't know," she said. "I don't think so."

For now there was nothing he could do. She was gritting her teeth, so he knew it had to be bad. She had seemed upset since leaving Maine, but Will had attributed that to Mike's decision to stay. What had Aunt Bess said about a fever? Preoccupied with his duties as the pilot, Will hadn't paid much attention. But right now he felt worried. Her color was very pale, almost gray.

Maybe it was emotional, due to Mike not coming. Will knew the power of sorrow. It could do amazing, destructive things. He had never given it any thought before Fred died, but he had seen with his own eyes. Sorrow had aged Will himself twenty years overnight. It had changed Susan from a light, care-free sprite into a fearful, superstitious child plagued by night-mares and asthma. It had transformed Alice from a loving wife and mother into a wild woman, turning to the world because her husband was still paralyzed by grief. Sorrow had ripped Will's family to shreds.

Glancing across the seat at Sarah, he tried to touch her. She flinched at the pressure of his hand. She was barely standing it, holding on for dear life. The tension in her arms was extreme. The cords in her neck stood out as if she were bench-pressing a great deal of weight. Will wanted to believe she was only suffer-ing from sorrow, but he could see that it was something more.

All he could do was fly the plane and get her home as fast as he could.

———

SARAH HAD NEVER felt such pain. She closed her eyes, trying all the exercises she had ever learned to endure moments like this. In childbirth she had been taught to breathe a certain way to make sure she got enough oxygen when the impulse was to hold her breath, to not let in any air at all. She had learned to focus outside of herself, on a word or a prayer or an image of the sea.

During the worst of chemotherapy, she had experienced no pain but a nausea so intense, she had sometimes wished to die. Meg Ferguson had worked with her on meditation practices. They had experimented with Zen, sitting cross-legged and following the breath in and out, giving each other mantras that sounded pretty and meant nothing. Sarah's had been "Allay-loo," and she tried it now.

Allay-loo, she thought. Allay-loo.

As the pain got worse, her thoughts broke through. The plane trembled in the wind, and Snow cried out. Will tried to reassure her. Sarah heard her own voice, telling Snow that everything would be fine, to think of the seals they had all seen on Elk Island.

"What about them?" Snow asked fearfully.

"When they dive," Sarah said. "They sometimes swim through turbulent water. Breaking waves, upwelling, fast currents. But they're sleek, Snow. Just like our plane. They're made to go through it."

"I'm scared, Sarah," she said, starting to cry.

"I know, honey," Sarah said, biting her lip. The pain was so intense, she saw stars. She heard her own voice, couldn't believe she was saying the words. Her mind screamed with agony. Snow's hand came around the seat, and Sarah held it. She squeezed hard. Perhaps the connection comforted Snow; all Sarah knew was it took a little of the edge off the pain.

Her hip was numb, and her leg tingled. Squeezing Snow's hand as hard as she could, she pictured Dr. Goodacre. On her last visit to him she had felt so reassured. Hadn't they talked about his father, his brother the angel? The focus had been off Sarah for a change, and she had felt so relieved. But what had Dr. Goodacre said about numbness? Tingling? He had told her to watch out for them, but he had stopped short of telling her why.

Sarah thought she knew. New tears came to her eyes. She had wept all morning for Mike, but now she was crying for something else. She had fought so hard, been filled with so much hope. Her birthday had been a dream. Flying over the mountains with Will, so grateful to be alive, to feel healthy again, Sarah had imagined it going on forever.

"Sarah," Will said, sounding so worried. Feeling his hand on the back of her neck, Sarah bowed her head.

"Thank you," she said.

"Sarah, what's wrong?" Snow asked from the backseat.

Wanting to give the child strength, Sarah tried to tell her nothing was wrong. She wanted to say her back hurt a little, that she'd take a little Tylenol and it would go away. She wanted to say the words, but she couldn't. Not about herself.

"Don't be scared, Snow," she said. "We'll be home soon."

"Hang in there," Will said.

Sarah nodded.

"Sarah, remember how scared we were when Mike fell through the ice? Remember how we thought he was going to drown?" Snow asked.

"Yes," Sarah said.

"But he didn't! No matter how scared we were," Snow said, "we were wrong. Because he came out just fine. Is this like that?"

The pressure of Will's hand on her neck felt comforting, and so did the grip of Snow's hand. As if when Snow had picked up on Sarah's fear, her own seemed to have dissipated. She was breathing quietly now, the rasping of her asthma less severe. Sarah felt grateful for what she had just said, because suddenly it all became clear.

"I think this is like that," Sarah said, thinking back three days to that terrible moment beside the pond. Staring at the black hole in the white ice, Sarah had thought Mike would die under the water. She had gazed at the spot, filled with terror as she imagined never seeing her son again. Pray, she had said to Snow. Pray.

And Sarah herself had prayed. She had closed her eyes and asked God to spare her son. She had begged for mercy, to let Will rescue her boy, to let Mike survive. Sarah even offered herself as a sacrifice if her son would live. Everything had happened so fast, she had almost forgotten. The rescue had been so swift, the outcome had seemed inevitable.

There had been a miracle. Sarah hadn't known then, but she could see now. Looking back, hours from leaving Mike on the island, Sarah could see. She had offered to die so Mike could live, and that was going to happen. Standing there on the bank of that frozen pond, Sarah had taken her son's death into her own body.

Knowing didn't lessen the pain, but it made it slightly easier to bear. Feeling the closeness of Will and Snow, Sarah closed her eyes and tried to find peace. She thought back several months to another meditation she had tried with Meg. Sitting on pillows on her bedroom floor, Meg had told Sarah to breathe in the word "love," breathe out the word "fear."

Sarah tried it now. Bumping through the air, being caressed by the Burkes, Sarah forced herself to breathe through the fire in her spine. She formed a picture of Mike in her mind, and she thought but did not quite say the words: Love . . . fear. Love . . . fear.

As Will flew them home.

CHAPTER

20

WILL LOOKED DOWN and saw Fort Cromwell. The town was right there, and the old fort itself, the Revolutionary War site that everyone wanted to see, all the paying customers he took up for sight-seeing tours. But Will hardly even noticed today. He was too worried about Sarah. Picking up the radio, he called the tower at Brielmann Field. It was his home airport, and knowing they were just a few miles away filled him with so much relief, he couldn't stand it.

"This is 2132 Tango," Will radioed in. "We're coming in at three o'clock, and we need clearance to land."

"We got you, 2132 Tango. Using runway one today, got two closed down on account of a stiff crosswind."

"Pretty gusty up here," Will said.

Glancing over at Sarah, he thought she looked worse. She seemed calmer, but her face was tight with pain, her lips almost blue. He considered asking Curtis in the tower to call an ambulance, but he didn't. He'd drive Sarah to the hospital himself. Getting clearance to land, he started coming in.

Attempting to put the landing gear down, he needed two green lights and got one. He had a main gear light, indicating that the main landing gear was down and locked, but he wasn't getting a nosé gear light.

Will didn't say anything. He could see the airport now, the

runway shining black in the sun. There was the tower, that pillar of safety that always let him know he was home. Out of habit and not yet alarmed, he checked the gas tank: half a tank left. Gauges on Piper Aztecs were not particularly accurate, but give or take, he had a couple of hours of flying left on this tank.

Looking at the panel, he saw that the nose light still wasn't coming on. He checked the fuse. Running his hand under the panel, he found the wire and jiggled it. No light. Exhaling once hard, he glanced over at Sarah.

"Aah," she breathed, teeth clenched. "Oh, God."

"Sarah, we're almost home."

"Hurry," she said. Looking over at him, she had animal fear in her eyes. She was in terrible pain. This was the first she had really let on, and Will knew it was because she knew she was almost there, she didn't have long to wait.

Okay. Calm down, he told himself. The nose gear wasn't going down by itself, the hydraulics weren't working. But there was an alternate means of extension, a handle he could pull to activate a CO_2 cartridge and blow the gear down. Will had never had to use the procedure before, but it had been built in for a reason.

He found the handle. Sarah's pain had him panicking a little, and his fingers closed around the handle, shaking slightly. He knew this method functioned best with minimal airspeed, and he pulled back on the throttle. Pulled back more, slowing the plane down.

"Dad, I think you'd better land right away," Snow said, sounding scared. "Sarah's sick."

"I know that," Will snapped.

Snow started to cry. Sarah was silent, but the look on her face was excruciating. Will tried to concentrate. He had slowed down as much as he could, but the pressure had caused him to misjudge, and he pulled the handle too soon. The cartridge went off, but nothing happened. He still didn't have a green light.

"Shit," he said.

"What's wrong?" Snow asked. "What's going on? Is it something bad?"

He ignored her. Circling the airport, he tried thinking about the problem. His palms were sweating. Sarah and Snow could tell something was wrong. His silence, the look on his face, the fact that he was not answering Snow's questions. She had been asking them fast and furious, but suddenly she had stopped. The plane was quiet except for the constant hum of the engines.

Will called the tower.

"Brielmann Field, this is 2132 Tango. We're experiencing problems with our nose gear. Not getting a green light."

"Fly by the tower, Will. We'll take a look."

Will got that rush of hope that he wasn't alone in this. He had the responsibility of two lives besides his own, his daughter's and that of the woman he loved, and he was really scared. Banking right, he flew back toward the airport. He spied his own hangar, Burke Aviation. He saw his car parked in the parking lot. And there was the tower manned by his friends Ralph and Curtis. He saw Curtis in the window, watching the plane fly by.

"Your main gear's down, Will," Curtis radioed back. "Nose gear's hanging limp, does not appear to be fully extended."

"What's that mean?" Snow asked.

"Thanks, Curtis," Will said.

"Dad! What did Curtis mean?"

Will didn't answer.

The fuel gauge registered under a quarter, and the needle was dropping fast. One never knew with Piper Aztecs; flying a charter, Will never liked to cut it too close. The plane had good range, but the gauges weren't always on the mark. He needed to almost run out, but not quite. Without nose gear, they were going to go in hard. There would be lots of sparks, a chance of fire. All he wanted to do was land for Sarah, but to save her life right now, he had to fly.

———

EVERY AIR POCKET sent jolts down Sarah's spine. She had lost all feeling in her legs, but the pain in her back shocked her. She had never imagined the human body could feel this way. She wanted relief, medication, Dr. Goodacre. She understood there was a chance that she wouldn't survive the crash landing, that none of them would. Will had taken a big loop north, and now they were coming in.

"Get ready," Will said.

"Oh, Dad," Snow cried.

Aiming at the runway, Will stared straight ahead. Sarah could see flashing lights everywhere. Police cars, fire engines, ambulances. Blue strobes, red flashes. Snow covered the land, and white foam coated the runway.

"Okay," Will said. "I want you to put your heads down. Fold yourselves up as small as you can."

"Daddy, Dr. Darrow," Snow wept. "He wiggled out of my hands, and I can't get him."

"Leave him!" Will said sharply.

Sarah had the impression of Snow reaching, stretching for the cat in the backseat. Will slapped the seat to get her attention.

"Susan, let the cat go. Put your head down! Arms over your head, you hear me?"

"Yes," she cried.

"We're going to hit hard," Will said, the words measured as he concentrated. "But we'll be fine, just fine. We're going to walk away from the plane as if nothing ever happened. Okay?"

"I'm scared . . ." Snow cried.

"It'll be over in just a minute," Will said, teeth set.

"Daddy . . ." she said, her voice breaking.

"Are you listening? As soon as we stop, the instant I tell you," he said carefully, adjusting the approach. Sarah felt them evening out. "Undo your seat belts. And get out fast. Start running, and get away from the plane. Fast, okay? You both hear me?"

"Fast, Dad," Snow said. "I hear you."

Sarah must have spoken, but she didn't know. She was in such a cloud, a haze of agony. Bending over stretched whatever was hurting her spine, made it jab deeper and harder, brought new tears to her eyes. She thought of Mike. For the first time, she realized how glad she was that he hadn't come after all. He was safe with her father, far from this danger.

"Sarah," Will said. "Snow. I love you."

"I love you, Daddy," Snow called.

I love you, Sarah thought but could not say. The plane hit the ground. It landed with a roar, scraped the surface raw, skated left and right, wanting to spin out of control. Will was holding on. His arms were iron straight as he fought the plane. Sarah heard him cursing and praying, heard the metal ripping apart around her. The metal screamed and tore. Propellers broke apart and segments flew against the window. Glass shattered, sparks flew from the friction.

And then they were stopped.

Will was out of the plane before Sarah could get her head up. Snow tumbled onto the tarmac, clutching the kitten. Will shoved her away, yelled for her to run. He flew around to Sarah's side, undid the door. Emergency personnel surrounded the plane. Sarah saw foam spraying into the air. She heard firemen calling, shouting for everyone to move clear of the plane.

"Come on, Sarah," Will said, holding the door open, undoing her seat belt. "You've got to get out."

"Out of the way, Will," one of the firemen commanded. "We'll take over."

Will stayed by Sarah.

"Fuck it, Will. Your plane's gonna explode! Now, move!"

Will ignored them. He stood very still, as if he had all the time in the world. With Snow far away and being helped off the field, Will had eyes only for Sarah. He held out his hand, crouched down to bring his face close to hers.

"I can't move my legs," Sarah said, looking straight into his blue eyes.

"That's okay, Sarah," he said gently. Reaching into the plane, moving as tenderly as he could, he eased her arms around his neck. She didn't think she could hold on, but she did. Supporting her back, easing her out of her seat, Will lifted her into his arms. She pressed her face against his chest.

Will carried her to the ambulance where Snow was waiting. He lifted Sarah onto the vacant stretcher. He held on as they strapped her in. Even after the ambulance drove away, lights and sirens blazing, he didn't let go.

21

THEY WERE ON the evening news. Snow sat in the library, covered with a blanket and holding Dr. Darrow, watching the whole thing. Channel 3 had caught them on film from the moment the plane had started to circle over the airport. There were other news crews on the ground, and Snow could hear the disaster-excitement in the reporter's voice as she described what was going on.

"They must have been pretty sure we were going to die," Snow said, riveted.

"Don't say that," her mother said. "It was awful. Julian and I were right here, waiting for you to come home, and the tower called to tell us what was going on. I couldn't believe it."

"We turned on Channel 3 right away," Julian said. "And I was ready with the pillow. I was pretty sure I was going to have to slap it right over your mother's eyes to keep her from seeing you go down."

"We landed fine," Snow said quietly, gently stroking Dr. Darrow. He lay on her lap, purring, curled in a tight ball.

"Thank God," her mother said.

"We thought it was going to be a big 'I told you so,'" Julian said.

"What's that?" Snow asked.

"You know, run away from home and bad things happen. I told you so," he said, smiling.

Snow wanted to ignore him. She stared at the TV. Her mother was being so nice, not punishing her yet, not saying anything mean about the kitten, but Julian wanted to pick a fight. She felt a coughing fit coming on, and she knew if she didn't speak, she'd blow up. "I didn't run away," she said. "I was with my father."

"There's Will!" her mother said, sounding strangely excited, as if she had just spotted a movie star. With the zoom lens Snow could see her father at the controls, so handsome and intense. The camera stayed on his face. Snow couldn't believe how calm he looked.

"That's not how it seemed," Snow said with wonder.

"What do you mean?"

"It was scary, horrible," she said. "I was screaming, Dad had to yell at me. But look . . ."

Every time the camera lit on Will's face, he was in control, showing no fear. He didn't flinch. Hands gripping the wheel, eyes focused straight ahead, he barely moved.

"Your father has a lot of courage," her mother said softly.

"I know," Snow said.

"Wow," her mother said, leaning forward to watch. She had a strange, lost look on her face. Snow couldn't figure it out. Was it sorrow or admiration? It seemed like a combination of both. "He knew you were going to crash, but he's staying cool."

The camera panned over to Sarah, and Snow felt the kick in her stomach. Sarah's face was viciously contorted, eyes scrunched up and mouth in a frozen grimace.

"She's not cool," Julian chuckled. "She's panicking."

"She was just as brave as Dad. You should have heard her," Snow said.

"Is she his girlfriend?" Alice asked. "That's what the reporters said."

"I don't know," Snow said. She wasn't going to tell.

"Something must be going on. He won't leave her side."

Snow just nodded. Her mother and Julian had picked her up at the hospital because her father had wanted to stay with Sarah. She had a pinched nerve or something, and the plane crash had made it worse.

Snow hadn't realized so much time had passed. During the actual incident, everything seemed to happen at once. The landing had seemed so fast and furious. But watching the crash on TV made it last forever. Every time Snow saw Sarah on the screen, she felt almost sick. She hadn't realized that Sarah was in that kind of pain. But when she saw her father, she felt relaxed and proud.

"So cool and collected," her mother said as the camera went back to Will.

"Yep," Snow said.

"He always was. In the worst emergencies." Her mother was frowning, picking at a loose thread on her sleeve as she leaned close to the TV screen. Snow thought it was weird, unusual, to hear her mother talking like this right in front of Julian. Almost as if he weren't there.

"What do you mean?" Snow asked, taking advantage of it. Her mother never mentioned her father, but the fact that she was doing it now made Snow feel safe.

"Just look at him," Alice said, hand over her mouth. "He thought he was about to crash with his daughter on board... he's calm."

"Like the day Freddie died," Snow said.

"No one died today," Julian said.

Her mother nodded, ignoring him. "Like that day," she said. "I thought he should have been more upset, but look..."

"My little emotional wreck," Julian said, tugging her hand.

A frown creased Alice's cheeks and forehead as she stared at the TV screen. Reaching across the sofa, she took Snow's hand. Without saying anything, she was making Snow feel so good. She wasn't yelling about anything, she wasn't saying mean things about her father. In fact, the opposite. She was paying him compliments just by watching him on TV.

"I sold him short," she said, still watching his face on the screen. "I really did."

"Dad's not cold," Snow said softly because she had sometimes heard her mother, when describing the day of losing Fred, say that he was.

"He's got that Navy training," Alice said. "We don't, you and I, and we really lost it. Didn't we, honey?"

"We did," Snow said, amazed that watching today's events on TV could be making her mother say these things. Snow always wanted to talk about the Day of Fred with her, and her mother never would. It had always been a closed topic.

"He's a loose cannon," Julian said resentfully. "I have the crooked nose to prove it. How'd you feel up in the plane?"

"Scared?" her mother asked.

Snow froze. The camera had landed on Sarah again, and she felt a lump in her throat. Something was wrong with Sarah; she was still in the hospital.

"Not knowing what was going to happen," her mother said, "is the worst part."

"Yes," Snow said.

"I'm pretty sure your dad was scared too," she said, staring at the TV. "Even though he never shows it."

"He shows it," Snow said. "You just have to know where to look."

"Some people collapse after the fact," Julian said.

Snow felt the heat rising in her face. Julian was right; that had happened to Snow's father, but she didn't want to hear Julian rubbing it in.

"Depression can be the most destructive emotion there is," Julian said. "I mean, if you can't be there for your wife and daughter when they need you most, when even the Navy discharges you . . ."

"The Navy didn't discharge him," Snow said hotly.

"No, I know he quit before that happened—that took guts and good sense," Julian said, disgustingly pleasant. He brushed his hair back, caught it in a ponytail, smiling at Snow.

"He was there," Snow said. "The whole time. So don't say he wasn't there for us."

"You can be there in body but not spirit," Julian said kindly.

"He was there for us, wasn't he, Mom?" Snow asked. Dr. Darrow, reacting to her tone of voice, began squirming to get away. Snow's chest ached. Her throat burned, and she felt the asthma vacuuming her lungs.

Her mother bowed her head. When she raised it again to look at the TV screen, she shook her head from side to side. Her eyes looked so sad, but there was a hint of mad in there too. Snow watched several unhappy thoughts bouncing around her mother's face, and she wished she could disappear.

"No. Uh-uh, he wasn't," her mother said.

"Let's not get into this now," Julian said. He had gotten what he wanted, and suddenly he sounded magnanimous, like the resident peacemaker. Snow's lungs were on fire. She had to gasp for air, but didn't want anyone to know.

"They're showing the landing again," Julian said, pointing at the screen.

Snow's eyes were watering too hard to see. Dr. Darrow's little claws scrabbled across her sweater, getting caught in the yarn. He snagged himself. Snow wheezed deeply.

"Good Lord, Susan," her mother exclaimed, grabbing Dr. Darrow. "You're allergic to that damn animal."

"Give him back," Snow tried to say.

"It's ridiculous," Julian said. "Letting her bring home a cat. Weren't there any grown-ups on that island? Or were they too wrapped up in themselves to notice you have a serious respiratory condition?"

"Give ... him ... back ..." Snow pleaded, holding out her arms. Mike had given him to her. Sarah had said he was descended from Desdemona, her mother's cat. Dr. Darrow reminded Snow of the happiest time she'd ever had, and she believed she would stop breathing and die without him.

Her mother handed her her inhaler. Snow pumped it, stuck it in her mouth. The whole time she was reaching with one hand for the kitten. The TV showed the crash again. The plane hit hard, sending the foam spraying everywhere. Sparks flew like crazy. Mesmerized by the crash, her mother handed Snow the kitten. Julian sighed with disappointment or disapproval. Everyone gazed at the screen, shaking their heads with amazement.

How could they have survived such a thing? Snow watched herself run from the burning plane, her father yanking on the door, pulling Sarah out. Carrying her across the tarmac, his face suddenly didn't look calm anymore. He looked insane with worry, just as he had after they couldn't find Fred. Sarah clutched his chest, face twisted up with pain. He carried her as fast as he could to the ambulance. Snow watched, holding the black kitten. Being home felt weird. She missed life on Elk Island. She wanted to go back. She wanted to be at the hospital with her father, waiting to hear about Sarah.

"Is he in love with her?" her mother asked.

"Looks that way to me," Julian said.

"Yes," Snow whispered, but only to Dr. Darrow.

————

THEY WERE WAITING for Dr. Goodacre. Will hadn't met him yet, but he got the feeling that he commanded everyone's respect. The nurses got a certain look on their faces when they said his name. Sarah herself trusted him. They'd been waiting in the emergency room, then sent down to radiology for a CT scan, and finally up to a room on the fourth floor.

"Is it still bad?" Will asked.

"It's better," Sarah said, lying still. Was she telling him the truth? Gazing at her, Will tried to see. She hadn't walked yet.

She wore a blue hospital gown, but she looked so beautiful and he loved her so much, Will wanted to lift her into his arms and carry her home right then. Being in the hospital made him nervous.

"They called him?" Will asked, making sure. He understood the way the world worked. The nurses needed clearance from Dr. Goodacre, Sarah's main doctor, to let her go. They had examined her, given her Demerol to take the edge off her back pain, determined that she had a pinched nerve. That is what the radiologist had told them: nothing more threatening than a pinched nerve. She had a fever, and that was from the swelling. Nothing serious.

"They called him."

"How long does it usually take?" Will asked, unable to disguise his impatience. Sitting on the edge of Sarah's bed, he held her hands. He lowered his head, kissed each of her knuckles. Rising, he kissed her lips and caught her smiling at him.

"Sometimes," Sarah said, putting her arms around him, "a long time. He's very busy."

"So am I," Will said. "I want to get you out of this place and get you home."

"That sounds very, very good," Sarah said, kissing his cheek.

"You're sure your back's okay?"

"It's fine. I guess I made myself pretty tense leaving Mike. When he decided to stay, it shocked me. Only because he had sounded so sure about coming back."

"He did," Will said, stroking her hand, watching the door for Dr. Goodacre.

"But once I knew we were going to crash, I was so glad he was back on Elk Island. I wished Snow were too. You were amazing. The way you landed that plane, brought it right down without wheels . . . how did you do that?"

"People can do incredible things when they're trying to save people they love."

"Love," Sarah said, smiling.

"Yeah," Will said, looking straight into her eyes. They were bright, almost too bright. His daughter's eyes got glittery when she had a fever, when she was overexcited, and that's how Sarah's eyes looked now. Her anxiety was as strong as his, and she was trying to hide it just as hard.

The door opened. Dr. Goodacre walked in, all business. In his dark suit with a yellow tie and gold stickpin, he looked more like an investment banker than a doctor, with about as much bedside manner. Standing beside Sarah, he didn't even smile.

"Dr. Goodacre!" she said, sounding delighted to see him.

"Sarah," he said.

"This is Will Burke," she said. "The hero! I'm sure you heard about the plane crash at Brielmann Field, the pilot who brought a plane in without landing gear and saved everyone on board. Well, this is the guy...."

Dr. Goodacre raised his eyebrows. Perhaps he had heard about the landing; he registered something like curiosity or admiration in his eyes, but he stopped short of saying so. He didn't shake hands. Will filed it away, to joke later with Sarah about him protecting his precious surgeon hands, probably registering them with Lloyd's of London, not wanting to hazard a handshake with a bone crusher like Will.

"I'll leave," Will said.

Dr. Goodacre nodded, but Sarah put out her hand and brushed his wrist. "No, you don't!" she said. She sounded excited, almost playful. But her eyes looked scared. "Please stay?" she asked.

"Of course," Will said, moving closer than he had been.

"Sarah, I've seen your films," Dr. Goodacre said.

"I'm sorry to haul you out for a pinched nerve," Sarah said. "You're way too busy for that, and all I can say is, I was upset about my son and nervous about what was going on up in the plane, and I guess...is it possible I got myself so tensed up, my spine compressed and pinched a nerve? Because that's how it feels, way down low, as if two vertebrae are pressing against something. . . ."

Dr. Goodacre had no intention of interrupting her. He stood there, his hands folded, listening to her carry on. Will watched him. He supposed this happened all the time, anxious patients relating their version of events, doctors trained to wait it out. Moving closer to Sarah, Will felt her body against his leg. He reached for her hand.

She stopped talking. Smiling, she faced the doctor.

Dr. Goodacre cleared his throat. He struck Will as being all business, a man who made himself cold in the face of terrible things. But a glimmer of compassion, of regular human kindness, was showing through in the way he didn't want to speak.

"The CT scan showed what we've been fearing," Dr. Goodacre said. "The tumor is back."

Sarah's smile didn't change. Her eyes flickered with hope. "No," she said.

"I'm sorry, Sarah," he said.

"They're not supposed to tell me anything before you get here, but someone did today. He said I have a pinched nerve. He was definite, right, Will?"

"Right," Will said, looking at the doctor. The doctor's lips thinned, and he shook his head as if he wanted to go find and punish the offending informer.

"A nerve is being pinched, yes. The tumor is located in a crucial area, Sarah. In the lower region of your spine."

"That can't be," Will said stupidly, thinking it must be a mistake. How could a brain tumor wind up way down at the base of her spine?

"It metastasized," Sarah said. The word scared her, Will could tell. Her smile stayed large, but her eyes changed. Very slowly, they filled with dread.

Dr. Goodacre nodded. "I'm sorry," he said again much more kindly.

Will stood. He faced the doctor, eye to eye. He saw a problem to solve. So it wasn't a smooth ride: They'd have to land
without nose gear, dive under the ice to save a kid. Sarah would
need operations, more chemotherapy, extra radiation, whatever
it took. Will didn't know much about cancer, but he knew how
he felt about Sarah. They'd plan whatever was necessary. "What
do we do?" he asked.

Staring at Will, Dr. Goodacre shifted his gaze to Sarah. The
solution was between them, after all. Will understood.

"We've discussed this," he said.

"It's like . . . we said?" she asked.

"It's extensive," Dr. Goodacre said. "The films show a spread
to the liver, the lymph system. I'd like to do some more tests,
send you down for an MRI to check for recurrence in the
brain."

"But what do we do?" Will asked again. This information
was all well and good, they had to know what they were deal-
ing with, but he wanted to get Dr. Goodacre back on track:
They needed a plan.

"Surgery?" Sarah asked.

Dr. Goodacre seemed to pause. Surgeons were always ready
to go in. Will had always thought of them as knife happy, making fortunes as they performed operations that were perhaps
better left to less terrible forms of treatment. His eyes widened
as he saw Dr. Goodacre shaking his head.

"No, Sarah," he said. "The cancer is just too invasive. It's
growing fast, like a vine around the spinal column."

"You're saying no?" Will asked. "She wants you to operate,
and you're telling her no?"

Not replying, Dr. Goodacre just stood there.

Will couldn't believe it. He wanted to leap up, take a big step,
and slam the doctor against the wall. Just shutting down on
Sarah after giving her news like that. He felt his heart pounding,
his palms sweating. Stay calm, he told himself. Messing up Dr.

Goodacre would do no good; it would only upset Sarah. And Will had to stay even for her sake.

Sarah had tears in her eyes, and they were rolling down her cheeks. Will wanted to take her in his arms, but he was paralyzed. Why had she had to cry so much today? Will just wanted to soothe her, to carry her away from this. He might have actually lifted her up, but the hospital was where she would need to be for treatment, to get better.

"How much time?" he heard Sarah ask. The question shocked Will, took his breath away.

The doctor's answer was just as direct. It went straight past Will and excluded him entirely. Will saw the moment in Navy terms. This matter was between Sarah Talbot and her doctor; they had fought a good fight, and the time had come to surrender. Will wanted to scream, to tell them to never give up. But even in his rage and despair, feeling Sarah's hand tremble in his, he could see the amazing light in her eyes and know that she wasn't giving up, it was all a mistake. This was someone else's diagnosis, someone else's tumor spreading.

"Two weeks," Dr. Goodacre said.

"Two weeks," Sarah repeated.

"No," Will heard himself say.

22

THE NIGHT WAS long, and it seemed to never end. Nurses came and went, surprised to find Sarah awake as they went about their jobs. Sarah said hello. They nodded and smiled. Lying in her bed, Sarah watched the night-shift nurses and worried. They all looked so young. Didn't they have husbands and children? What did their kids think when they woke up at home and their mothers weren't there? When their fathers told them their mothers were working, taking care of other people?

Sarah asked for a glass of water. The nurse who brought it to her looked familiar. Perhaps Sarah had seen her there before, during one of her earlier stays. She was small and slight, with curly dark hair and a quick smile. Although she could have filled a plastic cup from the bottle of warm water beside Sarah's bed, she went into the nurses' break room and brought Sarah a tall glass of ice water. The glass had wreaths and Santas on it.

"Thank you," Sarah said.

"You're welcome," the nurse said.

If Sarah was cynical, she might have wondered whether the nurse had heard about her CT scan. Perhaps Dr. Goodacre had said something or marked Sarah's chart to indicate what her tests had shown. Sarah didn't feel that way. She thought nurses were the kindest people in the world.

"Can't you sleep?" the nurse asked.

"No, not really," Sarah said.

"I can give you something for sleep," the nurse said, checking her chart. "Dr. Goodacre has it down."

Sarah shook her head. She was getting Demerol for the pain, and that was making her groggy enough. She wanted to stay as alert as possible. "No, thanks," Sarah said. "Can I ask your name?"

"Oh. It's Louise. Sorry, I couldn't find my name tag when I was getting dressed tonight."

"That's okay," Sarah said. "I just wanted to know."

Louise smiled, waiting for Sarah to say or ask something more. But that was all. Sarah just wanted to know her name. She knew that calling someone by name was one of the most important things people could do, that it made them feel connected to each other, that it made them feel alive.

Louise left the room. Alone, Sarah closed her eyes.

For some reason, she thought of her shop. Cloud Nine. She had loved the name, thought it celestial and full of hope. It had reminded her of her mother, sending her blessings down from heaven. Sarah had designed the logo herself, a gold "9" on a beautiful summer cloud, and she had intended it as an everlasting reminder of where her mother was, how much she had loved her.

Just as Sarah would always love Mike. Michael Ezekiel Loring Talbot. Just thinking his name filled her with so much passion, she squeezed her eyes tight. Less than twenty-four hours ago, Sarah had been certain he was coming home with her.

Less than twenty-four hours ago, Sarah had been sure of many things. The hospital was quiet. Louise walked into the room again. Coming toward Sarah, she paused for a moment to check the IV.

"Louise, do you have children?" Sarah asked.

"Yes, two daughters," Louise said.

"Girls," Sarah said, thinking of Snow. "How old are they?"

"Six and eight."

"Those are such great ages." As soon as she spoke, Sarah knew she would have said it no matter what ages they were. What year of Mike's hadn't been great? Even the recent ones, the ones filled with anger and hostility and running away?

Louise just stood by the window, perhaps picturing her daughters asleep. Who was looking after them? Did she have a husband? Was it the girls' father, the only other person who could possibly love them as much as she did? Or was she trusting them to their grandmother? Did she leave them with babysitters, as Sarah had done with Mike?

"What time is your shift over?" Sarah asked.

"Not till eight."

Sarah said nothing. She thought the girls would probably be on their way to school by the time Louise got there. She thought of Will, living apart from Snow, and she breathed slowly. She and Mike hadn't had it so bad. At least they had spent most of their years together, under the same roof, waking up and eating cereal at the kitchen table. She had walked him to school until he was seven. Tears were rolling down her cheeks when Louise sat on the side of her bed.

"I read your chart," Louise said.

Sarah swallowed, nodding.

"It's hard," Louise said.

The lights were out, but yellow light slanted in from the hall. Sarah felt cold. She pulled the covers around herself. Without being told, Louise reached into the bedside stand and took out an extra blanket. Placing it on Sarah, she sat down again.

"Have you talked to Dr. Boswell?" Louise asked quietly. "Have you discussed your options? They're doing a lot with chemo these days, different protocols getting better results all the time."

Sarah shook her head. She could almost hear the wind in the pines, smell the Elk Island air. She was an island girl from

Maine. Medicine couldn't save her from her own body. Sarah didn't want to be hooked up to machines. She didn't want to be part of any experiments. All of a sudden, she wanted Will and she wanted saltwater.

"All along," Sarah said, "I've thought I would know when the time came."

"Know what?" Louise asked gently.

"How . . . to leave."

"Yes?"

Sarah nodded. The tears ran into the corners of her mouth. It had seemed so much clearer last summer, before she had gotten any hope back. Mike was gone, she had been so sick, and there was no Will yet.

Sarah had discussed her prognosis with Dr. Goodacre and Dr. Boswell. She had known if there was any recurrence of the tumor that she would not seek further treatment. She had pictured her illness as a wave. It might slide out to sea, or it might return to take her. Coming from Elk Island, Sarah knew she could do nothing against the sea.

"How do I leave?" Sarah asked. She was trembling now, sitting with this kind stranger on a hospital floor where everyone else was asleep. Louise held Sarah's hand. Biting her lip, Sarah tasted salt and felt the pain burning through the last pain shot. She thought of Mike, and she thought of Will.

Louise didn't realize that Sarah was asking her a question. She was just a young nurse, overtired and missing her children, trying to comfort a sick woman who had just gotten bad news. She didn't realize that Sarah was aching with a passion, wanting someone to tell her how to do this new thing wisely. How to say good-bye to her son, to the man she had fallen in love with.

SNOW WOKE UP early. Dr. Darrow had slept with her all night, curled into a tight ball right under her chin. When he felt her stretch, he started to purr. His whole body vibrated, and he wiggled closer to her, nudging her skin with his cold nose. Laughing, Snow kissed his face.

Just lying there, warm under her down quilt, Snow could almost pretend she was back on Elk Island. She could practically hear the waves, feel the cold air whistling through chinks in the walls. She had felt so happy, part of Sarah's family for Thanksgiving. The air may have been chilly, but the house was warm with fireplaces, cats, tradition, and especially people.

No wonder Sarah was so wonderful, coming from such a place. Snuggling deeper under her covers with Dr. Darrow, Snow wondered how Sarah was. Was she still in the hospital? She had expected her father to call last night, tell her what was going on, but the phone never rang.

Although it was still dark outside, the alarm rang. Snow reached over to shut it off. Zero six-thirty, time to get up for school. How would Mike make it through life without school? Snow hoped he'd think about it, decide to come to Fort Cromwell on his own and resume his education once everyone got off his back and let him make his own decisions. Not that Snow blamed Sarah. Sarah was just a good mother, wanting the best for her son.

Climbing out of bed, Snow watched Dr. Darrow scamper to the window. He pressed his nose against the glass. Startled by the cold, he jumped back. Then he caught sight of some juncos at the bird feeder and began stalking them. Again, the glass got in his way. Laughing out loud, Snow picked him up. She wished she could stay home and watch him for hours. He was her kitten, hers and Mike's, and he reminded her of the island.

Dr. Darrow would make life bearable with her mother and Julian. He would be her private ally in this madhouse of money and nutso love. If Snow had to watch her mother glance at Julian one more time, attempting to determine what he was thinking, whether he was pleased or upset, Snow would go insane. She would need the real Dr. Darrow again.

Dressing for school, Snow decided she would miss the bus and ride her bike. On her way home she'd cruise by Sarah's shop to see if she was there yet. Besides, bike riding was the best way she'd found to clear her head. She wanted to think about her trip to Elk Island and what it meant. It was time to change her name again, and she got some of her best inspirations while pedaling home from school.

———

WILL HADN'T SLEPT. All he could think of was Sarah. She was alone at the hospital. After Dr. Goodacre had given her the news, Will had wanted to stay with her. He had sat on the edge of her bed for a long time, until the end of visiting hours. They hadn't said much. The news was too big to process. Every time Will thought of a question to ask, it seemed unreal.

They had watched the six o'clock news. It had shown the landing. The plane circling, close-ups of the broken nose gear, their faces through the plane windows, the actual fiery crash. Watching it on TV, Will could see how dramatic it had really been. They had been in serious danger; if anything had gone fractionally different, they all might have been killed. Mesmerized, he had stared at the screen. Holding his hand, Sarah had murmured things about how great he was, what a hero he was.

Will had shaken his head. What was a crash landing compared to what Sarah was facing now? He stared at the TV, feeling as if the events had happened to someone else. Seeing himself onscreen, carrying Sarah out of the burning plane, he squeezed her hand so hard, she exclaimed. If only it were that simple, he thought, watching the news. If only that was all it took to save Sarah.

When the nurse came in to administer more Demerol, she had seemed surprised to find Will still there. For one moment she had hesitated, deciding whether to kick him out or let him stay. Haven't you seen Sarah's chart? Will had wanted to ask. We don't have enough time for me to leave. But the rules won. The nurse told him to go, and Sarah didn't try to stop him.

Just after dawn, Will got up. He could think only of Sarah, getting to the hospital, changing her mind. Two weeks wasn't enough time. He needed much more time with her. They could have their forties, fifties, sixties, seventies together. Looking at George and Bess, their eighties. Five decades together if she could get healthy.

Drying himself off, he checked his watch. Nearly six-thirty. He made coffee and drank it at his kitchen table. The kitchen was small, impersonal. Moving into this apartment, he hadn't cared much about fixing it up. He kept everything clean, like the galley on the *James*. Snow's school picture smiled at him from the refrigerator door. She had painted his portrait in Saturday art class, and it hung on the wall.

Having something of Sarah here would make this place beautiful, he thought. Looking around the small kitchen, he tried to imagine Sarah's touch. He had never been to her home, but he had seen her shop, he had been to Elk Island. She had a style unlike any woman he had ever met, her love for nature and life so apparent. He pictured them decorating the place for Christmas, something he hadn't done for several years. He imagined doing it together, collecting ornaments here and there. Cutting pine boughs on drives to the country, putting up a tree, just living their lives together.

That's all: Will wanted to live life with Sarah. She hadn't done miracles, brought Fred back to life, reunited Will with estranged family members. She didn't wear a halo, she didn't make Will a better person. She just *was*. Sarah had come into Will's life, and now they were supposed to be together. He couldn't let her go. No matter what, he couldn't let her go.

Checking his watch again, he saw it was inching toward seven. Four more hours till he could visit Sarah. Had news about the plane crash reached Elk Island? Needing a connection with Sarah, he called her family.

"Mike?" Will said when he answered.

"Yeah," Mike said. "Is this Will?"

"It is."

Mike cleared his throat. He said Will's name again, and Will knew he was talking to George or Bess, telling them who was on the line. Will had no idea what he was going to say. He just wanted to be involved in Sarah's life, and it was too early to go to the hospital.

He pictured Elk Island, serene under its cloak of snow. He could see dawn breaking over the cold steel ocean, hear the geese beginning to rustle, picture the eagle on its hunt. Gripping the receiver, he imagined Mike at the other end, standing in the warm kitchen with his grandfather and great-aunt.

"You guys get home okay?" Mike asked.

"We did," Will said, realizing he hadn't heard. "Had a little trouble, but we landed fine."

"A little trouble?"

"Yeah. The landing gear got stuck, and we had a rough time of it. But we made it out safely."

"Did you crash?" Mike asked. *"Crash?"* George asked in the background.

"We came down hard," Will said, not wanting to alarm them more than they needed to be. Why had he called in the first place? His throat closed up. He had things to say that weren't his right. If Sarah wanted to tell her son and father about her condition, about the recurrence, let her call.

"But my mother and Snow are okay?"

"Snow's fine."

"My mother?"

Will hesitated. "She's in the hospital," he said.

"What for?" Mike asked.

Will paused. He couldn't tell Mike the truth. But he couldn't lie either. "Her back," he said.

"She hurt it in the crash?"

"No."

A scuffle occurred. Will heard the phone being jostled, voices talking, a sharp exclamation. "Give me that phone!" he heard George say.

"What the hell's going on?" George asked.

"Hi, George," Will said.

"What's wrong with her back?"

"She's in pain, George."

"It's the cancer," George said bluntly.

The seconds ticked by. It was up to Sarah to tell her father. She would want to inform her son, break it to him in her own gentle way. Will held the receiver and felt his eyes sting.

"Yeah, George. It is," he said.

"Shit," George Talbot said.

"The cancer?" Mike asked. He must have picked up the extension in the upstairs hall.

"I'm sorry," Will said.

The three men who loved Sarah most were silent, letting the news rush over them. Someone exhaled long and low. Will almost expected George to explode in anger, say she'd been keeping it from them all along, rant in his fear and fury. But he didn't. He just let out a long, thoughtful "Hmmm."

"Are they sure?" Mike asked. "The doctors?"

"Yes," Will said. "They're sure."

More silence. When was one of them going to ask "how much time?" Will was ready, prepared to tell them the terrible, unimaginable news. As he stood by his kitchen window, staring at the gray backyard, he felt his heart pounding in his chest.

"I want to go there," Mike said. "Grandpa, we should take the ferry today and drive back to Fort Cromwell."

"Good idea, boy," George said. "But I've got a better one. Will, you got another plane? How about flying back here to pick us up? We'll get there a lot faster, and you can fill us in on what the doctor's saying."

"No," Will said.

"No?" George asked, his ire flooding through the wires.

"Will," Mike said, his voice thick. "I'm sorry if I was a jerk to you. But we're heading back. Either you fly us or we drive, but we're coming."

"I was thinking something else," Will said.

"Well, forget it," George spit out.

"I want to bring her back to the island," he said. The pictures were filling his mind. The peace, the beauty, the love of her family, the nearness of her mother. He saw the chapel, so blessed and remote, at the easternmost edge of her island far at sea. The chapel, whose aisle she had never walked down.

"Is that wise?" George asked. "She needs the hospital, doesn't she? All the doctors and modern treatments."

"She needs Dr. Goodacre," Mike said. "And Mrs. Ferguson."

"She needs you, Mike. You and George. I'm bringing her home."

George exhaled again. Mike cleared his throat. Will was looking at his watch. If he left now, he could be at the airport in thirty minutes. His big Cessna could do the job, but he had to give it a fast service. It would take him the rest of the morning. He could be at the hospital by noon, just about the time visiting hours began.

"Goddammit," George said.

"Don't fight me on this," Will said. "I'm—"

"Grandpa, he's trying to help," Mike said, coming to Will's defense.

"It's not him I'm fighting," George said, all the anger gone from his voice, fathoms of bottomless grief there instead. "It's not you, Will. I'm asking God. Why Sarah? Why Rose and now my Sarah? Can you tell me that?"

"I can't, sir," Will said.

The next hour was spent making arrangements. Will looked through his book, canceled half his charters. He called Steve

Jenkins, a retired airline pilot who sometimes worked for him, and asked him to fill in. Steve was sharp, an excellent pilot, and as reliable as they came. The minute Steve said yes, Will left the office. He had given himself a mission, and all he could think about was flying Sarah home.

CHAPTER

23

GOING TO SCHOOL that morning, Snow hadn't realized it was a half day. The teachers had conferences on statewide reading scores, so classes were dismissed just before lunch. Riding her bike down the school hill, Snow wondered why they had even bothered having school at all that day. If they hadn't, she could have spent extra time on Elk Island. Timing was weird.

Snow prided herself on asking the big questions. Pedaling madly through town, she let herself wonder about the possibilities. All the stores had their Christmas decorations up. Wreaths and garlands were everywhere, white lights twinkling like an urban galaxy. It hadn't snowed in a few days, so the old snow was gray and disgusting with sand and car exhaust. Nothing like Elk Island.

Parking in front of Cloud Nine, she stared at the dark window. No lights, no garlands. Snow was surprised; she had thought Sarah would decorate right away. Was Sarah still in the hospital? A white paper had been taped to the inside of the window. Stepping closer, Snow read the note:

Cloud Nine will be closed until the Monday after
   Thanksgiving.
Until then, stay warm, and sweet dreams!

Snow frowned. Sarah had written that note before they'd left for Elk Island, which meant she *was* still in the hospital. Was her back that bad? Snow had a few twinges and bruises from the plane crash, but nothing serious. Suddenly she had an awful thought: What if Sarah's illness had come back? Jumping onto her bike, she rode home as fast as she could.

Zooming up Windemere Hill, she prayed everything would be okay. Fearing for Sarah, she wanted her mother. She hoped Julian was working, testing cars at the track or something. Snow wanted to find her mother, tell her about Sarah not being at work, get her to call the hospital for her. She wished her father still lived with them, that he would be home waiting for her.

Thinking of Sarah, all Snow's insecurities crashed in, filling her with such dread that by the time she reached the top of the hill, she collapsed against the front door. She found her inhaler and used it.

"You're home early," her mother said, walking to the front door.

"Hi...Mom..." Snow said, wheezing. "Teachers'...conferences..."

Her mother stood there, arms folded across her chest, a very I-told-you-so look on her face.

"What?" Snow asked.

"Nothing," her mother said, her lips tight. But then she made herself smile. Drawing Snow into a hug, she kissed both her cheeks. "Teachers' conferences, that's right. We forgot to check the calendar this morning."

Snow nodded, trying to get a good breath. She wanted to tell her mother everything, about why she was so scared. Sensing that her mother didn't like Sarah, she didn't want to come on too strong. She exhaled and spoke.

"Mom," she said. "You know Sarah Talbot?"

"The woman you spent Thanksgiving with?" her mother asked with a mean tone to her voice. "Yes, I know who she is."

"I'm kind of worried about her. She was supposed to be at her store, but she isn't. Do you think she's still in the hospital?"

"You stopped by her store on your way home?" her mother asked, frowning and totally missing the point. "Did you ask permission? Susan, when are you going to learn you have to let me know where you are? My God! If you'd had an accident, or if someone snatched you—"

"No one did, Mom," Snow said quietly. Already she knew she had made a mistake. She should have called the hospital herself, not asked her mother. She stepped away. It was a weird feeling, needing her mother and wanting to escape from her at the same time.

"You're grounded, Susan," her mother said calmly. "I was going to wait for Julian to come home to tell you, but now seems like the time."

"Grounded?"

"Do you have any idea how much you worried me?" her mother asked, her face getting all red. "When you didn't come home last Wednesday? And then to get a phone call from New Hampshire, on your way to an island with a family I've never even *met*?"

"You know Dad," Snow said.

Her mother shook her head. "Don't be fresh. Go to your room and think about this. I want you to really understand what's going on here. I'm not grounding you for the fun of it. I love you more than anything, Susan. And Julian . . ."

"Don't even say it," Snow said, backing away. She had never been grounded before. She knew she had misbehaved, she hated that she'd made her mother worry, but she wouldn't be able to stand it if she heard her mother say anything like "Julian cares about you" or, worse, "Julian loves you too."

"I will say it. Julian is your stepfather. He is my husband. You might not like him, but he cares about you."

"Aargh!" Snow wailed, putting her hands over her ears.

"He does! Do you know how hard it's been for us? Trying to make you happy, trying to make us into a family?"

"We are a family," Snow said. "Already. Julian's just not part of it."

"He's my husband now. Your stepfather, honey. He has no children of his own, Susan. He might not be perfect, but he tries so hard with you. Do you know what he said about that stupid cat? 'Let her keep it,' he said. I was fit to be tied that your father and *Sarah* whoever-she-is would let you have a cat, considering your allergies."

"Dr. Darrow?" Snow asked, her nerves tingling.

"Naming him after your doctor," her mother said, her eyes filling with tears. "When all we ever wanted was for you to get some *help* . . ."

"Where is he?" Snow asked, her heart pounding.

"I took him to the pound," her mother said, starting to cry. "You're allergic to him, honey. You can't have a cat, you know you can't. . . ."

"The pound?" Snow cried, the words tearing out of her chest. "He's my kitten, and he needs me!"

"They promised they'd find him a good home," her mother called, but Snow didn't wait to hear the rest. Flying upstairs, she ran into her room.

———

SARAH WAS WAITING. After such a short time, she had grown used to counting on Will. He didn't have to come, but she knew he would. When he came through the door, she lay with her head on the pillow and smiled. Just seeing him made her feel content, and she sighed.

"Hello," he said, coming right over to sit beside her.

"Hi, Will," she said.

"How are you today?"

"I'm about the same."

"Is the pain as bad?"

"No," she said. They were giving her medication, so the bursts weren't so sharp. But the pain was there. It was like having a toothache in her whole body. Now that Will was there, she could think. How strange that he would become as important to her as air or sunshine. Before he had come into her life, she had functioned just fine alone. But suddenly she needed him, just to be clear.

"Have you seen the doctor?" he asked.

"Yes. He was here this morning. I had my MRI, and I guess he'll be back later. I missed you."

"God, I missed you," Will said. As if he'd been waiting for her to go first, he dove on her in a massive hug. Closing her eyes, Sarah felt his strength in her skin, her bones. She didn't want him to let go.

"Don't stop," Sarah whispered when he showed signs of loosening her arms.

"Have you called Mike?" he asked.

"Shhh," Sarah said, closing her eyes tighter and hugging harder. She didn't want this to end. She didn't want the reality of plans and notification to start seeping in.

"Because I did," Will said.

Sarah's eyes sprang open. "You did?"

"Yes," Will said.

"You didn't . . . tell him?" she asked.

"I did."

"Will!" Sarah struggled to sit up. "You didn't. Tell me you're kidding."

"Why would I kid, Sarah? I—"

"You don't just tell Mike something like this, that the cancer's back. He's angry and so sensitive and he's scared, Will . . . I don't want to drive him further away when I've just started to get him back." Anger filled her chest, and she couldn't speak anymore.

"He wanted to come," Will said.

"What do you mean?" Sarah asked, her hands shaking uncontrollably.

"When I told him, he wanted to come here, to see you."

"He did?"

"Yes."

"Come to Fort Cromwell?" Sarah asked, her eyes filling with
tears. It was all she could imagine wanting. "Mike?"

"And your father."

"Oh, Will," Sarah said, burying her face in her hands. She
could hardly imagine it: Mike returning home and *anything* getting her father off the island. The image of her father on the
mainland, a bewildered expression on his old face, miles and
miles from the only place he had ever known, filled her with
such love, her body shook with silent sobs. She felt Will's arms
around her.

"If you want them to come here, Sarah," Will said quietly,
"I'll go get them. But I was thinking about something else."

"What?" she asked.

"I know you're in pain, I know it would be a lot to ask you
to sit there for the time it would take, but if you'd like, Sarah, I'd
like to take you home."

"Really?"

"Yes, Sarah. Really."

Sarah raised her head. She was picturing a blue sky, the endless sea, an eagle flying in wide circles, dark pines growing down
to the edge of the bay. She held his hand. It sounded so right,
more right than anything she had heard in a long time.

"Take me home, Will," she said.

———

AN HOUR LATER, Dr. Boswell gave her okay. She upped the
dosage of Sarah's pain medication for the trip, switching from
Demerol to morphine because the pain was so bad and could
get worse. Will was a guy with a mission. He took directions

from the doctor. He had called Meg Ferguson, and she was there, giving him various instructions as the hospital nurses got Sarah ready for the flight.

"Don't worry that you're giving her too much medication," Meg said, crying. "If she asks for it, give it."

"Okay."

"When you get to the island, do you have a nurse?"

"Sarah's aunt is on that now. She called a hospice in Maine, and they're setting everything up with a visiting nurse."

"Good. Hospice, Will. Hospice for Sarah. You know what that means, don't you?"

"I do know, Meg," Will replied patiently. Meg sounded bossy and kind of harsh, but she was blowing her nose, wiping her eyes.

"I wish I could be her nurse," Meg said. "I'd like to fly up with you, but I can't leave Mimi. . . ."

"Sarah understands."

"Shit, I thought she was going to be okay."

"So did she."

"I'd like to wring Mike's neck," Meg said. "You weren't around during the chemo and radiation, but he's all she ever talked about. And now she has to go chasing off to Elk Island, Maine, just to see her son one last time."

"That's not why she's going," Will said.

But Meg didn't want to understand. She was furious at the universe, at something bigger than herself, and she didn't want to be talked out of resenting Sarah Talbot's teenage son. Meg Ferguson was a visiting nurse, but she was also Sarah's friend.

"I've been carrying this around with me for a month," Meg said, reaching into her bag and pulling out a picture. "I've been meaning to give it to Sarah." She handed it to Will. It showed Will and Sarah standing together at the fair, between the hot dog stand and the Gypsy eternal flame. They were embracing like long-lost lovers, and the expression in Will's eyes amazed him. He had looked madly in love even then.

"Mimi took it," Meg said.

Will stared at the picture of himself and a woman he had just met. They might have gone their separate ways that day, never to meet again. Instead, they were connected forever.

"Can I keep it?" he asked.

"Sure," Meg said.

Will thanked her, sliding the picture into his breast pocket.

"What else do I need to know?" Will asked. They were standing in the hospital corridor, and he had his eyes on Sarah's door, waiting for the nurse to come out and say she was ready to go.

"That it isn't going to be easy," Meg said.

"I'm losing Sarah," Will said, the harshness in his voice suddenly matching Meg's. "I don't want it to be easy."

Meg touched his forearm. The door to Sarah's room had opened, and a nurse was pushing Sarah in a wheelchair. Will tried to smile so she wouldn't be scared. She looked so tired, and he couldn't imagine getting her all the way from here to Elk Island. Watching Meg crouch down, to say good-bye, he took a moment to pull himself together.

"Mimi wants me to tell you to have a good trip," Meg said.

"Tell her thank you," Sarah said. "She hooked me up with a good pilot."

Meg grinned up at Will, nodding.

"He's not bad," she said.

Will made a sound, wanting to say something funny, self-deprecating. But the picture in his pocket was burning over his heart, and all he could think of was the look in his own eyes.

"My friend," Sarah said, taking Meg's hand.

"Mine," Meg said, clasping Sarah's.

"You've been with me through so much," Sarah said.

"I have a lot of patients," Meg said. "But not many that have become friends like you."

"Your patients are lucky," Sarah said.

Meg shook her head, bowed it to wipe her tears. Meg's

stethoscope dangled from the pocket of her white lab coat. Her canvas bag was full of patient records. But just then she was just a woman who had come to the hospital to say a good-bye. Her training didn't make her any more able to handle what was happening.

Sobbing hard, she rested her forehead on Sarah's shoulder.

The part that killed Will was, Sarah was holding herself together. They were two women about the same age, both mothers, one of them going through something everyone feared. Sarah had leaned on Meg through all the months of treatment, and now she was being strong for the nurse who had let herself get attached.

———

ON THEIR WAY to the airport, Sarah looked at Will. "I want to say good-bye to Snow," she said.

They were at a stoplight. Will took her hands. The drugs were taking hold, and her arms felt leaden. Getting through the meeting with Meg had been hard, but she couldn't avoid the people she loved. She wouldn't. Her eyelids were heavy, and her mouth felt dry as cotton. Will was staring at her, and his eyes were pools of blue. Sarah had to struggle to focus.

"She'd want to come with us," he said.

"I know."

"Her mother would never let her."

"She doesn't have to come," Sarah said. "We can tell her she can't this time. But I have to say good-bye."

"Sarah," Will said, looking so worried. "The flight's going to be hard enough. It's going to upset you, seeing her. It's going to upset *her*."

"Please, Will," Sarah said. She didn't have the strength to argue. "She didn't get to say good-bye to Fred. Think of how she'd feel."

Will was silent, but he nodded. His hands were tight on the wheel as he turned to look at Sarah. "You're right," he said.

———

SNOW HAD CALLED the hospital. They told her Sarah had checked out, but she wasn't at her store and she wasn't home. She tried calling her father to ask him, but his answering machine was on at work and his phone just rang and rang in his empty apartment. Sitting on the edge of her bed, Snow filled with possessive panic. What if they were off somewhere together, forgetting all about her, just when she needed them most?

Dr. Darrow was at the pound. How could her father and Sarah be getting romantic together when her kitten was in mortal danger? Just picturing the pound brought tears to her eyes. She imagined a horrible concrete building filled with howling, abandoned animals. Just like an orphanage in England, one of the cruel ones with no heat and mean workers.

Would Dr. Darrow think she had abandoned him? She had loved imagining his joy, to go from being one of the extra cats to being Snow's beloved pet, and now he was shivering and alone, probably being attacked by bigger cats and possibly even dogs at the pound, thinking she didn't care anymore. Snow had to get him back. She *had* to.

"Susan," her mother called.

Snow's door was closed. She clenched up, hugging her pillow for comfort. Julian had come home early, and he and her mother had been sitting downstairs, waiting for her to come out. They'd have a long wait, Snow thought. Her mother's footsteps sounded harsh on the hall floors, as if they belonged to some warden in an uncaring institution.

"Susan," her mother said again, sounding slightly urgent and even somewhat caring. Snow pictured her standing just outside. She could practically see the worry lines in her mother's brow, the little frown she got when someone she loved was in trouble and not doing things her way, and Snow felt herself wanting to see her again.

"The name is Snow."

"Yes. Well...honey. Your father is downstairs. You'd better hurry."

Gasping with surprise, Snow tripped as she jumped off her bed. She stubbed her toe and didn't even care. What could this be? Her father never came to this house unless it was to pick her up or drop her off. Had he magically heard about the crisis, brought Dr. Darrow back to her? Running past her mother, not even stopping when her mother said wait, she wanted to tell her something, Snow flew down the great marble stairs, sweeping and circular like those in a mansion in a movie. Julian stood at the bottom, pointing at the library door.

"Dad!" Snow yelled, tearing into the library. "They took Dr. Darrow to the pound!"

"Honey," her father said, stopping her short. He put his hands on her shoulders and looked her deep in the eyes. Snow had only seen that look one time before. She drew a shocked breath.

"What, Dad?" Only then did Snow see Sarah. She was sitting on the burgundy velvet love seat off to the side, under the portrait of Julian's grandfather. Slowly, Snow walked across the room to stand in front of her. "Hi, Sarah," she said.

"Hi, Snow."

"We meet again!" Snow said, beaming. Julian and her mother were standing there, looking pained. Her father's face was grave, but Sarah was smiling in that beautiful, warm way of hers that made you forget other people's bad moods.

"We do," Sarah said.

"Did you hear about Dr. Darrow?" Snow asked, lowering her voice. "My mother thinks I'm allergic to him, but I'm not. I'm going to get him back."

"Susan, you have terrible allergies," Julian said with a very master-of-the-house tone to his voice. "I think we all know that."

"She didn't test positive for cats," her father said. "She knows I wouldn't have let her bring home a cat if she did."

"I'm getting him back," Snow said straight to Sarah as if the men hadn't spoken. She wanted to reassure Sarah that the Elk Island kitten would be properly loved despite the rocky homecoming. It suddenly struck Snow as extraordinary that all the important adults in her life had gathered in this room.

Smiling, Snow really caught Sarah's eye. Sarah smiled too, and Snow started to laugh. "Is this weird?" she asked.

Sarah shook her head. "I don't think so."

"Why not?" Snow asked.

"We're here because of you," Sarah said. When she put it like that, it made sense. Why shouldn't they all come together, considering they all had one thing in common: her! Snow was on the verge of cracking up some more, but then she realized she was on the edge of hysteria. Something awful was happening.

"This isn't about Dr. Darrow, is it?" she asked, sitting beside Sarah.

Sarah shook her head. For the first time, Snow noticed how pale she was. Her skin was almost pure white, glistening like a candle just below the flame. Her eyes were dull, which for Sarah seemed bizarre. She was trying hard to stay focused. Snow watched her stare and stare, not wanting to take her eyes off Snow's. As serious as it was, Sarah didn't stop smiling.

"What is it, then?" Snow asked.

"I've come to say good-bye," Sarah said.

"Where are you going?"

"Back to the island," she said.

"Alone?"

It took so long for Sarah to answer, Snow's father took a step forward to help her. "With me," he said.

"What?" Snow asked, looking around the room. "Can I go? I have to! If you're going, Dad, so am I. Tell him I can, Mom. . . ."

Sarah put her hand on Snow's wrist. Snow sensed her mother leaning toward them, but she didn't say anything. "No, Snow," Sarah said. "You can't come."

"What do you mean? Why are you going?"

"Susan..." her mother began, her voice thin. Julian put his arm around her.

"I'm sick again," Sarah said.

"No..." Snow said, clapping her hands over her mouth. Sarah couldn't be sick. She was too healthy! They had just gone cross-country skiing! Watching Mike fall into the pond, they had prayed for him to be safe, and he was. Sarah had had rosy cheeks, she had carried firewood, she had eaten big meals and asked for more.

"I want to be with Mike, and your father is going to fly me."

"This isn't fair," Snow said.

Sarah was the only one who knew what she meant. All the other adults took steps forward, into the center of the room. They were talking, saying she had to stay in Fort Cromwell and go to school, be at home, be with her mother. Snow heard every word, but she blocked them out. She wasn't talking about going to the island. She meant it wasn't fair that Sarah was sick.

Sarah reached out her hand. Her hair looked so great. Staring at it, Snow could hardly believe how awful it had looked just two weeks before. All yellow-gray, and now it was a cap of cool, iridescent white-gold.

"Your hair looks pretty," Snow said, lacing fingers with Sarah.

"Thanks to you," Sarah said.

Snow nodded. Lowering her head, she tasted the tears flowing into her mouth. Sarah's hand felt small and alive. Her life was everywhere: in her hands, in the room. Sarah had a force of energy about her. Snow could feel it now, actually felt it quivering and moving the air around her.

"Will I see you again?" Snow asked so quietly only Sarah could hear her even though the others were standing right there.

"I don't think so," Sarah said.

Snow nodded. With her eyes closed, she savored Sarah's presence. She's right here, Snow thought. Soon she'll go, but for now she's *right here*. Snow had never had that with Fred. She had never known that moment of transition, when he passed from her sight, from her presence, from her life. Holding tighter, she clutched Sarah's hand.

"I have some things of my brother's," Snow said.

"His socks, for example," Sarah said.

Nodding, Snow pulled up her pants leg to reveal the maroon alligators.

"Names have been important," Snow said, keeping her voice steady, informative. Her mother groaned, but Julian held her back. Snow heard the honest pain in her mother's voice, but she kept talking anyway. "The names have to remind me of him. He loved snow."

"I know."

"I've been wondering what to call myself next. It has to begin with 'S' because that gives me serenity. I've been considering ideas that make me think of Christmas, that would bring Freddie a little closer for Christmas."

"You'll think of something," Sarah said.

"I have," Snow said. Raising her head, she looked into Sarah's eyes. "Sarah."

"Oh, Susan . . ." her mother said, the sob shaking her whole body.

"I know you never knew Fred," Snow said, gripping Sarah's hands. Now that she was talking about this, she knew that soon she would have to let go and that made her hold on harder. "But it seems like you do. You talk about him with me. Whenever I want, and you seem to want to know him better. When we saw that whale, when I said he had angel wings, you knew I was thinking of Fred. Didn't you?"

"I did," Sarah said. She was holding on just as tight.

"You would have loved Fred," Snow said.

"I believe I would have."

"Don't be sick, Sarah." The words just came out. There was nothing Snow could do to take them back. She knew they were stupid to say, that it could only hurt Sarah because she would be well if she could, and they made Snow start to cry. She leaned right into Sarah and held on tight.

"I loved that whale," Sarah whispered, stroking Snow's head.

"You're going to see him again . . . when you get to the island." Snow sobbed.

"I will," Sarah said.

Snow cried for a few minutes. She felt her father's hand on her hair, heard him whisper something. Knowing it was time for them to leave, him and Sarah, made Snow cry harder. That brought on an asthma attack. She had to use her inhaler.

"I want to be called Sarah," Snow said. "It's your name, but it's about Fred too. You're connected because of the whale."

"Thank you," Sarah said.

Snow nodded, miserable. She clutched Sarah's hands. How terrible it was that in a few minutes all she'd have left of Sarah would be her name. Wearing someone's socks, taking talismanic names, were such poor substitutes for the real person. This was hurting her mother's feelings. Snow could tell by her mother's occasional sniffles, by the way Julian said "We'll deal with this later" in a big stage whisper.

"I'm honored," Sarah said. "But how would it be if, instead, you took another name?"

"Like what?"

"Like Susan," Sarah said.

"Susan?"

Sarah nodded.

Snow just stared.

"It's a beautiful name," Sarah said.

Snow waited, her mouth slightly open.

"It's the name your parents gave you," Sarah said.

"But it's not *enough*," Snow said. "It's just my name. It doesn't mean anything, remind me of anyone."

"Fred knew you as Susan," Sarah said gently, still holding her hands. "Not Snow, and not Sarah."

"But I miss him," Snow said, her face twisting. "And, Sarah, I'm going to miss you!"

"Oh, I know," Sarah said, smiling. "That's why I wanted to see you. Because I'm going to miss you too."

"But there aren't any new Sarahs."

"Maybe Mike will name a daughter Sarah. Maybe he won't..." Sarah said, smiling as if it didn't matter.

Bowing her head, Snow bit her lip. Sarah's eyes were sparkling again, more than when she'd first arrived, and Snow wanted it to last forever. But when she picked up her head, the clouds were back. Just a few, off in the distance, at the back of her bright blue eyes. Sarah held her gaze; she wouldn't look away until Snow did first.

"We have to go," her father said. He had one hand on Sarah's shoulder. Reaching out his other hand, he waited for Snow to take it. Snow's mother stepped forward. She put her hand out too. To take her parents' hands, Snow would have to let go of Sarah.

"Honey?" her mother said. She was just standing there, an expression of expectant worry on her face. She didn't have jealousy in her eyes for Sarah being there. She didn't have anger at Will for their situation. She didn't even have insecurity about Julian. She had only love, pure and simple, for her only daughter.

"Dad, you'll have a safe flight, won't you?" Snow asked, still looking at Sarah.

"Absolutely," her father said.

"Really safe," she said just to be sure. This was the moment to ask again, to beg her parents for permission to go, but something held her back. A feeling of peace settled over her shoulders, like a soft shawl of Aunt Bess's, and a shiver ran down her back. Sarah's hands were warm, holding tight. Staring into her eyes, Snow could see Elk Island: the dark bay, the northern lights, Mike.

"Your father says it's time to go," her mother said, still wait-ing. "Honey?"

Sarah nodded. Snow nodded back, then turned toward her mother. The sight of her mother filled her heart with love and gratitude, as if she had never really understood how lucky she was. Her father had his hand out, palm up. The big clock in the hall chimed: fourteen hundred hours.

"Honey?" her mother said again.

"The name's Susan," Susan said softly, giving Sarah one last hug, possibly the biggest and best one she had ever given, be-fore letting go of Sarah's two small hands and allowing her par-ents to pull her to her feet.

She stood there, her eyes closed, gently weaving. Sarah was going to leave. When she opened her eyes, it would be the last time she ever saw Sarah, *ever*.

"Thank you," she heard her mother say to Sarah.

"You have a wonderful daughter," Sarah said back.

Susan just stood there, rocking on shaky legs as she held her parents' hands, afraid of what she'd see because soon it would be gone.

"I love you," Susan said, not directing her words to anyone in particular. In a way it didn't matter who heard. Her eyes sprang open, and they were all still there.

CHAPTER

24

HOME.

The word held Sarah together, kept her focus, filled her mind all the way from Fort Cromwell to Elk Island. The plane engines hummed like low voices, like the rhythm of the MRI, saying the same thing over and over: "Home, home."

The drugs made her groggy. Meg had pumped her full of morphine. The hospital nurses had installed a Port-A-Cath in her arm, a little portable IV that hid under her sleeve, and Meg had taken a big needle full of drugs and stuck it in. As the pain recurred, Will did the same thing. The morphine took all her fear away.

The medication was killing the pain, making it possible for Sarah to fly across New York, Vermont, New Hampshire, re-fuel in Portsmouth, take off over Maine, fly down east to Elk Island.

Home, Sarah thought. Home, home.

"Yes, we're going home," Will said.

Had she spoken out loud?

"Are we almost there?" she asked, hearing her own voice. There was her hand on her knee, her other hand on the cold window. She could feel the cold on her fingertips, but she had no pain in her back or anywhere else.

"Yes, Sarah," Will said. His voice was low, as deep and resonant as the plane engines. She loved him so much. His voice blended with the motor noise in a way that reminded her of dreams, of strange movies from the sixties. Sarah was taking drugs, that's why. She was high as a kite, and she couldn't tell real from imaginary.

"This has to stop," she said.

"What?" he asked. She knew she had alarmed him by the quick way he turned his head. Sarah herself couldn't feel anything. She was wrapped in cotton, surrounded by fog. Her tongue was thick, her eyelids heavy. The sea had come into sight, but she was too numb to care. Turning her head took effort.

"No more drugs," she said.

"Sarah, the pain will be too bad," he said.

"I want to be alert," she said.

Will didn't nod. He didn't agree or disagree. He just flew the plane. Deciding to stop the medication made Sarah start to wake up. The pain lurked in her lower back, a heavy pull reminding her it was there. As the minutes went by without a shot, the pain grew sharper. But so did Sarah's senses.

By the time they flew over Elk Island, saw the snowy islands in the dark bay, Sarah was beginning to fill with excitement. She reached for Will's hand. Part of her wished Susan were with them, that she had stowed away like last time, that the minute they landed she would pop out from behind the last seat in the plane.

But mostly she was glad she and Will were alone.

Approaching the island, the plane cut white circles in the deep blue sky. Peering out the window, Sarah looked at the northern cliffs, the southern bay. She saw the little chapel off to the east, and she looked for the eagle. Maybe Mike would be waiting for them at the landing strip.

"We're here," she whispered, her eyes brimming with fierce joy.

Will squeezed her hand.

THEY HAD A welcoming crew there for her. Will landed the plane as softly as he could, mindful of the fact that Sarah's medication had to be wearing off fast. George and Bess were there, as grim-faced as the couple in *American Gothic*. Mike stood still, hatless and trying to smile. A stolid nurse stood beside him, a navy blue jacket over her white dress, hands gripping the handles of a wheelchair.

Helping Sarah out of the plane, Will felt her arms around his neck and felt her breath on his cheek. It was strange, he was so attracted to her, she was the woman he loved and he wanted to take her somewhere and make love, plan trips and their lives together. He had the passing thought that they should move away from Fort Cromwell, somewhere closer to the sea. The thought lingered. Lowering her into the wheelchair, he kissed her hair.

"Sarah," George said, his voice all gravelly and his face looking a hundred years old.

"Hi, Dad," she said. "Aunt Bess, hi."

"Sarah, darling," Aunt Bess said, leaning down, the only one unafraid to touch her. When she straightened up again, Sarah smiled up at Mike.

"Well, there," she said.

"Hi, Mom," Mike said. He hung back, frowning and shy. Will wanted to shake him. He kept his hands locked on the wheelchair handles. Sarah opened her arms. Reluctantly Mike bent over. But midway through, his hug turned real, and Will could see he didn't want to let go.

"How's she doing on meds?" the nurse asked Will. He glanced down. She was about fifty, short and stout, with a cap of salt-and-pepper hair. Her face was lined and gentle, her voice kind.

"She doesn't want to take any," he said. He felt the tension in his chest. Until landing, he had had sole responsibility for Sarah. Her decision to stop the morphine had scared him, but now he was able to share the burden with an expert. Let the nurse convince Sarah to take her medication.

"I'm Martha," the woman said, crouching down beside Sarah. "I'm a registered nurse, and if there's anything you need, anything at all, I want you to let me know."

Sarah stared at her as if she were trying to remember something.

"Do I know you?" she asked. "Are you from the island? You look familiar."

"I'm from Camden," Martha said. "But I travel around Maine quite a bit. Our paths might have crossed before. I'm a visiting nurse."

"Oh, the visiting nurse," Sarah said with trust in her eyes. She had to be thinking of Meg, Will thought. She gazed at the woman for another few seconds. Then, closing her eyes, she breathed deeply of the cold salt air. She seemed tired, worn out by her trip. Will knew the pain had to be terrible, and he wondered how she was able to seem so calm.

"Are you ready for some medication?" Martha asked.

"I don't want any more," Sarah said clearly, looking Martha right in the eye as if she expected her to try to talk her out of it.

"Many people decide they don't," Martha said.

"Are you sure, dear?" Bess asked.

"I'm sure," Sarah said, and Will saw her watching Mike.

"Let's go, then," George said gruffly. "It's too cold to be standing out here all day."

————

THE HOUSE WAS just as they had left it the day before. Sarah caught glimpses of the kitchen, the Christmas decorations she and Will had laid on the mantel. The fire crackled and cats scattered as the door slammed open. Everyone trooped in, and Aunt Bess went straight to the stove.

"Beef stew," she said, stirring the pot.

"Your favorite," Sarah's father said. He sounded subdued but hopeful. Sarah knew he wanted her to eat, but she couldn't.

"I'd like to lie down," she said.

Mike picked up her bags. Will lifted Sarah into his arms. She laid her head against his chest. His heart was beating fast. She could feel it with her right hand, which she laid upon his collarbone. The drugs had just about worn off, and her body was alive with pain. On the other hand, she was so alert, she noticed everything.

The smell of her childhood was everywhere. Aunt Bess had washed the windows, and they gleamed. Gelsey was jumping on Martha, greeting their new visitor. Susan had left a pink sweater behind: Someone had folded it neatly, left it on a window ledge.

Mike was scared. Sarah saw it in his posture, the downward cast of his eyes. He led the procession upstairs into Sarah's room.

"Not this room," Sarah said.

"No?" Mike asked, pausing on the threshold.

"That one," Sarah said, pointing. Will's room. The one with the big bed, where he had stayed on their Thanksgiving visit, the room where her mother had died.

"I can stay in your old room," Will said.

"Stay with me," Sarah said, unable to lift her head. "Please, Will?"

He squeezed her very gently, hardly pressing at all. The pain was very bad now, a clawing sensation at the base of her spine, as if she were being devoured from the inside out. Her lungs ached with every breath.

Martha had prepared the bed in the other room, but it didn't matter. Mike pulled down the covers of the big bed. Will laid her carefully on the mattress, easing her legs under the sheet and quilt. He stepped back to retrieve an extra blanket from the oak chest at the foot of the bed, and Sarah caught sight of her son's face.

His eyes were filled with terror.

"Come here," she said.

"Where?" he asked. He stood beside her, paralyzed, looking from left to right as if he didn't dare breathe.

"Right here," she said, patting the bed beside her.

Very gingerly, Mike lowered himself to sit on the edge of the bed. He was so big, a full-grown man. Sarah never got over it no matter how long she stared at him. In her mind he was forever six years old, but in real life he was enormous. It made her laugh.

"What?" he asked, hurt.

"I'm happy."

"How can you be?" he asked, his voice hoarse and his expression injured.

"I'm with you."

"Is this . . ." he began, hardly able to talk. "Because of me? Because I wouldn't go home with you?"

"This?" she asked, not understanding.

"You getting sick again."

Sarah shook her head. All she had ever wanted was to see her son on a shining path, but she hadn't known what that path was. Now she did. There were many choices in life, and they changed constantly. None was all right, and none was all wrong. As long as you took care, thought of others, tried to do the right thing. She felt so proud of her son.

"No, Mike. You were right all along."

"About what?" he asked, his face tormented with confusion.

"This is home," she said. And then she was so tired, she had to sleep.

———

DURING THE EVENING, Martha checked her. Or was it her mother? Pain did mysterious things to the unconscious mind. Grimacing in sleep, Sarah felt the cool hand on her warm brow. The slender fingers soothed her eyes, caressed her hair.

"It hurts!" Sarah cried.

"I know, love," the woman said.

Outside the window, the moon was full. It shone on the new snow, making a silver path into the dark bay. Tracks of gold-green whale fire glowed in the sea. The pine tree Sarah had decorated for her mother that last Christmas had grown taller. But it sparkled with candlelight from top to bottom, decorated again. The eagle on its nightly hunt crossed the land with three swift beats of its mighty wings. The motion stirred the air, creating a ghostly wind that whistled through clapboards and rattled the ancient windowpanes.

The pain was unbearable. It had settled in Sarah's spine, but tentacles reached out, strangling her bones and organs in a death grip. She cried, reaching out for the woman's soft hand.

"Please," Sarah begged. "Make it stop."

"I will, darling. I'll make it stop," the woman promised.

———

WHEN WILL WENT upstairs, after dinner with Sarah's family, he found Sarah standing by the window. She wore a white nightgown, and she was staring across the moonlit yard toward the sea. Seeing her up shocked him. Will stopped in the doorway, his heart pounding.

"Sarah?" he asked.

She turned, as beautiful as the first time he'd seen her. Her skin glistened, translucent. For a moment, viewing her in the moon glow, he thought he was seeing a ghost. But she walked toward him, pressed her warm body against his, kissed him with intense heat and human passion.

"What happened?" he asked.

"The pain's gone," she said. "I don't know how or why, but it's gone."

Leading him to the bed, she gently pushed him down. They

undressed, slowly at first and then, as Will felt more confident that he wasn't going to hurt her, more urgently. Her skin felt hot, as if she had a fever. She pulled him close. Will caressed her body, kissing her mouth, feeling her smooth and silky skin with his fingertips.

They made love. Will touched her tenderly, and she touched him back. She moaned when he entered her, and at first he thought she was crying out with pain. Pulling his face to hers, kissing him with their mouths open, Sarah reassured him that he was wrong. They wanted each other with everything they had. Will gave himself to Sarah, everything he was feeling, from the deepest part of his heart.

When one of them started falling asleep, the other would whisper their name.

"Will," Sarah said.

"Hi," Will said, wide awake again. Downstairs, the grandfather's clock chimed four in the morning. They had kept each other up all night.

"I can't sleep," she said.

"Neither can I," he said.

"Good," she said. "I don't want to sleep."

"Me neither." He didn't want to waste a minute.

"Will, I had a strange dream about my mother," Sarah said.

"Why was it strange?"

"It seemed so real . . . as if she were with me. Was Martha up here?"

"Once or twice," Will said, stroking her hair, not wanting to disappoint her or break the spell. Sarah seemed so content and carefree, as if she weren't sick anymore, as if she had never been sick at all. He closed his eyes to preserve the fantasy.

"Maybe it was Martha," Sarah said, "but I don't think so. I think it was my mother."

"Maybe it was," Will said, not wanting to tell her about all the super-real dreams he had had about Fred. She felt so beautiful in his arms, so warm and sleepy. Pressing closer to his body, she rubbed his chest, kissed his shoulder. What if this could last? What if her health had somehow returned?

Will remembered meeting her for the first time, on her birthday flight over the autumn hills of Fort Cromwell. Had he known then, had he loved her already? By the harvest fair, with Mimi's picture as evidence, he certainly had. It almost seemed possible, lying with Sarah in his arms, that it was meant to be from the very start, that they had been put together for a reason.

Pushing back the covers, he gathered her closer.

"Can you stand?" he asked.

"Yes, why?" she asked.

Climbing out of bed, he tugged the quilt off the mattress. He held Sarah close, pulled the quilt around them. His heart beat fast as he led her to the window. Together they stood still, feeling the cold air swirl around them.

"It's so beautiful," she whispered, staring at the moon's silver path on the blue-black bay.

"You are," he said.

"See that tree right there?" she asked, pointing at the silhouette of the tall black pine tree.

"Yes," he said.

"That was my mother's Christmas tree. I lit candles and hung them on the branches."

"Did she love it?"

"Oh, yes," Sarah said. She frowned, staring at the tree as if she could see the candles glowing right now, lights invisible to Will no matter how hard he stared. Why had he brought her to the island? She had said good-bye to everyone on Sunday, the flight had been a terrible idea considering the pain she'd been in and the fact they had just endured a crash the day before. It made no sense and it made all the sense in the world.

"Sarah . . ." he said, turning her away from the window.

She looked up at him, her eyes wide and shining.

"Will you marry me?" he asked.

"Oh, Will . . ."

"In the island chapel," Will said. "Today. Will you marry me?"

"Yes," Sarah said, making him the happiest man alive and letting him know why they'd come back to Elk Island. "I'll marry you."

———————

"I WISH I were there," Susan whispered, too bereaved to talk in a normal voice.

"I know you do," her mother said.

"We're glad you're here," Julian said.

He was trying so hard, Susan couldn't even bear to shoot him a hateful look. They were all sitting at the breakfast table, staring at their bowls of oatmeal and not eating. The baby bear, the mama bear, and the dorky stepfather bear. He had tied his ponytail back with a rubber band that had a piece of tinsel caught in it, and Susan dreaded to think he might have put the tinsel there on purpose.

Checking her watch, Susan saw it was time to catch the bus.

"I have to go to school," she said, pushing her chair back.

"Um, no, you don't," Julian said.

"Excuse me, but I think I know when I have school," Susan said haughtily.

"We're keeping you home today," her mother said quietly.

Susan looked up. Her mother looked terrible, as if she hadn't slept for months. The little half moons under her eyes were dark purple, almost like shiners. Other than that, she looked beautiful, as always, her blond hair glinting and her high cheekbones glowing. She wore a Christmas sweater, red cashmere with green cuffs and gold buttons.

"Why?" Susan asked, a pit in her stomach. "Did you hear something about Sarah?"

"No," Julian said quickly. "We would have told you if we did."

"We've made an appointment for you," her mother said. "With Dr. Darrow."

"Please, no," Susan said with horror. She thought of Mike, of what he would think. Picturing those scary twins, water wings on their pudgy arms, their auburn-haired mother dripping with new jewelry, the Darrow family pictures hanging on the wall.

"I've been a little blind," her mother said.

Susan ignored her.

"Honey?" her mother pressed.

"Blind how?" Susan asked reluctantly.

"To how hard it's been for you."

"Moving in here," Julian said. "Getting a new stepfather. We know it hasn't been all Mardi Gras."

"All? Try none," Susan muttered. In about ten seconds she was changing her name back to Snow. Maybe she'd go for Sleet. "You don't know the half of it, Julian."

"Tell me, then," he said.

"DOF, divorce, getting a new kitten and having him taken to the pound."

"What's 'DOF'?" Julian asked, an intensely earnest expression on his face. If Susan didn't dislike him so much, it would break her heart to see him trying so hard.

"Death of Fred," Susan said.

"Wish I'd known him," Julian said.

"Many people feel that way," Susan said, looking down at her socks. They were black-and-yellow striped, the ones Fred used to wear with his black jeans or brown corduroys.

"You never talk about him to me."

"You never want to hear."

"How do you know? You've never tried."

"He was cool, he was great, he was Fred!" Susan said.

"More," Julian said.

"He liked football and loved baseball. He played shortstop and he could run fast. Wicked fast. He called me Zuze. Also known as Zeus."

"Zeus," her mother said, remembering.

"He teased me about being Susan for some reason," Susan said. "Constantly."

"Well, he was a little older than you," her mother said. "He knew your great-grandmother Susan slightly. She was...let's just say 'strong' is an understatement."

"He called her a battle-ax," Susan said.

"Her home was her Mount Olympus," her mother said, smiling sadly. "I think that's what Freddie was driving at with 'Zeus.'"

"He definitely never called me Susan with a straight face," Susan said.

"Is that why you changed your name?" Julian asked.

"Of course," Susan said, blinking away the tears.

"Wow," Julian said, giving his spoon a meaningful tap. Like wow, man. Like heavy, Susan thought, staring at him. "DOF. Death of Fred. Wow."

"DOF," Susan repeated.

"That kitten, though," Julian said. "He was pretty cute."

"He was," her mother said.

"Dr. Darrow," Susan said bitterly, thinking of Sarah. "He was one of the extra cats. They trusted me, giving him to me. His great-great-great-grandmother was Desdemona, Sarah's mother's cat."

"Good bloodlines," Julian said, stirring his oatmeal.

"No kidding," Susan said.

"Maybe we acted rashly," her mother said.

Susan's head snapped up. "What do you mean?"

"Your father's right. Your allergy tests didn't come up positive for cats."

"I told you."

"Well, I should have listened," her mother said.

"You mean I can have him back?"

Her mother nodded. "Yes," she said.

"Oh, my God," Susan said, getting all choked up and tearful.

Her heart filled with joy, and she bowed her head, knowing how happy Sarah would feel to know that her mother's cat's grandkitten was being returned to his rightful owner. "Thank you, Mom."

"You're welcome, honey. It's just that I'm afraid the pound is closed today. I called first thing. We'll have to wait till tomorrow."

Julian smiled. He laughed, and his smile got bigger.

"Fear not, ladies," he said. "I have a friend . . ."

"What do you mean?" Susan asked. Julian always had a "friend." It was part of his being a big shot. If they wanted a table at the best restaurant, Julian had a "friend" who could arrange it. When the Rolling Stones gave a sold-out show, Julian had a "friend" who could get tickets. If they wanted to buy a certain Chippendale chair, Julian had a "friend" at Christie's who could find it.

"I have a friend who works for the town garage," Julian said. "One of my old mechanics. The pound's right there, in the same building . . . he'll have a key."

"Can we go now?" Susan asked, jumping up.

"On our way to the real Dr. Darrow's," her mother said, smiling.

"Really?" Susan asked. "You're making me go?"

Her mother nodded.

"Oh, God," Susan said. "If I have to—"

"If your mother says you have to go," Julian said, putting a tentative arm around her shoulders, "you might as well put your coat on."

CHAPTER

25

SARAH WOKE UP. She was in the midst of a small miracle, and she knew it.

Today was her wedding day. Will had woken up an hour ago, if he had fallen asleep at all. He'd kissed her, then went downstairs to get everything ready. Stretching, she tested her body. Her pain had gone during the night, and it hadn't come back. She walked to the window, and with every step she knew: Today I'm going to die.

Yesterday's brilliance had worn off, and the sky looked close enough to touch. It was a snow sky, lacy with fine clouds. Sarah felt the cold in her bones, and she shivered by the window.

At the sound of a knock, she turned around. Aunt Bess opened the door a crack. When she saw that Sarah was up, she hobbled into the room carrying a large box. She was quite heavy, and her hip was out of alignment. But the expression on her face was a mixture of pride and delight.

"Sarah," she said, her face turning pink. "When Will told us the news, I couldn't believe it. But we're so happy. All of us." She laid the box on the unmade bed, walking across the room.

"Thank you, Aunt Bess," Sarah said, allowing her aunt to fold her into her arms. The older woman's body was soft and plump, and the hug felt so loving to Sarah.

"Will's dear," Aunt Bess said. "I love him."

"So do I," Sarah said.

Holding her at arm's length, Aunt Bess seemed to study her. Sarah could see her aunt had gotten up early. Her teeth were in. She had washed her hair and put on rouge and lipstick. She wore a dark green dress that Sarah thought she had chosen because it was rather Christmasy. She wore the pearls and pearl earrings Uncle Arthur had given to her for their fifteenth anniversary.

"I've waited a long time for this day," Aunt Bess said, limping over to the bed. Leaning over, she opened the box. Sarah knew, even before she looked inside, that it was her old wedding dress.

"I can't . . ." Sarah began, feeling an old sorrow and panic. *Wear the dress you made for me to marry Zeke in,* she was about to say. But when she glanced down, she saw that it was a different dress entirely. She gasped.

"Your mother was so beautiful," Bess said, lifting the white satin dress from the box. "When George brought her home, I was overjoyed. I loved her like my own sister. Do you think it will fit?"

Sarah touched the fabric of her mother's wedding dress. The satin felt creamy against her skin. Glancing at the bureau, Sarah saw the picture. Her mother was wearing this dress, smiling at the camera, as happy as she had always been. Taking the dress into her arms, Sarah stared at the picture. The dress contained yards and yards of satin, but it felt light as air.

"I hope it fits," Sarah whispered, holding the dress against her thin body. She felt so tired, but touching the dress and looking at her mother's picture seemed to give her strength.

"It will," Aunt Bess said, turning her practiced dressmaking eye on the garment.

"Aunt Bess, my pain is gone," Sarah said suddenly.

"I know, honey."

"What do you think it means?" Sarah asked.

"It means you have something important to do," Aunt Bess said gently.

"Marry Will," Sarah said.

THE GEESE HONKED and waddled around the yard. George and Mike stood by the big Jeep, waiting for Sarah, Bess, and the nurse to come out. Will paced the walk. All three men were dressed up about as much as people got dressed up on Elk Island. Will hadn't brought a suit, and he was too big to fit into anything in the house. So while Mike and George wore their church clothes, Will looked like some Navy flyboy in his bomber jacket.

"You've given this some thought?" George asked.

"A lot of thought," Will said.

"Not enough so you thought to bring a suit," George said, narrowing his eyes.

"I had a few things on my mind, leaving Fort Cromwell."

"Grandpa," Mike started in a warning tone of voice.

"She's my only daughter," George exploded.

"She wants to marry him."

"Yes, well," George sputtered. "She hasn't always been so wise about picking men in the past." What would any of them think if they knew he was wearing the very suit he'd worn to give Sarah away at her wedding to Zeke Loring? And look how that had turned out. . . .

"Will's okay," Mike said, chin jutting forward as he defended Will.

"Swoops right into our lives, and now everything's all topsy-turvy."

"What's all topsy-turvy?" Will asked, pronouncing the word with a little hitch in his voice, as if making fun of George for using it.

"Well, the fact you nearly killed her in a crash, for one thing."

"It was mechanical failure. The nose gear wouldn't engage."

"Don't you service your planes?" George asked. The more he thought about it, the madder he got. Standing in the driveway, chest to chest with Will Burke, he wanted to fight him. A physical sensation came over him, the taste of violence, and he was inwardly begging for Will to throw a punch.

"Yeah, I service my planes, George."

"Nearly crashing with Sarah on board. Jesus Christ."

"I'm sorry, all right?"

"No, not all right. You think a little apology's going to make up for everything?"

"The plane crash, what else?"

"Her getting sick again," George yelled. "That's what!"

Will stood still. George had shocked him, that was sure.

"She needed to stay calm," George said, his eyes burning. "Free of emotional entanglements. Maybe she would have come to live on the island if she hadn't met you. We'd take care of her, me and Mike and Bess. Right, Mike?"

"Grandpa, stop," Mike said in a low voice.

"Getting herself all stirred up," George said, breaking down. "That's what happened. Her system just can't take it. Shit, Will."

"Yeah, shit," Will said, just staring.

George turned away so the others wouldn't see him crying. He'd lost Rose the same way. Tried to keep her lying down, free of emotions, but no: She'd wanted to get herself involved in everything. She had loved George till the end, actively, hugging him every chance she got. She had been passionate about him and Sarah, loving them with more than she had. All that passion had stirred up the cancer, and they'd lost her.

"Sir?" Will asked, standing somewhere behind George's left shoulder.

"What?" George snapped.

"Something I forgot to ask."

George gathered himself together. The air was frigid, and their breath came out in billows of white. George's throat ached so much, he thought words would crack it. So he turned and gave Will a rough nod instead.

"George, I'd like to ask you for your daughter's hand in marriage."

Standing there, feet planted in the snow, George blinked up at the sky. Goddamn snow was starting to fall.

"Please, George," Will said. His tone was soft, conciliatory. All the aggression had gone out of him.

Slowly, George nodded. Mike just stood there, not offering any objections. The snow was fine and white.

"Yes," George said. "I give you my blessing to marry Sarah."

"I love your daughter."

George squinted at Will Burke. He looked like a mess. Six foot something, a Navy man who'd lost his deck for too long. Gray hair and tired eyes. Looked as if he hadn't slept in days. At least he'd shaved. George cleared his throat, ready to call him "Commander." But the words came out a little different.

"I know you do, son," George heard himself saying. He pulled his future son-in-law over and gave him a backslapping hug just as the door opened and Sarah walked out. Dazzled by the snow, by the sight of the three men, she stood on the top step, gazing with wonder at the scene. Will was crying, and George kept him turned away from Sarah.

After all, it was bad luck for him to see the bride before the wedding.

———

THE CHURCHYARD LAY covered in new snow. By the time they crossed the island, snow was falling hard. The dark stone church had weathered many storms. It sat on the edge of the sea, low to the ground, the green wreath still on the door. George led Will into the church. He still hadn't seen Sarah. Bess had made a big production of making sure he faced away, sat in front while Sarah sat in back.

She sat there, in the backseat of the warm Jeep beside her

son, while the others went inside. Mike wasn't saying anything. Sarah felt nervous, and she thought she knew why. She was thirty-seven, she had a son, but she was getting married for the first time. She had butterflies in her stomach.

"You okay?" Mike asked.

Sarah nodded.

"Warm enough?"

"Yes," she said, although she was shivering.

"I drove over a while ago to turn on the heaters. The church should be warm."

Sarah turned, smiling. "You're so thoughtful," she said.

"You didn't used to say that," he said.

"I should have," she said, thinking of how much she had left him alone while she worked, to go on dates. "More often."

Mike shrugged.

"Snow wanted to come," Sarah said.

"Yeah?"

"We thought it better that she didn't. This time," Sarah said. "But I know she'd love to hear from you."

"Maybe I'll call her," Mike said.

Sarah nodded. "She likes you," she said, and that was the moment it hit her: She wasn't going to be around to find out what happened. "Oh . . ." she said, covering her mouth.

"What?" Mike asked, looking alarmed.

Sarah knew she looked stricken. She sat there with her seventeen-year-old son, knowing she wouldn't see him turn eighteen. She wouldn't find out whether he went to school again, whether he decided to stay on the farm. If he fell in love with Susan, Sarah wouldn't be around to see it. If they married, she wouldn't be there as mother of the groom; if they had children, she wouldn't be there as grandmother.

"Mike . . ." she said, staring at him.

"What, Mom?"

How could she tell him? She had no right to put this pain at his feet. Her body was tired and her bones ached with the sorrow of what was about to happen. She felt it coming fast, the death she had taken into her own flesh that day by the frozen pond, when Mike was fighting for his life and Sarah made her petition to God. How could she tell her son that all she wanted, all she had ever wanted, was to know how he was going to turn out?

"Honey," she said. "I want—"

"I know, Mom," he said.

"No, you—" She paused to regain even a shred of composure. "Be happy, Mike," she managed to say.

He looked worried. Her face showed everything, it always had. She had dressed for the wedding, put on a little makeup, but it couldn't disguise what was happening today. Second only to Mike's birth day, this was the most important day of Sarah's life. It was the day she was going to get married, and it was the day she was going to die.

Mike came around to her side, helped her out of the Jeep. They walked up the stone walk, already dusted with snow. Pausing at the steps, Sarah lay her hand on her son's arm. The churchyard was off to their right. Sarah's eyes traveled over the graves. There she was.

"Mom . . ." Sarah said.

Mike waited.

"She was so beautiful," Sarah whispered. "Your grandmother. Did I talk about her enough? Did I tell you stories about her so you have some idea of who she was?"

"Yeah, Mom. I'm here, aren't I?"

"What do you mean?"

"On her island. I'm with her all the time. . . ."

A sob rose in Sarah, and she hugged her son. He supported her with strong arms, holding her steady. He was a young man, but he respected the past. He honored his ancestors, and just knowing that made a question rise in Sarah's mind that she could not push away.

"Will you tell . . . ?"

"Tell what?" Mike asked.

The tension in Sarah had been great. She knew she should keep this to herself, to not upset Mike, but something about his tone, the look in his eyes, made her know she could ask. "Will you tell your kids about me?"

"Oh, Mom," he said, smiling with great strength.

"What?" she asked, needing to know what was making him smile.

"Look where I am, Mom. I'm on Elk Island. It's where I want to be, and that's because of you. I love it here, Mom. It's—"

"It's what?" Sarah asked, spellbound. She gripped his arm, looking into his eyes for the secret.

"It's our home," Mike said.

"Yes," Sarah said. "Home." The word so sweet and beautiful, so familiar and warm, it made her start to weep. All this time Sarah had been searching for Mike's shining way, his secret path, and he had found it on his own. The way home.

Mike held his mother close, looking out over the church-yard. Seeing where Sarah's mother lay gave her strength, and she dried her eyes, gazing at the headstone for a minute. Zeke's grave was there too, and she watched her son's eyes go there and linger for a moment.

"Are you ready?"

"I am," she said.

Mike took one last look at the sea, at the snow falling in soft flakes. Then he turned to his mother and took her hand.

"Come on, Mom," Mike said hoarsely but with gentleness. "Let's go in."

They opened the church door. The beautiful wreath smelled like pine, and Sarah's senses filled with Christmas. Stepping inside, she drew a deep breath.

There he was. Will stood at the front of the church by the altar. His shoulders were so broad, they strained at his jacket, and he leaned slightly forward in a posture of yearning. Sarah felt it herself. So much space between them, when the point was to be in each other's arms.

Reverend Dunston stood there in black and purple robes. His hair was white now, and he was old. He had baptized Mike, presided over Rose's funeral. Sarah had known him her whole life, and he smiled at her now. Trying to smile back, Sarah could only gaze at Will.

Aunt Bess and Martha were the only guests. They sat in the front row, beaming at Sarah as she hovered in the doorway. Mike never left her right side. Her father stepped out of the shadows, took her left arm.

"Rose's dress," he said softly.

Sarah nodded, closing her eyes as he bent his forehead to touch hers.

"Are you ready, sweetheart?" her father asked.

"Yes, Dad."

"Okay, Mom," Mike said. "Here we go."

The music was Bach. It was old and beautiful, and Sarah must have heard it a hundred times before. Aunt Bess had chosen it, and Sarah had said okay, and it played in high, reedy notes from an old tape recorder placed on the altar. Candles filled the church. They flickered in the darkness. Their smoke mingled with incense, and Sarah took a breath. A miracle had brought her this far. She was so close, she didn't have much further to go.

Her eyes never left Will's.

Very slowly, Sarah began to walk down the aisle. Her father and her son were by her side, her arms solidly in theirs. They wouldn't let her fall. Every step was a blessing.

Love.

Sarah Talbot felt it with all her heart. She had come to life on this beautiful island, been raised by parents who taught her the value of love. They had cherished her, their only child. When the time had come for her to bear a son, she was ready. Her parents had shown her the way. With all the mistakes she had made as a mother, knowing how to love Mike had never been a problem.

"Oh," she said, stumbling.

Her father and Mike caught her.

"There," her father said. "Do you need to sit down?"

Sarah wanted to make it to the front of the church. She didn't have far to go, but she didn't think she could walk anymore. The candles blazed around her. Dim snow light came through the blue stained glass, the saints and martyrs looking on. She had two strong men at her side.

"Help me get there," she whispered.

"We will, sweetheart," her father said, his voice full of quiet strength.

Only a few steps more to go. Sarah kept her eyes straight ahead, trained on Will's face. His eyes were deep blue, pools of love and sorrow. Be joyful, she wanted to cry. It's our wedding day! But tears were running down her own cheeks. Life was so short. Every moment was precious! She had known Will for such a short time, and look at all the love they felt.

Imagine what a whole lifetime could contain. Just imagine the laughter, the fun, the journeys, the oceans, the walks, the sleep, the children, the grandchildren, the dinners, the holidays, the flights, the cruises... every minute of life was a gift, and God had given her and Will just enough time to find their love, to know they belonged together.

Reaching the altar, Mike and her father paused. They didn't want to let go. Sarah strained, wanting Will. But she paused for one moment. Looking her father in the eye, she smiled. She kissed him, and she heard him whisper, "My beautiful child."

So when she turned to Mike, to receive his kiss and bestow her love, she knew exactly what to say. "My beautiful child," she whispered to him.

Will took her hand. They gazed deeply into each other's eyes, and Sarah felt his love to the depths of her soul. She was wearing her mother's white satin wedding dress. The fabric felt

cool and warm at the same time. Her body shivered uncontrollably. Taking her in his arms, Will held her until she was ready
to go on.

"Sarah," the reverend said. "William."

Will nodded.

"Love one another," Reverend Dunston began. "But make
not a bond of love: Let it rather be a moving sea between the
shores of your souls. . . ."

Time went so fast. So much love, such alarming and radiant
joy, she thought. Transformed by the sheer love she had felt for
this man in her arms, regardless of the shortness of time or the
vastness of death. Sarah tore her gaze away from Will's face just
long enough to look up once to a spot behind the altar, where
for an instant she had thought she saw her mother standing.

Her family had gathered around. Mike and her father and
Aunt Bess and the nurse standing in a semicircle around them,
guests at the wedding.

Her body felt so tired, so heavy. Faltering, she leaned harder
on Will. His eyes were blue and dark, so intelligent, so sad.
Above all, Sarah saw, Will's eyes were so very sad.

Reverend Dunston looked from Sarah to Will. As if it were a
regular wedding, as if the man were not holding the woman for
dear life, he spoke in a normal tone.

"Do you, William, take Sarah, whom you hold by the hand,
to be your true wife, to love, honor, and cherish in joy and in
pain, in sickness and in health, forsaking all others, until death
do you part?"

"I do," Will said.

"And do you, Sarah, take William, whom you hold by the
hand, to be your true husband, to love, honor, and cherish in
joy and in pain, in sickness and in health, forsaking all others,
until death do you part?"

"I do," Sarah whispered. Tears running down her face, Sarah
was staring at Will.

"Stay," he whispered, as if he couldn't help himself.

Will was supposed to be the brave one. The strong man, the hero of the day, the bridegroom faking happiness for Sarah's sake. Sarah was dying, leaving him, and he was supposed to be stoic and brave. He was supposed to be smiling.

"Oh," Sarah wept as she had once wept for her mother, but this was different. Her mother had been sick and getting old, but she was supposed to be young and healthy. She had everything to live for. Till death do you part . . .

She felt it coming, the death she had taken into her body. It was peaceful, and it was terrible. "What emblems do you have of your love and regard for one another?" Reverend Dunston asked.

They hadn't had time to get rings. But her father had taken her mother's gold wedding band from the small ivory box on his night table, and he handed it to Mike, who handed it to Will.

Will placed the ring on Sarah's finger. Repeating after Reverend Dunston, and looking directly into her eyes, he said, "With this ring I thee wed, and with all my love I thee endow."

Aunt Bess stepped forward. Her shoulders shaking, she attempted to hide the sobs that shook her body.

"Darling," she whispered, pressing something hard into Sarah's hand. "It belonged to your uncle Arthur. I want you to use it now. God bless . . ."

"Bless you, Aunt Bess," Sarah said.

Then, sliding the ring onto Will's finger, Sarah held his hand. Repeating after the minister, she gazed into his gray-blue eyes and said, "With this ring I thee wed, and with all my love I thee endow."

They clasped hands, and Sarah felt her heart soar. They smiled and smiled. She was never going to let go.

"Sarah and William," Reverend Dunston said, his voice rising. He read:

"Now you will feel no rain, for each of you will be shelter to
  the other.

"Now you will feel no cold, for each of you will be warmth to
    the other.

"Now there is no more loneliness; now you are two persons
    but there is only one life before you.

"Go now to your dwelling place to enter into the days of your
    life together.

"And may your days be good and long upon the earth and in
    heaven.

"By the power vested in me by the Church and the State of
Maine, I now pronounce you husband and wife. You may kiss
the bride."

Tilting her head back, Sarah felt Will kiss her lips. The kiss
was tender. Her lips met his, and his arms encircled her body,
and they were husband and wife.

"Will," she said, smiling.

"Husband and wife," Will said, grinning, making her remember how he had looked that first time they met, on her
birthday flight. The ride had lasted a long time—longer than it
was supposed to—but it was almost over, their time was done.
Time was a gift, and she and Will had loved every minute. They
had been on a journey, a secret path, and for Sarah it had led
back home.

Her son was there, standing behind them. Susan, Sarah
thought. Snow. Wherever you are, hello, my daughter. Her
heart fluttered. Angel wings moved the air. Her mother was beside her, and Fred. Sarah could hardly breathe. Tears blurred her
vision, and she could hardly see. Life . . . oh, life.

"Till death do us part," Sarah whispered.

"Forever," Will said.

"Forever," Sarah said.

She gazed at her husband, to memorize his face.

Forever.

EPILOGUE

IT WAS LABOR Day, and all the island grasses were golden. They moved in the wind, tickling Susan's legs as she walked along the narrow path. She had set out from the house nearly an hour before, passing places that she had first seen the previous November, when the island was covered with snow.

The church stood straight ahead. Approaching it, she felt her heart beating faster. She felt nervous about what she was doing, although she had been planning it all along. Her knapsack felt heavy, bumping her back with every step. But the discomfort didn't bother her: Susan had been wearing threadbare socks for years, and she understood the sacrifices people sometimes made for love.

Pausing when she got close, Susan caught her breath. The chapel was so beautiful, like something in an English painting: the dark stone, the steeple rising into the blue sky, summer clouds scudding across the sea. A bouquet of wildflowers was tied to the church door, and Susan wondered who had put it there.

Walking around the side, she came to the small walled churchyard. Susan undid the latch, then quietly went through the gate. Her heart wouldn't settle down. She felt nervous and shy, as if she were meeting someone important for the first time. Palms damp, she wiped her hands on the sides of her jeans.

Her eyes roved the small cluster of graves. She had thought she would have to search for a while, but one stone drew her immediately. Very slowly, never taking her eyes away, Susan walked toward it. As she got closer, her body began to tremble. Brushing the smooth granite with her fingers, Susan lowered herself to her knees. She couldn't stop the tears from flowing down her face, and she didn't even try.

"Hello, Sarah," she said.

Seeing the name etched in stone made everything so real: "Sarah Talbot Burke, beloved of the island."

"Not just the island," Susan said, frowning as the tears touched her lips. Why did that make her so mad? Did Elk Island think it was the only place Sarah had been loved, made a difference in people's lives? She felt the resentment, a big knot in her stomach. But suddenly she could almost hear Sarah's gentle laugh, telling that *she* knew what Susan meant, and that it would be okay to let it go.

"Fort Cromwell too," Susan said almost absently, as if to the air. "Beloved there too."

She glanced around to see if anyone was around to hear. People thought you were eccentric or crazy if you talked to the dead, but Susan had been doing it for years. Some of her most meaningful conversations had been with Fred.

"I've missed you," she said, gazing fixedly at Sarah's name.

The September sky was deep blue. An eagle circled overhead, as if keeping watch. Susan believed in messages from nature, like Fred's whale at Thanksgiving; it had made her feel better knowing he was looking out for Sarah.

"The eagle, Sarah," Susan said softly, tracing the stone's letters. "He's here. And so am I."

Settling down, she took off her knapsack and laid it on the grass beside her. She sat cross-legged on the ground. Someone had laid a bouquet, identical to the one hanging on the church door, at the base of the stone. Sticking out from beneath the tangle of asters, goldenrod, and Queen Anne's lace was a note in her father's handwriting. Susan glanced down, but she only wanted to stare at Sarah's name.

"Dad's here too," she said. "I know he was out here early this morning—I heard him leave the house. He misses you too, Sarah."

At the thought of her father, of what he had gone through in the aftermath of Sarah's death, Susan's heart shrunk a little, and she curled inward and wept.

"A lot," she said when she could talk again. "That's putting it mildly. He kind of shut down for a while. Even I couldn't get to him. But, Sarah . . ." Swallowing hard, Susan touched the stone again. "He had to go through it. He explained everything to me on our way out here . . . it's like what I went through with Fred. Love is the greatest blessing there is, and when you love someone as much as he loved you, you can't let go lightly. You just can't."

Shaking with sobs, Susan seemed unable to take her hand away from the carved letters of Sarah's name. She traced them with her fingers very carefully, as if she were reading something very urgent. But after a few minutes, letting out a shuddering sigh, she reached for her knapsack. She seemed about to open it, but instead she let it rest on her lap.

They had come to pick up Mike. Did Sarah already know? Was she sitting somewhere, radiant and smiling, because Mike had decided to finish his senior year at Fort Cromwell, that he was going to fly back with them, live with Will until next summer?

"Your father had a fit at first," Susan said, smiling. "He and my dad had these long-distance battles over the phone, yelling at each other, hanging up, calling back . . . it was a mess. Poor Aunt Bess. She'd call back when George wasn't around to apologize for him and tell us it wasn't *us* he was mad at, it was the situation . . . you know, having Mike leave the island."

Laughing, Susan bowed her head.

"The funny thing was, in the end, he accepted it. Good old

George! One day Mike went into his room, and there were all the old *National Geographic*s tied up in a bundle with a note: 'Bring these back when you get your diploma.' I mean, what was Mike going to say to that? Especially—"

Here the laughter stopped, and Susan gazed at the stone again.

"Especially because he knew that's what you wanted."

Her hands shaking slightly, Susan began to untie the cord on her knapsack. She had tied it extra tightly, knowing that what she had inside was very precious. Susan had the sentimental need to link things with the people she had loved and lost. She still wore Fred's socks. For years she had used names that had reminded her of him, and it still felt slightly weird each time she answered to someone calling her Susan. Although her mother was relieved—for her it made all the difference to have Susan going by her real name—and they even had Sarah to thank for *that*.

Carefully, she pulled the plaque from within the backpack. Cradling it on her lap, she sighed. It was at moments like this that she wondered: Had she done this for a real reason? Was there any way Sarah could actually know?

"Everyone loves you," Susan began. "Everyone. Your father and Aunt Bess, Mike, my dad... God, Sarah. My dad loves you so much. You were such a gift to him. You have no idea how much you taught him... to love, Sarah, but even more, to hope. My dad has so much hope now. He gets up every day, and he lives it for you."

Susan caught her breath. "He has to, he says, because life is so wonderful. It's a precious gift, and we never know when it might be shortened unfairly. You just never know," she whispered. Now she picked up her father's note, a thin piece of paper stained green from the wildflowers. "I love you, Sarah. Forever," it said. Knowing the message was private, between her father and Sarah, Susan gently placed it back.

"You meant so much to everyone, Sarah. They talk about

you all the time. Sometimes I feel that you belong so much to other people, the ones who knew you longer and better, I forget about us."

Us, Susan thought, smiling through her tears.

"Remember, Sarah? When we first met? I mean, I'd seen you at the airport for your birthday flight, but we didn't actually meet until that day in your shop. When I came in freezing cold, pretending I wanted to buy something, and you gave me that cup of hot cider . . . remember?"

A shadow passed across the grave, and Susan looked up. She wanted it to be the eagle, but it was only a low cloud gliding across the brilliant sun.

"I wanted you to be all mine," Susan said. "When those college girls came in, I felt jealous. But you know . . ."

Holding the plaque tighter, she bowed her head for an instant, gathering herself together. "You *are* mine. You're my stepmother. My dad married you, and it makes me so happy. You knew me, Sarah. Really knew me, and I think that's rare. To understand and accept all there is about another person . . . At home, when things are hard with Mom and Julian, I think, oh, how much I wish I could ride my bike down to see you. I know you'd understand."

Making a place beside her father's flowers, Susan stood the plaque she had made against the gravestone. It was a small blue wooden oval, a magical cloud with a golden "9," feathers falling like snow—a tiny replica of the sign at Sarah's shop. Susan remembered the first time she'd ever seen it, that freezing evening when she'd walked in.

"My father helped me make this," Susan said. "We did it in his workshop at the airport, all last winter, after you died."

For a minute, remembering the cold hangar, the silence as they worked the wood on the long tool bench, both feeling the loss of Sarah, Susan bowed her head and cried. But by the time the sign was ready to paint, spring had filled the orchards surrounding the airfield with apple and pear blossoms. Susan and her father spent those long hours together, many of them laughing and recalling their love for Sarah.

"When I was making the sign," Susan said, the tears making her throat ache, "I was thinking that that was our place—your shop, Cloud Nine. But, Sarah..."

She looked around, feeling the island breeze lifting her hair. Waves broke on the rocks below, and sea gulls cried from the roof of the church. They sounded happy, exultant, a choir of birds.

"You're with me all the time. That's the amazing thing."

Tapping the little sign with her hand, she smiled even bigger than before. "Cloud Nine is just where we started. But I have you with me always. At school, at home, here on the island. You were even with me and Dad in his workshop."

She read Sarah's stone again, making her eyes take in every word slowly. "Sarah Talbot Burke, beloved of the island," she said out loud.

The wind picked up. Susan's neck tingled. Looking up, she saw him again: the eagle. He circled once, a tight bend overhead. Then he ranged out over the moors, around toward the bay, dipping low behind a row of pines before he was lost to sight. It didn't matter. Susan knew he would be back. She and her father would take Mike home to Fort Cromwell, and next summer they would all return to the island. The eagle would be there, and so would Sarah.

Standing, Susan brushed bits of grass from her palms. She checked to make sure her plaque was solidly wedged against Sarah's grave to keep her company while Susan, Mike, and her father were away. It wasn't going anywhere.

"Beloved," Susan whispered, touching the letters one more time. "Of the island."

This time, the words didn't seem so hard to say.

ABOUT THE AUTHOR

Luanne Rice is the author of twenty-five novels, most recently *Last Kiss, Light of the Moon, What Matters Most, The Edge of Winter, Sandcastles, Summer of Roses, Summer's Child,* and *Silver Bells.* She lives in New York City and Old Lyme, Connecticut.

Visit the author's website at www.luannerice.com.

Visit our website at www.bantamdell.com.

LUANNE
RICE

LAST
KISS

A NOVEL

On Sale Now in Hardcover

LAST KISS

by
New York Times
Bestselling Author

LUANNE RICE

Luanne Rice returns to Hubbards Point, Connecticut, and characters from her beloved *Beach Girls,* to tell the haunting story of a close-knit community grappling with a heartbreaking mystery, and of a woman rebuilding her world and reclaiming a love she believed lost a lifetime ago.

Available wherever Bantam Books are sold

THE
LETTERS

A Novel by

LUANNE
RICE

&

JOSEPH
MONNINGER

THE LETTERS

by

LUANNE RICE

and

JOSEPH MONNINGER

In this remarkable collaboration, *New York Times* bestselling author Luanne Rice and acclaimed writer Joseph Monninger combine their unique talents to create a powerfully moving novel of an estranged husband and wife through a series of searching, intimate letters. By way of a correspondence so achingly real you'll forget it's fiction, they trace the history of a love affair and of a family before, and after, the moment that changed the course of two people's journey forever.